April Sealed
Our Fate

To David,
With affection,
Sincerely,

Jacqueline Richardson.

13ʳ April 2010

Jacqueline
Richardson

© Jacqueline Richardson 2009
April Sealed Our Fate

ISBN 978-0-9564552-0-8

Published by Normandy Press
'Normandy'
Rushmore Hill
Knockholt
Sevenoaks
Kent TN14 7NS

A CIP catalogue record of this book
can be obtained from the British Library.

Book designed by Michael Walsh at
MUSICPRINT
5 Lime Close Chichester PO19 6SW

and printed by
ASHFORD COLOUR PRESS
Unit 600 Fareham Reach
Fareham Road
Gosport
Hants PO13 0FW

I dedicate this book to Reg, as without him there would be no story to tell.

As life dictates, there can by no joy
without knowing sadness,
no love without knowing indifference,
and being soulmates, only when you come
to take me home will our love be complete.

ACKNOWLEDGEMENT

I would like express my thanks for the guidance and encouragement from so many loyal friends in my endeavours.

My sincere thanks to Paul Mahoney, who was such a help in creating photographs the size I asked him for.

Most of all to Dr Michael Walsh, who particularly guided me through the minefield of telling my story to the best of my abillty.

All royalties from the sale of this book are being donated to THE BRITISH HEART FOUNDATION.

PREFACE

This is a story of a man and a woman travelling on parallel paths of life, feeling the despair of indifference on one hand and the sadness of no progress of recovering health on the other, till their paths met.

From that moment, the two paths joined and soon after fused together into one, never to part, till one of them became a spirit. The one left still has loving memories that no one can obliterate and having known such love and true devotion is anxious to relate the love story which nothing can destroy.

It all began when both were in the early autumn of their lives and the unexpected seed of love was planted in both their hearts.

From that April day they felt privileged to have met.

PROLOGUE

As I walked up the path to my house, I put the key in the door and was struck by the silence before even taking my coat off. I made a cup of tea to calm and soothe the feelings of sadness and concern about my husband's condition. He had suffered a stroke in the early hours and was now under the care of the nursing staff.

The Doctor in charge had said to me: "Mrs Sheridan, your husband is not able to swallow, and must regain that ability within twenty four hours or the news will not be good. At the moment he has lost his speech and his right hand's fist is clenched but it may be with time and care he will improve."

I am afraid that I did not know anything about that illness and was not given very much hope, so I sipped my tea, phoned my Mother who lived in Monaco and told her my sad news. She assured me that she would take the first morning flight to Heathrow to be with me. The next day, on my visit to hospital, I was told by the Sister that he could now swallow, but was still unable to speak or unfold his right hand. The only comfort was the recognition in his eyes as I walked to his bed.

It was the 22nd of March 1977, his seventieth birthday but to him, I don't believe he was aware of that occasion.

As I realised there was no love lost between my husband and our neighbours, I explained to my Mother that selling our home, changing our surroundings could be beneficial to us both. So I decided to put our house on the market and when I had a buyer, I selected a few houses in this area that would be suitable.

I looked for a house with a medium sized garden for him to enjoy its peaceful atmosphere, with spacious and light rooms and so on. I took the bus to Petts Wood and found two modern houses which seemed to offer some comfort. The first two houses were a disappointment. Although both kitchens and bathrooms were dazzling my eyes with shining appliances, the reception rooms were bland with magnolia wall paper, carpets and curtains. I had the feeling I was walking through a tub of butter and there was no cosy atmosphere or touches of character where you could sit down and relax. So I nearly did not pursue the intention to visit the third choice, but decided to make the effort.

As soon as I reached the front door, I started to look forward to being invited inside. It was a semi-detached chalet house with leaded windows and as soon as the lady of the house opened the door, I was happy to have entered the place. Both reception rooms were spacious and light and the staircase was central in the square entrance. Downstairs there was a small study/fourth bedroom with a bathroom, separate WC and a small kitchen overlooking the back garden. Upstairs there were three bedrooms and in each was a vanity wash basin which would be useful to avoid using the bathroom. I asked if it was possible to bring my Mother the next day and from then on it was a question of arranging surveyors' visits, sorting out Land Registry, and the usual interminable letters to and fro which take time. I hoped it would be a new start where I could help my husband.

His dislike of his Christian name was such that he answered to "Sherry" – a contraction of his surname Sheridan. His sisters, colleagues and friends always used that name. He was now back home but he was a very different man; so many things he could not handle and it was obvious much care had to be given to make his life comfortable. My mother returned home. Although I had put a deposit on the house at that time, I knew the paperwork involved would take a long time. The owners of the house we wanted were in a chain, so I could only wait, but I was at the time very busy looking after Sherry.

Our own Doctor had advised me to purchase tins of baby food to facilitate his eating. But to my surprise even using a small spoon, found he kept aiming for his cheek instead of his mouth so I found it less irritating for him to feed him. Also I hired a man to call every day to shave him. His clenched tight fist somehow would not open, so had no ability to write or hold anything. A completely different routine had to be adapted so as to not tire him too much. Very slowly he could say a few words, but the difficulty to speak frustrated him so much when I think that in one hour he could finish the Daily Telegraph crossword, but no more. If only I could help, but all I could do was to keep trying.

It was now the 3rd of April 1978, and our taxi drove us to our new home on the hill. A bitter cold wind was blowing and the snow was crunchy underfoot. It had a wonderful view over Orpington and it seemed to be waiting for us to make us welcome. I had asked the removal men to bring Sherry's armchair before anything else so that he would be comfortable. I went to the kitchen overlooking the back garden. It was a riot of daffodils each with a top-knot of snow waving on each side of the path and the garden sloped away from the house. A horseshoe lawn was in a sunken part, one large apple tree cast its shadow and on the left, by the gate, a Victoria tree was almost hovering over the pavement. A small greenhouse was looking a little forlorn and further on was a garage. It was a pretty garden that would be a wonderful place of comfort for us both. The removal men were still busy and when I returned to the drawing room, and I found thirty-two packing cases and some suitcases which I started to unpack. I knew today, Monday 3rd April 1978, would be a tiring day, a little stressful, however I did not realise that I would never forget a date that would completely change my life.

At four o'clock, the knocker sounded. Surprised, I opened the door with a teapot in my hand and there stood a gentleman in a dark blue suit, a briefcase in hand, about 6 feet tall, twinkly blue eyes.

He spoke with a slight lilt, which I did not recognise. He said: "I am Mr Richardson – I live next door, if you need any help, please ask." I thanked him for his kindness and shut the door. Our first meeting lasted all of 15 seconds and I did not realise how important my choosing this house would be in years to come.

Getting familiar with things that worked or didn't (mostly the latter) I soon became aware that the items I appreciated like a wash-basin in the second bedroom was in fact a disaster. It blocked the opening to the water tank and the only way to reach it, in case of any leaks, was to open an eaves cupboard door in the next bedroom, crawl over wooden beams and spiders' webs about fifteen feet to reach it. When a leak started to appear in my kitchen, I had no idea where the trouble was coming from or where the stopcock was located. Luckily, on asking for help from my newly-found friend and neighbour, who obviously had a mirror image of my house, he asked me to wait a moment. He reappeared five minutes later wearing overalls and had a bag of tools with him. He had the task of crawling whilst I held a powerful torch for him. I was so embarrassed that such an awful job had to be done and I thanked him and imagined he would think twice about any other jobs. He was very kind and I appreciated the help given.

I decided to do as many jobs as I could even if I had no experience and became a tiler and grouter, a wallpaper hanger, painter and even managed to use an electric drill to fix a medicine cabinet on the wall. Money was somewhat short and doing jobs myself was the only way. Thankfully a lot of help and advice was given to me and I slowly improved my ability to become fairly handy.

May came and I had to work in the garden and plant shrubs and flowers, so my time was very taken, though by now my neighbour was often visiting with his wife to share coffee and cakes. Then one morning very early the phone rang. My mother was finding it difficult to stand and walk, she had pains in her side and sounded upset. I suggested she booked a flight to Heathrow and I would look after her as well as I could. Next day, I sent a taxi driver I knew to fetch her, but when the knocker went, I opened the door, and found the driver standing there carrying her in his arms as her legs kept giving way.

On the 20th September, Maman was in such pain. I called the Doctor who seemed to think she had dislocated the third lumbar disc.

As the weeks passed, I noticed my mother's mobility was getting worse. Nearly every night she tried to get up, but the thud on the carpet used to wake me up as my bedroom was immediately above. I dashed down and by sitting behind her on the bed I put my arms under her shoulder and lifted her back into bed. By this time Sherry noticed I was not there and shuffled out to the landing. I had to warn him to stay put and take him back to bed safely. Three weeks later, Maman was admitted to Lennard's Hospital, not far from Bromley Common Road.

On his way home, my kindly neighbour called to find out how my mother was. I offered him a cup of tea which was accepted and said to me: "Do you know how long we have been good friends?"

"Yes, just over five months – why?"

"You have called me Mr Richardson since I introduced myself last April. Could you call me Reg?"

"I am sorry, I didn't mean to be unfriendly, but in France you don't call people by their Christian name unless they suggest otherwise, but from now on I will call you Reg."

"Can I give you and Sherry a lift to Bromley to visit Maman? Going by bus is none too easy for Sherry and I am on my own this evening."

"Thank you, I very much appreciate it. I am hoping that I can find a bed in Orpington Hospital, so that I can walk there every day and bring her whatever she needs. I must be patient and hope a transfer can come about. Thank you for your help, what time will you be able to drive us to Bromley?"

"I will be round at seven. See you later".

1

Across the gateway to my heart,
I wrote "No thoroughfare".
But love came laughing by, and cried
"I enter everywhere."

Herbert Shipman

Christmas came and went. Sherry had no idea that the festival he had so enjoyed in the past was so important to me, and I suppose the stroke he had suffered had that effect on his memory playing tricks, my mother had been sent home for the Christmas holiday and while he was resting, Maman and I had a long talk, she was an understanding woman who realised that life was difficult for me now.

The worst of it was that Sherry and I were not husband and wife, as we had been, but child and mother. He wanted a lot of tenderness and reassurance as a mother gives a child, but often he would ask me, "What's your name?" It was heartbreaking to see the change that was happening to him. Also he had no idea of time; five minutes to make a cup of tea, and he would come to the kitchen saying he had been waiting an hour and missed me. He just wanted a hug.

Two or three times a week I would dash to a string of shops five minutes away and get back home within twenty minutes. It was necessary because Sherry would decide to find me, leave the house not even knowing our address and I often just arrived in time to see him on the door-step looking to see if I was coming along.

On the 29th of December I posted a letter and went to buy vegetables. Coming out of the greengrocer I bumped into Reg. He offered to carry my bags, and to my amazement told me of his feelings towards me. I don't remember saying anything, I was so surprised, yet so pleased that such a kind person should feel close to me. We had been such good friends for the last eight months, but although I liked him, I still felt very loyal to Sherry and could not forget he was my husband. Reg was a very private man and I felt he also was a little off balance about admitting to his feelings, so we walked home in silence. We still felt that we had committed ourselves to a heart-felt consideration that we had taken an identical path. Many things had to be fathomed, but only time, patience and complete honesty with each other could allow us to understand why!

For the next year, slowly, so very slowly, Reg and I got to know each other. My mother had been sent home, the x-rays and tests had not shown anything untoward, so she came home armed with a 'zimmer' although when trying to walk I found the only way was to pull her slippers to make her take steps. Reg gave her a transistor radio which kept her company in her bedroom downstairs. Often he used to pop in on his way home from the station and have a little chat with her.

One day, after his visit, he said that to make her evenings more interesting she had accepted his suggestion of calling at 6pm to carry her to the sitting-room to look at the TV and he would return at 10pm to carry her back to her room. At the same time, he noticed that when I accompanied Sherry up those stairs, he often said, "Let me help, he is swaying backwards," so he took him up.

For a whole month he did this, till it was considered necessary for my husband to be admitted to Orpington Hospital. After my daily visits in the morning, I could look after my mother and at least we could talk and I could give her more time than before. Reg always phoned two or three times a day to see if I needed anything at all. His wife went to business in London every day and apparently was interested in the St. John Ambulance Service which took a lot of her time, quite apart from any Special Events which meant arriving home at 10pm and many Saturday and Sunday occasions. I started to realise why their time was rarely shared, though never did Reg criticize in any way the situation and it was obvious that the status quo was accepted as a norm. He had kindly given me his secretary's office phone number and name of his secretary in case any difference in maman's or Sherry's condition change so that I wouldn't feel totally alone.

Luckily, I had made friends with kind neighbours and they would call in and cheer me up on those days I found difficult to cope. Nevertheless, the only person I found easy to talk to you was Reg. He seemed to be able to understand my feelings, and our shared moments became very precious.

A year after moving in our home, I decided to use every moment to bring the garden to life. I made sketches of favourite flowers, mostly scented, to bring colour to all sides of the garden. Reg used to give me the excuse that he had too many plants for his own garden, and kindly provided me with extra flowers and I arranged them carefully around dwarf shrubs and lavender bushes. I put evergreen shrubs and a fair amount of deciduous plants with flowers and scented foliage. When summer arrived I could coax maman to try to take a few steps and arrange for her to sit beneath the old Bramley tree with a small table by her side for her use.

The verandah at the end of the dining room was a little rickety and Reg arrived with nails and a hammer and made it safe and strong. By July, the colours and scents of summer were thankfully rewarding my efforts and I accompanied maman, this time with a walking stick, to try and walk down to enjoy the garden.

August the 23rd was Reg's birthday (59) so I decided to give him a present as he had helped me so much since our arrival here, so my intention was to give him a useful, very useful HAMMER. He was so surprised and we had a good laugh over my choice. I took a snapshot of him brandishing his hammer, and I still have that photo now. He had a camera on his coffee-table and as he offered me a glass of wine I put the delayed action button on and while we toasted his birthday we heard the click and our photo was taken. Both photos are the best ones we have taken, yet within ten minutes of my bringing him his present those two snaps were taken on the spur of the moment.

Since I didn't own a car, the garage at the end of my garden was unused and its entrance was at right angles to the main road. Reg asked me if I would consider selling that piece of land, as his own drive which sloped down towards his house was not at all practical. On rainy days the water poured down through his garage and in winter the drive was slippery with ice and snow; apart from emerging into a bus route it was not very easy. I said that as I had kept my driving licence going, I might at a later date buy a car, but if he wanted to use it, I would be quite agreeable to let him do so. But Reg would not hear of it. He asked if he could rent it and settle for it monthly, as it would be an easier way to park the car. I agreed reluctantly but he would not accept it unless he paid rent to me. I had a feeling he did this to help me financially, and I appreciated the gesture.

My daily walks after breakfast to Orpington Hospital were always the same. My mind was always hoping that a little improvement would be there, that memories of happy occasions would surface, but only too often we would hold hands, after taking a time to recognise me and after a couple of hours I would hug him and say, "See you tomorrow." It seemed a long trek up the hill to get home, dry my tears before reaching the front door and enjoy a cup of tea with my mother. I no longer could recognise my husband who had been so loving and was blessed with a sense of fun.

Reg holding his hammer

Reg & Jacqui toasting his birthday

I know I was fortunate to be able to express my fears to my mother and to Reg who I found so understanding and sensitive.

When the darkness and chilliness of autumn arrived, I decided to prepare for the vagaries of the weather and had a 'Tudor' style fireplace installed in my second reception room. Having a coal fire topped with logs would be very welcome. As soon as that was done, my mother and I chatted about having alcoves on either side of the mantelpiece and fitting them with glass shelves. And after that was sorted out builders said it would take three weeks to be done. The meter cupboard was under the stairs at the far end of the room and I decided to paint the door white, cover the surface with wine labels, then varnish it. The small wall at right angles to it I covered with mirror tiles and it lightened the room and gave a reflection of the back garden. I had only one thing to do to complete the comfort: I had to choose a three-piece suite. When I mentioned it to Reg, he offered to drive me to Bromley and asked if I would like him to share the time choosing it. Nice of him to offer, so we chose a dralon 'old rose' suite and it would make the room comfortable for the possibility of having Christmas lunch and maman would be able to sit in front of the fire. By Christmas week, I had arranged a 'manger' and when Reg called he looked at it and seemed genuinely appreciative of it. I told him if I didn't have time for a Christmas tree – a manger to me represented Christmas much more.

2

It was the 2nd of January 1980. I woke up to a day of icy winds and treacherous pavements. I decided to get the housework done first, clean the grate and lay the fire, dash out to carry coal in and more logs. With the temperature dipping I felt sure a roaring fire would be appreciated by Reg after his walk up the hill. At 2.15 I wrapped up well and walked to the hospital.

The sister tells me the doctor wishes to see me. When I see Sherry I realise why. He is very pale, eyes sunken in and seems to be vague. I feel faint at his appearance. The doctor says he is in no pain, but cannot tell when he will fade. I think it cannot be long.

Dreadful walk back, it's bitterly cold and I feel drained. Need to see Reg, light the fire and make tea for maman and me.

At 6.30 Reg calls. Poor man, he looks frozen and is so pleased to see a roaring fire. Give him tea and tell him my news, gives me a page a day leather bound diary and a calendar and asks me if he can give me a lift this evening. I decline, as I will return tomorrow after a phone-call to the hospital. I can't seem to even get my hands warm, promise that if I need a lift I must phone him at once. Reg goes home and I walk to maman's room as it's obvious she's upset and needs to be close to me.

The next day I phoned the hospital, told Sherry is very poorly so must go at once. I got a shock when I walked in the ward, he's in bed, eyes closed, seems so frail with a chest infection, temperature and laboured breathing. I kissed his cheek and call his name, he opened his eyes for just a few seconds, but was exhausted. I returned home and when Reg called at 5.30 told him my news.

Will drive me after supper. When we arrive Reg goes to his bedside and goes back to the car for a smoke, I tell him to go home as I don't know how long I shall stay, I can go home in my own time. The sister says they won't phone during the night but anytime from 7am if the need arises. Terrible night, awake at 3am and 5am. 6.45am the phone rings. My darling Sherry died at 11pm last night. Thank God I kissed him goodbye and he was aware that I was there.

Get dressed, tell maman my news, get my house keys and walk round to tell Reg. He's dressed to go to the office and takes my hand and I sit on the settee. He says I must have a cup of tea, he can take a later train. Gladys, his wife, walks down the stairs and says sorry to hear the news. I only stay 10 minutes and go back home. So many things to do today, get death certificates, go to the Chapel of Rest and say my last good-bye. Funeral is booked for Thursday the 10th of January, Reg offers to drive me to the hospital to collect Sherry's clothes and any other items. Mention I should like him to be by my side at the funeral as I don't want to be in the car all alone. Says it could cause me embarrassment, so don't know what will happen!

The next day, Reg decided to accompany me, so I was determined not to show any tears as any emotional distress might have upset Reg and as I appreciate his efforts to get Gladys to stay home with maman, it must have been a feat of diplomacy to have arranged all this.

The very close friends who came back to the house, just an intimate few who had known Sherry over many years, kept the gathering as Sherry would have liked it, without morbid thoughts. I am so very grateful to them all for remembering him as he was before his Strokes, and keeping the conversation a light-hearted experience.

Soon after the visitors left, I go to my mother's bedroom to see if she needed anything, she said no, so I kissed her goodnight and walked upstairs hoping I would have a whole night's sleep. Go to our bedroom, just going to draw the curtains in the bay window, when I see the lights go on next door, hear a clothes hanger click against the picture rail and see Reg waving good-night. Return the wave and draw the curtains. From that day, we always waved goodnight to each other.

Since I had moved to this house, Reg's wife had asked if I would mind letting the window cleaner in (it was the only way to get to the windows facing the back garden) Reg would settle the cost when it was done. I naturally agreed and since I didn't go to business it was no trouble. That particular day when the chap knocked on my door, I took the key and told my mother I was taking him to do the windows and walked round. I unlocked the front door and jumped in surprise as I found Reg in his armchair and apologized for disturbing him. He said "I didn't go to London this morning, this wretched migraine came and I had flashing lights and a headache. I'm sorry I startled you." I explained the window cleaner was here, so opened the backdoor and let him get on with It. I asked Reg if he'd like a cup of tea, and did he have any special tablets for it. "Yes, I have had one, but if you are making tea have a cup with me." So I put the kettle on and we shared a cup together. Not having suffered from migraines, I did not know how he felt, so I sat by the gas fire and thought it better to keep quiet.

Somehow, the silence did not bother me. Just before the window cleaner returned to the kitchen, I asked him on pure impulse if he would like to share some supper with me next Monday instead of having a sandwich on his own.

"It's very kind of you, I accept."

"I will give maman her supper first, so shall we say 6.30, if its convenient to you?" I settled the bill and left.

When I returned home, I told maman what happened and said I don't know what made me say that, but it would be someone to talk to for us both. Maman smiled and said, "I think it's a good idea, what are you going to cook for him? Do you know what he likes?"

No I did not, and would have to play it by ear.

The Monday came and he phoned to ask if red or white wine would be suitable. I was surprised but said "Red." He called at exactly 6.30 and gave me a bottle of *Chateauneuf du Pape* which would be great with *boeuf bourguignon* I had prepared, accompanied by vegetables and for dessert I made an apple pie which was fine with ice-cream. He accepted a second helping of that. Had coffee and I offered him a glass of Armagnac, I preferred a tiny glass of Cointreau.

He seemed to enjoy it and was very relaxed. We chatted and it felt as if we had known each other for years, yet up till today we had always kept our conversation very light-hearted and had never divulged any personal details of our past. I just knew him as Reg, knew nothing of his childhood, what his profession was and he knew even less of me, yet we seem to be on the same wavelength and it was very strange since we have known each other one year and nine months. The time suddenly startled us both as the hall clock struck 9pm. I realised it was getting late, so he put his coat on, thanked me and went home. Five minutes later the phone rang, it was Reg. "Sorry I had to leave, but I wanted to thank you for a lovely meal and such pleasant company." I said 'goodnight' to my mother and she asked how he enjoyed his meal. I said it was a wonderful evening, he bought a bottle of good wine and the time went too quickly. "Your eyes are sparkling and I don't think it was the wine. Goodnight." Was my mother aware of a spark having started a romantic interest to someone of forty-eight who had lost a husband and was not at all expecting anyone to be in the least interested?

He was married and being a very handsome and intelligent man, it seemed strange to spend most of his time, even sometimes week-ends separate from his partner. I could not understand it but it was so personal I had to wait for him to open his heart, I felt that until he made the next move I could only wait and be there for him. A week later, when Reg called and had tea by the fire, he asked if I would like to come to London and have a meal with him. I was surprised but explained I would love to, but would have to arrange with a friend of maman to keep her company and prepare a meal as I didn't want to leave her on her own. He looked disappointed so I said, "If you like, share a snack with me then I'll feel happier being at home, it's up to you."

He replied, "Well, if it's not putting you out; I will re-schedule meetings and take an earlier train, perhaps I can help by keeping maman company."

3

**"A spark can set a light a great passion,
but a deluge cannot extinguish it."**

Anon

On that Monday, maman called me to say she had just seen Reg pass her bedroom window, it was only four-fifteen, so I guess he went in to wash and change. At five o'clock the knocker went, Reg stood on the door-step, a sprinkling of snow on his head and shoulders so ushered him in quickly. He wore a Harris Tweed jacket, beige trousers, matching shirt and a Kent tie. Asked if there was anything he could help me with I replied, "No thanks, but I'll make a cup of tea, perhaps you could take one to maman."

I showed him to the dining room and he made a bee-line to the fire. I asked maman if it was OK to let Reg bring in some tea and whilst they were chatting away I put the finishing touches to our meal. A while later, he brought back the two cups to the kitchen and I went with him to the dining room.

I sat on the rug and with my back to the settee and enjoyed the warmth and crackling of the fire. Reg looked at me and suddenly got up and sat on the settee, took my face in his hands and kissed me so gently that I caught my breath, and returned his kiss after only a moment's hesitation. I moved my head back and saw such tenderness in his blue eyes. I put my hand round his neck and pulled his head down to mine. We kissed again as if we wanted to make up the time lost, his long fingers caressed my breast and his fondling made my nipples harden and I was even more excited. I undid the buttons on my blouse and removed it. He slid down on the rug and we took off our clothes without the slightest feeling

13

of modesty, and were soon side by side, allowing our passions and hunger guide us to a journey of discovery. He ruffled my hair and then as we got more and more aroused, he turned towards me and slid into me.

I gasped but enjoyed the warmth of him, he put his arms on either side of me, looked at me and saw the response in my face, we moved in harmony and all at once our rhythm became more intense and urgent. We were reaching the heights, we were both getting out of breath till we became one.

We listened to the cracking fire, and to each other's breathing. We twined our legs together and he cradled me in his arms, in such a loving way, I felt safe from everything and everyone. Then the noise of the clock in the hall striking 7 o'clock.

We dressed and I went to the kitchen to get something to eat, we were both so hungry.

After a quick snack, Reg took my right hand and without a word spoken, took me upstairs to the spare bedroom. We undressed again and slid between the sheets. I told him I felt cold so he put his arms round my shoulders and I leant against his chest. We snuggled like a pair of spoons and soon I felt warm against him. Within moments we both wanted to be close and faced each other, and without saying a word, we knew there was no going back. He said that by the fire he could not hold back and it all happened so quickly, but now he wanted me again. I had wanted him for a long time so we allowed ourselves to enjoy every pleasure we wanted to give each other. If only we could fall asleep in each other's arms, it would be wonderful, but time was our enemy and sadly we kissed each other good-night, got dressed and he opened the door and went to his house. It must have been nearly ten when we waved good-night at the bedroom window.

I peeped in to see if maman was still awake, but she was already asleep. I tiptoed to her bed, kissed her cheek and closed the door carefully.

We both looked forward to our intimate Mondays, and at least I was sure that he would have a substantial meal after his train journey home.

I told him of my idea of starting a collection of glass or china ornaments. Reg liked the idea and suggested that we chose the first item together. Next Thursday, he was driving to Gatwick airport to go to Newcastle for a conference but would fly back the same evening about 7pm. At 7.10 the knocker went. It was Reg, it had been a long day but it was lovely to see him again.

Next morning, Reg phoned from the Holborn office and said he'd heard last night some news which I might like. The St. John Ambulance Service has arranged for 2 female members to visit and stay at the Italian Hospital in Naples for three weeks next June. I just could not believe it, the only thing was that when I gave Gladys a cup of tea after working in he garden, she said she did not want her garden neglected so was told Reg would put in an automatic watering system as he intended to go on a golfing holiday.

When Reg called in the evening, we shared a cup of tea and he asked me if I would share the holiday with him. It was so unexpected I just could not take it in. Then I realised, it would not be possible. I could not in any way leave maman with such poor mobility and just go away. So I told maman what Reg had told me, and within minutes, she asked me for the telephone and got her address book out of her handbag and said "I know what we will do, you could do with a holiday. Sit on the bed and I'll sort it out."

I could not believe how someone of her age and unable to move much could decide so quickly what to do for both of us. She found a Paris number and dialled the Continental Exchange, phoned Helene, a childhood friend she had known since both were eighteen years old and asked if she would be able to come over to Orpington and stay a fortnight if she sent the return flight from Orly Airport to Heathrow, and as she can't manage to walk would she mind preparing their meals. She also explained the reason for asking such a favour and Helene immediately said she would be only too pleased to help. After a few words she rang off. Well, all you have to do is go to the travel agents and get the ticket. When Reg calls, I'll tell him what has been arranged. Also, please order a taxi to collect Helene and bring her to the house." That evening. Reg called and I told him maman had some news for him, and when he left her room, he was grinning from ear to ear, and hugged me saying he'd never met anyone like maman and how understanding she was. Where we would go, was to me not in the least important, being together was all that mattered.

Our first holiday! It was exciting but at the same time, I was very apprehensive. I would worry about how my mother was faring, also how we would feel and get used to each other's ways, if I would please him – a thousand questions were in my head, and yet deep in my heart. I felt the holiday would bring us together and that nothing would be able to separate our lives, however long we would have to wait.

The month of March came in with a roar, strong winds, temperature up and down, the perfect recipe for colds, sore throats and headaches. I was lucky. I kept well but not so Reg. Came home one evening with a sore throat and a shocking cough. Advised him to see the doctor, which he promised he would do so. Next day, he broke a lens in his new reading glasses so I offered to take them to the opticians and also get an appointment with his doctor. Much to my surprise he meekly agreed and said "You worry over me, don't you."

I did the necessary and also collected his inhaler from the chemist. A few days later, Reg recovered from his cold, he phoned from his Holborn office and asked me if I would enjoy a day at the sea tomorrow. Would go early, but make our way back around 4pm. The sun shone for us and we stopped en-route for a lovely breakfast. We ambled round the town and Reg bought me a beautiful ostrich leather handbag, stone colour, very smart yet roomy. He said to me, "Must only use it on your birthday, that's the 7th of April, isn't it?" So kind of him; I wondered why he got it so early. Realised when April came my birthday fell on Easter Bank Holiday and it had been organised well in advance by Gladys to visit old RAF friends who lived in Suffolk. I had not visited Hastings before and we enjoyed a lovely lunch on the front.

So for five days he would be away. I looked out of my bedroom window and although the curtains were open, all was silent and empty. Who would imagine that five days would seem so long. He had given maman a birthday card to give me on his behalf, expects to be back at about lunch time. Can't eat lunch till I know he's safely home. Calls round at 1.30 and I realise we have missed each other, go upstairs and enjoy a cuddle, it's been such a long five days.

Comforted myself with the thought it would soon be June and our first holiday together would be upon us. Thursday the 5th of June was Gladys' departure date. Reg was meeting her at Charing Cross to carry her suitcase to Leicester Square tube station for a direct tube to Heathrow. I had to walk to the surgery to collect a prescription, so offered to carry Gladys' case to Orpington Station. As far as I was concerned, my holiday started this very moment.

Maman's friend Helene arrived the next day and it was lovely to see her and speak my own language again. When she first saw me I was just a few days old and over the years she always wanted news of me. When Helene first met maman, she had arrived in London, not knowing the language and my grandparents had taken her in and maman had the job of teaching her English. She had been offered a position at

Fortnum and Mason as she was a trained dressmaker in Paris and also had a gift for sketching designs for clothes. So I enjoyed seeing her again and knew that both women would have much to chatter about whilst Reg and I were getting to really know each other on our first holiday.

4

Monday the 9 of June the alarm went off at four-thirty am. Reg had already put suitcases and a zip bag of shoes in the car. When we had said goodbye to maman (she heard my alarm) we left at 5.15am. As soon as we reached the countryside of Wales, I realised how different it was. Waterfalls and water features were reminding me of parts of Switzerland and was agreeably surprised about the beautiful scenery. I had never before visited Wales and it was pleasant to explore in Reg's company the views around us. We arrived at Llandudno at nine-forty five and Reg found a lovely hotel called the "Hydro" on the promenade and facing Llandudno Bay, and booked a comfortable double bedroom and usual facilities on the first floor. After a light lunch, we strolled in the town and booked seats for a show this evening. After driving 260 miles this morning I was surprised he wanted to go to a theatre, but after a good sleep in the afternoon he felt ready for anything. Reg booked a call to Orpington to tell maman we had arrived safely and all was fine. We had a quick chat and now we could start our holiday.

The next day, we took the cable railway to the "GREAT ORME" (679ft) had a walk and a good lunch. At last we could talk to each other without worrying about time. We found a wooden seat and after looking at the view, we were eager to find out about each other's past. So many events were similar, it was quite uncanny, we were both only children and had grown up without a father. There was only eleven years and eight months difference in our ages, a good balance when the man is older. Reg had lost his father at the age of three, his father had lied of his wounds in the Great War and his mother, grand-mother and aunt rallied to bring him up.

He got a scholarship to help him get a good education. At nineteen he joined the RAF. Whilst at High Wycombe, H.Q. of "BOMBER COMMAND", he married on the 17th of October, 1943. In 1945 he was sent to Valley, on the island of Anglesey, where he intended to drive me to see it again after all those years. He was sent to HAMBURG (SIGNALS FLYING UNIT) and a few months after the end of the war returned to England and civilian life. He went into the Electrical Industry and joined B.I.C.C. (British Insulated Calender's Cables). He worked for them for twenty five years and travelled to Canada regarding installing cables across the St. Lawrence Gulf in Canada and other sites in that large country. Reg was interested in all those explorations, but after those exciting projects were done, decided to go in the Gas industry. The North Sea oil explorations and in parts of Dorset intrigued him and he joined their ranks. He then studied Contracts Law to further his position and was seventeen years with British Gas.

When I met him he was Contracts Advisor and enjoyed the challenges of travelling as well as the friendships of his colleagues. He had a daughter, married with two children and a son three years younger than his sister.

He gave me no further information, so I asked him no more. By this time, as if to mirror his mood, the mist came down and we made our way to the cable railway and feeling cold and damp, we returned to our hotel. We enjoyed planning tomorrow's drive to Valley, I said nothing but had a feeling that returning to past places were often a mistake and sometimes caused hurt, but kept this to myself, I could well be wrong. The next day we followed the road after crossing the Menai Straits bridge.

As we got nearer, I was surprised at the amount of sheep by the roadside, little pieces of wool caught on twig and branches in the hedges, I have never seen so many sheep. I

Reg joins the RAF at nineteen

Jacqui aged 7 as a junior member of the Monte Carlo Ballet

mentioned it to Reg, didn't seem at all surprised, said it was always like that.

When we arrived at our destination, the look of surprise and disappointment on his face made me feel so sad, the place was full of brick-build married quarters, no more grass but cement runways, he did not recognise it at all, such was the change.

I begged him to turn back and realise the place had changed as much as he had. He was a boy in '45, he was now a man. I said, "Enjoy the now, not what things were like thirty-five years ago. Let's have some lunch and enjoy each other's company." Reg looked at me with such surprise, I bit my lip and hoped I had not upset him, but I felt he had to be jerked out of his black mood. As we sat down to our table he looked at the menu, then he said "I'm sorry, I was forgetting the past is best left alone, it's being together that is important."

Once our meal was finished, we eagerly made our way back to the hotel, we just wanted to be close to each other, all at once, I saw how vulnerable a strong man can be, he wanted me to comfort him, to tell him how much he meant to me. We were now equal, the tears I had shed so often over him returning next door, yet he told me because he does not have tears, he still aches inside when we are apart, he feels as much as a woman, but doesn't show it. I relied on his strength, but in fact, we were as sensitive as each other. I had learnt a little more about Reg, and I loved him more for being aware of other people's feelings, no doubt that this is why he showed such kindness to others. He certainly was a very special man and I was glad he wanted to be with me. Reg wanted to phone a hotel in the vicinity of the picturesque village of BETWS-Y-COED, a place of waterfalls and an ideal starting point for Snowdonia. But all hotels were full, was then recommended to try the "BRYN EGLWYS" Country House Hotel in BEDDGELERT, it is set in the heart of the Snowdonia

National Park and has lovely views over the river GLASLYN. Sounded fine and Reg booked a room for the next two days. It seems it had an interesting legend and it appealed to us both. We arrived at the village and found the drive leading up to the hotel. The curving drive brought us to a place and found a bank of Rhododendrons, they had wonderful trusses of pink, white and red flowers and on our right the Mock Orange with cream flowers exuded the most overpowering perfume. I got out of the car whilst Reg drove to the car park by the side of the hotel and wandered over to the shrub so tall and so attractive. We were shown our room and felt at once a friendly atmosphere, we were happy to stay in this place. I found a story of the Legend, and I hope the reader will be patient with me and read this legend, to understand how the history of it affects the feeling of this place.

In the 13th century Llewelyn, Prince of North Wales had a Palace at Beddgelert. One day he went hunting leaving the faithful Gelert who was unaccountably absent. On return, the truant standing smeared with blood, joyfully sprang to greet his Master. The Prince alarmed hastened to find his son, and saw the infant's cot empty, the bed-clothes and floor covered in blood. The frantic father plunged his sword into the hound's side thinking it had killed his heir. The dog's dying yell was answered by a child's cry. Llewelyn searched and discovered his boy unharmed, but nearby the body of a great wolf, which Gelert had slain. Llewelyn is said never to have smiled again, and he buried Gelert with honour there. Beddgelert means "Gelert's Grave" in English.

After a tasty breakfast, we drove to the Lamberis Pass and Swallow Falls, then went for a walk on the outskirts of Beddlegert along a waterfall, down again to enjoy a picnic by the edge of the Glaslyn River. After a certain overcast morning, the sun had decided to shine and the countryside was transformed. Reg was keen to know all about me and I was a little surprised that he was so curious.

I explained that I was born in London, both my parents were French, but at that time if you were a girl you were a British Subject by birth, but also a French citizen (in other words I am a dual National.) I have two passports, two identity cards, but had I been a boy, as in those days you had National Service at your majority, you chose for which country you would serve and from then on you were considered a national of that country.

"Is that system still in place?" Reg asked.

"I couldn't say, laws change as the years go by."

"Is your father no longer with you?"

"I don't know him and don't want to know him!" Reg looked surprised, wanted to know why I was so vehement in my reply.

"Why I feel so bitter was that my father was a mummy's boy and apparently when he married was much against having children and had to give more time and affection to his mother than his wife. When maman was pregnant he kicked her in the stomach and when his temper flared threatened her with his army revolver. In fear of her health, she visited her parents' home on the pretext of going there for tea with my father, and refused to return to the marital home with him. The result of it all, she asked for a divorce and when I was born I had a twisted right foot on which I could not stand. The family doctor asked a colleague of his to make a kid-leather covered metal brace which my foot was put in, bandaged for three hours, then removed for three hours, night and day. For how long I can't recall what my mother said, but it was a success. I suppose the bones of a new-born baby are so soft and pliable."

"You certainly have had your share of worries. I see your foot is absolutely fine now."

"In 1936, after a short stay in Coulsdon, Surrey, my grandmother's health was not too grand, so my grand-father and my mother put tenants in the house and moved to the

Principality of MONACO. My grandfather had a brother and a sister living there and the sunny weather seemed an improvement to the damp of England.

When the war started we were on holiday in Cannes and we were told if we went to the beach with our papers and one tiny attache case, we could get the last Submarine going round the Bay of Biscay to England.

Maman and I were accepted because of a British passport but not my grandparents, so we decided to decline so that the family would stay together not knowing how long the war would last." Reg said to me, "Strange, as I was joining the RAF, your chance to return to England was blocked, but who knows the sub could have been torpedoed and we would never have met. It makes you think how Fate can sometimes block or allow people's path to meet." Reg looked pensive, then said "Sorry, go on."

"When eventually maman and I returned to England, the VJ Day Celebrations had just occurred, the doctor who brought me into the world, came to meet us at Victoria Station and was shocked when he saw us. Maman was barely five stones and she was 5ft 7. You could count my ribs through the bodice of my dress and he was amazed to see how thin we were. We tried to get into our house in Coulsdon but the tenants (who owed a years rent) would not vacate and when my mother called them to court, they said they had no intention of giving the house back to "Bloody Foreigners" but when the judge found no rent had been paid, ordered the money to be settled and one month to return the house to its owners."

"How did you arrange things for schooling?"

"Well, maman took me to Purley Grammar School but as I could no longer speak English, I could not do the entrance exam, so the principal suggested a private school in Coulsdon and I went there, but on the day I joined the school, I was taken by a prefect to the class but could not understand a solitary word the pupil spoke, so it was very scary.

The head-mistress was very kind and spoke French very well so at least there was one person I could understand. I soon learned the language but many subjects on the curriculum were very difficult.

You understand I had to forget Joan of Arc, Louis XIV and learn about Henry VIII and his many wives, forget Napoleon and learn about the Spanish Armada. Then I knew no rivers except the Thames and found geography and doing maps a completely new experience.

Of course, maths were a nightmare, I did not understand the farthings, half crowns and guineas and even less inches, feet and yards so I was mostly marked as 2 out of 10, whilst the English girls were terrific at mental arithmetic. Mind you, the French lessons didn't give me any problems, but I had an arrangement with some of the girls on the phone, got help on maths and I helped with their French prep.

The only subject I had no problem with was Latin. Having been in a French convent in Monaco, and serving mass in Latin every morning before class, it became easy. So the teacher sent me to the sixth form which was a little off-putting to do Latin with them, and back to the upper IV with my new found friends for all other subjects."

"Tell me Jacqui, did you marry at a young age?"

"I am sorry to say I did, I was eighteen and in my salad days I believed that when someone wanted to marry you, the reason was because they loved you, wanted to look after you and cherish you, but I was far too young to realise that although he worked hard (he was an optician) he had what I discovered later this obsession of gambling (horses, greyhound racing) and when he lost, he thought he could re-coup it all by doubling the stakes, it was difficult. When things went wrong he lost his temper and lashed out at the nearest person, that was me. So I won't say any more, it's such a lovely sunny day and I am so enjoying your company."

Reg put his hand on mine, and we just looked at each other, grateful that we had to enjoy the holiday and no more sad thoughts.

The next day, we drove to Aberystwyth, took photos of the sunset and asked a chap to take our first picture together admiring the view from the cliffs.

The next day, Saturday, we were making our journey back to Orpington. We stopped for lunch at Worcester, bought presents for maman. Helene and a souvenir for my glass alcove, the first glass hand-bell for our collection.

We arrived after Reg driving 740 miles. We had a coffee and Reg suggested I spent the night at his place and after a light supper we walked round to his place.

I followed up the stairs and entered the bedroom. I was amazed at seeing two very narrow twin beds and before I realised it, said "Good Lord, I had no idea, how long have you had twin beds?" He replied "Fourteen years." It was beyond my understanding. So uncomfortable, I spent most of the night getting cold in my back, only in the early morning when he joined me did I get warm again. If we got the chance again to be together it will be in my comfortable double bed.

Monday the 16th of June, Reg had to go back to the office, so after our soiled clothes were put in his washing machine, I collected them, took them home and ironed them all. He suggested that in the week, he will get tickets to a show in the evening and also on another night see a play.

Sure enough, after supper gives me an envelope, it contains two tickets to see "My Fair Lady" at the Adelphi in the Strand. Goes home and waves at window at 11pm. Next day, I keep very busy tidying my bedroom and taking back to his house every item of ironing and sorting out which clothes to wear for the theatre.

I get the fast train to Charing Cross, Reg is already there anxiously looking for me. Have a quick walk and a drink before the show begins at 7.30. Nice seats and a beautiful show. Tonight he will be staying in my bedroom for the first time and thank God I will not experience a frozen back. Make breakfast and he goes at 7.40am. Mow the lawn and also the lawn in the front garden that spans across both our homes. Gives his green-house a good soaking. Feel so tired, go in kitchen, sit at table to start the vegetables and go to sleep on the kitchen chair.

Reg has a Masonic meeting on Saturday, so has accounts to sort out so will go home and get his paper-work done. Tomorrow we meet in London to see 'The Mouse-trap' Agatha Christie's murder mystery, have a steak supper and go to the theatre, but are both somewhat disappointed, it was not as exciting as we expected. Get train home, it's nearly midnight when we go to bed. Hints he'll take tomorrow afternoon off, I think he'll take the whole day.

Next morning, he asks me which of two country house's I would like to visit. Choose Sissinghurst Castle in Kent and we go after lunch. The sun is shining and the place is a blaze of colour, wonderful scents and it's my idea of what Heaven should look like, provided I ever get there!

Before leaving, Reg buys some strawberries for maman and Helene, and we make our way home. 10pm we get to light the bonfire in his garden (one thing I discover Reg enjoys thoroughly) and watch it burn from his shed. Go in after coffee, listening to records and eat two large pieces of apple pie with cream. Then he goes back home to sort the papers he needs in the zip case I gave him last Christmas. Smelling like smoked kippers we both showered to be free of the joys of BONFIRES!!

Next day, 6.30 am [Reg goes by train to Cardiff and I keep busy to make the day go by quickly. Don't know when the conference finishes, so have no idea when Reg will be home. 6.40pm phone call from phone-box, Reg says he's at Charing Cross Station. 5 minutes later bell rings. It's Reg, he'd rang up from Orpington Station. Lovely surprise. After our meal Reg has to pack a suitcase for three days as tomorrow, Wednesday, he is on a course at Bishop's Stortford, will be back Friday evening. Helene is leaving to get back to Paris and wishing me well says "You nave to be patient for worthwhile events to happen but it is worth the waiting. God Bless." Wednesday Reg gets the car out, says goodbye as he stops outside my front door and says "No tears, see you Friday when I put the car away." Wave to him and realise our holiday is over, Gladys is returning from the Italian holiday tomorrow evening. 8.15 pm phone rings, Reg had a twenty minute break so found an empty room and phoned me. "You seemed so unhappy this morning so thought you would like a call." He's thought of me a lot and thanks me for making our holiday so enjoyable. Seems certain we will have many more.

Mid-August. Reg's 60th birthday was mentioned and plans were proposed to him which he was not at all happy about, he was fine with the family being there, but not neighbours or friends, actually he did not want a fuss. The mistress of the house was organising a Public Relations exercise which Reg was acutely aware was for the benefit of both family members and friends. When I arrived at the party they were just about to take photos of cutting the cake and opening birthday gifts, but the camera didn't work so I offered to fetch my camera and use that.

One member of the family called the next day to bring back the camera and pay their respects to my mother. I was not surprised that when we had a chat, said that both Gladys and Reg go in different directions and is very aware that it's an act that's put on. So when Reg said he would appreciate a quiet, intimate birthday meal at my home, (apparently Gladys was visiting her daughter in four days time and staying two nights) I agreed to prepare for us a special meal. It was a wonderful evening, just the two of us, we put some records on to dance to and crowned our evening with loving each other and spending the night together.

The month of September announced itself with a worsening situation for my dear mother. I had given her a brass bell which I told her to use if she needed anything in the night and I could understand she was regarding calling me, but three times, sometimes four, I had to rush downstairs and try to help her to the bathroom across the hall, so neither of us got a complete night's rest. Maman was so concerned, she asked me to take a letter to the Doctor to explain that perhaps the only solution was to return to hospital or have more tests. The consultant's opinion was that she should be admitted to St. Christopher's Hospice but her condition would be revealed to her, so mentioned that it would be preferable to go to Orpington Hospital so that I could visit daily and walk there. If going to Sydenham I would not be able to afford taxis and could not impose such a trip to Reg, he had helped so much already. The doctor gave me the impression that she would not be expected to return home, but would be well cared for. On Monday the 28th of September the ambulance came to take maman to hospital and obviously I accompanied her.

She told me that she was glad that there would be nurses to help her and I could do with catching up on my sleep. Nevertheless, I felt so very apprehensive as I knew as well as maman that time was not on her side. At least, there will be drugs that will remove pain and stop the feeling of nausea which has been so unpleasant for her. I return to the house and receive a phone call asking about maman. Reg is coming home early as he knows I feel upset about today's events.

In six days time he will be having a holiday in Crete and for fourteen days I shall be without his support. He has promised to write, will post letters and I will keep mine for him to read on his return. Four days after his departure Reg wrote a letter to me, took six days to arrive but I am so pleased to have news. On the day of his return I gave him two letters I wrote to him, and a second letter is still in the post. We have missed each other perhaps more than we either of us imagined and Reg suggested our letters were carefully put away with all our other cards and mementoes that we accumulated over the time we have known each other. A mahogany writing-box I had given him last Christmas seemed a safe place and our various letters, valentine cards, birthday and Christmas card and Easter cards were lovingly kept inside. His second letter to me arrived the day after his return and he poured out his feelings so movingly that I have read it many times and over many years.

5

It was a cold November day. The wind was bitter on one's face and when possible Reg would kindly drive me to the hospital and drive me back.

On the 20th of November, maman was having her 81st birthday and we spoke of seeing her and bringing presents and cards that she could enjoy, but the evening Reg and I went to visit, after a few moments, maman asked me if I would mind leaving her and Reg alone as she wanted to speak to him. I left the ward and went to have a cup of tea.

When I returned about twenty minutes later, maman thanked me and Reg looked at me in a strange way, so I asked if maman wanted something in particular and was she alright. He said, I am sorry but maman wanted to speak to me in confidence, so I cannot say any more. Don't worry, she's looking forward to her birthday, she asked the Sister if she could drink some champagne on that day, and was pleased that she was allowed that treat, so we will get some, she told me the make she favours."

He never divulged their conversation and to this day I can only guess what it was. Unfortunately, on the 20th, Reg was having meetings in London and could not be there, but friends were so kind and brought presents, flowers and even the nurses who were so busy gave her birthday cards. She could not have had better care, and I brought glasses so that we could toast her birthday. The next day Reg went with me to see her and I showed him a beautiful silk rose that our good friend and neighbour Gill Slade had made for her especially. I still treasure it now. Friends in Austria sent roses to her. Gladys brought talc and cologne and as the champagne was still around we three had a glass each. I guessed that the condition of maman's health allowed the kind Sister to impose no restrictions to such a small request and I thanked her for her kindly gesture.

Tuesday the 25th of November, Reg phoned me as soon as he reaches the office, and as he is going on a seminar at Stratford-on-Avon for three days and wanted to know if I would write to him. I agreed, but at lunch-time, he phoned again and asked me if I would like to meet him in Stratford on Friday after 3.15 pm so that we would drive back together and arrive home at about 6pm. He asked me if I thought that it was not a waste of time for the sake of a drive home together.

I must tell maman, as I thought myself, she tells me to go and not miss the chance to be together. At the garage 9.30pm he brings a paper with name of hotel and telephone number, and here to meet him (Bus Station). Next morning, at 6.45am, wave him goodbye. I get a first class ticket (single) to Stratford-on-Avon for Friday.

Have to be at Paddington Station for the 10.17am train, change at Reading, also at Leamington Spa, then take a local train and get there at 1.17pm. Will give me time for a small snack before meeting him at 3.30.

On the Thursday, 10.20pm the phone rings. I was in bed, but dashed down to the hall. Reg thought he would phone to suggest I go inside Boots the chemist in High Street to keep warm as it's extremely cold and he hopes to finish by 2.15, one hour sooner.

So the next day, Friday, alarm goes off 6.30am. 8am taxi called to be certain to get to London Station in time. When I eventually arrive at Leamington, an American couple ask me if the local train is the right one for Shakespeare's birthplace as it's so small, it reminds me of a toy train. Safely arrive, it certainly is bitter cold. Have a steaming cup of coffee and a small piece of quiche. Walk down Bridge Street, pop into Boots, then decide to walk down Warwick Road towards the

Hotel. It's 1.50, when I hear someone calling me: it's Reg. He came out early and am glad to get into his warm car.

It's snowing and after going through Banbury, we stop at a Little Chef for a meal. Then we passed Dunstable and through the Blackwall Tunnel and after a comfort stop, we arrive at Orpington soon after 8.15pm. Say goodnight, Reg thanks me for coming all that way to see him. What a lovely day.

On the 15th of December, Reg suggested that on Monday 22nd, we both should celebrate our private Christmas lunch and exchange presents since he still had no idea what was arranged socially for the Festival. I told Reg I had always enjoyed a French Christmas so instead of stockings and pillowcases would he be upset to put his shoes in front of the hearth and we would put our gifts and private Christmas cards on top of the pile. He agreed and joined in the different custom and took photos of each other opening our cards. Also took a photo of the manger.

He brought a bottle of wine and I put it in the fridge. He arranged the parcels beautifully wrapped on my shoes while I put the finishing touches to the meal.

When I came in with the first course, Reg was in his arm-chair looking at the presents (I wrongly thought he would have preferred a Christmas tree) but no, he entered in the spirit of excitement I felt at opening one or two parcels before lunch and hugging him to thank him for making Christmas so happy. Reg somehow never asked me what I would like for any occasion, he just guessed what would please me and I am thankful to say, it happened the other way. We both loved surprises.

Christmas, one of my favourite Festivals was approaching and I had no idea or clue as to how I would spend it. Maman was still very ill, no one had as yet mentioned what the programme was. I knew Reg was unable to discover what was planned either.

I would visit Maman, but in her condition, any visitor was such a strain, and mornings were busy for both doctors and nurses, although it was allowed to visit anytime. Their daughter invited the parents to spend Christmas lunch at their home in Hertfordshire and my heart sank, the decision was taken. Reg was in such a quandary, didn't like to rock the boat, yet knew I would be alone and felt unhappy about it. He decided the next day, to try and change the situation, so phoned his daughter and persuaded her that a kinder gesture could be possible, so thoughtfully was told of her invitation to me to share Christmas lunch with them, but Reg insisted to give the Ward Sister his daughter's phone number in case of emergency and he would drive me back at once. Thanked them both and after a visit to the hospital at 11am Christmas morning, I was driven to Ware for Christmas lunch. We left at 12.25 and arrived back to Orpington at 1.40am. Reg had made my Christmas day, considering the situation. He gave me on my mother's behalf her Christmas presents and I gave my presents to them both and members of their family.

Boxing day Reg drives me to hospital, Maman seems smaller and paler every day and it's so awful to see the change in her. The neighbours on the other side of Reg invite me to join them as well as Gladys and Reg for a little drink and it's very pleasant to enjoy both the company of Judy and her Italian husband Louis and two children.

They have been very kind to me and my mother and when in difficulty we help each other without question. Her husband is a chef and has very irregular hours. Very lucky that the friends living across the road and around our house are so pleasant, and have for many years remained friends.

Monday the 29th of December, invite Gladys and Reg to a cold buffet and drinks on New Year's Eve. They accept and I start making a list of food needed. Reg promised to buy Champagne to drink the New Year in.

After our meal had a Tombola and enjoyed opening little presents. 10.35 phone Judy to have a drink and dessert with us. Reg offers to baby-sit as Louis isn't yet home. She returns home at 11.40pm to be with her husband and children and Reg returns to have a few glasses of Champers. Wonder what the New Year will bring. Have a strong feeling that 1981 will begin with sadness, but know that at least support and kindness will be given to me by Reg and the good friends around me.

6

When I first arrived at this address, the one room which was in dire need of a change was my kitchen. Unlike the spacious bedrooms and reception rooms, it was a dark and dismal room which needed attention.

To explain what I mean, the walls being very uneven, had been covered by cork tiles (dark brown ones) which gave me the impression that I was entering a mud hut. There was only one electric plug, an assortment of pipes going one knows not where, and few cupboards to store saucepans or plates. My good intentions of removing the offending tiles and lightening up the room, went out of the window as nursing my husband and my mother obviously was more important so at last (two years later) I arranged for a firm to design and furnish the kitchen so as to bring it up to date.

By the end of 1980, it was starting to look all right but of course, the necessary electric plugs and so on would have to be fixed so Reg very kindly offered to install electrical items because he said it would save a lot of expense and time. He asked me where I wanted the plugs fixed and also said cables need to be chased in the wall, as well as plumbing had to be streamlined in such a small space. I had only to purchase the items and cable and he would do the rest. It was so kind of him to offer to do it, 1 also bought tiles which would match the units. I was now able to fix them on and grout them, so that's a job I could do on my own. Reg suggested to me that if I lent him my spare key, he would start on the kitchen while I visited Maman in hospital. On my return, he was pleased to show me how things were improving and after a cup of tea, we discussed what other improvements could be done. I was so pleased that he put such a lot of care and skill to improve that dingy kitchen.

The next day, Monday the 5th January, while having our evening meal, Reg told me he would know lunch-time if Gladys would be able to go to St. Mary Cray evening class to learn Italian as neither her friend who accompanied her to Naples nor herself could understand the language and felt left out. The next day, it was snowing hard and as usual, on those occasions, the trains were delayed and making life miserable for commuters.

Gladys was expected back to Orpington at 6pm, so I suggested as the weather was bad, she calls and I will have a home-made soup, bread and butter ready for her and Reg before he drives her there in time for the class. Reg didn't arrive from London till 6.45 and after their snack off they go. He returns at 7.40 and at 9.15pm goes back to fetch her home. We have a drink at my house and then go back home.

My daily visits to hospital are getting more and more upsetting, when I return home, Reg very kindly makes me a hot drink and does not press me to express my feelings, sometimes the silence is comforting and I know he realises how sad I feel, and just a hand on mine is all I need to know he understands. The Sister said Maman asked for Communion and a blessing on Sunday and although quiet was less depressed. Reg drives me to hospital and Maman is so pleased to see us both.

We hold her hand till she goes to sleep and then return home. The next day, spent all morning putting the first coat of emulsion on the bathroom wall, must keep as busy as I can. After lunch I walk to hospital, maman is pale and fast asleep. Ask nurse should I wake her, says no, as she's deteriorating fast and perhaps would not know me. Stay five minutes, told best to go. They think she'll probably not wake up. 3.30pm Reg phones, so tell him news.

Has a Lodge meeting, but will call on return home. As promised he comes in for a few minutes.

I wave good-night at my bedroom window as usual, but worried about what tomorrow will bring. Tuesday, the 27th of January, wave good-bye to Reg at 7.40am. 8.25am the phone rings. The hospital Sister tells me maman passed away peacefully five minutes ago at 8.20am.

Phone Helene to tell her the news, as for 63 years they have known each other and shared their hopes and sad moments, so I feel honour-bound to tell her my sad news before anyone else. Then phone Reg, will cancel any meetings, and arrives lunch time to help me with Registrar and funeral arrangements. Phone friends, then Gladys calls on her way to London at 9.15, so tell her my news. Prepare soup for tonight's snack for them before the Italian lesson. 12.30

Reg arrives. He gets fish and chips to eat at home, then go to hospital to get certificate and effects. We than go to undertakers. They confirm the date of funeral by phone. Then home for a drink at last. It's 5pm. At 6.15 Gladys phones. Will call in a moment with her Italian book. Have soup, bread and butter. Reg drives them to evening class. Home again at 7.40pm. Cup of coffee to make me feel warm, keep shivering. Feel so tired, will be glad to go to bed. When I visited the hospital, I was asked if I would agree to have a post-mortem done as it could help the knowledge about cancer, so knowing my mother so well, I felt if anything about that terrible disease could help other patients, she would have wanted me to give my permission. I received, a few days later, a letter thanking me for agreeing to it, and also telling me that five areas of the body were affected. I can remember the cancer was in one breast, one lung, the thyroid and spinal cord, which was operated on stopping her walking. I cannot recall the fifth area. Also my mother had left letters to ask me to place her casket in the family vault amongst her parents and grand-parents, so had to do the necessary to open the family vault. A visit to the French consulate in London and certificates of every kind had to be sorted as soon as the cremation had taken place. Dealing with authorities is always such a long and tedious process, I wonder how long it will be before all things arc settled.

At the same time, my solicitors are requesting many papers (i.e. bank cheques, royalty accounts) which are sent to me from my mother's grandfather's music and all those papers being sent by post do not happen speedily, so must patiently await the legal papers to be checked carefully. I must do my best to carry out my mother's last wishes.

7

Absence is to love what wind is to fire;
It extinguishes the small, it enkindles the great.

Comte De Bussy-Rabutin. (1618-1693)

Saturday 25th of April, Reg and Gladys drives me to Gatwick and I am off to Paris carrying my very precious casket and wonder when I meet maman's good friend, Helene, how she will react when we meet tomorrow. It was an emotional meeting, she could not understand how her wonderful friend who shared so much with her was, as she put it, ("in that small casket") but at the same time is relieved that she is in no more pain or anguish.

I have booked a taxi for us to take us to me family vault and will also phone after the ceremony has taken place, to Reg as promised. He misses me, loves me and thanks me for phoning him. Tell him that on Wednesday the 29th when I arrive at maman's hotel in Monte-Carlo to clear her apartment and clothes and suit-cases, I will phone at 3pm, he's arranged with his secretary to be called if out of his office. Phoned also my mother's good friends in Monaco who have promised to meet my plane at Nice airport to drive me to my Balmoral hotel in the afternoon.

When I enter the hotel, find lovely orchids which have been put in my room, a lovely gift from Georgette and Bernard to welcome me. So very kind. As soon as opened my suitcase and phoned room-service for a cool fruit-juice, I phone Reg to say arrived safely. Misses me as I do him, he has been so kind to maman. I so missed his presence on Monday, but Sunday will soon be there when I return to Orpington.

I look at the reflections of the lights in the harbour and think Reg would enjoy Monaco, perhaps, one day.

I go to visit old friends of my mother's and tell them my news. Tomorrow is Friday the 1st of May and as is the custom in France I get a Lily of the Valley card and send it to Gladys and Reg. They usually represent "good luck" and many couples are walking about carrying posies of Lily of the Valley.

Bernard and Georgette drive me to Menton, then turn off up the hair-pin bends to the mountains, go to Sospel, Col de Brouis (1,800ft high) and reach a lovely village up in the hills where we had a lovely meal. Started our meal at 1pm, finished at 3.30pm.

Bought postcards then on to the Col de Tende, stopped at Limone Sui-Station (Italy) 4,200 ft, took photos and on to Vintimiglia, frontier town, showed passport 6 times popping over the frontier. Then home to the Richmond Bar. It's now 7.15. Drove us 1,000 miles. Feel tired and hope I'll sleep well tonight.

Next day, Saturday take all my mother's dresses etc., to the Red Cross so it will be of use. Notice many items in shops that I can buy to take back to Orpington. Finish most of packing. Notice a lovely men's outfitter but shut Saturday, but open Sunday and will get a lovely dressing gown, pairs of shorty pyjamas, one pair I'll put by for his birthday. 12.30 (local time) Sunday 31st of May arrive at airport 1.05pm. Reg meets me on his own, so pleased to see each other again. He intends to have a few days off soon. A few days after my return from France, sort out some of the souvenirs which I have brought back and as soon as we can spend an evening together enjoy his surprise when he undoes his little gifts, also Helene gave me two bunches of edelweiss flowers which she and her husband George picked on a holiday in the Alps: One for me and one for Reg. Since my return Reg finds every reason to see me and is even more attentive than usual, says he finds it difficult to have to wait for the holiday we hope to share as Gladys and her friend Iris are leaving for Naples on Friday the 19th of June till they return three weeks later on the 10th of July.

Reg would like to see Paris as the only times he has visited was with business colleagues at a suburb called NEUILLY, which is the financial centre of the capital. Asks if I will book a hotel from Sunday the 21st of June till Friday. We will decide later where in England we will spend our second week. Have phoned and written to the FLORIDA hotel and expect confirmation of booking.

The 20th May, when Reg calls, show him letter and translate it, it confirms our booking and contains a brochure showing hotel with details of facilities. Only four weeks to wait. It's a part of Paris I know well, walking distance to the opera, five minutes walk to Helene's flat so it helps to know the area. In my mind, I am thinking of places which we would enjoy, only 5 days but the most rewarding happening is sharing time, meals, conversations and the closeness a man and a woman of similar tastes who enjoy the sights, choosing entertainment and pleasing each other is appreciated after such a long time of waiting. It's our second holiday together and we both look forward to it. Only five days stretched in front of us and I had to stop myself from trying to see too many places and tiring ourselves out walking to all the tourist spots.

Every capital is proud of particular buildings which are special to that country, but we also wanted to relax, enjoy seeing places at our leisure. Of course, Paris is usually at its best in spring-time, but in the first few days of summer there was much to enjoy.

Getting to our hotel at 3pm and visiting Helene, we had a twelve minute walk to Place de l'Opera, found a restaurant and enjoyed a pleasant meal with a bottle of Cotes du Rhone.

We saw the world walk by and heard every language under the sun, strolling along wide pavements.

Although it was still early, we walked back to our hotel and suddenly I felt tired and weary, and once in our room, thought it was sense to hang up some of our clothes in the wardrobes. I dashed downstairs and came back with a large bottle of mineral water in case we were thirsty in the night, and so to bed.

The sun shone into our room and I phoned for breakfast. Now we were ready to explore a few places and book tickets, so we walked to the Place de la Madeleine. On one of the large pavements there was a little kiosk and booked two seats on those tall double-deckers to see "Paris by Night" for 10pm this evening. We would be able to view the City of Light in the comfort of a PULLMAN COACH, no walking and we could take a taxi from the terminus to our hotel. The large Church of the Madeleine was facing us and I wanted to go in for a little prayer, but as Reg was Church of England, I didn't want to press him, so asked him if he would mind waiting for me for ten minutes, I explained that I didn't know if he would mind entering a catholic church.

He put his arm round my shoulder and said, "I am sure God will listen to my prayer as well as yours. I would love to visit this lovely church." So we went in, lit a candle and wondered whether my prayer was similar to his, but we knelt side by side in silence. I gazed at the flickering candles praying that the overwhelming love we felt for each other would one day be blessed. We stayed much longer than we intended and walked to the "Place de la Concorde". Reg was very surprised at the size of the square, we walked the two miles up the Champs Elysees, booked two seats for the "LIDO" night club for 8 o'clock Wednesday evening. Sit by the "ARCHE DE TRIOMPHE". Carry on to the Palace of CHAILLOT. Notice the Eiffel Tower is closed to the public as they were painting it, so can't go up to visit.

We walk through the gardens and take two photos, then

Jackie by the palace of Chillot in Paris

Jacqui & Reg on a boat on the River Seine

lunch. Take a bus to St LAZARE main station, a few minutes walk to our hotel.

Have tea at a little patisserie that have a few tables to enjoy their lovely cakes. Buy a few things at the local Delicatessen to enjoy an intimate supper in our hotel room Was going to get a taxi to go to rue de Rivoli to board our double decker bus, but Reg gets a migraine. Suggest he takes a tablet for it and have an early night, but doesn't want to miss the tour and says it will go eventually. So we take a taxi and board our bus. Certainly have done a lot of walking today, but Reg seems to enjoy every moment. Home by midnight and look forward to get to bed and sleep.

Next day, Tuesday the 23rd of June, I ask Reg whether he would enjoy a lunch on the River Seine, and it appeals a lot so as it's a sunny day it could be very pleasant. So walk to the Madeleine and book two seats for lunch on the Seine, and walk across the Place de la Concorde and along the right bank of the Seine, sit under the chestnut trees and relax. Walk to the quay, have a drink in the lounge alongside the boat and Reg takes a photo. It is hot and sunny and we settle at our table and study the menu. A photographer takes our picture and having made our choice, look at the brochure showing all the bridges we pass under, one of which has the Statue of Liberty, but of course a more modest size than the large statue made as a gift from FRANCE to AMERICA and it always seems to surprise visitors to see it on the central span of the bridge of GRENELLE. Reg was interested at the different styles and attractive lamps which made the forty bridges along the course so interesting. In the centre of the river Seine we passed the two islands, one is the "Ile de la Cite" with the imposing Silhouette of "Notre Dame" with gargoyles against the skyline and the "Ile de St Louis", then we turn to go along the opposite bank. We enjoyed our meal and the wine and alas, we were back at the landing stage we had started from at 3am. We walk back towards our hotel but stopped at our usual tea-room for a pot of tea and chocolate eclairs. Reg, I am glad to say, was full of curiosity regarding the places we passed by, and suggested we could visit Notre Dame on the "Isle of the City" tomorrow. Then we strolled back to the hotel. After all the walking, it was lovely to enter our room, cool, quiet and even better to remove our clothes and enjoy a shower.

He showered first and when I had dried myself and came out of the bathroom, he was stretched out on our bed and patted my side to join him.

He had already removed the brocade coverlet and folded it, laid it on a chair. The cool white sheets felt good on my skin and we both felt eager to love each other and please each other. We turned our heads and without touching, we just looked at each other's eyes as we had so often done in the past, Reg's usual twinkling blue eyes full of devilment were now serious, full of tenderness it was as though we could see our souls, as before it all seemed familiar, our minds and spirit were one and we both needed our bodies to confirm being a single being. He stroked my cheek, kissed my eyelids and softly murmured "My Jacqui, you are so full of love and make me so happy, it can't be wrong."

I kissed him to show there was no need to feel unsure, our depth of feeling was too strong to be a passing fancy. I felt as aroused as he did and wanted him as close as possible. He bent down and kissed my breasts and caressed me while his hands were gently probing to be sure his passion did not hurt me, but by now he would have known that the hunger for him matched his and I caressed him; to make him realise my desire for him was overwhelming.

Somehow, however often we made love, it was always full of happiness and when we were spent we twined our legs together and enjoyed the closeness, he used to ruffle my hair, and kiss the soft skin behind my ears. We had long ago learnt simple gestures that meant pleasure to each other, many expressions we used were private to each other and would never be divulged. Our private jokes and sense of fun would remain ours and only when we both become spirits will those words be uttered again to each other.

The next day, Wednesday, 24th of June, was Midsummer's Day, and after our breakfast, we decide to take it easy, as tonight we go to the "LIDO" night club, so will be quite late. Strange as it may seem, at the age of 49, I have never visited a night club and we are both looking forward to it.

We stroll toward the Seine and go to visit Notre-Dame and go up the stairs to the very top. The stone gargoyles are quite extraordinary and we find the view over the rooftops of Paris quite amazing though unfortunately there is a mist and we can't pick out readily the main buildings.

We take a photo of each other and descend the stairs down to the entrance. We spend a lazy afternoon and reserve our energy for a late and hopefully exciting evening.

We receive a phone call from Helene inviting us to supper tomorrow evening as Friday we return to England. We send a postcard to Georgette and Bernard, our good friends in Monte Carlo and tell them we are here for only five days and go home on Friday morning. They had some time ago visited my mother when she was still able to walk and had met Reg and Gladys. They had been so kind and helpful when I visited Monaco after maman's funeral and hoped we would again have the opportunity to see each other in the future.

We took a taxi to the "LIDO" and were guided to a table for six, so I immediately said "Thank you but no thanks, it's our first visit and we wish to sit the two of us alone, so please do it." He looked at us and smiling directed us to a table for two in the middle, it was perfect. On the table were 2 black miniature top-hats with "LIDO" CHAMPS-ELYSEES written on it as a small ashtray. Everyone smoked in those days. A small posy of flowers, and an enormous programme of the show. It mentioned two orchestras, one Latin-American to dance to and one band, also to dance to.

The show was so sensational and I glanced at Reg, he looked absolutely entranced at the spectacular costumes of lack of them, the gorgeous Bluebell Girls that were fabulous. Each scene was so well presented, it was great. Enjoyed a bottle of Champagne and a good meal. After the first part of the show, the stage glided away behind gold curtains and the orchestra took its place.

Reg and I went down to the stage, as did many other diners and we enjoyed both the tunes and the pleasure of the Latin rhythm. Reg is a good dancer and stayed on the dance-floor a fair time. We eventually came back to our table to enjoy a dessert and a cup of coffee. Asked Reg how he liked it, said he had never seen a show like it. Then the second show took place and the lights dimmed a little and romantic music was played and Reg was keen to end our evening with dancing to tunes we had danced at home – just the two of us. We went on dancing till we noticed couples were leaving the floor to get their coats from the cloak-room and eventually only two other couples were still dancing.

A little while later we were the only people on the dance floor, we then realised we were keeping the band playing so we stopped in the middle of the music and taking my hand, he guided me back to our table and out of the building.

We walked a little to enjoy me night air, grabbed a taxi and home to bed. Such a wonderful evening, I doubt I shall ever forget our evening even if I become old.

Reg asked me, the next morning, if there's a florist nearby, take him to a small but well stocked shop and he chooses an enormous bouquet of Sweet Peas as he would like to give them to Helene this evening, also a bottle of Champagne.

She has invited us to supper, and we are both looking

forward to an intimate meal with such a kind and pleasant lady, who is also blessed with a sense of humour, so we will, I am sure, have a nice evening. When we get back to the hotel, we finish our packing and realise our holiday in Paris is nearly at an end. Tomorrow morning, Friday the 26th June, we go to the airport. Discover there is a strike in England, so wait two hours for our flight. Arrive home, Orpington, at 3.30pm and sort out the mail, and I start to undo the suitcases and washing as need clean clothes for our second week's holiday in the English countryside.

Reg and I work out that after an early lunch, we will drive to our holiday on Sunday the 28th of June. Had not booked any hotel but were making our way to Devon.

8

The sun was shining when we left Orpington, and we found a place near Honiton, called the "MONKTON COURT INN" . It's a lovely place and we are given a beautiful room with every comfort. We have a delicious evening meal by candlelight accompanied by a bottle of Sancerre, our first stop in Devon. Next day, we make our way to Torquay and Reg and I look for a hotel on the front. Find the "BELGRAVE" and get a room on the second floor (room 63) it has a view over a park with putting-green, a bowling green and a small lake.

Have a fish supper and book seats for the "Princess Theatre" comedy show with Russ Abbott.

After we come out of the theatre enjoy a leisurely walk along TORBAY, and the coloured lights under trees and bushes. The reflections along the sea-shore look like a necklace around a woman's neck and it's beautiful to look at as the sea is so still. Enjoy a Martini when we reach the hotel. Tired but feel close and happy.

Next day, Reg drives to Cockington village, with thatched cottages and an old forge. Then on to BUCKFAST ABBEY and take a few photographs for our album. Go the Dartmoor for a picnic, have necessary food, flask of coffee and a punnet of strawberries. Go on to Widecombe where toe fair takes place in September, then back to hotel. Cup of tea, start to look at Wimbledon on the T.V, but switch off preferring to enjoy a cuddle. All that fresh air, our eye-lids are finding it hard to keep open, so we decide to have an early night. The next day, 1st of July, the weather is dull, so it's a good day to purchase souvenirs. Reg buys a glass bell, the second one for our collection, also gets me a round leather covered bottle, I get for him a reversible leather belt. After lunch, we decide to play novelty golf. I have not the slightest knowledge of golf but

I did my best and had a good laugh at my efforts. Took a few photos. Had a cream tea and after our evening meal chose to see the Old-Tyme Music Hall at the hotel. Reg bought some raffle tickets as he usually did, but on this occasion it was for the RAF Benevolent Fund and when the show finished at 11 -45 they asked us to keep our seats while the raffle was called out. To my surprise they called out the winning number and it was mine. I have never won a raffle before and the Master of Ceremonies asked the winner to come to the stage to collect the prize. It was an enormous fur PANDA. It was in a sitting position and it was 27 inches high with a width of 23 inches. Reg was grinning when I resumed my seat, as it was such an enormous toy. I had difficulty in carrying it. We called it "LUCKY" and how I can give you its size is, it is now still in my bedroom and last month, it celebrated it's 25th birthday.

Friday the 31st of July, we were going home to Orpington. Reg went down to reception to settle the bill, we had finished packing last night but all of a sudden, I realised our holiday in Devon was over, it was like a painful knock in the chest and I was unable to stop the tears coming, it had been such a happy time, I didn't want Reg to see me like that, so when I stopped, I washed my face in cold water, combed my hair and when I opened the bathroom door, Reg turned and came over to me, just put his arms round me and I knew he had guessed what had happened. "Your eyes are red and your lids swollen, don't be upset, we will have many more holidays, I am sure of it."

He made me a cup of tea and I held on to his hand for comfort. 1 had a splitting headache but at 1 1am we left. Stopped at Yeovil for lunch but soon after while on a country road Reg stops the car and parks under a leafy canopy saying, "Feel tired, if you don't mind I could do with an hour cat-nap." Said I would just rest and wait for him to wake up. I didn't sleep, just occasionally watched him, very peaceful, his face rather tanned and relaxed. I don't know how certain people can manage to sleep for a chosen time and wake up so readily, but exactly fifteen minutes later, he woke up, said he felt refreshed and we carried on till we arrived at Orpington.

The next day, Saturday the 4th of July, I go in my garden and pick some raspberries. Walk to butchers and get some lamb cutlets, and fresh vegetables. Reg looks at Wimbledon finals on TV.

The day after tomorrow Reg is back in his office. Seems tense, don't know if it's because of going back to office or apprehensive about the return of Gladys, but I can feel his thoughts are elsewhere. I was quite busy sorting out clothes to be washed or dry-cleaned, so Reg helped me putting the shirts or undies in his automatic machine and I dried them on the line. Also when putting things on hangers admired once more a lovely knitted blue and navy suit which Reg spotted in a shop window in Teignmouth last Thursday and tried it on once more to see if it still suited me. Wednesday the 8th July, Reg phones at 9am from office, will do his best to be home early as intends to take me out for a meal. 3.15 Reg already home. Water green-house and puts on a grey suit and blue shirt, looks very handsome, decide to wear the knitted suit he gave me in Teignmouth. Likes it on me, so off we go. He drives to our favourite restaurant "THE CHANTICLEER" in Sevenoaks, but it's in the process of being changed, so drive towards Westerham and come across "Pitt's Cottage", a 13th century house which was William Pitt the Younger's home.

It's a carvery, very cosy, old beams, soft lighting and candles on tables. Had a good meal. While on our ride to Ide Hill took some photos to finish the film in his camera, so with our new photo album will put in our Paris and Devon photos.

Since our return from Devon we have spent our evenings and nights together but tomorrow Friday the 10th July in evening Gladys will be back. Reg makes the tea and bring it up to bed.

Can't stop the tears, tonight will come quickly enough. Ask him if he's missed her, says he hasn't as we've shared such a lot. Does not eat much breakfast, could it be that he's more upset than I think? Walks down the hill and waves.

Irons the last of his shirts and jumpers and he will put them away when he returns home tonight. 10pm he returns to his house and we wave good-night at the bedroom window. Flights are delayed and not expected till 11.45 so Gladys won't get home till 1am. Apparently Gladys because of delays arrived home at 2.15am. Reg was told her suitcase was ripped on her way out to Naples and she had to purchase another. To add insult to injury her new suitcase was also torn on way back to Gatwick, so wants Reg to drive her to High Street to get a new one, but Reg says there's no immediate hurry to replace it, next week will be soon enough.

Saturday the 18th I am still sandpapering kitchen walls, baking scones. Reg and I go to the tip, also while in the car take the opportunity of looking for suitable wall tiles. Just before Reg returns home after locking garage, tell him "I think Gladys is going off me, been cool for two days." He says "you may be right." Tell him "I'll not lose any sleep over it."

Wednesday the 22nd of July, Gladys tells me over the fence that Saturday and Sunday has to go to town re rehearsal for "Royal Wedding" and also the Wednesday 29th for the Royal Event, has to be there at 6am, so I offer to have a meal ready as it's such a busy time, accepts for Wednesday, I will have everything ready here, so no washing-up for her to bother with.

The next day, Thursday I receive legal documents from my Solicitor in Bromley, will pop in this evening to see if can help. Also tell him that Barbara and Ray, friends of Sherry and myself have kindly invited me to their Dinner Party tonight at 7.30. Will do some more tiling after my lunch and look forward to seeing him later.

He suggests to do a bit more tiling while I am out. 6pm see Reg walking up the hill, only says a quick "Hello", at my sitting- room window. Not surprised, she hovers at any time to see if talking together. When Reg calls to do a bit of tiling, asks me who is the other guest is it a man. Say, yes, but don't know his name, have never met him. Have a beautiful meal, the chap asks me if he can escort me home, thank him but only five minutes walk, so I am fine. Leave their house in Crofton Road at 11.3 5 ,11.40 open my front door. Next morning, Reg phones me from office at 9am and chats till 9.20. Asked if I enjoyed my evening. Seems curious about the man that was invited to dinner. Said he heard me walking past his window and listened for me. I think he listened for two pairs of footsteps, but I was not intending to be escorted by any man I have just met, when I am already committed to Reg.

Was told that Madge and Raymond, his aunt and uncle are arriving today to stay this weekend. Hope I will be able to see them as such a friendly couple. Break the monotony of tiling by spending a while in garden, as I return up my verandah steps, Gladys tells me Madge and Raymond have arrived at 11.30, invited me to a cup of tea at 3.30 as they asked her if they will see me. Reg phones me again at lunch-time, says he'll come home early, will be over re; tiles anyway afterwards. 3.30 go next door. Lovely to see them. 4.25 Reg arrives. I go home to continue my tiling at 5pm. Auntie Madge asks me if it's alright to see my garden, so take her round, it's only 75ft long, so it doesn't take her long, but if tired can sit on the wooden seat and enjoy the fragrance of the lavender bushes either side of the stone steps. Asks if she'd like my mother's dressing gown, it's been laundered and she gladly accepts, takes it back to Reg's house. I am trying to get used to hearing Madge and Raymond talk of their darling RUSSELL as it's his first Christian name and his side of the family always call him that. Monday the 3rd August, our favourite day of the week, Reg arrives at 5pm just finished preparing a juicy

Cantaloup melon as a starter. He goes home to change and enjoy a refreshing shower.

He is soon back after putting out his dust-bin and mine. Tells me Gladys seems surprised about my saying that now all my routine consisted of doing tiles, doing the garden, but nothing much else, seemed to think I was complaining and thought perhaps I would prefer to be free to go out with other people etc. I was so surprised, told him I was only happy when he was with me, find it hard not to be able to share things. After all, I want by choice to work on my home, as it's not been cherished before, and I am I know, a bit slow working on jobs, but I must look after my home. I must have explained things badly and appreciate all the help you give me each day. Reg listened intently and realised that what he had been told by Gladys was completely different to what I had explained to him. We had our meal and Reg, who had been quiet, pensive even, looked at me and said "I have known you over three years, we have been close and we have shared so many emotions, I am old enough to sift between opinions and the real truth, just wondered if you felt too alone to cope I know how I feel and I can't be swayed by anyone."

I realised that anything said would be easily twisted beyond truth, so I must keep any remarks to myself as lies to some people come readily.

Monday the 10th of August decide to only spend 1 hour working on kitchen as want to prepare a good meal for us tonight. Wash my hair and relax in my bath. 5pm Reg is home.

Talks of his Aunt and Raymond and how they enjoyed seeing me. Raymond and I had a game of rummy and we enjoyed the company. Reg wanted to walk in the garden to see how the flowers I had planted were doing, loved the scented roses and I discover how much he liked dahlias. After dinner, Reg started talking seriously. Does not want me to be apprehensive about his retiring as if he leaves it late, he might not get his pension index-linked and won't anyway get a full pension as he's only been at BRITISH GAS a few years.

Also said he's quite aware mat I am more careful in my spending right now than Gladys.

I told him it's amazing the need she has to buy expensive items as soon as she sees anything, it's almost compulsive. Say to him, if he still thinks we'll be happy together one day, and he says "yes, we will be, I know it."

Reg's 61st birthday is this Sunday the 23rd of August and I have a little list of things he might appreciate and must get two Birthday Cards (one official one) and a romantic one with beautiful words to give him the day after, as well as wrapping paper.

I understand the family is invited so that a barbecue can be brought out for its annual burn. Wrap his cassette-case in wrapping paper. Also his hose and sprinkler. Very pleased with presents, also his card. I tell him quietly that the other card will be given tomorrow evening.

The next day, Monday, I carefully packed in tissue paper his Royal Doulton Crystal Bell so that we can continue our hand-bell collection, I don't think Reg will mind keeping it on the glass shelves in alcove. I hope he likes it. He arrives at 4.30, so we can enjoy plenty of time to be together. Reg loved the bell, so all is well.

Have been quite busy lately, one of my neighbours has booked a holiday in St. LUCIA as his wife is rather delicate and would appreciate it, but asks me if I would look after their dog, so I agree to take his basket and instructions as to food. Have just collected him and taken him back to his home, enjoyed their time away.

Today my friend and neighbour Judy, has just asked me to baby-sit their two children as next Sunday has to collect her mother-in-law at Gatwick airport and drive her to ROMFORD and return to Orpington. Will confirm tomorrow

Thursday the 10th of September.

I like to tell Reg before agreeing to it, as I always think I must keep him in the know. He is driving to HINCHLEY tomorrow, staying the night at Madge and Raymond's.

Phones me at 6.45pm from a phone-box to say will phone again in the morning as to where to meet tomorrow Friday on his way home and spend a little time together. 10.20am Reg phones from motorway phone-box, his chest sounds bad, wants to meet me at 12.15 in car park, BROMLEY. Even if it's only for an hour. Make some sandwiches for us. Catch 11.10 to Bromley South station.

Go to car park and see Reg arrive at 12 noon. Says will avoid Bromley and go via West Wickham to Ide Hill. Arrive at 1pm. Have our sandwiches and stroll hand in hand in wood where bluebells were in abundance last June. Drive on to Westerham and have tea in a place we went to before. Return to Newstead Avenue 4.30. I walk the length of the road, whilst Reg drives straight to his drive. Chat in garden. Gladys gets him to dig out a diseased Christmas tree and cut down shrubs till 7.30pm. I give drinks over the fence. 8pm open garage for him and he pops in to kiss me goodnight. Tell him Gladys isn't friendly any more and never have drinks in her place. Says perhaps she thinks I'm a danger to her. Strange thing to say. Go up at 9.10pm. Feel uneasy. Yet he drove three and a half hours since before 9am to meet me and spend time with me. It must mean something.

Sunday 13th Reg gives me Sunday papers and I give him mine. I am going to Judy's to baby-sit at 8pm. We arranged that when he goes upstairs to bed, I'll wave from Judy's front garden at 10.15. Do so and at 11.50 Judy phones to say arrived at Romford. Eventually arrived at 1.30am. Get home at 1.45am.

9

What is an intuitive man?
One in whom persuasion and belief has ripened into
faith, and faith becomes a passionate intuition.

William Wordsworth.

Monday 14th of September, get up 7.10. Look out for Reg till 8.15. No one. See Gladys run down the road at 8.40. Go on terrace, windows of kitchen wide open, knock on dining-room windows and see Reg in back bedroom in his dressing gown. Phone him, says Gladys made appointment with the doctor for him for 11.45. Say come along at 9.30 for coffee.

Gets car out and go to High Street. I go to the bank while he visits the doctor. Have fish and chips lunch and go home. I walk to the chemist and collect his prescription.

On my return, make scones and enjoy some with a cup of coffee. Suggest he has a little snooze on the settee, while I sort out some supper for later.

Wants to know when I am coming back, said just call, I am in the kitchen. Seems not too keen to be alone. I look in a few moments later, seems to be asleep but as I reach the door he says " Will feel better if you join me, come and sit by me."

I do, but one kiss leads to another and we enjoy being close. Reg has a week's certificate so looks forward to being home with me for the next few days. Talks about the idea of finding a cottage in the country, tell him that if I get my house valued when it's finished being decorated etc, could have some money to find something. Say to him "I take it, it would be away from Orpington? He says, "Of course, would only find that in the countryside."

He seems to think that idea could only be feasible when he retired. Very close and happy together. He had a Lodge Meeting, asked me to phone to give apologies as not well. Reg goes home and to his bed by 9.30. Gladys returns at 9.50 (as per usual on Mondays).

Tuesday, I suggest that any shopping he has been asked to do, let me go by bus and you just potter, and I will take Gladys' duvet to be cleaned. Notice his garage doors have been delivered and are leaning against his garage, so will carry them in for him. Get home and prepare a light lunch and get him to take his tablets. After lunch. I put the TV on, cricket should help to make him doze off, as the commentator has a voice which would send a virile twenty year old to sleep. Ten minutes later, Reg is in the land of Nod, so sit in armchair and think of last nights conversation. After a good hour's sleep, Reg wakes up and I ask if he would like a drink. As if carrying on last night's chat I ask him if we will look for a cottage together? Says "Yes, but these things can't be managed quickly, let me arrange it." Seems that patience will in the end manage for us to be together. Feel he's so close now that I can find the patience if in the distance one can see happiness in view however blurred the image.

He goes home at 5pm. Sits on his terrace. Gladys arrives at 6pm. She says to me no French lesson till Reg feels better, perhaps later in the week.

My efforts in trying to make my home more comfortable are at last paying dividends. The small kitchen is now much more functional, I can put items in cupboards and in a small kitchen you need a place for everything. The dining-room has taken a long time being a large room, but now the fireplace takes pride of place, I have at last finished hanging wallpaper and doing the painting, the new curtains are comfortable and have a nice design and as time goes by, our collection of glass bells and personal mementoes are beginning to look great on the glass shelves of both alcoves. But I must not rest on my laurels, the sitting room facing the front of the house has not been cared for as it should. Each recess on either side of the fireplace have been covered with a plastic laminate, dark and does not do justice to a nicely proportioned room, so I decide to remove the plastic and will ask Reg which place he thinks is the most suitable to choose bricks and I'll make a sketch to design a more attractive fireplace. If I can get some fire-proof cement, I can mix it and with a spirit-level put the bricks to make my own fireplace.

I have put curtains in this room that were the same measurements on the bay-window from my last house, but intend to choose better material which will keep the warmth in for the winter.

After three weeks of mentioning it, Gladys wants a holiday, it's fixed for one week in IBIZA, going on Sunday the 11th of October. Reg asks me to write to him and keep letter till his return, he will also write to me. Has shown me a D.I.Y book for me to look at and will help in any way re my ideas of a brick fireplace. Last Friday, choose bricks and an iron bar to do with it. Next day receive the bricks and cement. Reg helps to lay bricks down re the surround and I tell him while he's away, it will keep me busy, will do my very best.

Reg seems to be all nerves and I notice when we have had a last cuddle to say goodbye, his right upper lid is throbbing and seems to be less than enthusiastic to have a meal. 10am Sunday, pops round to say goodbye, will count the days as I will.

Tomorrow, spend my day working in garden, I remove tomato plants, weeds and generally get things tidy. The weather is turning; a cold wind has whipped up leaves in garden and by the evening feel the need for warmer clothes. Go to bed early and start writing a letter to Reg. Only 24 hours have passed but miss him so. Wednesday, have a tickle in my throat and feel as if I am starting a cold.

Just what I need, I want to get work done and don't need that nonsense. Thursday, I decide to do some work on the front sitting-room, so start by measuring and counting how many bricks need to be split in half. Get a strong hammer, two different size chisels etc and when I look up, notice it's pouring with rain, so can't do that job outside. So open trapdoor in passageway to go down the cellar.

It's not a proper cellar, it seems to have patches of water on ground, but I get some bricks (and the tools) and it takes ages to split 13 halves and mix cement. Its now 11am and go on till 5pm, stop for a cup of tea. Take a couple of Hedex and then decide to leave it till tomorrow as my head aches and feel as if I am burning. Take temperature but only half degree higher than normal so can't be that bad.

Hope to heaven if I feel better than this by next Sunday.

Friday I go to the High Street, just as I walk past a furniture shop, I am stopped in my tracks as on the dining table in the shop there's a table lamp with an opaque glass bowl held by two cupped hands. It is identical to our private sign and can't possibly not go in and enquire the price. However expensive must get it, it will be such a surprise for Reg when we have our meal together next Monday. Do only one hour work on my bricks in the cellar and decide after a small supper to make a lemon and whiskey toddy and go to bed. I must be a dreadful sight, a runny nose, a cough that would make a seal jealous, and sore eyes.

Roll on Sunday, just hope my croak will disappear by then, it's still pouring and I am aching everywhere. Write to Reg a second letter, it's a depressing day, dark and miserable. Laid the fire for Monday and decide on a bottle of MACON-LUGNY for our meal. One more day to wait to see Reg.

Go to florist and get a red begonia to leave on the dining table of Gladys and Reg. Fresh flowers are always right in a home.

Sunday 18th October, still raining. Tidy the kitchen. The day drags on and on, but at last 10.30 pm, they are home. Ten minutes later knock on door, going to open garage. Surprised that I wasn't too well. Wrote me two letters but will hand them to me tomorrow. Pleased with flowers. Missed me a lot, came in for five minutes and just kissed each other. Tomorrow evening, will not have to rush. Wave at bedroom window when going to bed, missed our waves.

Monday 19th October, at 4.50 Reg arrives. Make a drink which we take upstairs. It's wonderful to enjoy each other after that separation. Go down at 6.30 and put supper on.

He reads my letters and I enjoy his letters. He loves the lamp and is amazed how close it resembles our special sign. Enjoyed our bottle of wine and put some records on to dance to. Said mat Gladys spoke of going to Italy next June with the friend she knows and it means at least another holiday for us. Added he's well aware of his responsibilities towards me, but I didn't ask him to explain.

So happy you're home again. Two days later. Res arrives at 5pm. Enjoy a drink by the fire.

This evening snack is ready so that not late to go to evening class for Italian. Reg returns from school 8.15. Goes to his home at 9.30pm. Was just going up my stairs when my door knocker goes. It's 9.40. It's Reg to say getting car out, Gladys wants to see a chest advertised. He returns at 10.30, open door and say "What a time to go looking for a chest!" Says he's going to have a coffee and go to bed. 10.55 he waves goodnight.

I will phone tomorrow. That looks to me like a wild goose-chase. Speaks to me on phone lunch time. Asked him if the chest was O.K. "No, he said, it was a waste of time." Reg has to spend three days in Newcastle, he phones me at 10pm to see how I am, this flu seems to be with me still.

Went to see the doctor as it all seems slow to clear, have got a touch of bronchitis, but have medicine to take. Reg will phone again tomorrow to see how I am doing. He should look after himself, he sounds very asthmatic.

Will be home tomorrow Friday. Next day, 10am Reg knocks on my door, he's getting the car out as Gladys has seen in the local paper an advert about wheel-back chairs, dining room ones, and has taken a fancy to them, so they go to Chelsfield and buy them, although she has 8 matching chairs that go with table and sideboard. Still it's her business. Sunday, he is off in the car to collect the last four chairs.

Return and gives me half an hour to help put a layer of stones on the hearth. I mix the cement as it always starts his wheezing.

Two or three days later feel very hot, have a temperature and Reg tells me to phone doctor, not to go to the surgery in that cold weather.

He sounds very stern so I do what I'm told. Doctor examines me thoroughly, think I have bronchitis at base of both lungs. Also examines my tummy which feels tender, thinks it could be an infection of the fallopian tubes, get antibiotics and an expectorant mixture. Must phone Monday if not better, then can have an internal exam at surgery.

November brings not just cold temperatures but unpleasant winds. I will have to sweep the fallen leaves, but not till I feel a little better.

Reg finds out I have no electric blanket and suggest while shopping at weekend to buy one, put a plug on it, so that I can keep warm while the weather is so cold.

Surprise, surprise, Reg tells me Gladys is very keen to get bricks and do a fire surround a little bigger than it is now, so that for Christmas a log fire could be lit. He told her that if she wants to put the bricks how she likes them, she can take her time and put them how she thinks it will be attractive. The following two evenings whilst Reg is away in Cardiff, I hear the clonk, clonk of bricks being placed on the fire surround and realise it's a copycat time.

When I mention it to Reg, says that Gladys wants him to light paper in front lounge, and if OK, will have a coal fire on Christmas day.

He says he doesn't think it's copying so much as wanting to make Christmas cosy. Apparently the daughter and husband and children will come over Christmas eve, and Christmas day so that will be impressive.

Friday, after an afternoon of purchasing Christmas presents and getting them delivered to my house, at last I get home to light the fire in dining-room and enjoy a coffee.

Reg calls at 8pm and amazes me saying Gladys thought she saw a good friend of ours cross the road to visit me. Say, no this gentleman did not, I thought Gladys has good eyesight. He took it as a criticism and become quiet. Ask him what's up and get angry thinking I was unfair to her. Very touchy. I am upset. What an end to the day. I always seem to get hurt.

How could he believe something like that when he knows how much I care. We have a drink, eventually hugs me and comforts me.

Next day, Sunday calls to bring indoors a few more bricks. Perhaps has realised that the remark made was intended to discredit me, and asked me if I'd like to go to Hastings tomorrow, it is such a surprise. Will meet at Tower Road at 7.15am. Bad night, I was more upset than I thought because when we stopped for breakfast, could only have a cup of tea.

Feel better after a walk on the beach and look round shops. Have lunch. Reg buys a tiny pottery panda (re "LUCKY", our fur panda from Torquay). Home by 4pm light fire and enjoy a quiet chat. We have a cold supper and listen to some records. Reg goes to his home, and phones me to say thanks for a lovely day.

The next day, Tuesday, busy myself with buying Christmas cards, I buy for myself a Christmas present, a good Llama wool coat which will protect me from cold winds. Get coal and logs on my return. Reg phones me to tell me what train he will get and I light the fire.

Fancies some wine and enjoy that. Brings me a set of tiny glass angels to put round the manger. Such a kind surprise. It's a cold day, so call at Reg's house to collect a few more bricks. See note on Gladys kitchen table "Dear Reg, there's some soup on top shelf of fridge, if you want it. Love Gladys" There's two cupfuls of brown liquid, won't keep a grown man alive for long. Prepare when I return home celery and ham *au gratin*. 5pm Reg arrives. We have our supper, tell him about his supper treat in fridge, says, "O.K. I'll get rid of it, when I get home."

Thursday 3rd of December, Reg gets car out at 9.30 and suggest we get shopping at Petts Wood. We separated as he wished get things in shops and so do I not to spoil a surprise.

I find a good shop and a chess-table in mahogany 20"x 20"and a pale wood which I think is olive wood. Just the thing Reg would like. Will be delivered next Saturday.

Have already purchased at Singers a padded sewing-box for Gladys' Christmas. They will be official presents, nothing to do with Reg and a private Christmas luncheon at home with special gift for each other.

Reg has chosen Monday the 21st of December. Next day, Friday the 4th Gladys knocks on my door to say after lunch is going to stay with her daughter. Reg arrived at 2pm to have sandwiches as he has a Lodge meeting at Rainham. Home at 10am. Goes next door to change and return with his pyjamas and dressing gown. Why I can't imagine. Shower and so to bed. Get woken up with a pot of tea on a tray. What a luxury!!

Weather is making shopping and walking difficult, it's five below zero and the snow has become ice. Advise Reg and

Gladys to walk on the flat path abutting house as trying to walk up drive and pavement is like trying to skate without blades. It's so dangerous. Reg phones and says he has asked his aunt and uncle to come over for Christmas, wants to know if I can put them up.

Will arrive Christmas Eve. Tell him they are very welcome, will make a list of what needs doing so that they are comfortable. Reg calls and asks me for a shopping list as the ground frost is bad and he doesn't like me idea of me crossing that busy main road with shopping. Tell him I'll be alright but won't hear of it. Keep items to a minimum and he calls for shopping bags. Asks if he can use my phone to ring our good friend, Phyl, as she's riddled with arthritis, is in her seventies. Just hear him say " Hello Phyl, don't try to go out shopping it's like an ice rink, will phone in ten minutes for a list of things and get your pension if you like."

Just like him to worry about others, have a quick hot drink and the phone rings again. Gets his list written and off he goes. A few days later, the thaw comes and after a few hours of slush, it's all O.K on pavements.

As our special Christmas lunch is approaching, I organise our special "DEJEUNER A DEUX" for Monday the 21st December, date preferred by Reg. Get up at 6.45, it has snowed again.

All the trains are delayed by the cold. Reg arrives at Victoria, as no trains to Holbom or Blackfriars. Hurry to High Street. Buses also seem to be in problems, I wait 1 hour and twenty minutes for a bus home. Light fire, change. Prepare vegetables and so on. 1.30 Reg is home, so now Christmas has began. Just finished packing my Christmas gifts to him. I will put them in front of the hearth when he puts his shoes on the floor.

The manger is already arranged on top of the sideboard. Put his glass angels around the base.

Looks good, have laid the table and put some fresh flowers in centre. Reg hugs me and wishes me a "Happy Christmas", will just pop in next door to collect his gifts and come back. As soon as our presents have been put in piles with our cards at the very top, Reg takes a photo and one of the "manger" and we turn to each other and enjoy the sheer pleasure of being together. We have a glass of wine and start to undo our gifts.

Have been so spoilt, it's so exciting. Reg joins in the fun of looking at the presents as if he were a boy. I put on the new watch he gave me and he shows me how to use the transistor tape player, looks at the personalised red velvet book called "Love, a Celebration" which has small poems and whilst he looks at it, take a photo of him. Admire my two nighties (1 blue, 1 pink) Reg loves his Crystal Brandy Glass, also his GIVENCHY "Gentlemen" after shave and leather credit-card wallet, but enjoys a lot a mahogany portable desk with a compartment for letters, one tray for pens, underneath the tray a large bottle of REMY-MARTIN COGNAC. I look at two white china hands and think it will take the odd rose or two to stand on glass shelf.

I was naughty then and used to smoke Sullivans and Balkan Sobranie and have two boxes of those. As usual we have spoiled each other and have enjoyed seeing each other open our parcels. After our meal, I washed his Brandy glass and asked him if he would christen it. I didn't have to ask twice, but asked to look after his desk, we would keep letters to each other and cards. Goes to his house at 8.40pm. Phones me as he usually does, says how wonderful it was to share an evening together and thanks me for everything. The official Christmas could never match our intimate one, not until what Reg says, "One day, it will be."

The next day, 22nd of December, Gladys phones me after breakfast to ask me if I can purchase a hot water bottle for her for Raymond and Madge to have.

Don't quite know how they will use it, as my guest bedroom has twin beds but no matter. Now what is it that I have filed in the recesses of my mind. It always begins the same. Ah, yes, I remember; "Reg thought it's a good idea if———." That expression, I have heard over a period of time, for avoiding a task of some sort knowing that as Reg has been so helpful over the years, no task would I refuse to do even if it takes a little effort. So I'll start again. "Reg thought it's a good idea as Madge and Raymond are sleeping in your house if you do the evening meal for us all as you shall be making on Christmas morning their cooked breakfast." That's news to me.

Mention it to Reg, says in an embarrassed voice, "I did not put it like that." That's all right, I tell him, I have many faults, as you know, but I don't suffer from laziness, so don't worry, tell me what they would enjoy and I'll make their supper. Get presents for all of them packed so that when Christmas morning arrives, I can bring them to their house. Have a bit of difficulty to get wrapping paper around the presents but after a few well chosen words, I eventually achieve my goal. Finish packing at half-past midnight.

On December the 28th Raymond and Madge are tucking in to a breakfast, Reg calls and has a cup of tea. I have made a small Christmas cake for them to take back home as making their way to Wolverton this afternoon. Reg is going back to the office tomorrow. Thursday, New Year's eve Gladys and Reg have been invited to my house for a New Year's eve buffet and to toast the New Year in. The second half of 1981 has been difficult, I wonder what 1982 will bring.

10

I have started the year doing something I have never had the will-power to achieve before, but I have made a New Year's Resolution, though it was taken on the 1st of January, I have only found the ability to start on Monday the 18th of the month, and also because I was getting out of breath kissing Reg goodnight I decided to stop smoking. It took me three days to stop the usual amount of cigarettes, but must admit had tremendous encouragement from Reg who had smoked since he was nineteen. He smoked a pipe in the Air Force, went on to cigarettes and when I met him used to enjoy small cigars. So he decided to stop as well and when I wanted a smoke, started to suck sweets. The first day I smoked 7 cigarettes, the next day I had 5, and on the 3rd day smoked half a cigarette mid morning and the second half after lunch and that was it. Unknown to me, I suffered withdrawal symptoms, I used to go to bed, while reading a book, found my knees were shaking, then could not get to sleep. I had no idea that it could have such an effect, but to make sure I could achieve it, I kept a large box of Sullivans at home to see if I could stop choosing a cigarette when I felt I needed something. We both managed it and I believe that neither of us smoking helped a lot.

January and most of February has been very unpleasant and frustrating months for people using trains to London, as apart from snow and ice, train strikes have caused much hardship to commuters.

When one strike is on, many firms organise alternatives like coaches collecting staff very early in the mornings. When one is pleased with strikes being settled, a new problem arises.

Rail guards start a go-slow and so the frustration carries on. Then on the 10th of March there is a tube and bus strike, let's hope by the beginning of Spring all these difficulties will be solved.

Wednesday, the 17th March, Reg invites me to go to Folkestone and Canterbury and we arrive at the latter at 9am. The wind is bitter cold, have steaming cup of coffee, look at the lovely shops and have lunch at a 15th century Elizabethan restaurant. Go to visit the imposing Cathedral.

Look at souvenirs in the entrance and Reg chooses a lovely brooch-cum-pendant and chain in the form of the Canterbury Cross. It has four pink stones and four green ones. He asks me if I would like it, and wear it as a memento of our visit.

Love it and ask him to attach it round my neck. We make our way home and arrive early afternoon. My birthday is looming up and on the Wednesday the 7th of April, I will be 50. My good friends in the bungalow opposite (Phyl and her husband Les) phone and sing "Happy Birthday". 8am go upstairs to my bedroom and hear hanger rattle on wall, go to window, Reg is there in pyjamas and waves. Will call in a while. Gill Slade, my neighbour who is a flower arranger, calls with a lovely card and a few delicacies she and her husband John have brought back from Paris. Phone my mother's best friend, Helene, in Paris to thank her for her card. 9.45 Reg calls. Cup of coffee and a kiss. Asks me to wait a moment and goes back in his house. He returns with a lovely birthday card and a red velvet box in which there's a three-strand gold necklace. Very delicate and I am completely taken aback by such a pretty piece of jewellery and his generosity. We drive off to Tonbridge, see "The Chequers Inn" on the far side of a green and we go there for a celebration lunch. Pleasant meal and good wine. We always enjoy each other's company. Reg gives the impression of being "laid back". I believe that's the modern term, but I have known him too long to be fooled by this relaxed appearance. Like most Englishmen, their sensitive feelings are well and truly hidden. What seems very well controlled show inside emotions are churning. When you know and love a man deeply, body language shows the true feelings that exist and no amount of control can fool you. I enjoy our laughter and his sense of humour, but I also know that we both feel frustrated when we have to go in different houses and although apart, think a lot about each other.

As Reg says so often: "One day, I know it will happen."

On the 15th of April, Gladys is thinking of having her 60th birthday do on the Saturday, 22nd of May, as her brother Arthur and his wife Doris can make it, though the actual date of birthday is the 11th May. On May the 3rd Gladys mentions talking to Robbie and George on the phone, but hasn't yet said if they can come to stay for the party on the 22nd. I think it's peculiar.

Apparently, when Reg calls at 6.15 with the Sunday papers, tell me that Robbie and George are coming, but Gladys wanted to tell me after telling Arthur and his wife Doris that she'll have to send them to my home to sleep. It seems she hasn't the courtesy to ask me, but decides to put up her Suffolk friends at her home, and her relatives can have second best.

Still I get on well with Doris and Arthur and will make them as comfortable as I can. When the party is going on, Gladys asks for photos to be taken, but only of family members.

I walk out into the front lounge, when George comes in and says "As they are being filmed, why don't we have a cuddle on the sofa?" I reply: "No thanks, I'm not interested." Walk back in reception room and wonder what Reg would think if he knew what George said to me. I never divulged it, it would have annoyed him and disgusted him behaving that way.

Could not get to sleep till 4am. Awake at 6am, get up at 6.30. Go in garden then take up some tea to my guests. See

Reg on terrace, says all three are still in bed. Has a heavy head, will call later. Make a cooked breakfast. 9.15 Reg calls and takes his brother-in-law back home, but Doris kindly stays to help with washing-up.

Early afternoon, the Suffolk contingent go home and later Arthur and Doris make their way. Sorry to see them go, but relieved that the party is over, and go home to strip the beds and generally get my home in order. Six weeks and four days till we can be alone and enjoy a holiday together – it seems a long time.

The weather forecast was apparently promising so having done the weekly shopping yesterday, Friday, today was going to be sunny with a light breeze. So Reg calls round after breakfast to ask if I have any plastic sheeting as wants to creosote the fence panels. Luckily I have some and ask if I can help him as his garden is 75ft long and will take less time if we all help with it.

At 10am, some panels are laid on the plastic on the lawn and we start. Gladys brushes them to get marks off and strands of loose shavings.

Reg and I brush the creosote. 11am we stop for coffee, carry on till noon, then Reg drives to High Street to purchase 4 more litres of creosote. Stop for sandwiches and after lunch carry on painting 8 large fence panels, 5 small ones. 5pm tea break. Start again painting 3 panels in front of greenhouse. Finish by 7pm. Help to replace small panels, but one neighbour helps Reg to put the large ones up as he's quite tall and finds it easy. Starting to ache in places I did not know I had, but Reg is so pleased that it's done and I am so happy I have been able to help a little.

I think it's like measles, it's catching. Gladys has now suggested that Aquaseal must be painted on the garage ceiling and that the drains should be cleared. Also before going back to office, the careful measuring of wooden shelves in lounge should be done, so that glass doors are fixed and her coffee service can be displayed there. The mowing of front and back lawns must be attended to in case it rains, etc, etc, etc …

Now should Reg have any time left, would he peel the potatoes, gives a quick hoover while the greenhouse plants are given a shower. Tomorrow another St John event is taking place in London, so uniform and Tricorn hat has to be ready, so that becomes important above all else. I go to my front lounge and start to remove wallpaper. Reg calls with Sunday papers and I give mine. Thanks me for my help and asks if I'll meet him at Tower Road 7.30am, is having a day off and we will go to the countryside together. Such a surprise, had no idea that it was his intention. Wonder where he will take me.

I was out of the house at 7.20am, a little misty but the weather could not spoil the anticipation I felt, as any time shared in Reg's company was always enjoyed. He found a place on the road to Hastings to have breakfast. By 9am we double back to a place called BEDGEBURY PINETUM and I was quite surprised at the variety of majestic trees, different colours and shapes of large shrubs. I had never before visited a Pinetum so was interested in such a peaceful place. It belongs to the National Trust. The fog had disappeared and it was a sunny day. We ambled and chatted about holidays. We had not as yet chosen a particular place, I left it to Reg, as I felt his company was much more important than the destination chosen.

As we walked, we came upon a beautiful lake full of water-lilies. Just as we sat down on a wooden bench, Reg whispered: "Look, seven of them, keep still." A drake and seven ducklings swim in front of us, then two more tiny ones, then they climb on the bank and all ten of them ambled at our feet. Tame, so very tame. Those little ducklings were so fluffy, we could not believe our luck.

We never moved or spoke till they had decided to return to the lake and swim away. We then drove to Goudhurst village.

Have coffee, scones with jam and cream at a very small and cosy tea-place.

Later we purchased two punnets of deep red strawberries, tomatoes, celery and one carton of Jersey cream off a farm by the side of road.

Get a crusty Coburg loaf on way home. Have a lovely supper with our purchases and enjoy what is left of our beautiful day. As always when we are together alone, time goes too quickly and soon it's time to kiss each other goodnight.

Try to book by phone "The Belgrave Hotel" at Torquay where we enjoyed last year's visit, but the hotel is full, so try the "Corbyn Head Hotel" and we are lucky this time. So tomorrow a letter is sent with cheque for deposit and Reg posts it in London.

Book for Sunday the 17th July. At last on the 11th July, we started our holidays we had looked forward to and chose the "Mansion Hotel" right on the front, beautifully laid gardens were very tastefully done and after doing the usual booking and putting suitcases in the room, we went for a walk and enjoyed the scenery. I had not visited Eastbourne before. Reg showed me the "Grand Hotel" where he was stationed at the age of 22 before he was married and doing RADAR.

After a leisurely lunch, we booked two seats for the "BLACK AND WHITE MINSTREL SHOW" for tomorrow evening. Monday 12th July, Reg takes me to Beachy Head where the 1st RADAR Station was, beautiful views. Did quite a lot of walking and enjoyed the countryside.

The next day we go to the shops to buy beachwear, as my swimsuit is too tight, and we decide to go for a swim. The tide is out so walk on sand instead of shingle and enjoy our first swim together.

Take more photos. At the end of the promenade an exhibition of oil paintings is in progress and have a look at them all. Didn't know till then, Reg had also enjoyed when much younger doing oils, though I myself can enjoy water-colours but can't manage the technique of oils. We book an Agatha Christie play called "The Unexpected Guest" with Pat Phoenix of Coronation Street fame and Anthony Booth.

The next day Wednesday, we go back to Orpington and use the next two days, washing and ironing clothes, keeping all lawns cut and tidy till we go off again towards Sidmouth and on to Torquay and a hotel we don't know.

Still the area is colourful and we look forward to a second week's holiday.

On Friday the 16th July, we drive to Sidmouth stay the night and go on to Torquay. Pleased with our hotel, have a very spacious bedroom and a balcony with two chairs and are pleased with good facilities. Meet other guests and go dancing the evening away till one in the morning.

The next day, we drive to Totnes, small town with attractive shops and arcades. Reg looks for a delicate Juliana glass bell with a gold rim to add to our bell collection. Also there is a kind of fair, many people are dressed in TUDOR clothes and see a Town Cryer in a beautiful costume ringing his shiny bell and gives us the Old Tyme version of the television evening news, and it was fun.

Many stalls were scattered in the square and each one was full of interesting goodies and also food. One particular stall was beautifully set with corn dollies, large and small and I was fascinated by the skill of the people who made them. Even stalls were set out with attractive linen. I remember being interested to gingham bread roll holders which folded and I bought two of different colours, also amazing crockery of all shapes and sizes. Reg and I always liked the buzz of country markets, each stallholder wearing a colourful costume. We eventually leave Totnes with sandwiches, cream and jam scones, and punnet of strawberries. We go to Dartmoor and have a picnic, take photos and enjoy the beauty of the countryside. Go back to the hotel and we meet two new guests who have just arrived and after supper, invite them to join us for coffee. The fair-haired lady is called ANNETTE GRIFFIN and has brought her aunt with her as I recall, the aunt had not been well and appreciated her niece's invitation to relax a few days. The management invited Annette to give the guests a song and we very much enjoyed listening to that lovely song, "MEMORIES". Her bell-like voice was great and she was much applauded. The band started to play and we danced the rest of the evening.

The next day, was also a sunny day and Reg decided to take me to Cockington Village by horse and trap. He asked the coachman if he would take a photo of us sitting in the trap.

Enjoy the ride, go to the Old Forge and get some souvenirs. Go back to hotel and then on to Paignton to see the "DANNY LA RUE" show. It was good. The next day we make our way home as traffic bad. Exchange addresses with Annette who lives in BRISTOL and take photos of each other outside the hotel. On way home we stop for lunch at Stonehenge and eventually reach Orpington after 220 miles. Monday, Reg is going back to the office, so after an afternoon of mowing lawns and getting washing sorted, I pick vegetables and fruit from my garden and give a few to neighbours as there are more than we need.

11

All I ask of a woman is that she shall feel gently towards
me when my heart feels kindly towards her,

and there shall be the soft, soft tremor of unheard bells
between us, it is all I ask.

I am so tired of violent women lashing out and insisting
on being loved, when there is no love in them.

D.H. LAWRENCE

Our next four days are bittersweet for me. Though Reg is
returning to the office and my day will be a normal day
of jobs to be done at home and the garden, when the evening
comes my joy will be welcoming him home, sharing our meal,
show him how much it means to me to have his company and
like married couples who care, share the intimacy of spending
the night together.

Soon after I will have to content myself with fleetingly
hug him as he knocks on my door at 7.15am as going down
the hill to the rail station, enjoying his voice on the phone
as soon as in office, lunch-time and in afternoon. Seeing him
sometimes on way home and waving at the bedroom window
late before retiring to bed. Since Reg and I have become close,
up till now, whenever I have criticized what I feel is unfair
or unkind, he has been loyal enough to tell me off as he feels
loyal and won't listen to, anything to hurt her, but though
I respect him for his attitude, I notice that now he realises
that loyalty has to be earned, and being a wife doesn't give
one the right to reject her husband. The love that was once

there, eventually has been transformed into duty. But since the middle of 1982 it has been noticed that we are very close and bitter remarks and untruths are said to discredit me in any way possible. Now for the first time, it is becoming apparent that the play-acting shown to both family and friends is not fooling anyone. Nevertheless, it is much more difficult for Reg as I notice both migraines and asthma attacks, as well as nervous indigestion are worse after any unpleasant difference of opinions, usually expressed in banging wardrobe doors and throwing things which I hear hitting the dividing wall of our house. At such times, I cringe and get frightened that things could hit his face or eyes and pray the anger and bad temper gestures will stop.

I come to the conclusion that I must keep myself as busy as I can because I live too much for just time with Reg and I hurt inside when I know he has to return to his abode, so enrol in an evening class of painting at Bromley and my neighbour and friend Gill Slade who lives opposite suggests I can have a lift, as on the same day and time she's giving a class on flower arranging. Very kind of her to suggest it and learning more about painting would be wonderful. Return home at 5.15. Reg already home. Calls and I offer him apple pie and cream with a cup of coffee as no one home.

Monday the 4th of October, I put alarm to get up early as Reg is driving to Stratford-on-Avon, to wish him a safe journey. 9.50pm Reg phones, had a bad car journey, raining hard most of the way.

Going for a walk to the river before going to bed. Says if I come over to meet him Friday, to bring garage keys. Will try to phone tomorrow evening.

Reg has found time of direct train to Leamington Spa, 9.50 arriving 12.45. If train cancelled, phone him at hotel, so it's all set for Friday. Had thought of my coming over Thursday and staying the night but as Saturday we'll be together all day, it didn't seem worth all the arranging. I leave home by taxi 7.30 am but no buffet-car on train, so no breakfast. Meet Reg on forecourt of Station and drive out of town through Banbury, stop at BRACHLEY and have lunch. We then go on road to Dunstable Downs and stopped car on a picnic area overlooking a gliding club where his Mother used to take him when he was a boy often. Eventually, we reach the top of Charterhouse Road at 8.10pm. Say goodnight in the car, what a tiring journey. Get out of car at Newstead Avenue and walk home from there.

Gladys getting her uniform ready for tomorrow's competition (St. John) at the Albert Hall. Wave goodnight and think how pleasant our journey home was. Next day, do shopping together, I get a lovely pineapple and prepare slices of it and soak it in KIRSH. I know Reg will enjoy it. He brings a bottle of wine for our lunch, and the day stretches in front of us. Gladys has told Reg she has found a holiday in Yugoslavia for a week, from Saturday 16th of October - 23rd of October. Feel sad but Reg says will write to me as I will write to him.

Glad I now know the dates because I intend to visit Helene in Paris and can book my flight and my hotel. Phone her but says there's room in her flat, not to bother with hotels. Very kind of her.

Saturday 16 of October, Reg and Gladys are only leaving at 3.30pm. Reg and I have at 12.30 physically expressed our goodbyes and Reg has said I will be in his thoughts all the time the miles are separating us. Glad that it's only seven days. 3.30 they both call to say goodbye, Reg kisses me on the lips in front of Gladys quite naturally.

Feel so sad, but the ringing of the telephone jerks me out of my dejection. It's Frank to confirm he will be at Gatwick airport next Friday at 8pm. Very kind of them both to drive from their home in Epsom to the airport, take me home to

Orpington, then drive back all that way. Joyce and Frank have known me and my family since I was sixteen years old, so we have been good friends for many years.

I shall be home about nine hours before Reg, and I shall be so glad he's safely home, look forward to seeing him and hold him in my arms. After breakfast, phone Helene to say I'm safely home and thank her for looking after me. Wash hair and cut it, get flowers to put on dining room table next door, and get some basic food to put in their fridge.

Phone Gatwick to find plane has just landed, 6.40 pm they're home.

The next day, Sunday, at last when he comes in for his French lesson, we can show each other how much we have missed each other for the last eight days then chat about my pleasant stay with Helene who has sent him her sincere regards. I show him a little bottle of REMY-MARTIN COGNAC, he asks me if I will keep it here for his use (I personally don't like brandy at all) a bottle of GIVENCHY after shave. Told him Helene took me for a walk in the PARC MONCEAU and nearby a beautiful flower shop attracted my attention. I bought an oval glass frame with beautiful dried flowers tied with a pink velvet ribbon around the stems. Loved that, it was tastefully arranged. One day, will hang it on the wall of our cottage. Treated myself to a lovely pair of black and red shoes. He admired those. Helene and I went to a huge department store called " LE PRIMPTEMPS" and we bought a few unusual things there, but Helene was getting tired, so I suggested taking the lift to the top of the building to have tea, a deserved sit down and enjoy a pastry or two.

After chatting together, we exchanged letters telling each other how much we missed each other's company.

At the end of October, my eyes were giving me trouble, Reg urges me to see my Doctor as they are sore and red. I am given anti-inflationary drops to put in every two or three hours and must collect a letter to the Eye Hospital if not better. Reg puts drops in my eyes every evening before returning home.

It's now the beginning of November, so buy wallflowers to plant in my front garden, there are a choice of many colours and heights, so I get fifty of them as they smell so sweet and will make colour in my garden. Also plant short red tulips, multi-stemmed and arrange them hoping the colour schemes all blend. Reg had a lot of travelling to do and today. Monday the 8 of November he calls at 7.30am, suitcase in hand to say goodbye as spending five days in Newcastle. Phones me at 9.30 pm just to see if I'm all right. Thursday afternoon, I go to painting class, learn a lot regarding mixing colours etc and enjoy my afternoon, also realise I have a lot to learn regarding also shading.

At 6.15 Reg phones, looks forward to meeting me tomorrow afternoon when he gets off the train at King's Cross, we will spend a little time together before getting home to Orpington. Taxi to Charing Cross and put heavy suitcase in a left luggage. Go for a walk and end up at Fortnum and Mason Food Hall, and go to their tearoom for a gorgeous tea. Walk back through Burlington Arcade and on to Charing Cross. Get train to Orpington and arrive at 5.15. We walk to our houses separately and feel so tired but happy to have been in each other's company.

Tomorrow it's the Lords Mayor's Show so will prepare Reg's lunch as no doubt Gladys will not feel like cooking a substantial meal in the evening.

I spend Monday afternoon in Petts Wood, I decide to visit one particular dress shop as their clothes are smart, well-cut and I want to find two outfits for my visit to London tomorrow and Wednesday. Reg has booked in at the Russell Hotel and I am intending to find something elegant for those two days.

One two piece is just what I wanted with my new PARIS red and black shoes. Also a very fluid black dress with red piping in small areas of the dress. Meet Reg at 4.15, just got off the Northampton train and we take a taxi to the Russell Hotel.

Spacious room, have tea and cakes brought up and later in evening walk to our usual restaurant called the "SHUTTLEWORTH" in Aldwych, a place which has beautiful food and decor and where Reg has invited me to lunch when visiting London from about 1980.

Enjoy a leisurely walk back to the hotel and so to bed. Have a continental breakfast at 7.30, then Reg has to go to office and I have till his return at five-thirty to wander down Oxford Street and Oxford Circus. Buy early Christmas gifts, get tired, go back to the carvery at the hotel and enjoy a splendid lunch.

Go back to our room, look at TV and do crosswords. Reg is back at 5.30, has a shower and gets ready in a Dinner-suit for a Director's Dinner at the Grosvenor. He looks very handsome. Returns at 10.30 pm. I have had a lazy evening of TV but feel happy to see him back.

Next day, Thursday, can't believe how fast these two days have gone, after our breakfast, walk towards Holborn, then Reg puts me in a taxi to Charing Cross and I make my way to Orpington and in afternoon to my painting class.

On Saturday, as usual, Reg and I go to Bromley tip to get rid of garden refuse which is mine and his. I always do that for the two of us before returning to get list for weekend food shopping. Gladys is very curt with him and doesn't even say "Hello" when entering car to go to the supermarket. We are both now getting the silent treatment, difficult if enquiring re items of food wanted for weekend. Sunday, spent doing many jobs, Reg decides to climb Victoria plum tree to use electric saw as weight of fruit last September has cracked large branches which could fall and hurt anyone below. Then help Gladys in their greenhouse to sort out plastic sheeting. A new bolt is all of a sudden vital on the back door at their house so gets tools and attends to it, after which it is considered wise to put another bolt on front door.

It's nearly 3pm before the weekend delicacy is produced in the shape of a cheese sandwich. Eventually without waiting for any further jobs to be done, Reg calls with his Sunday papers and I give him mine. Quick hug and a sit down. Reg says asked Gladys what she wanted for Christmas. She said didn't know of anything in particular but instead could he take her out to a theatre once a month because they never go out, said it's not possible as they both have commitments and meetings so it's not a goer. Reg said you would think she never goes out but she mostly returns from St. John very late and doesn't worry about my supper. I feel shattered, don't know what he will do. So anxious, can't eat my supper. 9.55 waves at bedroom window, gestures loose tummy, keeps going to the loo. Typical Sunday, a long list of jobs to do, will be relieved to go back to office. Monday, make his favourite meal and must make his evening a peaceful one with a lovely fire to enjoy and a glass or two of good Bordeaux wine. When he calls at my house at 7.25am realises he forgot to write cheque book to pay in 3 cheques, so asks me if I would get it from his bureau and fill it up. I'll take them to his bank this morning.

Phoned me at 8.30am as meeting will start at 8.45. I do the necessary at bank, and on my return light fire and start to weigh ingredients for the Christmas cake. Home at 5pm, so all is ready to welcome him home.

The next day, Tuesday 30th of November, I was beginning to think Reg and I have a guardian angel who is looking after us very well. Expecting gas man, no one calls, so Reg tells me to ring them. Lady apologises, suggest another day or go round and read meter and check amount on computer. Go round to read his meter at his house, see letter on floor, notice BRISTOL postmark, it says "2 Newstead Avenue. Try 2a – my

Above: Reg trying on his two new hats at Christmas 1982
Below: Jacqui looking at her Christmas presents

next door neighbour Peter must have brought it round and put it in letterbox." Take Bristol letter home and will give it to Reg when he calls tonight. Show him letter, contains letter to us, and two photographs taken outside Torquay Hotel. Reg can't get over it, the fact that if not asked to read the meter would not have noticed the Bristol postmark and Gladys would have hit the roof.

Reg says we must have a guardian angel looking after both of us. Will have to contact Annette and tell her. Next day, Reg is visiting Cardiff. Gladys is going to a St. John Ambulance Christmas party, so won't get home early. Reg phones at Charing Cross, wants to know if OK to come home.

The fire is lit, but not knowing when he would return have only a homemade soup to give him. Looks so tired. Has coffee and a Brandy and goes home at 9.30pm. 10.50 Gladys is back. The following week Reg asks me if I will kindly translate into French Christmas cards and letters inside them to Helene of Paris, Georgette and Bernard of MONACO, my friends of AUSTRIA Inge and Gerard OSWIRT, so suggests he writes them as soon as he has time and I will translate them so he can copy them.

Managed to find the phone number of Annette in Bristol and phone, explain that we are not yet able to be together but appreciate receiving the photos of our pleasant holiday in Torquay.

As Reg has suggested for the past two years, December the 20 (Monday) is being planned as our private Christmas Day celebration, a Christmas lunch with candles and fresh flowers on the table, decorations especially a Manger, a log fire and our respective pairs of shoes in front of the fireside with our presents and cards on top. What else could anyone desire? Just the two of us. Bitter cold day but at 10am drive to Sevenoaks, Reg is keen to get a hat as is now noticing the cold and find a very good shop top of Sevenoaks, they have quality clothes for men and find a fur hat. It fits beautifully, and also tries a tweedy hat which can be folded, Harris Tweed. So warm, but rain-proof, very smart.

Persuade him to have both, and say it's my Christmas presents. Didn't expect me to say that, so I'm pleased the icy wind will not get at him. Have a coffee and make our way home. Reg writes his labels and we both start making our pile with Christmas cards on top. Open two cards, one funny one and one for the first time a card "To my wife", can't get over it. He has spoilt me and I do appreciate the gifts he has given me. A beautiful mohair cardigan from Italy, three pairs of stockings, a book called "The Christmas Story" by David Kossoff, illustrated with paintings of well-known painters, one radio earphones, box of home made chocolates, telephone index, one black/gold alarm clock looking like a Paris lamp-post with "MOULIN-ROUGE" sign. A silver and crystal pineapple, the surface is full of prismatic surfaces.

I know Reg enjoys decent clothes so hope my little gifts will be liked. I gave him two leather reversible belts, one LP record called "What goes up might come down", recorded by David Gunson who used to be with Coastal Command on Shackleton Aircraft and with tongue in cheek is in demand as an after-dinner speaker describing the niceties of nose-wheel steering.

Reg and I both have a sense of humour and I know that his record will be enjoyed. A set of Irish Coffee glasses, one pair of stretch overshoes in zip bag which are useful when it's pouring, one place setting (bronze and rosewood) and two hats, one fur for icy weather and one Harris Tweed for rain and warmth. I also gave him a cheeky card and a romantic one with lovely words. Have our lunch and enjoy the crackling fire. It's been an intimate Christmas and a day full of surprises, quiet conversation, Reg puts on the radiogram favourite records and we ended our evening dancing to one of our favourite PERRY COMO songs full of sentimental words.

Unfortunately, at 9pm we both have to put out our dustbins, then kiss each other goodnight and Reg sadly walks back to his house. I go upstairs and wave goodnight. What a happy day it has been, Christmas by the fireside, just us two, certainly has a certain magic. We pledge that whatever the future holds, Christmas Day will always be shared together.

The next day is spent delivering by hand cards and Christmas presents to friends and neighbours.

Reg phones me from office, thanks me for yesterday Christmas lunch and will call on way home. Just received by post, one of his official Christmas presents, a decanter with the words "Russell's Night Cap" written on it. Will put gold and red paper round it, also receive the mahogany and olive wood chess table so must use at least four sheets of paper to wrap it properly, a shoe-shine box I have already packed and a green jacket with unzippable sleeves for use in garden. Gladys' presents are nearly packed but will finish it Christmas Eve.

Madge and Raymond, Reg's aunt and uncle have been invited for Christmas and I have packed their presents, warm woollies as they feel the cold so much. New Year's Eve I am doing another BUFFET so after that it will be the ending of 1982 and who knows perhaps 1983 will smile a little more towards us. Reg gives me another leather bound diary (a page a day) for the coming year, also calls with a glass folding book with a poem painted on it. I thank him for thinking of me.

12

As the weather gets colder, my good friends Phyl and Les who live in the bungalow opposite me are getting more and more unable to manage simple tasks in their home and as their only daughter lives in Sussex, and we have become good friends, they ask me sometimes for a bit of help. Their home is at the top of many steps and only if they use their back entrance can they manage to go and get shopping at the parade of shops. This morning was Twelfth Night and Phyl was finding it impossible to get her decorations down. Her husband was in bed with a pain in his side and even refused a cup of tea, so I hurried over and took the Christmas things off the walls, I can reach almost anything being 5ft 7½ inches, but Phyl is only about 5ft, also suggested to get the doctor, as such a pain must be attended to. I start to remove my own decorations, put them in cardboard boxes and pull the retractable ladder to attic and put everything away. Reg is away to Stratford-on-Avon for three days as from tomorrow Wednesday the 5th of January, say goodbye at 6.40am, said will phone tonight, but as Gladys has not mentioned it perhaps is having a snack at her son's and going on from there. 10.30 Reg phones as promised. Will phone tomorrow evening. Get some ironing done and go to bed at 11.45. Strange, still bedroom curtains not shut. Wake up at 2.30am, still curtains open.

Today the 6th January, I get up at 6am and curtains are open. Usually, if going away, it's mentioned in case one hears noises, and it's burglars. Wonder if taken unwell at Italian class. Wonder if I should ring hospital. See light on at Phyl's house, ring her to ask what she thinks I should do.

She says go as you have a spare key, in case she's not well or fallen. Do so, Christmas decorations still up, call out from hall, no-one in either lounge or kitchen. Go back home,

Phyl suggest I phone Farnborough Police and St Mary Cray. Phone Orpington Hospital, no one. Then go in and in case she's ill upstairs and look round rooms. No bed slept in. Go back home, ring other neighbour Gill, ask heir re evening class, say only starting next week. 5.45 Phyl phones to say, lights in hall. Sure enough, light in kitchen, so she's back. 6.10 knock on door, it's Gladys and her grandson Thomas. Says just arrived and thought they'd say they're here and find out how I am.

I said I did not know you were away. Sit down, the boy is tired, been to a Service at Brompton Oratory, round museums, boy says tired out as carrying rucksack full of his toys. Hungry too. Doesn't mention she didn't bother to say was staying out all night at her daughters. Goes back at 6.30pm. 10pm Reg phones, tell him how anxious I had been most of the day, he said can't understand. Ridiculous to have gone back there again after spending last Sunday at their daughter's house.

Friday the 7th of January, Reg is coming home. Do shopping and return home 12.30. Have some lunch, 2.45 hear door bang, see Gladys and boy walk past, needless to say do not knock.

Three fifty Reg phones from box. Meet him at bottom of Tower Road between 4.15 and 4.30. Nearly 4, see Gladys and grandson coming up the hill. Meet Reg at 4.30 and we drive to Sevenoaks.

Have lunch and stop at Toys Hill and have a talk. Told him I was very hurt by Gladys' behaviour and won't ever put myself out again. Reg says he knows she makes use of people and gets close to them at Christmas, then drops them, won't allow anyone to be close, won't like to rely on anyone.

I said to him she's only interested in herself, as long as she does or gets what she wants, no one else matters. Says he's sorry I was so upset, not to talk about it any more. Drops me at Ruskin Drive and I walk home. Today, Thursday the 27th

January 1983: it's two years since maman died, I think of her often, miss not being able to talk to her. I share my hopes and enjoy having a chat with her. Such an understanding mother, trust she is watching over me, come to that, as she was so fond of Reg, watching over him as well. Reg phones me at 12.15, has a lot of work and will be home late tonight.

Go upstairs in front bedroom, bang goes the front door at Reg's house and see Gladys run round front of house, go in bedroom over the entrance hall and see her get in a red estate car with large dog in the back, car waiting for her outside my front door. Very careful not to get in car in front of her own house. Then the car drives off.

At 1.30 I go to painting class in Bromley. The next day Friday, I have to take papers to my solicitor re my late mother's Royalties which will be sent to my bank and Reg who has to drive to Sydenham kindly gives me a lift to his office and goes on his way. Whilst in Bromley buy kitchen items I need, have lunch and meet Reg at 2pm on his way back. Drive to Westerham for tea, and on to Toys Hill to have a chat. Back home at 6pm. Whilst on our drive, Reg ordered three cubic yards of top soil for his vegetable patch and also a Victoria plum tree for my garden, as my lovely 40ft tall Victoria plum tree has at last met his maker and had to be cut down for safety's sake. Tomorrow Saturday the 29th Gladys is again involved with St John and at 8am runs down the road to catch the train.

After a cooked breakfast we make a list and go to Locksbottom to do shopping. Back fairly soon and Reg gets his top soil delivered, the only place to put it is on the drive in front of his house.

Prepare lunch as time is going. Do gammon and vegetables, Reg brings a bottle of Beaujolais-Villages and finish off with vanilla ice cream. Wash up and Reg and I look at T.V film together. 6.50 Gladys is home. Tomorrow Sunday, another

St John is taking place so 8.20am off she goes. While Reg is taking a shower I cook breakfast, then after a while we get our respective wheelbarrows and shovels and start the job of shovelling earth and wheeling it down the drive and into the vegetable patch at die bottom of his garden, start at 11am and go on till 1pm. Stop for coffee and start again at 2.30, carry on till 4.15. My arms are starting to ache so tell Reg, will stop now, hope I helped a little. He thanks me for my help and at 5pm goes home for a wash and change. Gladys returns at 5.15 and Reg will return at 6.30 with Sunday papers and I will give him mine.

Reg says told Gladys that his neighbours Judy and Louis and their two children are moving to Sevenoaks. So Gladys says perhaps they should move to a smaller house, Reg says as they are moving and so is their daughter, they should do the same. Apparently thinks she's never satisfied with what she has, also wants something else. What can one say to that, never hear criticism before, but it's starting to be noticed now. After all the time and effort, the drive seems almost as full of soil is when the lorry emptied it's load. Will have to get down to it next weekend.

Next day, Monday, it's starting to snow, very windy and cold. So decide to clean grate, lay the are and get logs in. Phone Phyl and ask her if she needs anything as ground is slippery. Will pay her papers, and get her a loaf. Suggest I have lunch with them, as weather is so awful. Whilst there, cut her hair and put it in rollers as she will never be able to get to the hairdressers in this. Very pleased, so do it. Saturday the 5 of February, Saturday mornings, the day we regularly carry garden refuse bags, etc, into the boot of the car and go early to Bromley tip to get rid of every piece of heavy rubbish and do it together, but it did not start in a very pleasant fashion. It was nearly 8.30am before Reg arrived and put his car by my back gate and start to pick large stones from my garden, Gladys hovering around. Suddenly, she decides to stop me lifting and helping Reg to lift a large concrete slab and puts her arm out across my waist and holds me away. Brings a large newspaper round to protect his boot. Reg says to Gladys "We won't be long, get rid of those heavy stones and do shopping after." Gladys gives me a terrible look which made me shiver and Reg saw it, I am glad to say. She then turned back and shut garage door. Reg said to me she looked very angry. I suggested he went back to soothe her but he said, "Blow it, let's go. Funny woman!" I said she doesn't have to be annoyed with me, but with you."

We drive to the tip, return by 10am. She says she doesn't want to go to the supermarket, only to shop by the green. Walk into shop behind Reg in complete silence. There was never such a performance, not even at the Old Vic. And so ended Saturday the 5th of February, in deadly silence, pursed lips and when I arrived on the terrace in the back garden a striking of a match on a cigarette, and a chair with its back to my terrace. Every gesture an invitation to Reg to find a refuge in his shed and enjoy a little peace and quiet. Sunday is a usual day, not of rest but of furious activity, sweeping remnants of soil on the drive, sweeping water down it, cleaning drains. Going up and down to his shed for either the workmate or a collection of tools for vital jobs which need attention.

Only when I bring a tray of coffee and cake on my terrace can I be sure Reg will be able to have a break.

Thank heaven, 12.45 French lesson, so can enjoy being together for a short while. When Reg brings the Sunday papers, Gladys said she phoned her friends (RAF Suffolk friends) who told her intention to visit Seville next September and hopes they will go with them. Her friend also asked if she was still looking for a cottage, says it will be easier to find a bungalow. Reg said didn't comment.

Halleluiah, Sunday is over. Tomorrow Monday 7th our usual evening will be short because Reg is going to his

Lodge. 4.30 it's starting to snow. The sky is leaden and it's obvious there is more snow to come. As soon as returned from an Abbeyfield meeting, I get a coal fire going. 6pm Reg phones, just come out of meeting and walking to Lodge. I start preparing sandwiches for him and myself, get cake out of oven and cups and saucers ready on a tray.

Reg arrives 8.30. Took a taxi to catch fast train. Asks me if I would like to spend tomorrow with him, will phone office and take a day off. Wonderful, goes in at 10pm sneezing a lot, so decide to get some cold pills out ready for tomorrow. As soon as he calls, that's the first thing I'll give him, tea and Hedex tablets. Well, it's different, if not very affectionate, but hope it will help. Reg calls at 7.20am and before he has time to refuse, give him two tablets with glass of water, then a cup of tea. Had sat next to a friend last night who had a bad cold and he has well and truly caught it. Suggest perhaps he should stay in the warm, will clean the grate and light a fire and he can relax, but won't waste his day off and wants to take me out, treat me to lunch as if its vital. I would be just as happy seeing him have a rest and look after himself but, when he has decided something there's no changing his mind. So after a lovely lunch, coax him to make our way home, toast ourselves by the fire and just for once be lazy and let me look after him. Once home, ask him to make the tea while I light the fire. Till 6pm we can please ourselves and keep warm. Give him a few more tablets to take before getting into his bed tonight. 7.40am Wednesday, when Reg calls to say goodbye, give him more tablets, reminding him to take 2 every 4 hours.

Says will come home early as doesn't feel too grand. Visit Phyl and Les to see if O.K., pay their newspaper bill and have a quick coffee with them. Get home at 11.45 and light the fire. Have a feeling Reg will be home earlier than he said. Sure enough at 1.15 he's coming up the hill. Give him a hot drink and add a log to the fire. Lunch time we share some soup and I give him another two tablets. Reg snoozes in armchair while I make a cardboard heart and glue on cloves, melon and sunflower seeds. He's put on a thick rib pullover as I told him to put thick woollens on in this weather, but has been snagged in shoulder, so put that right whilst he drinks his coffee. 5.35 Reg goes back home and Gladys is back at 6.12. Still snowing. It's Italian evening class, so after snack, Reg gets car out of garage. 7.10pm and drives her to the class. Back by 7.40. Ask if he'd like a coffee with brandy in it.

Look at TV. Go to garage with him as he gets car out again to fetch Gladys. As he puts car back he calls for his goodnight kiss 9.45. Hope his cold will get better soon.

The next day, snow is still with us, Reg calls on his way to the station, said he had a disturbed sleep. 1.30 I go to my painting class. Home by 4.30. Start to clean the grate and light fire. Reg must be home as taps on wall and I tap back. 6.10 Reg calls. Only stay 30 minutes. Says he arrived home at 3.15. Was sitting in his armchair without a light when Gladys arrived back from an Italian class with a chap who gives her a lift. She's invited him for a cup of tea, was surprised to find him home. It's still snowing and getting thick underfoot.

Reg said no more hut it must have been quite a shock to him, so didn't refer or ask any questions about it. Reg told me though that Gladys said to him if he's going away next week, might go to her daughter for a couple of days.

Friday all the trains are delayed, some are cancelled, Reg phones me at 9am. Only just arrived at office. Had this morning given me his paying-in bank book as told him going to High Street to pay utility bills, so pay his gas bill, electric etc. as well as my own.

Also get two Valentines cards, one funny and one with lovely words for next Monday, St. Valentine's Day. Monday the 14th February, St. Valentines Day, is a festival Reg and I have always enjoyed, and today we are spending the day together, yesterday I have arranged flowers, tiny red silk flowers and green leaves tied in small bunches using white ribbon with print of red hearts printed on it, put on red straw mats with white porcelain hearts. I still have them carefully packed in a see-through box and I had put in as a centrepiece on my sideboard. Reg appreciated the time I took to put out the St. Valentines symbols in our dining room.

I have made a Pavlova for our dessert, and shaped it as a heart and on top of it sprinkled sugared rose petals. Also at one of Gill Slade's "Floral Art" classes we were shown how to arrange particular St. Valentine's hearts made of something resembling raffia to hang against the wall, decorated with red satin ribbon, silk roses and a spray of statice or some people know it as sea lavender that dries very well and makes it look a delicate spray.

Reg likes it and I go upstairs to get my two cards for him, he has sent a funny one by post and says he hasn't had time to get another. Feel disappointed, but he goes in bathroom and returns with an enormous card for me and a cardboard box. Open the box, and find a beautiful red and white heart-shaped box full of my favourite chocolates, it has flowers in the centre and white lace all around. I was so surprised, it was so lovely to be spoilt, I was so pleased. The funny card showed a very sexy kitten saying: "Valentine, you look wonderful. Don't just stand there ... Open the card and it says "UNDO SOMETHING!!!!" We later have lunch and take our time over it. Have a roast shoulder of pork, new potatoes, sprouts, saute parsnips. Pavlova, whipped cream and peaches.

Linger over coffee and I bring Reg his Crystal Brandy glass of ARMAGNAC and enjoy a tiny glass of GRAND-MARNIER. Had only one glass of wine with my meal to make sure I don't start to feel sleepy, as I want to enjoy every moment. There's time enough to sleep when I go to bed tonight.

Later on, I ask Reg if I can take a few photos of him in his Masonic Regalia, says he's never had photos taken in them, but agrees to fetch diem and I take the photos. They came out well, and I do so cherish them. Look at TV and at 8.30 time has caught up with us and we kiss each other goodnight.

Tomorrow he will be at Stratford-on Avon for four days. Only leaving at 1 lam so will have time for a good cooked breakfast before his long drive. As ever we wave to each other at the bedroom window at 9.15, so glad we shared such a happy day.

Next day, we go to get garage open and I wish Reg a safe journey. Take some mince pies to Phyl and Les and invite them to lunch tomorrow.

In evening Reg phones, is staying at his Aunt and Uncle's cottage, they send their love, less snow than in Kent, will keep in touch by phone tomorrow. Bitter cold tonight, so glad to put my electric blanket on.

Thursday, Gladys is off for two days and after lunch going to painting class and struggle with painting a stormy sky. One day, I'll get it right! Reg phones me 9.30, looking forward to seeing each other tomorrow. Giving a lift to two chaps to London but will reach Orpington by 4.30. Will phone me then. 3.30 Reg phones, just outside Bromley. Will meet me in 15 minutes bottom of Tile Farm Road. Drive on and have tea and cakes. Go on to Toys Hill, but it's already getting dark.

Have a chat but we both feel cold, I suspect after all that driving Reg must have been so tired, so ask him if we can go home. Suggests he drops me at Ruskin Drive at 6.40pm. I walk home and Reg puts car in garage but say Gladys is at back window so left garage open, so can return to say goodnight to me.

The weekend of 19th and 20th was as usual a hive of activities as after bitter cold night there is ice to clear away, branches of Dogwood are suddenly overgrown so need to be cut right away, and a series of vital jobs must be done by the man of the house. Never mind, tomorrow Monday a return to the office will be restful physically and a meeting in Cardiff Thursday will provide a tasty breakfast on the train from Paddington will be a pleasant experience compared to cup of tea and a biscuit munched walking down to the station every day. The next day, Wednesday, calls at 7.35am, very frosty morning. He will contact me by phone as usual, though it's a busy day for me. I am on duty at Abbeyfield House, and must visit the residents. Have just finished preparing some lunch when Reg phones. He's just going to the market to try and get leg-warmers for Phyl, as a belated St. Valentine's present, as she so does feel the cold. How kind of him to think of her, he's so thoughtful. Said if he can find them, will pop in to her on way home, so that she has them for this cold weather. Light the fire. Reg arrives and I give him a hot drink. Returns home and is back at 8.30 for his lesson. Says Gladys brought holiday brochures saying thought they could look through them for holidays in September. He didn't answer. Also she's hoping for promotion in St. John. Reg admits he doesn't know why she still wants more pips. So I said to him, "she still puts St. John as more important than you." Admittedly perhaps so, he'll think about what I have said. Have a coffee, add Cognac in his. Have our lesson and goes home at 9.40pm. Just before going mentioned holiday dates to Naples. Have been confirmed to Gladys.

In the middle of March, Gladys had to decide about phoning her friends Robbie and George re the five days of Easter, and Reg thought he would tell me so that if 1 wanted to visit Helene in Paris, I could arrange it. I told him that being alone in the house at Easter, knowing he was away. I didn't want to stay home missing him, so would enjoy Helene's company, it would make time go quickly.

He had said to Gladys, "I'm not that keen to go," but perhaps it will make us realise how much we miss each other.

I walk to travel agents and book my ticket to Paris for Friday the 1st of April. I also book my taxi to Gatwick. Over the past few days have spoken about the chances of sharing a holiday while Gladys is off to Naples for three weeks.

Suggest perhaps he would like to visit MONACO, the good friends who live there and visited maman in Orpington would be pleased to see him again and would fetch us at NICE Airport. Reg seemed interested and kept asking different questions about it. Said I would phone the hotel and Bernard would pay a deposit for us which we would reimburse when seeing him.

Then I will confirm by letter the date of arrival and departure. Will show him letter and translate it as soon as I receive it. Phone the French Consulate and asked for brochures of the Principality of MONACO so that Reg could see them on his return from Suffolk. A few days before my departure to Paris, we gave each other Easter cards, Easter egg and a large gingerbread heart iced with flowers, I gave him an Easter egg with SPARTAN assorted chocolates (all of them hard ones he likes so much). I collected some French currency and had only to phone Helene to give her an idea of my time of arrival. Had phoned a taxi driver in Paris that I had dealt with before, was reliable and helpful so had no worries at all.

13

Today Thursday the 31st of March, Gladys and Reg are driving to Suffolk. Of course, Reg goes to London office knocks on my door at 7.25am as usual. Will phone lunchtime. After my breakfast Phyl phones to ask if I can dig a few of her rockery plants and have a coffee with her after visiting my surgery for eye-drops. Bring them both an Easter card and dig up plants. They give me also a lovely card and Les gives me a green watering-can. Lovely, mine is getting past it. Very kind of them to think of me. Return home and put out my small suitcase as away four days. Cut my hair and wash it, as Reg phones. Will pop in at 5pm. Reg gives me two pairs of stockings and says will be with me all the time, showed me his diary and flight number. Tuesday 5th. Returns indoors 5.15. 5.35 returns and gives me a kiss before getting car out to put on his drive. 6.50 both say goodbye. Look forward to seeing you again, Reg, be safe.

10.30pm start to pack and wonder what April '83 will have in store for us, it is always a month which like the rebirth of nature seems to mean a renewal of deep feelings which sweep us into a turbulence we are notable to avoid. Wonder if his holiday will be peaceful in the lovely countryside in Suffolk, or will be embarrassing!

The first of April was very frosty and after we landed at 8.25 and queued at passport control, got out at 10am, my taxi-driver was waiting for me and recognised me. It's now pouring with rain, but arrive at 11am. Lunch is nearly ready and Helene and I enjoy seeing each other again. While she's having a little sleep after lunch and she has given me a spare key I go to the Galerie Lafayette, LE PRIMPTEMP, and find a lovely Italian sports jumper for Reg. Sneezing and coughing, so make my way home to Helene's flat by 4.15. She's enjoying Tennis Championships from MONACO. She's always enjoyed playing tennis as a young girl with my mother and never lost interest in the sport.

I brought her a small teapot and tea cosy, a few packets of tea and packets of BIRDS CUSTARD, so is pleased to make a lovely cup of tea for us both. Feel shivery, so take 2 Hedex tablets. Go to bed. God Bless Reg, hope I feel better before we meet again.

Saturday 2nd April, must get shopping before the shops close for Easter. Unfortunately, it's raining so hard, have to use my umbrella and walked for two and three-quarters hours but it was worth it. Bought many things which I thought Reg would enjoy, mind you, I also acquired a large blister on my heel and arrived back to the flat laden like a mule. It was 5pm. I felt tired, and cold and enjoyed a hot drink. Showed my purchases to Helene and she thoroughly enjoyed the variety of presents I will take back with me. After a delicious lunch, which Helene prepared I took the metro to Montmartre, Place du Tertre, and bought a colourful picture of Paris for Phyl and Les. I know they would be pleased and could put it in their lounge.

Tomorrow Easter Sunday, shops will be closed from 2pm so was glad I finished my shopping.

After lunch, get a loaf at bakers and two delicious pastries for our tea, and spend a lazy two hours laying next to Helene under the quilt looking at TV. The only interruptions were my sneezing and blowing my nose. My nose is as red as a tomato. Hope to God I feel better and not so dreadful to look at when I see Reg again.

Only two more days and we will see each other again. Feel very guilty, poor Helene has a sore throat and I have given her my bad cold.

Easter Monday, after a very cold night am not surprised

that it's snowing. Wonder it it's the same if not worse in Suffolk.

The next day, I get a few basic food stuff in the shops, so that Helene has necessary things in her fridge and does not have to go out in this snow.

Pack my bag and all the gifts in a bag I brought with me. It's 8am here but 7am in Orpington.

The taxi is waiting for me at 10.25 getting me to the airport at 11am. Can't find Reg's favourite aftershave, so get another, hope he likes it. At last, we are above the clouds and I can relax and look forward to our meeting. My bag of presents weighs more than my small suitcase, so get a trolley and suddenly see Reg standing there grinning like a Cheshire cat, it's been so long. Leave trolley and run into his arms, such a long five days, it's so good to hug him.

A stewardess asks me if it's my luggage, as I left it in the middle of the corridor. I noticed she was smiling as I apologized. I guess she must have noticed my excitement at seeing Reg standing there. We collected the car and went to Pitts Cottage for a lovely lunch. Reg told me arrived back yesterday, Gladys asked if I wasn't going to see you. I said that I was involved with Abbeyfield, so will see me tomorrow. Get back home at 3pm. Cup of tea, at last we are together and enjoy that intimacy we have so missed. Give him the summer sports top and it fits perfectly.

Before I unpack the rest of my gifts, Reg tells me about his stay in Suffolk and I feel very upset about it.

It seems that Robbie and George asked Gladys and Reg if they would join them on holiday next September. Reg said September was too busy and October he had his Lodge commitments. Then Robbie asked Reg if he would join them while Gladys was on her three weeks holiday in Naples. It was obvious Gladys had approached her friend to make that suggestion, so that he would be apart from me. When he replied he would go for a golfing holiday as he did last year Robbie said, "I think his affections must be elsewhere." Also showed him a picture of a cottage, dilapidated, it would need a builder to put it together again. Reg missed me and I think realised my criticisms were well founded. Also, apparently the weather made both journeys, going and returning very uncomfortable. It is amazing that a woman of sixty can't see that to ridicule a man in front of other people does not help to resuscitate the feeling of love that must have existed twenty years ago, it only insults his pride and does nothing to re-awaken tenderness or affection. No wonder those five days were so hurtful to him and must have made him wish he did not dutifully indulge his wife's whims come what may, since it is expected and not earned. Poor Reg, no wonder he's having those migraines so often, things are much more difficult for him than for me.

No wonder he says so looking forward to our two weeks holiday at the beginning of June, it will be wonderful and a rest from commuting will also be appreciated. Wednesday the 6th April, phones me lunch time to arrange meeting at KINGSWAY tomorrow for my birthday lunch. Leaves with me a parcel to be opened tomorrow morning with two cards for me.

Open box. It contains a glass dome on a stand and contains beautiful real flowers and butterflies. Looks very pretty. Cards are full of lovely words, the comic one is saucy but good fun. Took taxi, lovely driver who laughed when Reg called him 'young man' as he's the oldest cab driver in London (82 years old). At Selfridges find a short cream coat. Reg buys me 4 bunches of sweet smelling Freesias. Home by 5.45. Without Reg, my 51st birthday would have been very lonely. God Bless you Reg. It had started this April and already the excuses for trying to separate us by any method was on.

Reg's well conditioned loyalty will not accept any criticism from me, and I get upset by the list of jobs given out on Saturdays and Sundays even knowing he has a migraine or an asthma attack which seems thoughtless and unkind, but when I voice my opinion he only says thanks for worrying over me.

Because of so many occasions of sometimes unpleasant remarks, Reg and I hurt each other and then immediately regret it and try to take steps to mend the hurt we have caused to each other. Reg right away before even returning to his house, would show how sorry he feels, and ask me if we could spend the next day together to show each other how vital we need to be in each other's company. Even whilst away on business, he phones me just before going to bed to see if I'm all right. Nevertheless, I must let him come to his own conclusions, our hopes are the same, but he must see for himself that time has passed and only duty but no love can be rekindled.

It is all too late. Perhaps two weeks holiday will help to soothe his mind, recharge his batteries and being away he will be able to think what is the best course of action.

Keeping up appearances from her point of view is no longer fooling either family or friends. He has lived on his nerves so long, he must feel sometimes that he's drowning.

Unbeknown to us both, when we first met, I was sad because my husband was so ill and would not be able to recover, and Reg was aware that the delicate flower of love had already faded and we recognised in each other a need to give comfort and become close. Our becoming close was inevitable and I now feel that first day of meeting, our destiny had been written in the Book of Life.

The whole of May, continued in the same manner as April. We both feel our holiday can't come soon enough. The day before travelling to Monaco, I must mow my back lawn and also phone my friend Georgette who will be at NICE Airport with her husband Bernard as they are coming to meet us off the plane. They are a very lovely couple who have been good friends to my mother and it will be good to see them again. As soon as my lawns are done, do the wide front lawn. Cut my hair and wash it. Reg arrives from London office and has had a haircut.

Put luggage in car and lock garage. We must leave home at 7.30am. Supper and can now relax and go to bed. Tomorrow will be a big day. Do hope Reg will enjoy our first week's holiday in the Principality of MONACO. It will be his very first visit and I feel eager to show him the places I have enjoyed in my childhood.

Saturday the 4th of June was a lovely sunny day, our flight is delayed by thirty minutes due to heavy traffic. Leave by TRISTAR (380 seats) at 11.25, land at NICE at 1pm (that's 2pm French time). Glorious sunshine. (79°F).

Georgette and Bernard are there to meet us. The car journey is spectacular as instead of taking the coast road which is full of bends, he takes my mother's usual route which is called "THE MOYENNE CORNICHE" (the middle Corniche) which is about 1000ft above sea-level with wonderful views of the Med and only takes about 40 minutes to reach Monaco. Reg is quite taken at the different trees and plants which are, of course, typical of the sun-soaked countryside. We get to our hotel, lovely room, large bathroom, and a balcony where the view of both the harbour and the Rock on which RAINIER and GRACE'S pink Palace is dominating the panorama.

Go back to our friends flat and give them a few presents. Get car out of private garage and take us to LA TURBIE, a village overlooking the Principality (1500ft altitude).

Stop the car at hair-pin bend where Princess Grace's car shot over into the greenhouse of a gardener and lost her life. When we reach the village, the two men enjoy a PASTIS (local alcoholic drink) and we two ladies enjoyed a Martini.

Jacqui and Reg in the exotic gardens in Modaco

Then decide to have a light supper, a large pizza cooked on a wood fire, an ice-cream topped with whipped cream and a coffee. We accompanied that with two bottles of "COTES DE PROVENCE" Reg seems amazed at the hair-pin bends and the altitude. Home by 10.15pm. The men have two whiskies and we go to our hotel.

What a good day it has been and before going to bed, we go on the balcony and look at the reflections of lights in the harbour, the yachts bobbing up and down and the silhouette of the Palace against the skyline. Reg seems to be taking it all in and says how pleased he is with my suggestion of visiting this place. Our first day has been full of happiness. I feel very lucky to share time with Reg. And so to bed.

Sunday, had our breakfast in our room and afterwards go to the market which is in full swing until noon, when all the stalls disappear and the square is washed. All the shops in the covered market are closed but till 12 you can buy anything you want. Fruit, vegetables, meat, fish and in the covered market even cooking utensils, even on Christmas morning the market is very busy up to noon. Return to our friend's flat at 11.30am as pre-arranged as they have organised for us a very pleasant Sunday luncheon, so off we go. Drive up in the hills to yesterday's venue at LA TURBIE, then on to ST MARTIN DE PEILLE. Lovely restaurant, and sit on the terrace. Aperitifs, then a starter consisting of Parma ham, radishes, salami, butter olives and gherkins and home-made paté.

Then a separate dish of home-made Ravioli. After that. Leg of lamb, potatoes and stuffed aubergines. Vanilla ice cream, coffee. Provence Rose and Beaujolais Villages. Took photos with them around garden and fountain. Drive home and we go to our hotel to rest and get cool, as temperature is in the eighties. At 7pm, we go to meet Georgette and Bernard. They are taking us to MENTON on the coast via CAP St

MARTIN, a lovely pine covered place along the coast road which has beautiful villas, each one different to the next in style surrounded by gardens full of lemon trees and Oleanders which are in every colour you can think of and smell delicious. Have our evening meal on the terrace with lighted candles and enjoy another tasty meal. Home by 10.15pm. Tomorrow I will show you MONACO and we will not even bother with the clock, amble where we please and go where the fancy takes us. Strangely, Bernard and Reg seem to understand each other more with mime than anything else, if Reg is stuck I just translate what Bernard has said and the other way about.

They both seem to have the same sense of humour so it's easy to chat. Bernard comes from Marseilles, excitable, uses his hands to describe everything and has a strong Provençal accent, yet his lovely wife Georgette, always impeccably dressed with fair hair, comes from the North of France and has a different accent and those two are so fond of each other, it's lovely to be in their company.

Monday the 6th of June, after a leisurely breakfast, at about 10am I decide to walk towards a place called the "PRINTANIA" a kind of British Home Stores where all kinds of things can be bought at a reasonable price. We firstly get an olive-wood chopping-board, a lovely golden wood, for the kitchen, also a sachet of 2 fresh vanilla pods, a bottle of CINZANO BIANCO and a small bottle of COGNAC. Walk back to hotel and have a glass of Cinzano and a small biscuit, also a little sleep. Take a bus to the "ROCK", Show Reg the Convent where I went to school, then on to the square facing the Palace.

Have a small glass of beer as it's getting hot and visit the Cathedral. It's a beautiful building built of marble taken from the quarry south of "LA TURBIE", the village on top of the hill we visited on our first day. Prince Rainier and Princess Grace were married there. Then walk a little way to the gardens abutting the edge of the rock and there is a Statue of ALBERT I in St. Martins gardens, he was the Great Grandfather of Prince Rainier, and a mariner who collected rare species and put them in the aquarium on the lower ground floor of the OCEANOGRAPHIC MUSEUM a few minutes walk from the gardens.

We take photos in that place. We continue our walk to the square where the daily market is, down a long road leading to the Harbour. Found there was now a supermarket and bought two large cups to have our morning tea. Got back to hotel, tired after all that walking because in Monaco there are few roads on the level. It's either climb or go down steps. Have a lazy afternoon, then suggest a restaurant I know by the harbour called the "STELLA POLARIS", the food is good and they don't close till the customers decide to go home. After supper, we stroll along the edge of the quay and look at all the yachts, small, large, luxurious ones like the ONASSIS yacht which is often berthed there. Of course, perhaps you are not aware that there are no harbour fees, so yachts favour getting supplies, food and other things before making their way to other ports. I don't know if nowadays the rules are the same. But it seems to me that's good business. We have walked quite a lot and we are both ready to turn in.

Tuesday 7 of June. As soon as breakfast is over, we walk past the market, pass the Railway Station and reach MONEGHETTI. It's not far from where my family use to live, and every shop is familiar. We have a rest on a park bench in the square, then walk down to Bernard's "Richmond Bar". Have an aperitif with them both. Back to our hotel for a cold lunch as it's such a hot day.

After a rest, we take the bus to the Exotic gardens. Take photos. Have choc ices outside the entrance. The gardens are fantastic as they are designed on the side of a cliff overlooking the Med. Paths and little bridges have been designed for people to admire the amazing variety of exotic plants which have been transported from the South American deserts and which enjoy the same climate. There are enormous "Mother-in-law Cushions" large and prickly circular plants which you would not want to sit on, extraordinary flowering cacti and agaves.

You have to walk through the paths to see the multitude of plants to appreciate them. I took photos of Reg admiring them and enjoyed his surprise at the truly weird shapes. Walk to the hotel and have our supper there. Had coffee in the lounge and went for a walk in the Casino gardens overlooking the sea. Then tired out but happy go to the hotel.

Wednesday the 8th of June After putting another film in the camera, take the bus to the OCEANOGRAPHIC MUSEUM and AQUARIUM. Buy postcards, Reg buys me a lovely book on the museum. I explained to Reg that although the large building was filled with unusual animals by ALBERT 1st, it was many years later the headquarters of JACQUES COUSTEAU who used to use the large rooms for conferences about his expeditions and television programmes that were so popular on BBC Television. It's quite an interesting place. Also in the ground floor room which was not just long but had a high ceiling there was a skeleton of a whale and all the children use to be taken by various schools to see this enormous animal. We lunch at our hotel, then after a siesta we decide to go to one of my favourite tea-rooms called "L'EPI D'OR" and enjoy tea and pastries. Reg is getting very tanned, all I manage to do is acquire freckles all over my nose and cheeks.

Thursday the 9th of June (83°F). We call on Georgette to see how she is as her cold was giving her trouble, then take a coach to MENTON and have a walk in the market and spot an attractive porcelain CICADA. I believe it's called a wall pocket which you can put flowers in and hang against the wall, also get two glass drink measures, one for spirits and one for Cinzano. Find the restaurant where we had supper on Sunday evening. It's a hot day, so only want cool things. Enjoyed a melon in Port, a pizza, a bottle of red "COTES DE PROVENCE", ice cream and coffee. Very hot and sunny, almost bums my skin. Take a coach back to the Casino and walk back to hotel. Sit on our balcony and chat about our holiday.

Reg has enjoyed all the different places we visited and says he hopes we will one day return. Says Georgette and Bernard have been so good to us, but have also respected our privacy and knows seven days goes quickly and we so enjoy being together, so we are very grateful for their consideration.

After supper, we sit in the Casino gardens and then visit the gambling rooms. Reg cannot understand the fascination of the Roulette or Black Jack (minimum stakes £100). Still it's strange to see the seriousness on the faces of some gamblers to see if they have won or not. For a laugh, we put a few coins in the machines outside the gambling rooms and promptly lose them. Still it's an experience to witness such a compulsion. Personally, I would rather enjoy a good meal or go for a swim in the Med. Go back to our hotel, Reg makes me a cup of tea and go to bed.

The next day, stroll up Rue Caroline and purchase a pair of folding sunglasses for Reg, then enjoy a coffee. Buy some flowers for Georgette and take them to her. Have a beer and go to the "STELLA POLARIS" for lunch. A storm is brewing, lightning and thunder echoing round the mountains surrounding MONACO, also a little rain. Find a pretty little jug for Phyl as she collects them.

Go back to see Bernard re time to airport tomorrow. Gives us a large bottle of PASTIS to take back to England and will collect us at 1.15.

Leave them at 9pm and have a walk along the BOULEVARD DES MOULINS, the one and only road which is level, also the one with the most beautiful shops, we also pass the church of St. CHARLES and some nice restaurants and tea-rooms.

After looking at most window displays, we stop at the ROXY, almost opposite the BNP BANK and we enjoy a snack and go back to our hotel.

Saturday 11th of June. Our last day here and I admit I feel sad to leave, I have seen Reg relaxed, smiling at the new experiences he has had, laid back and not walking on egg-shells as he has done before our holiday started, and feel glad that we have for our first week's holiday the fun of being taken around by such good friends. We settle our hotel bill and tip the chap who served us our breakfast. Go for a walk, stop at a dress shop where Reg had seen an attractive sun-dress. Wants me to go in and try it, even the size I needed required an alteration, the girl says will be done by noon. Navy and white. Go to park, return to shop, it's ready. Reg likes it, suitable for walking in the garden, simple, but appealed to him. Bernard is at the hotel and there's little traffic. Register luggage, told delays from London, so plane taking off at 3.30 instead of 2.50. Eventually take off at 3.45 (French time) land at 4.30 (English time). Home by 6.30, tired but happy to arrive safely home. Go in garden and notice my back gate which was bolted by Reg is undone and some muddy foot prints are outside my kitchen and dining room. Someone has been asked to see if I have been home this past week, it's fairly obvious. Ask Reg to re-bolt garden gate but say nothing. Spend Sunday the 12th of June putting clothes in washing machine, pop over to Phyl and Les with a few presents and mow lawns. It's just a day of preparation for tomorrow's drive to Bournemouth.

Next morning, after a cup of tea, wash my hair and Reg asks me to wash his. Small breakfast and by 10am we're off on our second week's holiday and after an uneventful journey arrive at the Chesterwood Hotel, at 3pm.

I feel the holiday week is going to be very different to our

Monaco holiday, but just as pleasant I think Reg will feel more in charge as he won't have the language difficulty and when someone chats to him won't have the bother of asking me to translate. Personally, I like having a man in charge, protecting me, looking after me, and now he is in his own country can be in charge of the situation. I am looking forward to our second week's holiday as I know Reg is.

It probably seems old-fashioned but Reg gets a little frustrated by a woman flexing her muscles of independence and prefers the more feminine side, and by remarks he has made, I know that he appreciates more the softer approach of a woman.

We are now more able to guess each other's likes and dislikes so it's so easy to please each other.

The setting of this hotel is wonderful, it's run by a family and all the staff are very helpful and pleasant to talk to.

In front of the hotel, there's a good size swimming pool and beds of flowers and shrubs. A hedge around it all of evergreen plants makes sure the privacy of the guests is maintained. All rooms are spacious and the ones facing the sea gives us a lovely view. It seems tea is being served in the lounge and afterwards walk down the coast road and into town. Book seats at the Pavilion Theatre for Thursday evening, then walk round to the Winter Garden and book two seats for Wednesday for MIKE YARWOOD. It's chilly and very windy, so don't go out for a walk after supper. The swimming pool is all lit up and the lights are on the PIER and neighbouring coastline.

Decide to go to bed early, after a tasty meal, as well as a few glasses of a white MOSELLE wine. And so to bed.

Tuesday the 14th of June, tea brought in 7.15am in pretty cups with roses on them, no doubt a family run hotel looks after its guests and its luxury. Go down to breakfast eventually and take an open-top bus to town, take wind blown photos of each other and buy a few things in the shops. Lose our direction and take a taxi back to hotel for lunch.

After, walk down cliff path to sandy beach, sun is hot. Play a game of Mini Golf, then enjoy an ice-cream and back to hotel. Notice our waitress, Bernadette, is wearing a lovely lace apron. Tells us she purchased it at Poole in the new covered market. Will go there tomorrow and look at that shop.

Join other guests at the dance in ballroom and enjoy dancing till 11.30pm. Nice relaxing day, good food and friendly people.

The next day, we took a bus to Poole and found a modern shopping precinct with escalators up to a gallery of little shops and found the lace shop we wanted. Bought a hostess apron (white) got a tray-cloth for Phyl and Les, a pink lace apron for Gill Slade, my neighbour on the other side of the road. Returned to hotel at 2 in the afternoon, lazed around the pool and swam a little.

Went to the theatre in evening and went to bed at midnight. Friday is our last complete day in Bournemouth and after a gentle walk to Boscombe and a stroll through the lovely gardens, we decide to pack and leave early in the morning after settling our bill. Back in Orpington by 3.30 and my back gate for the second time is open, though I especially got Reg to push bolt in before we left. Give little presents to both Phyl and Gill. Reg phones his daughter to find out about the health of her mother-in-law, who is so ill. Speaks to his son-in-law who asks if he enjoyed being away. "Wish it was on a permanent basis." "You'll have to arrange that with Gladys."

Go to bed 10.30. Tired, go to sleep. Monday, 20th June Reg had a wheezy night, kept coughing, gave him extra pillow. He says if chest still worrying will ask me to make an appointment with the doctor. Goes in his house to see if "Father's Day" card from his daughter, but none as usual, then he goes to office but will return home at 1.30pm. Give him a light lunch. Then asks me if I'd come by car with him to doctor.

Chemists are shut, but will collect his medicines tomorrow morning.

I am counting that there are only two days to go when we can enjoy time together, so today Tuesday after a trip to get his medicines, we go shopping. At 1.30, we go to Sevenoaks, have a lunch and go to Penshurst Place. Take many photos in the gardens as it's a lovely sunny day. Get home at 5.15. Make a cold supper and afterwards Reg asks me if I'll shorten his trousers as it's fidgety to him. Then go in front garden and finish planting flowers. Do some watering. Reg goes go his place to phone his daughter re: news of her mother-in-law's health. Just as the call finishes, the phone rings. It's Gladys phoning from Naples, asks if he's been away. Says yes, when he tells me, feel a bit put out, says her friend Iris phoned her husband so Gladys thought she's do the same, says only copied her friend, saw nothing in it.

Thursday the 23rd of June, Gladys returns from Naples and the holiday is over.

Reg is on edge and can't concentrate on anything. Suggest I meet him outside Selfridges for lunch tomorrow, then we'll be together a little while. Says if I have things to do in the house, we could postpone lunch in town, leaves it to me.

When I hug him he said "Right, see me at 12.30 outside Selfridges." Get the fast train and enjoy our meal together. Tomorrow another Saturday afternoon out at St. Paul's, so Reg and I get the shopping and bring it back by 11 am when Gladys is off again.

Still an afternoon of peace which is appreciated by us both. Tomorrow Sunday, will be a day of jobs in the garden, with the only break being lunchtime when the weekend cheese sandwich will be the highlight of the day.

Reg's health worries me so, he's getting migraines and whenever an argument flares up his asthma sounds appalling. I wonder sometimes whether his Ventalin inhaler gives him much relief. After a visit to his doctor, phones his office as can't go next week as doctor wants him to rest and take things easy, he has given him three lots of medication. I know he's not well as he's always on edge and loses patience so easily.

As from the 1st of July, the gloves are off, and whenever Gladys has a conversation with me, it's contradictions, criticisms and generally showing off.

Even Reg gets a fair sprinkling of verbal abuse and I cannot understand how he can keep his opinions to himself, but his body language certainly gives it away. Many times notice his clenched hands and his white knuckles.

Today, Reg makes a cup of tea and brings it on the terrace. Chat about tennis, he mentions Lacrosse, Gladys says few schools play lacrosse only Hockey, sounds as if I used to play it at school in 1846 not 1946.

Everything I say, she contradicts or pooh-poohs. Says can't understand why I don't know the scoring of either cricket or snooker. So when programmes like 'Pot Black', a favourite snooker event on TV, she says the scores out loud to show how knowledgeable she is. When I return to my home and see Reg, tell him I would have enjoyed his tea more if I hadn't had to listen to inane remarks and critical comments from Gladys, and don't know how he stands it. He points out that when he mentions tennis she disagrees with him too.

Sunday the 3rd of July, Reg calls while she's sitting under a sun umbrella reading a magazine. Reg said had a bit of an argument. She said she wanted the leaves to be swept from the front door. He said "Good God, why is it you have to have this Victorian idea that because visitors are coming, you need to turn everything upside down. Use the hose, it will do it even better!"

She wishes she hadn't mentioned it, so she's all in a huff. Next Friday, his aunt Madge and uncle Raymond are coming over for the weekend, so even the shrubs have to have a short back and sides, it's quite pathetic.

14

True love will neither suffer sharing or mediocrity.

ANON

Friday the 8th of July 1983, auntie Madge and uncle Raymond have a lazy afternoon, they are 77 and 78 years old and although young at heart, do feel tired travelling but they always enjoy Reg's sense of humour and his kindness.

Whenever they visit Reg is relaxed and always remembers how his aunt helped his mother look after him when he was a young boy.

Get up early, and bake a lemon drizzle cake that we can tuck into coffee time when they call to say hello. Today, Sunday, they make their way back home to Buckinghamshire. Take a few photos on the terrace. 4pm Reg says please come to train station to see them off. Gladys very curt, doesn't say goodnight. Friday the 15th July 7.35am Reg pops in on way to station and says "Had a bit of an argument last night, she said she wanted to fix the holidays for September as she has a lot of commitments with St. John and wanted to know what date etc." Reg replied, "If you want a holiday, I can only have one week and not abroad, we can go to the countryside if you like, but that's it." Gladys said, "For the last two years he didn't seem interested in any other arrangements", to which he replied, "I'm sorry, but that's how I feel, full stop." She told me it would be nice to go away for Christmas, but Reg said "I am going away for Christmas, so that's not on."

I am collecting Reg's glasses from the opticians in High Street, pay for them and ask for receipt.

When waving goodnight at window, Reg gestures a 7, that's when Gladys is off to Croydon, another St. John's event. Next day, Saturday 16th, get shopping bags and at 8.35 off we go.

Afterwards, put away all perishable food and after coffee go to the 'House of Holland', large store with all kinds of garden furniture. Find an attractive pair of wooden seats with a table between them and a hole in table for a sun-umbrella. Will order one but new lot expected Wednesday so will phone.

Go to Homecare Texas and buy eight rolls of white wallpaper, two large cans of white emulsion, one small gloss (conker brown) for wooden uprights, brushes and adhesive. Home by 12.15. Now I have what I need to start on my front lounge. Pick a few raspberries from my garden for us to enjoy with cream after lunch. Gladys said would be home by 5.30-6pm, That will be G.M.T (Gladys Mean Time) so of course arrives at 7pm.

Wednesday 20th of July phone re: my two-seater which I discover is called a Jenny-duo and ask them to put one by, Reg and I will collect it and put it together. Next day, ask Reg what Gladys has concocted with her friend Robbie regarding holidays next September. Reg knows she's doing everything possible to get him away from me. Tells me not to worry, leave it to his judgement.

Carry on working on my lounge and painting. Don't stop even for tea, and open both windows. 10.30 go in kitchen for a glass of water, see Gladys mowing lawn. Carry on working till 1.30 (5hrs) have put two coats on door. Lunch. 2.15 start again. Finish doing picture-rail and ceiling edge ready for roller. Take off gas safety grill to clean it. Remove log fire cover and wash. Screw it back, gas fire now clean.

Stop a moment, 4.15 (so far been working in lounge seven hours.) No sign of Gladys. 4.30, while drinking a cup of tea with a distinct flavour of Dulux Paint (vintage 1983) Reg phones. He will try to be home by 6.50, but at 5.50 arrives. Only stays five minutes. Goes to his garden, at 7pm calls with rollers. Invite Gladys to come over for a Martini or two and am glad to sit down as aching all over.

Next day, Friday 22nd of July, Reg phones me early from his office, asks me if I'd like him to have a day off, either Friday or Wednesday, will arrange it. Just received an appointment for my left eye at Queen Mary's Hospital, Sidcup for the 5th August, today fortnight.

Phyl and Les invite me to join them for lunch 1.30. Very kind of them. Go back to painting with roller. Very fast and easier than with brushes. Back home by 2.10. Still no phone call. 3pm Reg phones, will be home by 5.10. Putting the second coat on down-drop and carry on till 4.30. Clean rollers and any paint off my nose. Reg pops in and says it looks good. Returns at 6pm to say going to supermarket, just come to look at my progress. Gladys has just said to him, "I suppose we'll have to see what needs to be done in the way of decorating, if anything. I still think the house is too big." Reg says "You said it could be cut in half Gladys says, "That's not the same" Reg replies "In that case employ a charlady, then you won't have so much to do."

Gladys, after shopping wants Reg to get fish and chips as doesn't feel like cooking. She's so excited that the Royal Tournament is on TV and so won't have to miss anything of it as doesn't have cooking to do.

Saturday the 23rd of July. As usual get rubbish and newspapers to tip at Bromley, and at 9.30 go to the butcher and greengrocers. Home by 10.15. At 10.40, Gladys and Reg come over for coffee and scones.

As soon as Reg mentions getting my garden seat, Gladys has note from Post Office to say parcel awaiting her for collection. From that moment, it was like a video on 'fast forward' and today Gladys asked Reg to go to nine different places when he only offered to collect my garden seat and if any sun umbrella was there, to get it. But it became a manic race which was exhausting. As soon as my seat was put in the boot of Reg's par, Gladys went back as wanted a porch light (has already one in porch, one outside shed, one hanging in apple tree). Then on to Marley, does not like them, so back to the 'House of Holland', find it takes maximum 40 watt lamp bulbs. Then go home. Lunch. 2.30 Reg calls to say Gladys wants plastic wire for plants and if Argos has them, same time get umbrella, but sold out. Tell Reg I can try to get one in the week and carry it OK. Not to bother. Told Army and Navy (Bromley) have a sale, so Gladys wants to go. While I collect my parasol, Gladys sends him to Debenhams, suddenly wants to buy stockings at Allders, then wants to go to B.H.S to the lighting department upstairs. Also gets an urge to purchase a brass curtain-rod with a pineapple each end. Home by 5pm, thank Reg for collecting my wooden seat but feel so angry, this sudden need to dash about all afternoon, he looks absolutely shattered.

Had a terrible night, couldn't get to sleep till after 2am. I feel very tired. Reg was popping in for lesson after 12 noon. Reg says Gladys said to him, "We did not do what we decided to do yesterday or today."

"What do you mean?" Reg replied. "We haven't looked round to see what decorating needs doing." Because I am busy decorating my lounge, expects him to copy me and do his.

Also concerned that she's discussing dates in August to visit her friends in Suffolk.

Tuesday the 26th continue to paint bay-windows, also picture-rail and part of wainscoting. Put brown gloss on upright beams. Also get the box of 'Jenny-duo' but picture of assembly looks very complicated, hope it does not give too much difficulty to Reg to put together. Next day, Wednesday, Reg has a day off and after breakfast Reg starts on putting my wooden garden seat together. Could not have done that alone, that's certain, but by noon it's all done.

Go to Riverside Inn for lunch. Home again by 2.45. See rest of film on TV. Take last three photos in camera seated on new seat. Have half an hour enjoying the sun in garden and Reg goes in at 5.30.

Next day, Thursday, I am busy putting wallpaper up. Very slow at it but manage to get five lengths up, so hope Reg will be pleased with my efforts. Wednesday the 3rd of August, Reg is taking a day off and as I need to replace my lounge carpet, ask Reg to measure the lounge (11ft 4" x 16ft) so I shall be able to choose some carpet and have the firm lay it for me, so my lounge will be completely finished.

Reg gets the car out and we go to Orpington High Street. He goes to his bank and I go to Boots, then pay his gas bill and on to Harris Carpets. I leave £60 deposit and they'll phone me next week to ask which day I shall need it laid.

Have a quick lunch, he collects his suit from the cleaners and home by 1.45. Reg looks at his cricket on TV and then puts the loungers on lawn and have a little sun-bathing for an hour. 6pm he goes home. 6.30 Gladys arrives.

Phone Phyl to invite her after my supper for a coffee. She and her husband offer to come with me to Queen Mary's Hospital tomorrow as I have to have an examination to my left eye.

When they go, I put the 9 o'clock news on TV, but above the news hear voices of Reg and Gladys. The voices are getting louder and higher in pitch. Whatever is going on now. Hear footsteps up and down stairs and doors slamming. 9.45 go upstairs to my bedroom, hear click against wall, Reg looks out and waves, he gestures she's up and down stairs like a yo-yo. Wave goodnight.

Go down again to warm some milk, notice by 10.15 no lights in kitchen, unheard of Gladys going to bed early as that. Wonder what's going on now. We'll find out when Reg says hello first thing in the morning on his way to station.

Next morning, Reg calls and tells me of last night's event. Gladys (9.30pm) suddenly asked Reg "What's happened to your blue suit then?" "I've had it cleaned, why?" "So you came home early, did you?" Gladys started to raise her voice and said "I don't understand, you never talk to me for the last two years. You don't seem to have any intelligent conversation." He replied, "There's not anything to say, that's how I feel." She then added, "Jacky seems to know more about your movements than I do, Bill doesn't go to her house to help her with different chores, but you are there all the time." Reg said "That's completely different, I knew maman and Sherry and I promised maman I would help anyway in the house. If you're finished, I am going to bed."

Told Reg I'm worried that she might throw things in your face and say "Well if you go on seeing Jacky, you can pack your suitcases and go," then she can have the house and you'll be in difficulties.

Reg answered, "I am not interested in the house but if she makes more remarks in that vein, I shall tell her I'm going away for six months to get away from all that." I said "Do you think she would do that?" Reg said, "No, she's too interested in the monetary side of it to rock the boat."

So I told him if she really lost her temper he could always live here, but as he says that's too close. So I said, "I could sell my house and we can get somewhere wherever he likes." He said that's very nice but he's talking in the short term, if she's going to be funny, he'll retire and go away for 6 months.

It's cleared the air and he's made it clear he's not going to be dictated to because I said "What if she makes an ultimatum that you must not see me again or she'll throw you out." Reg answered, "The house is in my name and don't worry. Told him I was sorry he had such an upset. Reg said, "It's all right, I slept like a log." Perhaps clearing the air was a relief to him.

See Reg walk down to station and wonder what sort of day he'll have. He phones me at 5.20, just leaving now, says might not be able to pop in. Says I leave it to you, but if Gladys thinks by her Views knowing you're not going to dare call, she will have achieved her aims."

"Yes," Reg says, "but you leave it to me." When he arrives, pops his head in window, says, "I'll come to see you later." Hear more voices. 7pm he calls, tells me that his son-in-law's mother died today, so Gladys going tomorrow to her daughters to stay with the children whilst the parents do the necessary arrangements for the funeral. What a day. Everything happening from all sides.

Friday the 5th August. Reg phones me at 12.30 to wish me all the best on visit to hospital. My good friends Phyl and Les accompany me and am given another appointment for 5th January 1984.

As soon as home put new bed clothes on. Prepare sandwiches, Reg arrives at 5pm as going to his lodge at Rainham and must have some supper before leaving at 6.45pm. At 9pm open the garage.

10pm Reg is back, goes next door to phone as arranged. Gladys still there, will return tomorrow.

Saturday 6th of August, Reg wakes me up with a cup of tea and we go to tip as we usually do Saturday and get rid of garden refuse, newspapers and such. Get shopping for weekend and have coffee and buns when we get home. Reg peels the potatoes for their evening meal as he is expected to and comes to my house for a good lunch.

Feel so sad that our happy time is nearly over when Gladys returns. Reg doesn't like to see me sad but I so miss him when he's in there. Tell him I feel so afraid at times in case it all goes wrong. Asks me, "Do you think that you are wasting your time?" I tell him, "You could change your mind or be swayed back to fall in love all over again with all the effort she's making." Reg says, "There's no possibility of that when there's been no love for the last twenty years, so there's no worry on that score. We will have our cottage."

125

I go in garden and start working, 6.45pm Reg calls on way to shut the garage. We have our last kiss and hug.

Wednesday the 10th of August.

Today is Cassie's funeral. Unbeknown to me it was just a sad occasion for her immediate family, but it turned out to be a day of momentous recriminations, a day of hurt from all sides — words that can't be forgotten or erased. Everyday seems to be more frightening since bad tempers and hurtful words are being thrown about like shuttlecocks.

The day, nevertheless, started as usual. Get up early, click on wall, wave good morning to Reg standing there in pyjamas. Reg gets car out at 1 1am. Long drive to cemetery and on to Enfield for a bite to eat, then a journey back to Orpington. Went to Petts Wood but closing-day. Back home at 3pm.

Have lunch with Phyl. It's now 7.40pm, garage still open but no-one called. 8.50 Reg walks round, stops without coming in saying "Won't stop, we've had a few words," I say. "About us?" "Partly." Shuts the garage, then on the step, says "Don't worry, it's mostly about us, she's not getting anywhere, it's about not being close anymore and about splitting up. I'll tell you in the morning,"

9.25 see Reg at window, says "Five minutes." 9.35 still not upstairs. 9.45am see Reg at window, after noise of doors and wardrobes banging, Reg gestures "sleeping in back." Phone my friend Phyl, she tells me light just come on in small single bedroom over porch. All lights on in front bedroom. Something must have happened for lights in small bedroom being on. Will find out in the morning, what on earth has happened.

Thursday 11th of August.

Get up 6.30am. Reg calls round at 7.30 and tells me what happened last night. As soon as he has explained it all, go up to my bedroom and put in my diary every word said so that I don't omit anything. After they had supper last night, Reg wrote Jim's address so that I could send a card and a donation and told Gladys "Just written Jim's address and taking it to Jacky and see how she's going on, then going to the garage Gladys says "You always say you're going to the garage, but you go to see Jacky. It seems to me you are more concerned with her house and jobs than you are with this place. You still haven't done any decorating."

"You said you hadn't decided what you wanted done, so come off that one."

"For the last two years you haven't been close." So he said "It's been more than two years and it's obvious we haven't a chance of getting back at all, so let's be clear about that." So Gladys said "What do you want to do then, if we split up then we had better sell the house and split the money."

Then we talked of trivial things like Reg obliging me by driving to Bromley to get my sun umbrella and all sort of little things. Slammed the door so hard I thought it would break. So Reg said "Right then as things are I'll get my clothes etc, and sleep in the little bedroom and that's that." So I said to Reg "Is there anything I can do, find you somewhere else to live PRO TEM while you arrange things?"

He said "No, I'll stay in the small bedroom but you had better be careful." So I told him, "She'll not show her temper or any criticism of you to me or I'll blow my top." So that's it for now.

Reg says he brought her a cup of tea, but she didn't move, still in bed when he left the house.

Will keep in touch with me from office. Goes home at 6pm. He goes to his shed and she arrives and walks down the path. Eventually, says 'hello' to him. He walks back and as he does he winks at me.

It's now 7.45. 8pm they eat in silence. Only at 9pm the TV news comes on. 10.15 all lights out downstairs. Put coat on and walk round the front of the house, light on in small room above hall, so Reg still in his little room. What a day, even across the back garden you can feel the atmosphere, it's eerie.

Friday 12th of August.

Reg as usual knocks on my front door at 7.30. Pops in for a few minutes to tell me what happened immediately after going to his shed last evening. (I believe it's a relief to him to unburden all this before travelling to London.)

After he walked to his shed at 6pm last night, Gladys walked to end of garden to ask if he wanted egg and chips, said "No, thank you."

She made egg on toast for herself. He asked if she was doing any ironing in the small room/study downstairs. She said no, so he went in there to do his accounts. 9.15 she asked if he wanted a coffee, he had that and she went up to bed at 9.30 and he went to his room at 10.10pm.

Reg phones me at 9am from office. Tell him I'll try again to find a furnished flat, tell him there's one in the "News Shopper", a maisonette (£70 per week) but he says it's too much. Phone a friend in Epsom about names of estate agents, most are £200 per week. So disappointing. Reg phones me again lunch time. Ask him if he would like me to look in case it's good. Phone at 2.15. A couple are visiting it and will return at 9pm to say if having it. I arrange to visit, take taxi 3.10. It's very private, downstairs bathroom, spacious and clean, galley kitchen, narrow to the point of intimate, two bedrooms, one sitting room. It's in front of a wide green and good enough for six months. Back home at 4.15. Phone Reg and tell him about it. If couple don't take it. He can visit on his own first thing in the morning, and decide for himself. Reg says will be home by 6pm train. Will call later. Returns at 7.30, he said he's going to test the car and will get something to eat out. Ask me to go out in garden so that Gladys can see me. Reg returns at 9pm. No lights indoors. Reg says she's out Phone Mr. Mendoza, owner of maisonette. Will phone back. 9.30

this chap asks every question of Reg's Status, everything. 9.30 appointment to view in morning.

Saturday 13th of August

Get up 6.15am. Have barely slept. So tired. 7am tap on window. Reg ready to put bags over wall. Go to tip. Back home by 8.10am. Bought fresh bread. Reg just looks in to say going to view maisonette, looks very smart in business suit, asks if Gladys wanted to go shopping, she replied did not know yet, Reg said he'd be back in an hour to which she replied, I might be there or I might not.

10.20 Gladys' front door bangs, see her go out carrying a small black bag. 10.55 Reg phones from the phone-box near flat to say "I have paid deposit and all's well with the flat." Home by 11.05. Goes to his house to find a note from Gladys to say will be home by 8pm tonight, but out all day Sunday.

I go to our usual string of shops and get vegetables to prepare a salmon salad for our lunch and onto butchers to get a roast for lunch Sunday. As soon as 1 return, get a straw carrier bag and start to pack things necessary for the kitchen, washing up liquid, tea towels, sponge, toilet and bath soap, tin full of tea-bags, coffee jar etc. Then Reg can take it with him in the car and have the necessary items in his new flat. While I am making a list of what he must pack (clothes, shoes) and other things which are in the eaves cupboard. Go in garden and cut clematis, sweet peas and fill up to three bags of refuse. Reg goes back at 7.30 to have a sit down. At 8.30pm Gladys is back, but next door for a change silence reigns. Not a word or a door slamming. It's all quiet.

Sunday 14 of August.

Get up at 7am and do some hand-washing. As I hang underwear, the kitchen door opens, Gladys looks at me with a look of disgust, I say to her "I say, water sprinkler is still on down there. " She looks at heaven with a look of disdain, and goes to shut it. Returns into kitchen and shuts the door without a backward glance. She leaves the house at 9.30. Hear Reg say "Oh, I'm not bothered about that." Apparently, she'd said she would be home by 6-7pm. Reg is in his study drafting a letter to Gladys to leave on Tuesday.

12.30 get dressed to go out to lunch at Reg's suggestion. Drive to Petts Wood to a restaurant called Knights. Have a good meal and return home. We sit in garden in afternoon. Can't help feeling every day this week events are reaching a climax, a chance to recapture the love which stopped being nurtured twenty years ago has been lost and it's futile to be angry about it. The whole thing is sad but can no longer be brought to life. Goes in his house for a bath and then an hour later phone rings, it's Reg to say he's in Biggin Hill. When Gladys returned they had a talk, she took the suggestion of selling the house quite well but Reg said he had to go out as looking for a room. So telling me will go back later and go straight to bed. Feels so tired.

Monday 15th of August

Have a lot of shopping to get today and after phoning Helene to tell her our news, go and pay gas bill and get a soft acrilan double blanket, two pillowcases for Reg to take to flat on the day he goes, he will have to make his bed and spend his first night alone. Just as I reach home phone goes and Reg has bought a sandwich to eat in his office as rewriting letter to Gladys and make copies. Also writing letters to his son and daughter. Said will phone later. Will be home at 5pm. His chest is bad, has headache and his tummy is upset. He's getting worked up about tomorrow. Goes home at 8.45. 9.15 Mr. Mendoza phones to say his wife will bring keys mid-morning. Putting net curtains in the lounge. Small bedroom will be decorated in three weeks. Ordered a fridge-freezer from Currys, will be delivered at flat. Any problems at all to ring him. Phone Reg to tell him, he sounds pleased. Don't see Gladys arrive as doing a bag of groceries for Reg to take.

Go to bed, but keep thinking have I done everything. Understand the lounge carpet is being laid first thing in the morning in the front. Why does everything happen at once?

Tuesday 16th of August.

Awake at 2.45am. Need a cup of tea, wipe up the dishes used last night, put them away. Feel it is quiet and can carefully do the things for Reg to take with him to the flat Realise that first thing, the carpet people are calling to lay carpet, so need to get a certain amount of packing sorted without leaving everything to be done in the morning. A few zip-bags are put in Maman's old bedroom downstairs to put shoes, socks, belts inside them. When I feel as much as can be done in advance is ready, I go back to bed at 4.30am.

Two more hours to sleep before the alarm goes. Reg arrives at 7.30am. Give him tea, then breakfast. 10am carpet man arrives, Reg helps him to carry the roll of carpet in. I pay the chap a cheque for the balance and let him do his job. Reg asks me to help take suitcases etc into my hall, so his wardrobe is empty. While he's getting out of eaves cupboard wine bottles, spirits, two decanters and his Christmas present from me of chess-table, cameras and his microscope. My settee is replaced in lounge and then the landlord brings the keys. Make two separate trips to our flat and I make up his double bed as tonight he will spend alone, and must get his clothes and toilet things ready to go to business in the morning. Go to phone-box a few yards from our front door to have a taxi to take me home by 6pm. 6.05 hear next door slam. She's home. Windows and doors banging next door.

Reg phones at 9pm, been sorting things out, suggests he stops and gets into a hot bath, relax and stop looking for jobs to do. Tomorrow while he's in London, I shall do any cleaning of cupboards, putting provisions in the kitchen, polish wall-tiles and hoover every room. Tomorrow I will spend all day making the flat welcoming and we will spend the night together. A hot meal will be waiting for him and the next day the fridge-freezer will be installed, so it will be as comfortable as possible. We need to get a telephone installed, so that's another job to do. Feel tired now, wonder how Reg is, it will seem so strange tonight in a new place, but it is perhaps better that he has no distraction, he can go to bed when he feels the need to, and get himself adjusted, hope he won't miss his spacious old house, and will find his new abode comfortable enough.

Wednesday 17th of August 1983

Get up at the usual time, hear on the news that all trains to London Bridge, Cannon Street and Charing Cross are stopped because of a fire at a signal box, 230 trains cancelled. Poor Reg, how will he reach London. Says might affect trains for 2 or 3 days. Don't see Gladys go out.

Reg phones me at 10am. He has been two and a half hours in train standing and squashed, thought he was going to faint. Will try to return home after lunch. As soon as I get to flat, start to clean inside and out of kitchen cupboards, discover cigarette cards and sweet papers over floor. Clean washing machine, wash floor and top of cooker. Start to put the vacuum cleaner together when doorbell goes. It's Reg. So glad to see him. Cup of tea and clean inside of chest of drawers and put lining paper in it.

Look at TV. The landlord brings new net curtains for the bedroom. Thank heavens the fridge-freezer is being delivered tomorrow at 4pm. Reg says feels relaxed in his little flat. God Bless.

Thursday 18th of August.

Get up early, make breakfast and at 7.15am Reg makes his way to the station, takes him 15 minutes. Then I get down to it, taking dirty curtains off and wash ledges, polish windows. Replace clean curtains. Leave flat at 8.35. Go to Petts Wood to choose heavy curtains for my old house, will phone Saturday morning regarding calling to measure French windows. See Phyl, have coffee with her. Return home and pick a bucket of apples. Leave to walk to the flat, must ask Reg the short cut to avoid one hour and ten minutes, such a long walk. 4.30 fridge-freezer is delivered and Reg arrives at 5pm. Had another long journey. He starts to sort out papers, shows me a photo of his mother at the age she married his father. Very attractive woman. Polish dressing table and Reg rearranges furniture in the lounge. It's not as large as our lounge in Orpington, but it's cosy and Reg has chosen a favourite armchair and seems content while we look at the TV. 9pm Reg phones for a taxi for me and tonight I return to Newstead Avenue.

Friday 19th of August

Reg phones me at 8.45, trains still bad. Had to go to Victoria Station. I realise that now I must look after two homes. As I must sell this house, it must be looked after, the dustbins must go out Monday night, the electric and gas meters must be read and the garden has to be cared for, but more importantly, the flat (costing so much to Reg) must also be cared for as being small, everything must be put away carefully. Sometimes, I walk to the rail station to meet him and we stroll home together. Reg shows me the inventory and items in the flat. He phoned uncle Raymond to tell him events, said they had decided to part sell the house and if he wanted to get in touch before his hospital visit on the 8th September, to write to my address. Naturally, Reg or I, or both, will meet aunt Madge and uncle Raymond off the train and take them to the hospital for his check up.

Saturday 20th of August

Reg phones me at 8.30am from a phone box, going shopping, will phone later as he knows I am awaiting the curtain chap who is going to measure the French windows and will send estimate for doing the curtains. 10am Reg

Reg's mother aged 18

Reg's father aged 27

phones me again to say has bought the shopping for today and tomorrow lunch time and will now walk to estate agent to advise re his house being viewed etc. Eventually, I get a taxi and arrive at flat as there's much to do and I must help if I can. Reg wants to bring the wardrobe in second bedroom but can't turn the corner, so decides to pull it to pieces and re-screw it in the larger bedroom. I wash it in vinegar and line it. Then all the underwear and woollies can be put away tidily in the large drawer at the bottom whilst I am finishing that; look for Reg in kitchen to start on some lunch, he is on his hands and knees cleaning out the oven which he says is very awkward as there is little room, as most galley kitchens only are suitable for match-stick figures but not a fourteen-stone man. I must say Reg has worked very hard to make the flat clean and tidy, and has been a big help. Tonight, I am staying with him and though tired, feel so pleased that it's all coming together. Reg is also happy that I have helped him to make our little flat feel homely. Tomorrow, Sunday 21st of August, our first Sunday together, my swollen ankles have gone down after a nights rest but Reg doesn't yet find it possible to take things easy, as soon as breakfast is over I suggest getting a Sunday paper, but when I return he's vacuuming the rooms. After lunch we go for a walk and he shows me the cut-through as the walk to the old house takes a long time. After a relaxing cup of tea, I return to Newstead Avenue to get things sorted by removing any more apples on the lawn and mowing the back and front lawns.

Tomorrow, must get Reg's birthday present and birthday cards, so will do that in the morning.

15

**"Nothing worthwhile can be achieved
without a lot of effort, but
it's all worth both time and tribulation."**

Anon.

Today, Tuesday 23rd of August 83, it's Reg's 63rd birthday. I go to the flat with his birthday present and some shopping. He arrives from office at 4,15. Reg suggests going to our favourite restaurant called "Knights" and we enjoy a lovely meal and a bottle of wine, walked home and realised it was a week since he left Crofton Road.

The next day, when we have had our evening meal, over coffee we discuss all the changes and complete transformation that will affect our new life together. Emotionally, we are both ready for any amount of difficulties which will be thrown at us, as many things have to be organised.

I have my house to be completed vis-a-vis decorations and Reg has to get his house viewed and valued, on that score my efforts will be certainly more straightforward.

When Reg phoned to enquire from Gladys if she will show the house to the agent, she wanted him there, but he said that wasn't possible, so hopefully the valuation will be carried out next Friday the 26th August. Apart from that, Reg has to inform the Inland Revenue that he is now a single man and the date he left Crofton Road.

It's all a time of frustration, dithering re the sale of the house, and it's all a time of trying to cause the least arguments. Reg feels he doesn't want to wait till he's sixty-five to retire so decides to mention it at the office so that they have an inkling of his intentions. He realises that a fair amount of notice must be given, so thinks seriously about the next move.

I am very aware that Reg and I had this far enjoyed the space and facilities of a fairly large and well appointed house and we have had overnight to adjust to a small maisonette which though quite adequate, was a complete change to our last abode. Thinking back, I can only but appreciate that Reg handled the change with fortitude and tried his best to bring every comfort for both of us. This was a time when hard work and courage was paramount and more than ever my appreciation of sharing my life with Reg was even happier than I could hope.

For the last five years we have seen each other every day, shared meals together, had holidays together and comforted each other at sad times, and I always appreciated being escorted by someone invariably well-dressed, and whose appearance was absolutely impeccable, but they say you don't know anyone till you live with them. Usually, that implies criticism, but in this case I was amazed at what I noticed as from the first evening shared with him. While putting the last details to our meal, Reg strolled out of the bathroom naked and completely relaxed went to our bedroom. I was carrying a glass of Scotch in each hand and he said, "Come and have a drink with me while I change."

I then realised what I had never seen before, he put on his underwear, and brushed his suit before putting it on a hanger, put a jumper on and a pair of sports trousers, took a pair of socks, which were all tidily in a chest of drawers and a pair of moccasins. Tidiness like that I had never witnessed and I realised he must have noticed how untidy I was. In his case love wasn't blind, it was considerate enough to ignore my shortcomings and not criticize, he doesn't know how grateful I was that he said nothing. At the age of fifty-one, I decided that I would make the effort to put some order much needed, and by example I eventually became tidier, but I thank him for not saying anything.

A small desk in the comer of our lounge, was carefully stacked with Lodge papers, legal documents re 51 Crofton Road purchase, utility bills which Reg was paying on his old house, everything orderly and I guess in a small flat like ours, it was vital. Although I was busy in the house at Newstead Avenue, I was always back in the maisonette to prepare our meal and if in good time, go to the station to meet him. On Thursday 30th of August, Reg phones the estate agent to ask if his house had been visited and valued as arranged. When he phones me at Newstead, I suggest he phones back the agent to say I will collect letter and bring it to him, to avoid time wasted by posting it. I collect it and give it to Reg. He shows me the letter and is pleased that at least something is happening.

The next day, 31st of August, the documents regarding 6 months lease on our maisonette was duly signed, Reg got his deputy to witness his signature and that was at least duly concluded.

A couple of letters were redirected to us and when he opened them, found two pages of details of flats and maisonettes in Bromley, so Gladys was already looking for a place of her own, so put them back in a newly-typed envelope and sent them on to her.

Friday, the 2nd of September, Reg gets his Lodge papers together as tonight he has a meeting in Rainham, Essex. He phones me at 12 noon to say that his solicitor colleague in the City, suggests that if things get acrimonious, he will put him in touch with a Divorce Lawyer who specialises in that sort of thing. Reg phones again at 4.30. Just off the train, will have a snack and if possible phone me before making his way to Rainham. At 5.30 see his car on the drive, 5.45 the car is gone. Ten minutes later he phones to say Gladys doesn't understand why he's gone, where can she contact him. Seems she's worried about her pension. Doesn't want to get rid of the house unless it's all done legally, and thinks he might return. Reg is somewhat taken aback about how monetary her remarks are, worrying about twenty years hence and pensions. Won't decide re house, says more things to discuss. Wants it all done legally. A week later, Gladys phones Reg at his office in Holborn about collecting seven refuse bags to take to the tip as her son who lives 15 minutes away is unable to oblige. What happened, I don't know, but we neither of us were surprised at this absence of filial consideration. Ten day later we contact the telephone installation department to order an ex-directory telephone which will be installed on Friday the 23rd of September, we look forward to that. The next day I get up at 6.30, bring Reg a cup of tea in bed and get some toasts on the go. As he kisses me goodbye he says "You know it's as if 51, Crofton Road never existed." Then he shut the door, and walked to the station.

I was so surprised I wrote what he said in my diary two minutes later. He had lived in that house many years, I had been nervous that the large and comfortable house might have been missed by him, but no he had somehow erased it from his mind. Perhaps memories in that house spoiled the initial pleasure when he actually moved in, but it certainly was said with much feeling. Friday the 23 at 10am the telephone engineer calls with a new telephone and I feel so relieved to have that facility, but as luck would have it, a fault is discovered in the cable at the top of the pole so should not have counted on that. Hope the problem will be solved quickly. We have to be patient till next Tuesday the 27th when it can be properly connected.

Meanwhile Reg is still keen to look around for a new home for us and we go to Horsham, visit places in the surrounding area but to no avail.

Saturday the 24th Reg leaves by car to his lodge at 1.30, won't be home till about 8pm. I visit my friend Dora who owns a dress shop in Kent Road, I often get the odd items of clothing and we have known each other since the early seventies, asks me if I'd like to view her flat above the shop, as the girl student who rents it is out, as perhaps if it's suitable would help us. Surprised at the large rooms but amazed at the scruffiness and so on, but notice the space even though there's little furniture there.

I believe that Reg realises that sorting out the sale of his house or Gladys accepting the separation is difficult for her to accept, so think perhaps this situation will drag on and on, so feels will have to re-assess our financial position. Dora tells me her tenant is leaving on the first of October. 1 tell her that Reg would have to see the flat and we do have a tenancy agreement, so could not consider in any case to live in the flat without doing a lot of improvements to make it comfortable as there is such little amount of facilities. We'll see and have a talk about it. Dora invites us to her home in Charterhouse Road to suggest to Reg and I that if it's possible to put some order and improve the comfort of the flat, would he manage to find time and the energy since he was going to the City, to take the task on. I naturally said I would tackle anything that I was able to do in the way of stripping the old carpet in the kitchen and cleaning it thoroughly, but anything to do with woodwork and putting up brackets I would not be knowledgeable enough to do. Reg said that Saturday and Sunday he would spend there and take note of any jobs that would need attention.

Arrived back home at 11.30, knowing a little more about things, but also realising that much effort and time would be needed for us both to make things possible. Reg at last, receives a reply to his letter to Gladys, at last she's accepted he does not want to get together with her and she wants him to tell her what his plans are regarding the house.

After two days spent in Southampton on business, Reg is back and on Friday the 7th of October after breakfast we both go to the empty flat. This is the first time Reg has seen it and is amazed at all the things that will have to be done. For some unearthly reason in the process of moving the student managed to break a lock and a door-frame to the sitting room. The black finger marks on all painted surfaces does not create an attractive pattern and all three electric appliances in the kitchen are rusty which doesn't excite a prospective tenant one little bit. The gas cooker belongs to a generation of solid cookers which can be cleaned and given elbow grease comes up smiling with a good shine, so that appliance can be cleaned and come up a treat. A carpet on the other hand. I must tear off, hoping some sort of lino or vinyl covering beneath it will save the day. We will see. The spacious lounge is good with a three seater and a gas fire, but no shelves, coffee table or anything else. The bedroom, double bed and a gas fire has no wardrobes, chest of drawers or curtains, so we will have to improvise. A bathroom is there with a twin tub, a large bath and a wash basin. Toilet is down a long flight of stairs so will have to trip down if the need arises. Not a washing up bowl to be seen, so will have to purchase a few things, mostly of washing up liquid and cleaning agents before I will have a cup of tea there; also a kettle. I hope Reg is not too disappointed or even shocked but after noticing all that, just smiles at me and says, "I think we can make it cosy all right," what a relief, I was a little concerned about his opinion.

So now, realised there are three homes to look after, one to keep clean with garden etc, our maisonette where we live and one flat which needs our attention, so must do my best as Reg is still busy in Holborn and travelling is tiring.

Thursday the 3rd November, Reg has the day off and goes to Petts Wood to order planks of wood, brackets and such like, while I prepare a beef casserole for tonight's supper. I go to my Ripley House painting class and Reg meets me at Chislehurst roundabout. While I prepare vegetables Reg surprises me offering to prepare dumplings. I had no idea he could do that, or even want to, but he made very light ones and we both enjoyed them I remember now Reg telling me he used to watch his paternal grandmother make them when he was a boy and I suppose he was shown how to prepare them and hadn't forgotten. He seemed to have hidden talents and as time went by I discovered many more.

On Saturday the 5th of November, the residents around us had prepared an enormous bonfire in the middle of the green and we decided as darkness fell, to amble over and enjoy the excitement of the Guy Fawkes festivities. A lot of the neighbours had pooled their resources and organised a small fireworks display and we both enjoyed the fun of it.

Went to Dora's flat in case there was a reply from his letter to Gladys. A small letter was awaiting him where he proposed to pay for her removal cost, gas and electric bills at the new address when she finds one. But letter says she doesn't agree to his proposal, but will write again in a few days. Reg realising that events are now moving very slowly, tells me that he will write to our landlord and explain that his domestic arrangements are resolving themselves in a shorter time than previously envisaged. In effect the position is such that he could vacate at the end of December 1983. Whilst he is conscious that his tenancy does not at present terminate until the end of February 84, he writes to seek his agreement to an earlier termination date. We both hope our landlord will look favourably to our request.

Four days later, Reg and I take a long weekend away to search for our home, there must be a cottage somewhere that we will recognise when we see it. Thursday the 8th November, we drive to Horsham, then on to Petworth for lunch, then Winchester to look at the town, pass Ringwood and arrive at Boscombe, Phone the Chesterwood Hotel at Bournemouth, the receptionist recognises his voice, has a double room available for us and at 5.30 we are there. Lovely to be back, we spent a week there in June, never thought we'd be back so soon. Friday go on to Southbourne, visit the estate agent. See a tudor-style house, ask to view it, find it's already sold, so back to Bournemouth, feeling a little disappointed. The next two days were like a marathon, from Ferndown to Swanage, back to hotel, then next morning Worthing, Shoreham-on-Sea, Eastbourne. Stay the night.

Visit Tenterden, lovely bungalow but would need a compass to find it again, so return to Orpington and feel tired and wonder when we will be fortunate enough to come across our home. It's there somewhere, but time is not right yet.

I get started to get a decorator to paint and wall-paper my square hall in Newstead Avenue as it's the only part of my home I have not decorated and it's the first place buyers will see when they call, so Saturday the decorator will put back the carpet after putting the gloss paint round the front door. Must be there to put the chain back on so the painting dries.

Reg gives me a lift to my house and go to the flat and start on jobs. Suggest he does the grocery shopping apart from the meat. I'll do that. At 10.15 go to his doctor's surgery to collect his prescription. Get medicine and meet Reg at 11.15 and we got down to work which needs the two of us. Fix two wall cabinets in the kitchen and move cooker so that room is more spacious. Have a sandwich lunch, and at 4pm we return to our maisonette.

Next day, Sunday, Reg walks to the flat and does more jobs while I do some ironing. Will meet him there at noon. After coffee, get down to serious tasks. I hold the door - whilst Reg uses his power saw to make it 21" wide, then hold it for him while he drills holes for brackets. Then saws rods for heavy curtains in bedroom. Fixes them on wall. Go at 2.30 and get lunch ready. Pleased with our efforts and enjoy a sit-down.

Monday, the 12th of November, 8am I am already at Newstead writing a Christmas list and Reg phones me to tell me he has written the letter to his firm about retiring a little earlier than is the norm, so wait for a reply.

When 5pm comes, Reg calls and helps me to put furniture back in hall, fixes brass curtain pole and curtains.

Take taxi to maisonette and I make a list of items to bring to flat, but begin to sneeze and feel I have a cold coming.

Reg and I are somewhat concerned that having no wardrobes we don't know how to keep our clothes tidy and dust free, so our landlady (Dora) suggests two clothes rails to accommodate both our things.

Reg fixes a strong wooden batten on the wall for a brass pole and we go to a charity shop and purchase some wide and long red velvet curtains and one other curtain for the kitchen. The red curtains go on a brass rail and covers down to the floor all our suits etc, so that is a good job done. We find a small chest of drawers at a sale so that our underwear can be tidily put away. Reg has now caught my cold and we are sneezing in unison. I get some tablets for it and our usual nightcap is replaced by a nice lemon, honey and cognac toddy with a sprinkling of powdered cloves, taken in bed. I'm hoping we can sweat it out and feel the benefit by the morning.

Today, Reg has received a letter from the solicitor acting for Gladys. It's an aggressive letter threatening him he'll have to answer within 21 days or else take court proceedings. Name of solicitor rings a bell, believes it's his son Colin's solicitor. Reg is surprised.

Monday 21st of November I phone the G.P.O regarding transferring our telephone to the other flat, will disconnect on the 30th of December as we move on the 31st December.

Reg decides to buy a new fridge and we order one in the High Street, Orpington, as the rusty one is not acceptable and will be delivered in two days time. On that day, Wednesday the 13th of November. His firm is giving a Christmas dinner, and Reg will stay overnight at the Russell Hotel, I will stay at Newstead. He packs his evening suit and phones me at 8.40am from his office. Tell him I am just getting ready to do some work at the flat, take off the carpet and underlay in kitchen, sweep, dust, cut carpet into squares, and put in plastic bags. Wash floor and put other carpet and vacuum clean, just as the doorbell rings. The fridge is delivered and it's beginning to look like a kitchen. The curtains are fixed and I am sure Reg will be pleased with the transformation.

Go back home to Newstead. 6.40pm Reg phones. His colleague has shown him where a divorce lawyer can be contacted and will ask for an appointment in the morning. Will phone as soon as dinner is over and has reached his hotel. Sure enough, 11pm he phones to say goodnight, see you tomorrow.

Will tell him then about my visit from the estate agent and what price he values my house. He phones me at 8.30am with a croaky voice, feels he's got a cold, so we will be in tune, me with a sore throat and a headache and Reg with a croaky voice. We always share everything, even colds.

He's home at 1.20pm, meet him off the train, doesn't look very well. Has a high temperature, so give him Beecham Powder and suggest he goes to bed. Cheer him up saying our landlord has written to him. Give him letter, reads it out to me, he's accepted our earlier departure and all is well.

On the 17th of December, we contact our good friends Anna and Bill who live two doors away from Reg's old house. Invite them for drinks and finger-food, they have been so helpful to us and we hope they'll come over to our little place.

Prepare different savouries for the occasion and look forward to their company. They will be our first visitors. Anna is Danish and Bill was with R.A.F, and over the years they have both been good friends to us and were only two of four good friends whom we invited to our little home.

Christmas eve (Saturday) we collect the turkey and Reg takes it back to put in the fridge as well as bacon, chipolatas and the usual goodies. Take Christmas presents to my good friend Gill and her husband John, also to Phyl and Les in the bungalow opposite and give them an invitation from us both for Boxing Day, they have been so kind to us and we both look forward to their company. Phone my friend Barbara but speak to her daughter Lynn, who tells me her dad, Ray is coming home from hospital for Christmas and are just going to fetch him from London. Get back to the maisonette and start to wrap up the parcels for Christmas, will put them on our shoes in front of the fireplace tomorrow morning before breakfast as feel too tired.

Sunday the 25th December '83, our first Christmas together, our small lounge is strewn with parcels of every shape, size and colourful wrapping paper. Don't know where to start, then realise the turkey must be put in the oven, so do that then our magical Christmas begins.

Have a mid-morning coffee with mince pies and cream interlude. As usual we have chosen each other's presents with care, knowing what pleases and with much love. Strangely enough we have both given each other twelve presents and amid our gifts there's a mixture of practical as well as favourite things like clothes, books, chocolates, tapes and cosmetics. I was so thrilled with an envelope containing a refresher course of driving lessons, also a beautiful Cameo brooch in a pretty box from Hatton Garden Reg was pleased with a suede and wool green cardigan, a soft dressing gown and a glass painted photo frame with his photo in it. Just before starting to undo our presents, we took photos of it all.

When I think back, only perhaps children can feel such excitement or people who are full of love can enjoy the fun of undoing parcels to see the look of surprise in each other's faces and hugging each other in the privacy of our home. What a wonderful Christmas, I still look at the photos of it all and the pictures we took of our Christmas table just before sharing our meal.

Boxing Day our good friends Phyl and Les came and we enjoyed having them with us. Their friendship and loyalty were given to us from the day we met them and though they were both in their seventies have always helped us in any way possible.

As we are leaving our maisonette on the 31st of December, we made a list of what needs to be tidied and cleaned and polished so that our abode is up to scratch. Although it was not left very tidy, we don't intend to do the same as our landlord has been very obliging to accept our going sooner than originally planned, and has been fair, so we both make the flat tidy and polished before leaving. A lot of our winter jumpers etc, I put in the chest of drawers at our next address and some of our provisions (tinned food, pasta, rice and cereals) I put in plastic carrier bags and place in kitchen cupboards ready for our arrival on New Years Eve. Have also brought from Newstead, spare towels, sheets and blankets, also pillows so that it's all awaiting our arrival on Saturday. I put a box of cutlery on the table and a bright new kettle on the stove. The regulation box of tea, coffee and sugar has place of honour for our tea-break when we both start to work on our flat, so we will be cosy.

On the day of our departure Reg left the keys at his landlord's house and wrote a letter to the effect that he was unable to tell him of his new residence, but as he will be travelling around would he please write to him as appropriate at our flat, to which address I suggest you remit my return of deposit. Also wrote to thank him for his courteous and helpful co-operation in what has been a most enjoyable tenancy and in closing wish him a Happy and Prosperous New Year.

16

A new year, new hurdles to leap over, but two hearts
happy to share good and bad.

We move into the flat and realise we have taken a further
step towards climbing a stony path. We have to sort out
the difficulties regarding selling our respective houses, awaiting
his firm agreeing to an earlier retirement, also the reply from
his solicitor regarding asking for his divorce, so 1984 will be
a year full of a mixture of joys and disappointments, so there
is nothing new there for us.

The next nine days we received news which will cause
delays. One letter was from the Inland Revenue saying that
the particular form which must be filled was asked for after
the date allowed and so he was still taxed as a married man.

The next letter from his solicitor said that although Reg
hoped for the divorce he was seeking would take two years,
Gladys had decided not to agree, so a period of five years will
be imposed. Poor Reg is so disappointed but did not realise
that she would act in that way. I was not at all surprised, but
told him that being together was in itself more important and
we can both look forward to that day when being married
will only confirm what we already feel for each other.

The next letter was from the Corporation he had worked
for, agreeing to his retirement on the 31st of March '84, so
at least that cheered him up.

On the 11th January I decided to purchase some wallpaper
for the bathroom and while Reg is in his office, I start to paper
the walls and get four strips put up after having washed the
woodwork and cleaned the bathroom suite.

I feel it's best to do as much work for our comfort because when he retires, will want to concentrate on looking for a home and that seems as difficult as finding the crock of gold at the end of the rainbow but we have faith that our cottage is somewhere out there waiting for us to stumble across it and since September 1981 when Reg said, "One day we'll find our cottage, I know it."

I feel sure our patience will be rewarded. I organise with builders to put two new posts and a garden gate in the Newstead garden and tomorrow the 18th of January the builders will start. That is the last thing to be made good before I ask the estate agent to put my house on the market. By the 1st of February I am ready by arrangement to show people round so we will see how it goes.

I get in touch with the driving school so that I can make use of the driving lessons bought for me by Reg for one of my Christmas presents and book my six lessons starting on Wednesday the 22nd of February. It's such a long time since I passed the test and then there was not such a lot of traffic.

Reg urges me to get back to driving as I will probably need that facility when we find somewhere in the country. Of course, he's right, but I wonder if I will manage to get back into it. The 5th of March, Reg has a weeks leave, so we spend a couple of days looking for a place but after looking around, both feel a little dejected as on our return from Eastbourne we find a copy of Gladys' solicitor's letter sent to Reg's solicitor who's asking for everything but his blood. He makes an appointment for next Thursday suggesting he has council (i.e. a barrister) to sort it out.

We have now had ex-directory telephone re-installed in our flat and one morning the phone rings and Reg takes the call. Much to his amazement his daughter spoke getting all annoyed because was told it was ex-directory and only found out from her brother the day before. So much for asking his ex-girlfriend to keep the information to herself, but he had to listen to comments about being 'holier than thou', teachers have a habit of being forceful as if addressing five year olds, and regardless of age or being related assume that they are right to criticise. Poor Reg was bewildered and hurt, but I calmed him down and told him not to let it upset him.

The date of Reg's retirement was getting nearer so I bought a retirement card and was glad to let our good friends know that at last after 42 years in business and six years in the R.A.F, he would soon be able to be free of train journeys to London, driving to different parts of England, and be able to enjoy the freedom of taking up any hobbies or pastimes he wanted.

Reg was glad to receive from friends and colleagues beautiful and humorous cards from them, but none came from his son and daughter. The bitterness apparently was transferred from their mother. I noticed he eagerly opened his cards but as none came from them, the disappointment was obvious in his face, said nothing but I know he was hoping for a few good wishes from them. Still they will both have to live with their conscience for the rest of their lives.

On the Friday 30th of March Reg asked me to come with him to share part of the morning. Speeches were said. I met a few of his colleagues and friends and after a while I said goodbye as a farewell luncheon was organised and he would come home when it had all taken place. A beautifully bound red book was presented to him and photos were taken. The book was full of signatures and he was presented with gifts which he treasured and are still with him. As he said when he returned home, "We can now concentrate fully on finding our home, we have spoken about it such a long time, our cottage is out there somewhere and we will know it right away, we will spend this weekend relaxing, then we will decide next week where to start looking."

Thursday the 3rd of April, we were shocked by bad news. Our loyal friend, Les and had a heart attack in front of his wife Phyl, just outside their back door. I was stunned, that poor woman must have been so upset, they were such a close and loving couple. Her son-in-law and daughter who lived in Sussex quickly came and helped with the formalities, and when the funeral was arranged for the 10th April naturally Reg and I drove to the crematorium.

The next day, 11th of April we got a phone call to tell us a bungalow's 'For Sale' sign was just being fixed in the front garden, no knowledge of price or anything else but name of estate agent. Phoned my good friend Anna and asked if she could drive me there. Agreed to make an appointment for next day 10am and we went there. Reg had gone to London and would only be back in the afternoon. It was a glorious sunny day, I didn't know the area but as soon as I saw the 'For Sale' sign and parked in the drive I felt so excited, I was shivering. It was a long drive between two large oaks and we wondered whether it was an omen to see on the wall a wooden nameplate called "NORMANDY". Unfortunately the two brick steps in front of the door were broken, paint was peeling on the wooden upright which supported three rows of lroof tiles, some broken, but nevertheless I was so wanting to see the inside.

A young woman opened the door with a little boy in her arms and we walked into a very narrow hall, but were surprised when she opened the door to the living room as it was a split level room, giving on to French windows. The garden was long but the focal point was the most tall and graceful oak I have ever seen. The ceilings were beamed and I was sure that this was it. I had to look past the cosmetic appearance as wallpaper, curtains and carpet were my least favourite colour, dark brown, but with a little imagination you could visualise white on walls, colourful curtains and a carpet which took away the illusion of treading on earth. Anna and I looked at each other and I knew she could also see the potential of the place. The owner then re-opened the door to the hall, on the right was a little girl's bedroom, opposite on the left a small room which was her little lads bedroom. Opposite was a bathroom, a fair size but it contained an avocado suite, tiles to match and a lowered plastic ceiling. We went back into the lounge and to our surprise she opened a door on the left which was the parent's bedroom. How strange for a bedroom to exit into a reception room. Then on the right another door opened on to a tiny study. Then we noticed a mahogany stable door with a step down into a square kitchen, good size but noticed a tall fridge/freezer in the middle of the work surface and at the other end by the back door an electric double oven. Still apart from the illusion of Twin Peaks the size and shape of the kitchen had many possibilities.

We asked if we might go in the garden and realised that if we both chose this place we would have plenty to do all round, but the garden had a lot of charm as well as variety of weeds in all the beds, two dead brooms, a stick of rhubarb like an exclamation mark by the back door and under the rickety arch at the top, were swings imbedded in concrete and a greenhouse and shed. On looking at the oak I had admired, realised the size of the trunk was enormous. The lady said that it was supposed to be a 400 year old specimen and I could certainly believe it.

I said I was interested, but could I book an appointment to view for my husband as he was in town till about 4.30pm. The vendor had already another person viewing this evening so that was settled. I spoke to my friend Anna, who felt sure Reg would be very interested, so left a message for him to phone me back at the flat.

Reg called and mentioned that I seemed very excited, so will visit and no doubt will notice things from a man's point of view, and I felt he would have to be as interested as I was and we would have to share the same enthusiasm to be sure about it.

While he was visiting, I looked at the T.V but couldn't really concentrate; I just prayed he would feel as I did. Eventually I heard the door shut, his footsteps on the stairs, turned the T.V off and rushed to him to find out all about it. "Well, don't keep me in suspense, what did you think?" He looked at me with a worried frown and said "Well ... I've put a deposit, told the vendor we want the bungalow, at last that's the one we have hoped to find."

I can't express how I felt, all those years of thinking about it, and at last there it was, nearly at the top of that long hill, almost on the edge of a village, beautiful trees, it was so exciting. Unfortunately we were in a chain that causes frustration to house buyers as well as sellers and we hoped fate would smile on us, but who knows.

The month of May was a month which made us wonder just how long this chain was, people changing their minds about buying, someone becoming redundant and having to back out, it seemed interminable. There were times when we wondered if our cottage was not going to become ours.

The after effects of all the moving and all that had its side effects on Reg's health, he started to have vertigo, the whole room felt as if it was spinning round him, he would go very white in the face, had to grab the table or the nearest furniture and to top it all felt very sick. He had never experienced that particular feeling before and I was very worried about it. He was given tablets but they took a time to have any effects. That particular trouble gave no warning of its coming and all of a sudden even if he was just sitting in an armchair that dreadful sensation took over.

Viewers were looking at my house in Newstead Avenue, but as soon as they called seeing a woman alone, they all tried to knock the price down, guessing that I was keen to sell my house which was too big for one person alone. I resisted this unfair attitude, but was aware that at one point I would have to accept a smaller figure just for the peace of mind both to Reg and myself, avoiding a lot of work in the garden and keeping me house in good order, the most desirable outcome was getting away from slamming doors and vicious looks if I was tending the garden. So I doubled my efforts to get personal papers tidied and put in a briefcase and get things ready to bring to our flat for our convenience.

Now by the beginning of July, the sunny weather and the gardens coming to life brought many more viewers and I cheered up at the thought of being free of such a worry.

A couple who visited seemed very keen and after discussing it with Reg and telling him they were offering £3000 under the asking price we both thought it was worth it to be free of such a responsibility. So my house was sold and I need to organize writing to the Assurance Co. to get a rebate on my policy and have the house insured till midnight on the day I move.

Also ask the Gas and Electricity Board to read the meters on the 24th of July 1984. Advise telephone about stopping my bill by the end of that day and sending the bill. Reg kindly posts my Rates bill for me and believes that the time of moving from Newstead is done I could do with a holiday, just the change of scene would do us both good, so phone Bournemouth and book hotel from the 29th of July to the 5th of August and we both look forward to it.

No more dashing to the house, mowing lawns and housework, just in case a person was viewing. Not living there the charm of the place just seemed to vanish. Monday the 23rd was a frantic day from 8am till 7pm when thirty-two tea chests were packed. I polish the parquet flooring in the second reception room then go to the shed and while the men are busy packing I get everything tidy for collecting stuff out, late in the day. A freezer needs shifting as well as gardening implements, mower, wheelbarrow and the like. The next day Pickford will return to move furniture etc, must be there by 5am for the meter reading. 7pm I phone Reg and he arrives to drive me home.

Tomorrow will be even more busy but it will be the end of a chapter and I need to say goodbye to a house which has seen the two sad losses of both my husband and my wonderful mother, yet has blessed me with meeting the man who cared and comforted me in my grief yet showed me such kindness and love, these last five years were such a mixture of emotions but through all that Reg has been strong and protective, he has no idea how grateful and how privileged I feel to have met him. As every day passes so we both recognise that we are getting closer, we have shared the good and the bad and just being together is all we need.

Tuesday the 24th of July Reg drives me to the house and we arrive at 7.50am. He returns to the flat and at 9.15 the van arrives and parks by my back gate. Sure enough I see Gladys peer into my front lounge so go to front door as Pickfords is bringing out boxes. Sees me and looks viciously at me. I stay in doorway as she walks across the road and down the hill.

I hoover upstairs before the removal men take the vacuum cleaner away. One other van arrives. Still moving stuff, van is full so will have to get a smaller one to finish the job.

Reg arrives with the car at 2.30pm and takes me to the flat. Feel so relieved it's all over. Reg is very attentive, he knows I am tired and need him close. In five days we'll be away for a rest by the sea and I must admit I am so looking forward to it. Just being without chores and having time to be together, go for walks by the sea and chat about looking forward to getting into our cottage, can't believe that at last we will be able to enjoy a peaceful setting away from traffic and noise.

As I had said to Reg a long time ago, now that I had at last sold my house I intended to share with him the monies received for the sale, so that with his amount it would help in the cost of buying "NORMANDY". After all sharing was all part of caring, for each other and to make the house comfortable money would have to be spent on it.

As he would have to pay for the property Gladys was looking for and some, I doubt if the Crofton Road house he had paid for would bring him but just a few coins. Unfortunately I was proved right, as I later discovered when it was eventually sold and we read the solicitor's letter.

After a stroll in the park we find a bench and enjoy the splash of colour of flowers and shrubs around us. Reg is looking forward to planting our garden as he loves colour and scented flowers, so I will endeavour to make our garden a haven of peace for both of us to enjoy. He tells me that being born and spending his childhood in Weston Favell (it was then a village on the edge of Northampton) he was used to village life and was looking forward to being part of the community in such surrounding. Of course, like all towns they have spread and so many villages are now inside the boundaries of large towns.

The chain on the side of our seller is still causing many delays as it's stretching our patience sometimes. We are still receiving notices of houses for sale and as time is going we decide to view them as we just don't know if our cottage is still in the offing.

We visit a place in Park Avenue, Orpington. Spacious house, beautiful Wrighton kitchen. Also our estate agent sends details of two other places in Pratts Bottom and we go to visit. Very nice houses but both had cesspit drainage and that was not acceptable Completely different styles, but as I wrote at the end of the page in my diary: "My heart is still with 'NORMANDY', please God make it a possibility for us, we so feel it's the cottage we both desire."

17

It is now just a year since the departure of Reg from Crofton Road, but the delaying tactics are still going on, and it is frustrating to the extreme as he's paying the bills as he promised, so no urgency from her to leave as the cost of living there is free.

Anna Goddard, my good friend who lives next door but one in Crofton Road, is visiting Hendon RAF Museum with her husband Bill and as we had chatted some time ago about interesting mementos to be found, asks if I would like them to purchase something and bring it back for Reg's birthday on the 23rd of August.

Speak to her on Monday and she has kindly bought a lovely brass Lancaster Bomber on a wooden base in the shape of the map of England and Scotland and I know he will love it. Having been in Bomber Command Reg will be pleased that I have thought of such a gift, Tuesday the 21st of August meet Anna at 11am so that I can settle for the gift and carefully take it back to flat and find a good hiding place till I buy wrapping paper and make a nice parcel. Also as he's broken his electric trouser-press I phone Army and Navy and order a teak one, will post the cheque for it this morning and ask if we can receive it as soon after the 23rd of August. He always uses his trouser-press so I know he'll be pleased.

Today, everything is at last working in our favour, re the conclusion of buying our cottage. Our solicitor's secretary phoned to say the 7th of September is completion date, will phone to confirm when the exchange is. The next day, receive the Deed of Trust for my signature, also a will document for me, but the one for Reg hasn't yet reached his office.

The solicitor is returning from holiday on Thursday the 30th, so when we next visit we will sign in front of witnesses both our wills.

Reg is still troubled by this giddiness and took a taxi to Doctor's Surgery, given more tablets for the next seven days. Today, Thursday the 23rd of August, is Reg's birthday and I give him one of his presents (the other one is in the post, I guess) and he is very pleased. Hope he won't have too long to wait for his second present.

A week later, our seller phones to say the contracts have been exchanged and her solicitor will phone ours. At last, it's coming together. At 12.45, Army and Navy deliver my second present to Reg. He is so happy, unpacks it to look. Repacks it to take it to our new home. After lunch, go by car to solicitor's office in Bromley. Do the signing for my will and Reg's also. This morning Reg approached the Gas and Electricity Boards about taking supply out at 'NORMANDY', also gives his filled form to the GPO about re-direction of mail. Call at shop in High Street, regarding a washing machine which will be delivered the day after moving in. Phone the seller to call tomorrow morning, to give cheque asked for leaving shed and green-house. Tomorrow Saturday call at 'NORMANDY' and take a couple of photos of frontage, no doubt in,years to come, it will be interesting to notice the improvements we will have made.

Reg has wanted to have the weekend by the sea, but I said as he's not a hundred per cent very well, would be better to take things easy Next week, on Thursday the 6th on the eve of our move, his aunt Madge and uncle Raymond have to travel by train from Wolverton to a London hospital for a check up. So we both travel to Euston Station to meet them and accompany them. Tiring, but we both feel we must help them as both in their seventies. Very interested in our welfare and Reg and I tell them as soon as we are settled, they will be our first visitors to stay in our home.

Glad to be home again and after supper we just relax and think about tomorrow's eventful day. Reg tells me that he asked the solicitor to put our house deeds in his safe and also says he's put the house in my name. I was so surprised as I thought it would be in both our names as we have both shared the expense, but no, tells me that it is his decision and believes it is the right thing to do.

We go to bed tired, but still chatting about tomorrow and yes, remembered to prepare the traditional tea-making implements so that we can look after the removal men and ourselves when the need arises.

We woke up and realised that our safe if not comfortable flat was, after a stay of eight months, going to be exchanged for a completely different surrounding. The Public House on the opposite corner of our road was rather noisy when the regulars poured out in the evening and we were so looking forward to green fields and hearing bird-song.

It was a lovely sunny day and after our first hiccup we filled the car with necessary suitcases of clothes. 11am we received a phone call saying couldn't vacate the cottage as the solicitor of their new house in Essex had not received the money. Said she couldn't leave, so we phoned our solicitor who assured us the monies were paid and the cottage had to be vacated by lunch-time. Nothing is straightforward, is it??

After many phone calls, it was all sorted and we get there at 1.30. The removal firm arrived at 3pm with our furniture and fifty-two tea chests, some in the garage, the rest distributed in different rooms. Took a photo of Reg amongst those boxes looking bemused. Suggest making a cup of tea, and we both look forward to a break. Make two large mugs of tea and forget there's one step up from the kitchen to the lounge and sprawl on the floor, one mug goes left, the other right and my dignity and my good idea to make a drink goes flying out of the window. Reg kneels down to help me up, but it was so ridiculous, I am shaking all over, not crying as if I'd hurt myself, but laughing so much we both are on the floor giggling at such a stupid mistake. So after getting up and picking the mugs up, ask Reg to put the kettle on and make more tea, not forgetting the step. I go to the front bedroom to make the bed so when we feel tired we can just get into bed whatever the time is. Decide to hang some curtains, but curtain pole has been removed and the centre rose has been taken off, so can't put any light on.

Reg and I enjoy a cup of tea, then as time is going , it's getting dark, so Reg suggests I put the wall lights on. Can't believe it, both fittings have gone and live wires are sticking out like a letter V. Go in lower part of lounge, switch light on, its a 25 watt bulb, so all comers of room are in darkness. Not a very friendly gesture. Reg and I get undressed by the light of a torch, there's a very large Lawson Cypress in front lawn and the front garden is 84 feet long, so don't think anyone would waste their time peering into our bedroom. Too tired to even worry, just want to get into bed.

Large gold cypress on the front lawn at 'Normandy'

For all those niggly things, it's been a lovely day, at last we are in our own home, what more can a couple wish for.

Next day we get the delivery of our washing machine and Reg plumbs it in for me. Go in garden to find out what and where plants are growing. I make a list since there are many jobs we will need to do. Right at the top of the garden, through the rickety arch, there are remnants of large cement blocks which held the children's swings so that we must remove or we'll trip over them. On the lawn, on the right the water feature has been removed leaving a deep trench with rocks jutting out at all angles, so I will try to dig the earth around them to remove them, but don't know how deep they are. Can do something with that. Along the left hand side of the garden, about 10ft in, two very tall and large spruces are too close together, branches twining and looking dead, so will phone the tree surgeon to remove as unsightly and look completely out of place. Also next door, the whole length on other side of rickety fence. Ash trees are closely planted making the garden dark. By the kitchen door the two dead Brooms are still there and one stick of rhubarb. Must remove them as well as the weeds and find the edge of the border, also replant shrubs, some evergreens, some deciduous, a few with flowers which become berries. In the front garden, the drive is rather narrow, just about 2ft wider than the width of a car and the lawn nearer the house is about two and a half feet at a lower level, so when there's been a shower, many is the time Reg has slipped on the grass ending up on his bottom, so we'll have to reorganise the drive. Perhaps widen it and edge it with conifers to create a hedge. Anyway, plenty of time before we need to do that.

On the other hand, Reg and I have discussed the idea that since we would much prefer the parent's bedroom would be better as a dining room and as we have a tall roof, perhaps a room in the roof with an en suite would be a good idea. Mind you, we both dislike dormer windows which are like a square boil against a wall, so prefer a gable window facing the back garden, with a view of that beautiful Oak and the large field outside our back fence.

Imagine waking up and having a cup of tea with such a lovely view through the French window. Wonderful.

We discover how lucky we are to live in this village, there are two nurseries and with stocks of plants of every kind. One specialises in dwarf conifers and the other at the other end of the village has wonderful specimens of shrubs and so I am told, get many prizes from the Chelsea Flower Show. So we have all the choice in the world for our garden. Reg and 1 divide our time between the garden and the house, and everyday we slowly see our home improving. On the 3rd of October, we invite our old friend and neighbour Phyl and her visiting sister Molly to come over for lunch. It's lovely to see them, it's the first day since our moving in that we haven't been doing jobs. Very glad, as Reg has been so busy and he could do with a little relaxation.

Phyl and Molly love the cottage and also the garden. Reg drives them home to Orpington and I put him off on his return from doing any other tasks, it's just a rest and a chat after our meal.

Five days later, Reg is amazed to receive a letter from his daughter because since he wrote to her on the day of his departure as he also did to his son, not a single letter has been sent. All six pages of it, but when he read the last few lines of the last page, ten lines of it upset him and he was surprised that a 38 year old daughter of his could be devoid of understanding. He read the letter to me and I noticed the change in his voice and the slight shaking of his hand.

I quote "I had been thinking that if you did feel that you weren't really happy calling over to see us "EN FAMILLE", could always meet you for lunch or something up in London during school holidays or similar, in the same way.

I would feel awkward visiting you if shall we say, Jacqui was there, sorry, but it takes time!! Anyway be in touch please, and if you move send us your new address and phone no. No more of this ex-directory business! Lots of love to you. Penny."

So fifteen months have elapsed since leaving Crofton Road, yet when I lived at the old house, whenever her two children used to stay for a long weekend, we three used to play ball in my garden, my Mother and I used to always remember her children at Christmas, yet after all that time feels she will be awkward if she visits hey dad, I have never heard of such hypocrisy. Hurting her dad's feelings is what hurts me, after all, she has always been loved and cared for by him so this 'holier than thou' attitude does not ring true.

He filed the letter away and said he would reply when appropriate. I said nothing, he must do what he feels is right, so the subject was closed. Our landlady, Dora, told us she would redirect our mail should any more letters be sent to our old flat.

We met our neighbours to our right. Brian Hickman (retired) was a dental surgeon whose practise was 100ft from my old house, and his wife Diana, who was full of fun. On the other side, Sylvia and Arthur Nightingale (also retired) made us very welcome, they invited us to their home one evening for supper.

Sylvia suggested I joined the WI, thanked her but said that I wanted to help Reg with both the garden and the house which certainly needed attention, but as soon as we felt we had made it comfortable, would be glad to join in the activities of the village.

It takes time to get to know neighbours and make friends, but felt that they were aware and could see us working in our front garden, so understood our home was our priority. By the end of October, had replaced broken glass panels in the garage door, also put glass panels in the new dining room door to bring more light in the lounge so fixing them in was a rather tedious job with the beading etc.

On Thursday the 25th of October, the architect, Mr. Thomas, phones to make an appointment for 10am tomorrow to discuss our idea of a bedroom and en-suite in the roof space. The next day, he arrived and explained how it can be done tastefully, without spoiling the character of our house. Will send drawing of the inside of the loft and also of the gable window giving on the back garden.

In fact, it is a good thing to have it done because in the past, there had been a very bad fire and the timbers above the old fireplace in both lounge and small downstairs bedroom, were blackened and without much strength, so would be safer to replace beams and joists above us. At last, the new bedroom for us was going to be designed and we both looked forward to it. Mr. Thomas, goes at twelve o'clock and Reg carries on fixing fifteen glass panels in the dining room. While he's busy I plant seven bushes in the right hand bed in the back garden. All our work gives us an appetite and enjoy our supper, look at snooker on TV, and go to bed with backache, but pleased with the progress. Reg is very keen to get sweet-smelling roses so go to our favourite nursery up the village and get two apricot roses, one called 'Compassion', one 'School-girl', also plant two Clematis on either side of the arch.

The next Monday, November the 5th, Mr. Welling and Mr. Jordan, decorators who have looked after my house since 1975 and become good friends called in the morning as arranged by telephone, about demolishing our chimney which was badly cracked and would be dangerous. Reg asked them if it would be possible to bring down the chimney pot. Mr. Jordan brings it down, tells us it's an original 1930s which in those days were handmade. Will come back in the middle of next week as we would like a serving hatch in the wall of the kitchen into the now new dining room, so will call again, probably Thursday 15th of November.

Friday the 9th of November, Reg receives a letter from his solicitor and a copy of Gladys' solicitor. More unreasonable demands are made wanting her settlement before the sale of 51, Crofton Road. Won't vacate seven days before completion so that Reg can sort his effects, says will put his stuff in one room. She has obviously found her bungalow and is afraid to lose it, so she's pressing us now.

Wednesday the 14th, our decorators arrive to measure up for tomorrow to start on the serving hatch. Have left dustsheets for us to cover any furniture left in the room. 9am start to work. Have to use a Kango hammer drill as it's an outside wall (it was once until another room was added), so wall is 1ft wide and powder and dust are everywhere.

We go outside because it's no good to Reg's chest and clean leaves off guttering. I climb ladder and go on the two flat roofs. Get four bags of leaves that are on the roof. Lovely view from up there. The men go home at 4.30, so have done a good days work. Next morning they return to put in the wooden surround. We purchase doors and hinges to enclose the hatch, it's just a question of staining them and it's all done.

On Monday the 3rd of December, Reg says he is writing his letter in reply to Penny's received on the 8th of October, so I know he won't want anything to disturb him, so I get on with some ironing and don't put the radio on in case it disturbs him. When he returns to the lounge, ask him if he'd like a cup of coffee, and give him a piece of cake to go with it. After our break, tells me that I can read his letter, as he thinks it's appropriate to hers. After the usual niceties and mentioning the holiday in Cornwall she enjoyed with her husband, Reg replies to her weird remarks as follows; "The period since leaving 51, Crofton Road in August 1983, has presented many challenges, the temporary nature and standards of one's abode or abodes, the entry into retirement and two spells of trouble with the chest.

"As you know, without any legal obligation to do so, have all maintained payments of all outgoings on 51, Crofton and of course until the house is sold, I am unable to establish a more permanent base, however when this is accomplished you and the children would be welcome to visit. I have not been away on holiday since my retirement but if health and finances permit I hope to get a bit of sun during 1985.

"Of course, I look forward to seeing you, as much as I do Jim, Thomas and Ele. However, I did not wish insinuation to produce conflict and unpleasantness until matters between Gladys and I have been finally resolved. I find the manner of actions has endorsed if not completely should any doubts as earlier actions and plans. I trust you will respect my views and perhaps we can arrange to meet after matters are finalised unless you had decided that "SIDES" be established.

"I was completely at a loss to understand why my gifts and the cards sent by myself and those sent by Jacqui were not acknowledged. Thank goodness, many other close friends were much kinder. In the meantime it seems a card or note would be welcome and reflect less prejudice without full knowledge.

"I appreciate your wish to see me alone when we next meet, but please let it be clear that thereafter there be no prerequisite should you wish to meet, visit or stay wherever 1 am residing at that time. I have no telephone at present, etc, etc, etc."

The next morning the letter is posted and we wonder how long it will be before the next move. Our good friends Bill and Anna Goddard phone. We invite them to spend the evening with us on Friday the 14th of December. We also receive our first Christmas cards from both our immediate neighbours and appreciate that friendly gesture. Unfortunately there was no fireplace in our new home, so Reg bought a Christmas tree and we decorated it and put it in the comer of the room. Put our presents beneath it and spoke about making a fireplace of sorts in the comer of the lounge left of the French windows. Mind you, it would be a big job, so we shelved that and just exchanged ideas as to design. One day we will do it and organise the Christmas we used to enjoy by the hearth. As we both wanted, we had our Christmas festivities just the two of us. It was lovely, our second Christmas since being together was a possibility and although our commitments were dear, we still managed to give each other presents and enjoy our favourite festival.

Sunday the 30th December we are invited to lunch at Barbara and Ray Walkers home. Bitter wind, snow is in the air and we feel 1985 will begin with snow and ice. January is my most hated month, I lost my husband Sherry and my Mother twelve months apart in 1980 and 1981 and it's a month I always equate with sadness.

By the month of March, we had planted two flowering Cherry trees and on the eleventh had the builders to look at the attic about getting a tender for the work and will contact the architect.

On the 16th of March there was still snow on the ground, but it was sunny. The men arrive to remove our spruces. By 9.20 both trees are down and by 12 all wood is cleared. We receive a letter from the solicitor about Crofton, the completion date is the 3rd of April, the same date as my moving into Newstead but 7 years later. On the 27th of March Pickfords remove Reg's furniture which has been allowed to reluctantly be collected and some of it has to be seen to be believed.

Two cardboard boxes which must have been collected from the attic contained a chipped collection of glass ashtrays with the ash still in them. That went into a container to take to the tip. A second cardboard box had plastic kitchen bowls, two old saucepans, one frying pan (circa 1940) and a chip pan with the outside of it decorated with burned-on fat design which was put in an old box for the tip. How sick can you get! On the other hand the dinner service for eight, which he paid for, was kept except for two dinner plates, two side plates and two soup bowls. The dining room suite was kept and the gold dralon three-piece suite, and the narrow twin beds, which were in the marital bedroom for the last fourteen years. We decide to use the mower which has been returned. Surprise, surprise, it won't work. Belt is not on, so put new belt, still won't work. So joins its mates at the tip. Everything is either broken, glued, chipped or dirty.

Reg received bill and details of monies to go to Gladys. £49,000. Reg pays solicitor fees, estate agent, the balance he will receive from the sale of 51, Crofton Road of £53,000 is a measly £2,750.

Return home for lunch, and start arranging our 'herb garden'.

On the 9th of April, Reg phones Penny to arrange to meet her tomorrow. Wednesday the 10th, Reg goes to see Penny at her home at Bishops Stortford at 9.45am. He tells me he'll be home at 6pm. Plant Lavender bushes, Lemon Balm and other herbs and keep busy. At 4pm Reg is already home. Penny and the children were there and he enjoyed the welcome, didn't ask him his address and he said he hadn't yet a phone.

Our front garden is like a field, the bottom lawn is two feet higher to be level with the road and needs raised beds to plant flowers, so order 100 slabs and cream bricks to give an interest to the bland look of our front. Took the man twenty minutes to unload. Reg makes a sketch of a long but not too deep bed outside the bedroom window, also thinks of some change was due to a diagonal stone wall near the lower field by the road, we could remove a few feet of it, make two low raised beds and in the centre put two steps to walk up with a blue conifer on each side, the idea was good and so bit by bit, we achieved it. At a later date, we would widen the drive and plant some conifers to edge it, but that was a big job which we would have to plan carefully, so that was shelved for the moment.

On the 18th April, Reg receives the last gas bill of £140 for Crofton, only the telephone bill to come and at last he can feel no more reminders of that house. Since having moved here we are having to get used to power cuts as we have overhead cables and it only needs a large tree to fall and no electricity. Glad to use gas for cooking, so at least it doesn't ruin our meals. At the end of our back garden, right of the large oak tree, we are able to plant runner beans, perpetual spinach, courgettes and tomatoes and we both enjoy the pleasure of fresh vegetables. I fear, when the oak gets bigger, the shade will not allow us that pleasure, so we make good use of it Reg is keen to get as many jobs done to make us comfortable before we have visitors, so we both try to improve our home and garden. By the end of May, he decides to write a typewritten letter to both Penny and her husband Jim and one to Colin and his partner Wendy to make his position clear and sends the following letter.

Dear Penny and Jim,

Having passed through the trauma of almost two years of 'make do' accommodation, I am pleased to say that, after due consideration Jackie and I will be moving to the address above as and from the 1st of June 1985. Needless to say, it will be very nice to have a home in which one can take an interest and pass subsequent years in peace.

I have asked and Jackie has agreed to adopt my name upon moving to our new home.

Madge and Raymond are both delighted with the news and will be staying with us for a few days later in the month.

I trust that you both and the children will do Jackie and I the pleasure of keeping in touch and also visiting us when time permits.

It is nice to be able to issue such invitations to our relatives and friends.

Looking forward to hearing from you and seeing you both and the children in due course.

As ever, with much love

Dad.

18

After the usual letters to and fro from the council to get permission for our improvements to our bungalow, Reg phones the architect who tells him our loft conversion will start on the 17th of June. Madge and Raymond are expected the 7th (Friday) to spend the weekend with us. Reg is looking forward to it and we hope the sunny weather holds for us all. We drive them back to Sevenoaks Station and put them on the train.

Tuesday the 11th, Reg goes to the tip and tells me expecting a phone call from Colin, his son, so that I can direct him on how to find our house, because there are no house numbers, only names, so good instructions are vital, as it's awkward to find us, this hill is very long. At 3.30 Colin phones and soon finds our home. After a cup of tea, the two men stroll into the garden, Colin seems attracted by the vast expanse of land outside our back gate and looks at it for quite a time. At that time, a few acres were used for growing cauliflowers, and thereafter whenever he and his girl Wendy visited, Colin always strolled up to our garden gate and liked to look at the field beyond.

Sunday the 16th June, we work in the garden all the morning. Take lunch under the oak tree as it's so cool underneath. Don't go in till 3.30 and see a letter on the mat-It's a Father's Day card delivered by hand from Colin and his girl Wendy. Reg is very pleased to be remembered and phones Colin to thank him. Told that Wendy was taken to hospital in Lewisham with abdominal pains. Will phone tomorrow evening to tell us what the doctors say.

Next day, the builder and architect meet here to discuss tomorrow's start. Colin phones to say Wendy was discharged at lunch time, suspected bleeding ulcer was not correct.

Next day, Reg goes to the bank and also sends flowers to Wendy. By lunch time, the manager introduces us to two men who will dismantle the chimney breast and airing cupboard. Skip arrives and is put on top of front lawn by the edge of the road.

As from now, we have a collection of timber, men, plasterers, tilers and every kind of skilled men working on our attic. One doesn't realise how many skills are needed to get two rooms put in and though dust and bricks and lots of wood are everywhere the end result is worth every inconvenience. Mind you, all sorts of mishaps happen and you can't imagine all the things that can go wrong, but with the help of continuous mugs of tea being drunk the transformation is happening.

As you come into the hall there is a large opening on my right, takes some getting used to, but the stairs are starting from there so will have to get used to it a while. Also there's a large hole in the ceiling in the small bedroom, a ladder is leaning against, can't resist climbing up to peer into the attic room, cables galore over floor, looks strange but can imagine our bedroom up there will be great.

The water tank must be moved so water is necessarily cut off, so have to get buckets from the water butt to flush the toilet. Mains water switched back at 3pm. Still raining hard, hasn't stopped since 8am.

This morning Friday the 21st June, Reg received a letter from Penny thanking him for his note and its content for her birthday, also a thank you note will be sent from his grandson. She sends her regards to me. Finishes thus: "No allergies to gardening now you've got settled, you know."

She can't know her dad very well, Reg has helped me in the garden ever since we've moved and is far better than I at propagating plants. We spend a fair time planting and making our garden full of flowers and shrubs, so has obviously been given a wrong impression of her dad's abilities.

Two days later our stairs are delivered. It's Reg's sixty-fifth birthday. As so many bills are to be paid, suggest to him that instead of a meal out, we have one at home, and make a special meal and we both enjoy it in the intimacy of our home. After supper, as it's a balmy evening, sit on the terrace and enjoy the peace and quiet, look at the silhouette of our big oak and can't help wondering just how many events, coronations, wars and extraordinary historic happenings it has witnessed. The shape and majesty of that beautiful tree has to be seen to be appreciated. We often say to each other how lucky we are to have come across this place, it has answered all the hopes we had to find a haven of peace. It erases the sad moments we have experienced and on a nostalgic note, we go in and get ready for bed.

Next day, Saturday, a friend calls with flowers for Reg, have a cup of tea. Hear water pouring, presumed I'd left a tap on, but then realise it's coming from the dining room. Water pouring down the central rose on to dining table, carpet is soaked. Open door to hall, water is pouring through the pine ceiling, bathroom, lounge, electric heater over the wash basin in shower room upstairs has exploded. 2" of water everywhere. No cold water in pipes. Reg finds stopcock for shower, wc and basin, also stop water coming in, so phone builder to bring a cap so that water can be turned on. That was the first of our unfortunate mishaps.

Monday, the 2nd of September, Reg tries again George Hall's telephone number. He and his wife were friends of Gladys in the old days in the RAF and he wanted to let him know his new address in Kent, so tried again and this time it answers. Reg was surprised to hear him say Gladys has been on holiday with them at their caravan but seems to think Reg knows this. Reg says had no idea as he's not seen nor spoken to Gladys for 2 years. George asks if he has any message to give to Gladys. Reg very firmly says he doesn't want to have anything to do with her, can't forgive her and has never been so happy these last two years. George says his wife and Gladys have gone to the market and Gladys is going home tomorrow. Reg will send him our address.

The work goes on and another hiccup happens, this time in our kitchen. The workmen are taking the second flat roof off over kitchen. Reg is working on electric wires for the light. Big crash, chap put his foot through the ceiling just over wall units, no-one hurt, but plaster and fibre-glass over floor, units, breadboard, everything. So another piece of material will have to be fixed on our ceiling.

It's just one of those things, but clearing up is what takes time. Luckily the man was not hurt, only his dignity.

To help with the cost of all this, we decided to buy the wall tiles and put them on ourselves in the en-suite, but it's a long job. Altogether 79 tiles were put on lining a new tile-cutter which took a little time to get used to, but in a confined space it's very tiring to get comfortable especially round the pedestal basin etc. But we eventually finished and we were quite pleased with the result. The only thing left was the emulsion paint when the tiles are finished, that was the easy bit. We are now in mid October, but only now can we say our new bedroom and en-suite is finished. We intend to wallpaper it to our taste and fix the curtains. The new double bed is already waiting and the carpet will be laid in a day or two. Such a lot of work and some discomfort but we are very pleased with the result, it was certainly worth it.

Tuesday, the 15th October, we are surprised to answer the door and Colin is on his own. Wendy has gone to Devon to visit one of her sisters, so he thought he'd call. Has brought with him, such a surprise, a telecom telephone, cream/black, also cables and suggest visiting next week to install it in our upstairs bedroom. Such a kindly thought, we both think it will be great in case of emergency or illness. Very thoughtful of him.

Have driven to Green St Green to the supermarket on my own so avoid bothering Reg to drive for food shopping. Must practise more. Enjoy the driving, but must do more to really get proficient. November lets us know how very cold this part of Kent is. It's minus four and lawns have a lovely sheen, like Crème de Menthe, we are busy in our new room, Reg putting emulsion on ceiling, I am finishing the curtains for the French windows, putting a lining-paper in chest of drawers. Reg has just started to make some shelves for books, lights to read by, cups of tea etc, so it will be useful and when we sit up in bed we'll have a lovely view through the windows of the oak and the fields beyond our back gate. At the foot of our bed, on a chest of drawers, our TV is there, also next to it on a cupboard a tray with a jug kettle, cups and saucers, so I can make cups of tea and bring it to Reg every morning.

Friday the 16th of November, Reg gets a letter from his solicitor to say Gladys won't give him a divorce, so it will be another two and a half years to wait for. We are not surprised one bit. Reg still has a sore throat and aching limbs, so it looks like a dose of flu. Give him tablets and hot toddy every night but will take its course.

Colin is supposed to be calling this weekend but no news. Still no news from Penny. Reg phones Colin, Wendy tells him he's got a bad cold. Sunday 24th of November, Colin and Wendy call at 3.30 with belated birthday present for Reg. A large rechargeable torch with is very useful when these power cuts happen. Colin and Wendy called at their mother's home and Gladys said to Wendy about the divorce, "What's the hurry, is Jackie pregnant or is Reg on his last?" What a nice thing to say! Also Colin and Wendy have been invited to Ele's confirmation next Saturday so that they can give a lift there and back to their mother.

Sunday, Colin and Wendy arrive with a pine table and two chairs they said they would bring and put together for us. They told Gladys they can't drive her to Penny's for Ele's confirmation so Gladys is taking the train. Both Colin and Wendy said they thought they were being put upon. On Monday the 23rd of December, Reg collects Madge and Raymond from Sevenoaks station. We have lunch in our new kitchen. We decided to share Christmas with them as we don't know how much longer they will be able to stand the train journey. But anyway always enjoy their company. After lunch, his aunt and uncle have a rest on their bed and after washing up, we sit on the sofa and chat about our Christmas. I mention to Reg that it's a long time since his daughter has either seen him, hasn't phoned or written a letter. Says nothing surprises him now, it's six months since he was invited to lunch on his own and we wonder why that long span of time, yet her brother has been over with his girlfriend and has helped his dad with many tasks.

I know Reg is Church of England as is his wife and son, so don't quite see how Penny is of the Catholic faith. Tells me that when she became fond of the man who became her husband and was of that faith she became a renegade to her faith, the faith she was brought up in by her parents, to become a convert and as many converts is quite obsessive about it. I believe she chose that route because of wanting to marry a RC, so to her mind, that was reason enough however hurtful it may be to her parents.

That may explain why the telephone conversation developed the way it did. Youth always finds a reason for the road it takes, but never even tries to understand one parent's direction.

9pm on that Christmas evening, the phone rang and I answered it in Reg's study. It's Penny, can't believe it, wants to speak to her dad. Call Reg to me phone, picks it up and as I start to leave, puts his arm round my waist to stand by him. He asks her if she has dispensation from the Pope to get in touch with him. She says she wanted to know if she and the children could visit us at 10.30am on New Years Eve, will leave in the early afternoon, but Jim won't come as working that day. Reg and I looked at each other and after giving instructions as how to reach us by going up Rushmore Hill, we retired to the lounge and thought about the phone-call.

Wendy's birthday was on the 30th December and Colin and her were going to pop in so that we could give her a gift.

Reg says that he supposes that his daughter and her children will no doubt go to her mother after leaving us early in the afternoon, which is understandable, but being told her husband is working on New Year's Eve is really not believable however hard working or experienced the man is.

Some people can bend the truth like a skilful acrobat and always presume that people who are told these untruths are gullible enough to believe them.

New Year's Eve came, expecting them at 10.30, but arrived at 1 lam having taken the wrong turning. Twelve noon, Colin and Wendy arrive. Give Wendy her birthday present but surprise, surprise, they decided to stay for lunch, so all at once it's seven of us for the meal. Penny always refers to her two children as "the kids" but they no longer are, they're teenagers. Ele is thirteen and is an attractive dark haired teenager, has her father's good looks and Thomas, sixteen, is already tall and has done well in his G.C.E exams, and Reg is very proud of his grandson, says to me after they've gone that learning and using his abilities will always help him in adult life to achieve success.

Was told half an hour before lunch that Ele has become a vegetarian like her mother, so must rearrange the menu. Penny seems very curious about our new home and no doubt notices how different it is from her dad's old house in Orpington.

Just as they were leaving Penny gave us belated Christmas presents. From the youngsters BRUT aftershave for Reg and for me dusting powder. His daughter gave him a crystal decanter and to me a crystal dish. After a few homemade cakes and tea with Colin and Wendy the house once again became quiet and Reg and I thought we would stay up and see the New Year in and have a glass of wine and toast 1986, hoping our luck and happiness would continue. We would carry on to improve our home and put our stamp on it. Our next venture was a new porch, so still have to get used to workmen and mugs of tea to do, but the final result was worth it all. Many things we could do ourselves and would enjoy pooling our ideas to individualise our little place.

19

1986 is a year filled with more improvements to the comfort of our home, but also proves to be a year of meeting many people in the village who have become good friends. I had no idea that there could be such a variety of associations, clubs, opportunities to get to know the inhabitants of our village.

People invited us to join them in all sorts of activities, it was really an exciting time for Reg and me. Having lived in a town before our move here, and although the immediate neighbours were friendly and helpful, the community spirit that existed here was quite extraordinary.

Snow and ice began in February and it came with a vengeance. On the 6th of that month our porch is started on. The next day, two sections of wall and the wooden door frame, the base is already cemented, the window frames are in garage awaiting the opportunity and the weather to be put in their place. On Monday the 10th all windows upstairs are covered with ice. It's 14° below. Even the kitchen door is frozen. Have used my hair dryer to melt ice. Understand that we are 700ft high from Sea level, highest point in Kent and it's cold, very cold. St. Valentine's day, the window frames are in and have put the wooden frame to support the tiles. It looks great already. We exchanged Valentine Cards and Reg spoils me with a big box of chocolates.

We had ordered a small Crittall conservatory which we wanted outside the kitchen door and until it was delivered, had ordered bricks, cement etc to get a base sorted out. Colin put some of the glass panes on our conservatory, a very awkward job, Reg and I then mix cement to lay over conservatory floor (12ft x 8ft) and because we haven't the knowledge of doing those sort of jobs, found it very tiring.

We used four bags of it but had to purchase another load to finish the job.

On the 24th of March, Reg and I had a welcome break and drove to visit our old friend Phyl, who was now a widow and we both had a soft spot for her, took some whisky and a box of chocolates for her birthday. She makes us so welcome and we told her of our efforts and would invite her again, so she would see our progress.

She made us coffee and we tasted her homemade cake, a wonderful cook Phyl was, and we spent a happy morning. Storms were starting along the coast and winds were uprooting trees around us.

Monday the 7th April, my fifty-fourth birthday, had lovely cards from Reg, (one romantic one, and one saucy one) also, find presents put in our new porch. Colin and Wendy are coming to have a meal with us tonight, lovely red roses are sent to me from the florist from Reg and Colin brings flowers also.

Such an exciting day for me, five scented roses which Reg bought for me from our favourite nursery are planted Sunday. Reg cuts bricks and lays them down on lawn to get right pattern for the hearth. I mix cement in garage and bring bucket as it's raining on and off continuously. Get it finished by the afternoon.

April 28th, Colin and Wendy call at 10am, bring a large oak post for the fire-place. It's 7 feet long and 4½" square, lovely shade.

Two days later, Reg is busy cutting a thin sheet of plywood as a pattern for the chimney breast before cutting the wood to fix against the battens. Mixes a cream to fill in large cavities where the oak beams will go in wall.

It looks fine even though it's in its early stages. Next day, mix powder so that when it's creamy I can spread it on and make patterns. Later will apply white emulsion and the last job will be to put up the brackets for the glass shelves.

Have seen an attractive coal-effect fire with fan-heater which will be perfect on the two rows of brick flooring, it will make a focal point and Reg is looking forward to see the finishing touch on it. So this Christmas we will again have our presents in front of the hearth as we used to.

Towards the end of May, having a lounge that was through an arch and a fair way in, it was rather dark and we thought it was a good idea to measure the width of the far wall and we could go to town and order a large mirror to cover that wall, it will make the room lighter and reflect the back garden, so that the lawn, flowers and rose covered arch would be seen from our lounge.

On Wednesday the 28th of May I received a phone call from a Mrs. Daphne Hall, a lady living a few minutes down the road, to say would I be willing to help the over 60s Lunch Club which takes place in the village hall on the first Tuesday of every month. Told her will phone her back in a quarter of an hour as my husband and I were still busy doing our house, but would like to help in the village. Told Reg that all I had to do was get tables and chairs ready, lay the tables, serve the people there, help to wash up, have lunch with the helpers and come home. Reg thought at once that being involved would help to meet people and become part of the community, so I rang back and was told the next meeting was on Tuesday the 1st of July and appreciated my agreeing to help. Reg and I had already booked a weeks holiday on the 1st of June so would join the over 60s club after our return.

I enjoyed my first occasion at the village hall for the over 60s lunch club, I met Mrs. Eileen Jones who I think was treasurer, Mrs. Beryl Stevens and Mrs. Marjorie Roberts and was explained what was needed to be done. Also met Mrs. Daphne Johnson who was taking the money for the meal in the foyer of the village hall. People were making their way to their regular tables and all at once there was a hubbub of voices as everyone greeted each other. People bought raffle tickets and although I counted thirty-eight members, the chatter and the laughter was quite noisy. I got to know more names of people and enjoyed seeing them tuck in to their meal.

One lady, Mrs. Neave, living in Pound Lane who used to chat to me found it difficult to walk, so suggested to her that I fetch her in the car and of course take her home. She agreed and we became good friends. The meal was very tasty and I was eager after taking Florrie Neave home, to tell Reg all about it.

Another event we did not know about was the Carnival that took place every two years, organised by a committee, it was always a very exciting day and had a parade of floats, a theme, a celebrity was invited and a charity was chosen which would benefit from the generosity of every person in our village, as well as the visitors. The event took place at our recreation ground and it was full of stalls, every organisation took part, it had barbecues of our local butcher's sausages, chicken, hamburgers and tents of teas, drinks etc. People living on the route of the parade which was judged by the V.I.P of the village were seated in their front gardens and we thoroughly enjoyed them all. Some themes were the "Wild West", people wearing Stetsons and cowboy outfits and Red Indian costumes. One year we had "Fairy Tales". Every Carnival had something different. On that first one we met so many people, some were fairly close neighbours who invited us to their home for a cool drink and a chat.

Reg and I were glad to live here and we were to get involved in all aspects of village life. We often went for walks around the lanes and roads of our village, one day we walked up Old London Road, noticed a sign up some steps advertising 'strawberries' so we went round the side of the bungalow, and came across a picnic table covered with the most luscious boxes of shiny strawberries, a tall man came out of the conservatory, seemed a little shy, but greeted us with a smile and we bought four boxes. I was keen to make a strawberry flan for our son and his girl and also wanted to enjoy them with cream for our dessert. His wife, Liz, came out and Reg and I joined in the banter. We had no idea such a field of strawberries were so close to our home, and we became regulars. Nearly every day we came across new villagers and as Reg was so relaxed, it seems we got to know many people and were asked to join different activities.

On Friday the 25th July, Colin's thirty-fifth birthday, new neighbours were moving into the house me other side of our neighbours Sylvia and Arthur.

We introduced ourselves to the newcomers. The lady is called Gill, they have two little girls, one Katie, and the younger one is Elizabeth but is called Libby. The husband is called Rob and is a Doctor. Took advantage of glorious sunshine and had coffee and home-made cakes in the garden. Enjoyed their company and hoped we would see them again when settled in.

Reg celebrated his 66th birthday quietly at home, we invited Colin and Wendy who had this past year helped their dad and I to do jobs in our house and we much appreciated it. Had our evening meal at home, Colin gave his dad a barbecue and I gave Reg a well padded jacket for going in the garden when the cooler days come along.

Five houses away, up the hill, was Rushmore Lodge and we booked four tickets for their barn dance and barbecue on Saturday 27th of September.

People told us it was a good evening. Mr. Granville, the owner, had a big barn in his grounds and it was set out with bales of hay to sit on, music and square dancing was on the agenda and wine and food were provided, so we asked Colin and Wendy whether they would like to join us. We even had Morris Dancers. We met many friends who introduced us to other villagers and we had a thoroughly good time.

Just before the autumn was turning all the trees a beautiful golden colour we planted twelve golden conifers in a sweeping curve by the side of our drive which by now had been widened, and by the time the trees had grown would form a golden hedge to give us privacy. Also we bought two five-feet blue Lawson Cypresses 'Columnaris' which we planted on either side of the top steps, separating the top lawn to the sunken lawn and they are still standing guard but tall and proud. Such a lot of work we both did, but feel very proud of Reg's efforts as after all, he was now sixty-six years old and was still having asthma attacks, but must say they were not as frequent as in the past. The migraine had so far vanished and I was hoping that now in such a peaceful setting, that such an unpleasant occurrence would not worry him again.

As the Christmas came, Reg bought some Christmas tree lights and we both placed one small set at the apex of our chimney-breast and draped the tiny lights each side like an inverted V. On the oak mantel-shelf, I made some plant decorations by using three large potatoes covered in silver foil, used a skewer and in each hole inserted holly twigs, pieces of yew, interspaced with artificial small bunches of fruit and flowers, so its made it look festive. When the small Christmas lights were switched on, it created a magical atmosphere, also Reg strung lights over our central opening into the lower lounge, and over our Christmas tree, so now we're equipped for an exciting Christmas Day.

As we promised ourselves, we spent Christmas Day, just the two of us, Reg had put a record of Christmas Carols on in the lounge and then woke me up with a cup of tea and wished me a 'Happy Christmas'.

After putting the bird in the oven, we had breakfast and started our yearly ritual of taking our cards from the top of the pile of presents and started the fun of undoing parcels.

We had a break at 11am for hot mince-pies and cream and coffee, then carried on with undoing our presents.

Boxing Day, was as usual a day of looking in detail at our Christmas gifts, reading, tasting chocolates, trying on a lovely pendant, seeing Reg try the Icelandic black and white jumper which I hoped would keep him warm and cuddly. At eleven am. Dr. Rob Thompson, his wife Gill and their two little girls called for coffee and home-made cakes and biscuits.

The day after, Saturday, Colin and Wendy called as invited for supper. Arrived at 3.30 pm, still daylight, so could admire their new BMW car. The 30th of December, we are invited to our friends Barbara and Ray Walker for a buffet party.

New Year's Eve, Reg and I saw the New Year in and drank a Champagne Toast, and wished each other all the happiness and good health.

1st of January, 1987, we are invited for coffee and mince-pies to our neighbour Ann and Peter Trebell, four houses up the hill, it's one of their son's (Martin) birthday.

Next day, the 2nd January, Penny, Jim and their daughter Ele arrive for lunch. Ele is now fourteen, soon next month will be fifteen and with her long dark hair, already looks very grown up. Go home at 6pm, give us belated Christmas presents. Next day, receive an invitation by phone to our next-door neighbour, Sylvia, for supper at their house next Wednesday. Phone Penny to thank her for her presents. By the 11th of January, it's snowing all day. It's also windy so drifts are covering the entrance to the conservatory. Start to dig entrance to drive. Took photos in back garden, also icicles over our conservatory. Rob, our friendly doctor, comes over to help us dig out the snow to make a path to our front door. The drive is 84ft long, so it's an arduous job and we are both so pleased with the help given. 1987 certainly has started well, the weather is cold but the friendship of the neighbours is warm and we are both glad to be in this village.

20

By Tuesday the 20th of January 1987, there's still a single lane, due to snow ploughs, blocking edges of road. The local bus was forty-five minutes late. Although getting about to purchase shopping, the amount of snow covering large oaks and beeches as well as small shrubs, has completely transformed the look of the place. The dull grey colour of the road has now a white carpet and our green lawns have now a white mantle and delicate footprints of birds and marks of paws from animals looking for food. ^ Only when the sun fleetingly peers out from a cloud, does the landscape look lit up as if someone had switched on powerful stage lighting. I know it's inconvenient to the people trying to get to their business but once you are retired the beautiful sight of the snow being viewed from the warmth of your home cannot fail to impress.

On Monday the 16th of February, my neighbour and I walked to the village hall in total darkness and I was introduced to the members of the W.I. and joined. I did not know many names but it was suggested that I would take the task of doing the 'Register', take the members dues and get to know everyone. I was also asked to join the darts team, though I did say I had never played before, but still I was pressed to become a player.

Reg and I had spent the last two and a half years working on both our home and the large garden which certainly needed a lot of "tender loving care" and so we felt, that the most vital jobs had been done and we could now enjoy lot more relaxation and accept the friendly invitations of friends around us. Reg had made friends with a most pleasant gentleman in the village who often invited him to have a game of snooker with him in the village hall, also was asked to join a group of people that had a Whist Drive in the next village, Halstead, just a mile away. We joined the Horticultural Society and twice yearly took our flowers, roses and pots of flowering shrubs to be judged, though never thought they were good enough to win prizes, but we did get a few, I guess they were encouraging us to carry on supporting the village. Also cakes and all sorts of edible treats were wanted so that kept us busy.

After lunch, when the judges had looked at all our efforts, everyone poured into the hall, hoping that some sort of white card mentioning a prize was put in front of our plants.

Also some members grew beautiful fruit and vegetables and they were neatly presented, very tempting to look at. Apart from produce, there were also tables of crafts, needlework and such.

I put in an embroidered tablecloth and was thrilled that I had won a prize. The village was always crowded on those occasions and anyone whose name was called out, were always clapped by the members. Some of the ladies I had met, also made flower arrangements and they were really works of art. So twice yearly we took part and also clapped the members who had made delicious wines, jams, mint sauces and all manner of goodies.

As time went by, we began to feel that we had been in our village a fair time. In the mid-eighties the villages where the inhabitants spent their time supporting the endeavours of different societies, helping each other was the norm and everyone knew the name of newcomers, joined either sporting clubs and the Pantomime in the village hall or the local theatre in the next town. The community spirit was in good health and thriving, so we enjoyed our life together amid our new-found friends.

At that time, when summer was in full swing, many gardens in the village were open to the public, a small fee was asked for the entrance, also you could always count on a cake stall or/and a cream tea. Plants were for sale and whatever size the garden was, there was always unusual plants to admire and I have lost count of all the places Reg and I visited.

Professor Sir David Smythers lived in a fine flint house in the centre of the village, since his retirement from a medical career, he had become a prolific writer and always had concern for the good of the village. He had a large garden sweeping down the valley from his home and was cared for by his head gardener who lived in a small bungalow in the grounds of his house.

In the past, I understand that the size of it necessitated at least seven gardeners who tended not just the flowerbeds but the varieties of fruit trees, shrubs and vegetables as well as hedges and I can well understand why. Once a year a weekend was devoted to opening his garden to the public, many people in the village visited as well as many from surrounding areas came to give their support. Reg and I had often walked past his home, but the surrounding hedges protected their privacy and we often wondered what sort of garden it was.

We understood that the entrance fees were being donated to the nurses Association and Reg was very keen to subscribe to anything as worthwhile as that. When we entered the forecourt of his garden, Sir David was there chatting to people and I was pleasantly surprised when he spoke to Reg and I though we had never before met him. Any good cause that helped was a good reason for Reg to take part. When in 1937, Reg was living in his village near Northampton, it was then the custom to take part in Hospital Balls and it was then at 17 years old, that Reg joined a dancing school as he liked dancing, to be able to take part in any performance which supported charities, I can understand why he was such a good dancer and we both enjoyed dancing whenever the chance presented itself.

We both carried on transforming our garden which was devoid of shapely flowerbeds and choosing with care certain flowering shrubs.

I suppose when I look at photos we took when we moved in, I must say, it all looked very bare but the acid soil we had was making it possible to have azaleas, pieris and Moroccan broom with its pineapple scented flowers to grow and thrive, so we had at last achieved the garden we had hoped to grow. Sunday the 16th of August 1987, 1 receive a phone call from a cousin who had in the past got in touch with my Mother who was living in Monte-Carlo at the time, explaining to her that after seeing the film 'Roots' he was trying to delve into the history of my ancestor EMILE WALDTEUFEL, who was a composer of music and was trying to find as many members of the family as possible and particularly was wanting to acquire mementoes, photographs and details of his music.

My mother at me time did not particularly want his intrusive curiosity and was not prepared to divulge those private details to someone who was in fact from another branch of the family. But like a dog with a bone, this cousin still pursued his ideas and after I had left my last address found where I lived and tried to see if he could get more joy with me, so said he had approached the BBC to remind them it was the 150th anniversary of the composer's birth and would they be interested in celebrating it on the BBC.

This cousin was not aware that in previous years, my Grandfather, the composer's eldest son, had already done two broadcasts at the BBC and I had myself listened to them at home. I believe he thought he could take on the task himself, but when they asked his relationship to the composer, he admitted that I was his direct descendant and knew where I lived, so I phoned the number given and spoke to the Editor of Live Music, Radio 2 Music Dept. He had been told that the Composer of the 'Skater's Waltz' and over 400 other pieces of

Opposite page:
The Radio Times *of 12 December 1987*

Sport

Cricket: *Second Test*
PAKISTAN v ENGLAND
Reports from Faisalabad at
7.05am, 8.05, 9.02, 10.02, 11.02,
12.02pm
General Desk 10.02pm

4.00am Dave Bussey

The Early Show
Producers MEL HOUSE, TERRY CARTER
and NICK BARRACLOUGH

6.00 Steve Truelove

The Saturday Show
including at
7.45 **Down to Earth**
with **Alan Titchmarsh**
Producer DAVID BELLINGER
BBC Pebble Mill

8.05 David Jacobs

Producer ANTHONY CHERRY

9.00 Sounds of the 60s

Typical of the variety of popular
music in the 60s was the success
of a song originally recorded in
1929 by Rudy Vallee. *Tears*
proved to be a million-seller for
Ken Dodd – and today he
remembers more hits from
that period.
Producer STUART HOBDAY
BBC Bristol
*Compact discs; 'The Best of the Rock
'n' Roll Years', Vol 1 1956-1963 (CD 656)
and Vol 2 1964-1971 (CD 657) from
retailers*

finding 'in-form' players for
the national side.
IAN ROBERTSON and
ALASTAIR HIGNELL report from
Gloucester and Leicester.
Racing: PETER BROMLEY is at
Cheltenham for the feature
race:
1.55 £17,500 Glen
International Gold Cup (2½m)
The Four Seasons
The continuing journey
through the archives
of *Sports Report*
3: *Winter of 79/80*
Controversy reigns as
Britain's athletes decide
whether or not to go to the
Moscow Olympics; PAUL RINGER
is sent off at Twickenham;
DENNIS LILLEE introduces the
aluminium bat in the First
Test against England at Perth.
Rugby League:
John Player Trophy
The first semi-final.
Commentators EDDIE HEMMINGS
and DAVID WATKINS

5.00 Sports Report

Producer ROB HASTIE
Editor MIKE LEWIS

(MORWENNA BANKS)
Mike Channel (ANGUS DEAYTON)
Sir Leonard Why
(MICHAEL FENTON-STEVENS)
Sir Maurice Watt
(GEOFFREY PERKINS)
Nigel Pry (PHILIP POPE)
The Fifth Man (?)
Transcribed by GEOFFREY PERKINS
and ANGUS DEAYTON
with additional material by
MICHAEL FENTON-STEVENS
Music by STEVE BROWN
and PHILIP POPE
Producer
SIR ANTHONY GUY DONALD KIM TYLER
(First broadcast on Radio 4)
*('Radio Active: The Flu Special' on
Thursday 10.00pm)*

1.30 Sport on 2

see panel

6.00 Brain of Sport 1987

**Derek Kempthorne, Ian
McNeill** and **Nigel Devereux**
battle it out at Leeds Rugby
League Football Club in the
last semi-final.
Questionmaster **Peter Jones**
Referee CHRIS RHYS
Producer JOANNE WATSON

6.30 Look What They've Done to My Song

Steve Race celebrates the role of
the arranger in many spheres of
popular music and plays a piano
arrangement of his own.
Producer ALAN OWEN

7.00 Beat the Record

More musical teasers with
Keith Fordyce
Devised by DON DAVIS
Producer ANDY WILSON
*If you would like to take part in 'Beat
the Record' send a card with your
name, address, daytime telephone
number and a few words about
yourself to 'Beat the Record', Radio 2,
BBC, London W1A 4WW*

7.30 VHF/FM rejoins Radio 2

7.30 Emile Waldteufel

(1837-1915)
To commemorate the 150th
anniversary of the birth of the
French composer Emile
Waldteufel, a younger
contemporary of Johann
Strauss II, a selection of his
music, familiar and unfamiliar,
is played by the
BBC Concert Orchestra
led by MARTIN LOVEDAY
conducted by **Alexander Faris**
with guest artists
Linda Watts (soprano)
Roderick Elms (piano)
Rod Franks (cornet)
Presented by the composer's
great grand-daughter
Jacqueline Richardson.
Producer TIM MCDONALD

1.00 Bill Rennells

presents **Nightride**
Producers PAM COX
ROGER BOWMAN and
GRAHAM BELCHERE

3.00–4.00 A Little Night Music

Producer IAN GRANT

VHF
90
12

Music programmes and
are in stereo except whe
indicated
News 7.00am (VHF/FM)
9.00 (VHF/FM), 1.00pm,
World Service News
8.00am (VHF/FM)

4.55–11.35am Test Match Special

Second Test
Pakistan v England
Ball-by-ball commentar
Faisalabad on the fifth a
day's play.
MW only from 6.55

6.55 *VHF/FM* Weather

7.00 *VHF/FM* News

7.05 *VHF/FM* Morning Concert

Brahms Academic Festi
Overture
CHICAGO SO/GEORG SOLTI
7.16* Liszt Il penseroso;
Canzonetta del Salvator
(Années de pèlerinage: I
JORGE BOLET (piano)
7.23* Canteloube Two b
N'ai pas iéu de Mio; Lo C
(Songs of the Auvergne)
KIRI TE KANAWA (soprano)
NEIL BLACK (oboe)
THEA KING (clarinet)
ECO/JEFFREY TATE
7.28* Johann Strauss (s
Tales from the Vienna V
JOHANN STRAUSS ORCHESTR.
VIENNA/WILLI BOSKOVSKY
7.39* Respighi Symphon
poem: Fountains of Rom
SAN FRANCISCO SO/EDO DE W.
8.00 World Service New
8.10 Mendelssohn Overt
A Midsummer Night's D
CHICAGO SO/JAMES LEVINE

music, and that I no doubt have details of his life and music as well as manuscripts to be viewed, he and his producer invited us both (i.e. this cousin and myself) to have lunch with them to discuss possibilities at 'ANTOINE', Charlotte Street, London, on Thursday the 20th of August at noon. I presumed that in the BBC there were many talented writers who given the facts could write the programme, but as I was the Great Granddaughter and they wanted me to present the broadcast, I had to write it in my own style. They were both interested to know that I had manuscripts of waltzes that had not been ever played or orchestrated. Also asked if when I had achieved the task of putting his life on paper, I would allow them to visit in order to choose which music to use. Also said they would ask Mr. Alexander Ferris, the composer who wrote the lovely music of the TV serial 'Upstairs, Downstairs', he would sight-read the music and make his choice.

So I started to research and take notes of his childhood and the difficulties encountered.

Here is a condensed version of the story I told. It was a mixture of early poverty, a romantic meeting with the woman who was later to become his wife, and at last a recognition of his music. Both his parents were musicians and his mother taught him to play the piano. His studies were interrupted when he contracted Typhoid Fever. After his recovery, his family moved to Paris. He wanted to earn money to buy himself a piano, so got a job in a firm selling pianos, he was employed to play to prospective buyers and show to advantage the tone of those pianos. By the time he reached twelve he had saved for a piano and found an attic room in Montmartre. He gave piano lessons.

Many pupils were recommended to him and then he was presented to the Empress Eugenie, wife of Napoleon III and after hearing his melodies was nominated Court Pianist. He was twenty-eight years old. One year later, the Emperor asked him to be Conductor of the Orchestra of the State Balls. One summers day whilst working on his music, through the open window of his room he heard a lovely soprano voice coming from the window opposite, but noticed she had no accompaniment except the note of a tuning fork. So the next day, after his last pupil departed, he opened his window wide and as soon as the voice started to sing, he picked up the tune and played his piano till it stopped in mid-sentence.

He looked and noticed a dark-haired young woman leaning out and trying to see who was playing for her, so he introduced himself and invited to meet her. She was even more hard-up than him but was determined to become a singer. Born in Toulouse, she hadn't the fare to travel to Paris, so walked all the way, a distance like Glasgow to London. From their first meeting they found they had much in common, not least their love of music and although they loved each other and wanted to marry, they decided to be patient and work towards achieving a measure of success before taking such an important step. Organising the musical programme of the State Balls, he had the opportunity of playing his own music. Sometimes he conducted the orchestra, but often played the piano. At one of those musical evenings, playing a waltz he had first composed when he was fifteen, a guest asked to meet the composer as both he and his wife had so enjoyed the music. It was the Prince of Wales, later to become Edward the Seventh. Waldteufel asked permission to dedicate his next waltz to the Prince and Princess of Wales on the 11 September 1875 and he received a letter from the private secretary, Francis Knollys that he would accept the dedication and would he be good enough to let him have the score in question prepared for an Orchestral Band. In 1873, he married the girl with the lovely voice. By now he was conducting his orchestra at the Paris Opera while she sang, but soon there was a family to look after and at last the Patronage of the future King of England opened the doors of publishing houses.

He was invited to play his music at Covent Garden, Berlin and even as far as Russia. Johann Strauss the younger was a close friend of his and whenever the chance arose they played a game of billiards together. Although they both enjoyed comparing their 3/4 time waltzes, their compositions were quite different. Strauss was distinctly Viennese, Waldteufel was very Parisian. The latter often preferred to play the piano, but most of his pieces were composed in the night, so he had a mute fixed under the keyboard to soften the sound, so as not to disturb the neighbours or his wife and three children. We had the piano until 1977 when my mother decided to donate it to the Conservatory of Music in Strasbourg, his home town. One day I hope to visit as there's a plaque on the house of his birth in the Music Quarter and a road named after him. Eventually I finished the writing and hoped the BBC would approve.

Emile Waldteufel ~ aged 70

21

As summer turned to autumn, and the beautiful colours of trees and shrubs transformed our countryside, so the weather started to change, we were rather concerned with sudden gusts of wind, temperatures going up and down and though the Met. Office assured all will be well, as we all know now, mistakes do happen and on that fateful night, the 16th of October 1987, I woke up frightened by the incessant rattling of our tile-hung wall next to the French windows in our upstairs bedroom which was shaking our home. I felt very frightened and urged Reg to go to our downstairs bedroom as didn't feel safe or able to go back to sleep with all that noise. He agreed that it was a little less noisy and we tried to sleep, we had a very restless night. At 3.45am I woke up suddenly, through the curtains saw bright lights and noise and bangs which I could not begin to guess the reason for it, and at once the electric alarm clock showing the time in green went out, another power-cut. When we eventually woke up in the morning, we washed and dressed but when we opened the front door we were absolutely shattered by the devastation around us, our next door neighbour's beautiful beech tree was right across the road, thank God it fell away or their bungalow would have been crushed, a large branch of oak on our left had broken and across the entrance of our drive the overhead electric cables were draped across so it was impossible for a car to get out. People were slowly walking down our road with an expression of disbelief at the sudden destruction of our lovely trees. Reg went to get his camera and took photos of it, it was the sort of scene you witness on television of the damage a hurricane inflicts on some faraway country, but this was here, in our village, and of course the South Coast of England if not further along other coast-lines had suffered also.

The 1977 Hurricane
above: our devastated garden. below: power cables draped over our exit.

Within the hour, we could hear petrol saws trying to get through some of the large trees across the road, whether it was the council or private individuals trying to open up the way out of our village I don't know, but it was certainly a gigantic task. We went in the back garden, found large branches over the lawn but worst of all our green-house was empty of glass and the metal frames were twisted badly. Glass was found the full length of our back garden, and it had to be carefully removed. Fences were in heaps against our neighbour's walls and we realised that with the best will in the world, it was going to be a long job. Thank God, all our immediate neighbours had not been hurt, trees can grow again, but although precious, human life is more so. So now it means can't use our central heating as though it's gas, the electric pump can't work. Thank Heavens, we have gas for cooking, candles are now the only form of lighting and as Reg said, it's very romantic across the dining room table for an evening but, longer than that, it could become frustrating. TV was not on the agenda, but a small radio with batteries told us many people whose houses were hit by large trees were much more unlucky than us. We heard the damage that hit the South Coast and on that day, our good friend Phyl, of Orpington, lost her only daughter. She was the first victim of the hurricane, recognised her unusual surname on the news, had gone to deliver flowers and as she drove past, a large tree fell on her little van and killed her. Tried to phone our good friend, but the telephone was out of order.

When sad events occur, that's when you realise what real friends do to make life better. A few days after that terrible night, our neighbours were doing their best to clean their drives and gardens, cut wood to use on their fires and make some sort of order. Friends with small children must have found all this very difficult, though some had generators which helped a lot. One couple who used to play whist in the Halstead village hall, were very proud of their ceramic hob but without electricity was no use at all, so we invited them to share an evening meal with us in the kitchen, with the candles dotted about, but a beef casserole and a pudding was at least warming as the evenings were getting somewhat chilly.

The couple living immediately in front of our home, kindly invited us to an evening meal, they had a generator and made us both very welcome, were kind enough to escort us down their long drive, across the road and up our drive armed with a powerful torch.

The next day, our Doctor's wife offered to us the use of either a bath or a shower as they had a generator. Had no idea how long it would be to get all those cables replaced, so we worked things out from day to day.

Our TV aerial had also been ripped away from the roof and landed on our neighbour's lawn, so would have to get a new one and our usual electrician to erect it for us.

At last at 4.30 pm the electricity is back. Engineers have worked all day and have come from Yorkshire to replace these cables after 11 days and 13 hours without power. A friend in Orpington said to me she had been without electricity for 24 hours. Told her how lucky she had been, as we found 11 days and 13 hours much more uncomfortable, so she soon stopped complaining.

Slowly village activities were getting back to normal, frenetic efforts were made to clear roads and replace shattered fences, the photographs in the national paper showed the damage the hurricane had done and it has to be said many people sustained crushed houses by massive trees, so we often said that for all the inconvenience we were luckier than others.

We had our aerial replaced and could at least have the use of our TV. On Tuesday the third of November the over 60s Lunch Club took place and W.I. Dart matches started again.

The BBC producer phones to ask how the script was getting on, told him it was finished and invited him and Mr.

Ferris to come over for lunch on Friday the 6 of November if they wished to see some manuscripts.

At noon, they arrived and we had lunch. Afterwards, I gave Mr. Ferris ten manuscripts arranged for piano and he looked at them, hummed the tunes and was enthusiastic that apart from opening the concert with the tune most people know, that is to say "The Skater's Waltz", was keen to get the other ten pieces orchestrated and played as they were completely unknown to him and were tuneful. So he took the music with him and would get that sorted out. I went to Sevenoaks and bought a cocktail dress for the occasion and Reg was pleased with my choice.

I received a telephone call from the BBC to explain the time-table for Wednesday the second of November. They are sending a car for me to take me to the "HIPPODROME THEATRE" North End Road, Golders Green, where the programme is broadcast. I asked if it was possible for Reg to be there, said it was absolutely fine, he would be allowed in the recording-room where you have the view on the orchestra and the stage where I, the singer and the instrumentalist had to be in view of an invited audience. Told me the time Reg would need to be there, as hoping I could have a rehearsal with the orchestra.

It was exciting but I was nervous as I had not the experience of such an event. When I arrived, the producer introduced me to the orchestra and I was shown to the stage. I had to sit on a dais, get up and walk to a music stand on which my narrative was, after each part I had to turn, walk back to the dais to sit down. I can't tell you how I was nervous in case I tripped, but had to do it eleven times as there were eleven pieces of music to be played. The programme lasted one hour. I was taken to the third floor of the building to change in my Royal Blue dress and find my way down from the dressing-room. Thank heavens, when I returned to the recording-room Reg was there and I was introduced to the singer and the other artists. I was asked to go on this dais on stage to do a voice test, to balance the sound. The producer was very helpful and was now in evening dress looking very smart. When the programme started the lights dimmed and I was amazed looking up to see the circle and all those faces looking down. Still I am glad to say it went well and at the end of the concert, the producer kindly brought over for the lady singer and myself a gorgeous spray of flowers. I hurried to the recording studio, Reg hugged me and said how proud he was of me, said he enjoyed the programme and after saying our goodbyes we drove home, rather relieved that it was over. Ten days later on Saturday the 12th of December at 7.30-8.30, the concert came on air on Radio 2. Reg bought a Radio Times and was so pleased to see my name on the page. Wednesday Reg drove me to Bournemouth to the hotel we often went to for the Christmas Festivities, and we came home on Monday the 28th after a wonderful five days, the food was wonderful and it was really good fun. What an eventful year 1987 was, not just a hurricane, but a BBC concert to write, and the experience of being part of presenting a programme.

1988 was a leap year. Now that so many trees had been knocked down, there seemed to be more light, the canopy of trees around our cottage too have gone and the vivid colours of spring flowers were more vibrant. Now the time had come to seriously repair damage and replace fences, re-glaze the greenhouse and prepare it for growing the flowers for our garden. Everywhere in the village, people were mending their homes and gardens. As April came on that special day, the Sunday 3rd of April just before breakfast, a rather late one, we got up at nearly 10 am, Reg disappeared in the garage, and a few moments later re-appeared with a basket of spring flowers, sweet smelling Freesias and other flowers and greenery which took my breath away. He put the basket on the coffee-table, took me in his arms and said "Happy ten years. It's ten years since that day I knocked on your door, thank you for everything." We sat on the settee and I was so happy that he has remembered, but then Reg was a man who always celebrated any event that touched us both. Birthdays, Valentine's day, Easter, Christmas, we both enjoyed giving each other cards, sharing a meal and enjoying every minute of those occasions.

When my birthday arrived, four days later, a beautiful card was put on the table, and then another pile of cards was brought for me to open from friends. Mid-morning, his son Colin and his girl Wendy called with flowers and a present. None came from his daughter who always sent cards at least a week late. Reg had booked a favourite restaurant in Sevenoaks and we enjoyed our 'Special day' till midnight, and so to bed.

As from September, letters were sent to Reg informing him of any progress with advising his wife about the petition and giving fourteen days to acknowledge it and the process of law took its own laboured progress, but being so happy and content I could not begin to imagine how happier we could feel, so I listened to the letters read to me but stopped believing that our hopes would ever be realised. As summer came, after removing a Christmas tree that was very dead towards the top of our garden, Reg had the idea of buying some trellis and stout posts and make an arbour. We would put our wooden seat under it, a table and plant Victorian roses to climb to the top of it, also a deep pink climber called 'Galway Bay' and another with pastel and delicate shade. When it was done we both had a go at putting paving stones and we had the pleasure of relaxing with a tray of tea and home-made cakes, as the lawn descended towards the house, we could look at our efforts and flower-beds, also had a view of our back gate to see who was visiting us. Reg and I spent most of our spare time in spring and summer enjoying that, as we both liked the outdoors.

Our enormous oak tree was getting taller and wider and our vegetable patch became so shady it was obvious that there was no more possibility to grow vegetables that need sun and light. Apart from that slight blip, our garden still gave us a lot of pleasure. When more plants were needed, Reg had a knack of propagating lavender, rosemary and many other plants and was more successful than me. We quite often had visits from Colin and Wendy, but only rare visits from his daughter, apart from coming for the odd meal or to visit on New Years Day with the rest of the family. Nothing changes. On the 23rd of November, Reg received his decree nisi and was told that all being well, six weeks later he will have the confirmation that the divorce will be made absolute. Reg heaved a sigh of relief as on the ninth of January 1989 he was advised it was now absolute. Now he said our plans can be made, however much some members of the family tried to change his mind. Of course, that unpleasant move was not told to me for some time as it would have caused me a lot of hurt, but his family obviously did not know their dad very well, when Reg has decided after much thought what his intentions are they cannot be changed.

22

Always marry an April girl,
praise the spills and bless the charms.

I found April in my arms,
April golden, April cloudy,

gracious, cruel, tender, rowdy,
April soft in flowered languor,

ever changing, ever true.
I love April, I love you.

Ogden Nash

January the 1st 1989, the family all descended on us for a buffet meal to celebrate the New Year.

The routine of village activities started again, WI committee meetings, darts matches, we played against Chipstead WI and on Thursday the 25th of January we had a dinner party and enjoyed pleasant company. The Friday tenth of February, Wolverton phones to say Uncle Raymond was taken to hospital for tests as he had a fall. Reg speaks to his wife. Auntie Madge, will visit next week, probably Wednesday the 15th to see them both.

Tuesday the 14th of February, St. Valentine's day, as we always did each year, two beautiful cards were put on the table, but before I was allowed to open mine, a heavy box carefully wrapped in pretty paper was given to me by Reg and he asked me to open it before anything else. I was taken aback by the small porcelain box in the shape of a heart, in the centre of the lid a small painting of a Pierrot and eight little hearts all around him. I opened the lid and on a heart-shaped paper was written: 14.2.89 Jackie, will you many me, my love? Reg xxxxxxxxx

I was so touched by such a romantic way of asking me that his face became blurred as 1 felt the tears filling my eyes, I couldn't speak, I just stepped towards him and I kissed him very gently. That told him what he wanted to know. I opened my Valentine card and with my pen added to it. "Yes, darling, I will." He looked at his card and read it, took my face in his hands and we kissed each other so gently and afterwards just looked at each other, no more words were needed to be said, his blue eyes conveyed all he wanted to say and it was the happiest Valentine's Day ever.

We went to the sitting-room and started to make plans, wondered where we would choose for our honeymoon, I also was given an engagement ring with a Ruby in the centre surrounded by 36 blue diamonds, made a list of guests, we only wanted a modest gathering of loyal friends who were so happy for us, so only twelve guests were invited, (two were away and only found our invitation on their return) and six members of the family. Reg asked me if I felt OK about asking his son and daughter to be witnesses, as we intended to have a Registry wedding. Wendy, Colin's girl, told us of a good photographer so we phoned him to call on us to discuss details.

Also Reg suggested to me a place to have our reception and other details would only be possible to arrange once we had a date.

Unfortunately, the next day Wednesday, Reg took the train to Wolverton in Buckinghamshire, to visit his uncle Raymond and see if there was anything he could do to help his aunt. No doubt, knowing Reg he probably asked Madge for a shopping list and bought sufficient food to avoid having to leave Raymond on his own. He phoned and said all was well, and he would be back tomorrow. While Reg was in Wolverton, Wendy met me in West Wickham to take me to see a florist she knew and it was all organised. A posy of flowers for me and corsages for Reg and other members of the family.

A week later we went to the Bickley Manor Hotel to view the room where we would have our wedding breakfast. His son, Colin, offered to us the use of his address and our friend Phyl offered her address, so all would be fine.

So the 22nd of April would be our wedding day, Colin suggested to deck his car with white ribbon and drive us to the Bromley Registry Office. Reg booked our hotel "L'Emeraude" in the island of Jersey and also the short flight We sent our invitations to our friends and looked forward to our big day. I eventually found an outfit which I thought would be suitable and then I went to Tunbridge Wells to a hat shop and purchased a lovely navy hat with a white silk rose on the front. Also navy court shoes, and was only necessary to book a manicure, pedicure and get my hair done.

Reg had ordered a lovely silver grey suit and everything was ready. We chose a wedding cake but as we were an intimate circle of guests, we decided a two-tier cake would be suitable. Re my bouquet, I will put all petals and delicate greenery in a few flower-presses so I can still see the remaining colours of the flowers of that wonderful day. Friends and relatives gathered in a fairly large ante-room. We were chatting to all our friends but as I looked across the room, Reg was a little nervous as I was, in fact at the end of the afternoon, one of my friends teased me about my hat. She said to me, "Did you know you are wearing your hat back to front, that lovely white rose is supposed to be in front, not at the back." I had not even noticed, I was too happy to have even realised my mistake. We left the guests in the afternoon made our way to the house to collect our suitcases and on to Gatwick Airport.

As soon as we landed, we hired a car for the week and were pleasantly surprised at the comfort of our hotel. We had chosen it simply by the name and only discovered when

Signing the register on our Wedding Day
22 April 1989

Leaving the Registry Office

looking at their brochure on arrival, that it had formerly been one of the island's Stately homes. It was on a hill and pretty houses and gardens tumbled down, one more attractive than the next As we walked down to explore on foot people working in their gardens, smiled and sometimes spoke to us as hand in hand we admired their flowers. The blue skies and warm sun mirrored our happy mood, and we explored many lovely places. I had no idea that such a small island was so rich in interesting places to visit. I still have maps, postcards of our hotel, leaflet of pottery studios, also we visited an Orchid Collection where many varieties of flowers, different in both colours, size and intricate shapes are viewed growing as they would in their usual habitat nestling on trees and I must say we neither of us guessed they were so many. Also saw a Woodcraft Centre called l'Etacq and as a souvenir bought two wooden carved plaques, each for our own Zodiac Sign, one was Hazel, the other Alder. We asked a man walking through with his wife to kindly take a photo of us in a beautiful garden so that we could have a photo to remind us of that day. The next day, we drove along the coast to see the beautiful light-house of La Corbiere and went for a stroll on the empty beach of St. Ouen Bay. I guess in late April the sea would be too cold to venture in. But the views of the clouds racing across the sky were a real sight and I remember that day well.

The week flew by, but we enjoyed every day, but time was ready for our returning home and looked forward to see our little home again.

Sunday the 30th April, find a pile of letters on the kitchen table. Colin and Wendy had left bread, potatoes and in the fridge, milk, bacon and cheese. Much appreciated that gesture.

Two days later, we get a visit from Colin and Wendy to tell us some news. They are going to get married and want to chat about where around here they could book for their reception, they know the date and the church in Bromley, so

Reg suggests perhaps "The Spinning Wheel" in Biggin Hill would be an idea. So will let us know if it can be booked and more details regarding times and so forth. We neither of us were too surprised at the news because it was in the late 1980 that Colin's previous relationship with his last girl-friend was breaking up and he left and decided to live with Wendy. Although they were both working in the Ambulance Service and saw each other most days, they had in the last nine years found their qualities and faults, so had had time to discover each other's ways. Better take time than dive into something without knowing much of each other, so we now were told 3pm St. Joseph's Church, Bromley, on the 17th of June, then the reception at "The Spinning Wheel". We wish them well, we know Wendy loves Colin truly and will do anything to please him, so we sincerely wish everything good for them.

To go to Colin and Wendy's wedding, 1 decided to wear a very pale primrose yellow outfit 1 had bought in Paris which would be right for summer and look elegant. It had a finely pleated skirt, a camisole with a little embroidery on the front, and a long-sleeved jacket I purchased a primrose yellow silk rose, took off the white one on my navy wide-brimmed hat and also put a thin ribbon on the rim. I would use my navy clutch bag and matching navy court shoes. Reg wore his grey suit and looked very smart as he usually did. When we arrived at St. Joseph Church, we took our seats on the fourth row and noticed Gladys was already there right on the front, as being the Groom's mother felt it was appropriate.

Colin's sister, her husband and their son and daughter were not yet there, but at last out of breath they appeared. Eventually, the bride looking flushed and in a lovely white gown arrived on the arm other father, Colin turned round looking very smart and the ceremony began.

When the service was over, we drove to the Kent countryside and arrived at "The Spinning Wheel", looking forward to seeing photos taken, had not the slightest idea that the day which we were glad to witness would become a most hurtful setting for a family member's cowardly behaviour, and it took me by surprise. I thought that bullying was part of school life, never did I imagine a grown up could find the opportunity on such a special day. After all, it was Colin and Wendy's day, no one else.

The person who had been pressed to cause hurt, chose the moment when Reg said to me, "Won't be a moment, just going to ask Colin if it would be possible to get one photo of us four without causing any problems." He disappeared and chance presented itself by grabbing my arm with hysterical strength and making demands clear to me. I was bruised and shaken by that show of unleashed anger. The person walked away and I was in tears, the only people who saw that were the wedding guests, one young lady who was close and might have heard, put her arm round my shoulders and suggested accompanying me to the ladies cloakroom to dab my eyes in cold water.

When I returned, Reg asked why my eyes were red and my lids were swollen. Told him quickly what the suggestion was made to me and he just said, "Rubbish, I am not letting you out of my sight now, come on!"

I won't say what was said to me, but the person concerned will know and if a conscience exists, will be aware of that day's deed.

No doubt, members of the family, apart from Reg, still have no idea of that person's vicious behaviour. After the meal, we adjourned to a small private room while music was playing and dancing was going on. We drank coffee, but were in no mood to have a drink. After an hour Reg managed to talk to Colin and his Bride and we made our excuses. We were both keen to go home and get away from whispered comments from other members of the family.

Certainly funerals and weddings seem to bring out the most basic instincts that human beings have no reason to be proud of. We both felt happy for the newly married couple, but the incident that occurred made Reg feel embarrassed by the behaviour of one close member of his family.

Hugged him and told him not to dwell on it, by the time a person reaches twenty-one, they are responsible for their behaviour, you must not blame yourself. Nevertheless, that incident will not be forgotten by me.

As was quoted in a BBC lecture in 1967, "Far from being the basis for the good Society, the Family, with its narrow privacy and tawdry secrets, is the source of all our discontents."

23

R eg had by now made friends with people who invited him to join the Committee and had in mind to resurrect a Bowling Club in our midst.

There had been one whose green was where we now have a car-park behind the Village Hall, in those days the game of Bowls was a man's sport, so no ladies were allowed to play.

In these modern times, prizes would usually consist of silver-plated shields on a wooden base and cups and trophies, but in those days the prize was a pig. The first bowling green was organised in 1924-25, but by the Second World War, although many people tried to keep things going, by 1950 the Club lost support and it all finished. But a new committee was formed in 1989 and a lot of work was put in to bring to life a new Bowls Club, on land belonging to the village club, also a pavilion was bought and revamped. Many committee members organised Coffee Mornings, so that the items needed to use playing that sport could be purchased. Instead of two rinks as in the past, the green was large enough for six rinks, the only problem was that no one in the committee had any experience or knowledge of the rules of the game. So a gentleman experienced in having played a fair time, agreed to teach us and become our Captain. So that many practise days were only used in learning how to play, the etiquette of the game was shown to us and with much help from regular players who joined our club, we started to learn. Reg who had played every sport imaginable, nevertheless had never played bowls, but as a golfer and snooker player, it certainly helped him to become a good bowler. We had no idea, apart from getting a set of woods, how many other things had to be acquired. No-heel bowling shoes, grey skirt and white blouse, grey trousers and white shirt for men, also white gear for special matches as well as waterproof wear because unless it's torrential, we still carry on playing in the rain. A measuring tape and chalk to mark the bowl. A special bag for carrying your gear from your ear to the club, a leather to clean grass and mud (if any) and polish to keep woods clean. Also, we had to get a firm to manufacture our club brooch with our emblem on it (i.e. The Knockholt Beeches) and a badge to be stitched on your blazer and necessarily a hat.

On the 16th of July, we had a gathering at our green for drinks and nibbles, two days later we had a meeting at the village hall to discuss the details of running the club. Reg told many friends about the forthcoming start of our club, the usual start of the season for out-door bowling is the end of April to the last day of September.

We hoped enough local clubs would give us a game as we were raw beginners. We eventually had one hundred and twenty members from far and wide and in the spring of 1990 we would shakily begin to play and do the best we could.

A bowls dinner was organised on Friday the 10th of November. This year we spent a quiet and happy Christmas at home, the two of us and also New Year's Eve was an intimate day at home. We hoped that 1990 would continue to be as happy a year as it had been those past six years of togetherness.

But the New Year started on a worrying note. We had a phone call from Aunt Madge's neighbour, to tell us an ambulance was collecting her, but didn't know what the trouble was.

Reg, rightly, didn't hesitate and took the train to Wolverton (Buckinghamshire) to see what the trouble was. It seems Madge had pains and they would be doing tests to find out what was wrong. Reg returned the same night looking concerned and tired. Got home late in the evening of Sunday the 7th of January. On Thursday the 11th Reg and I returned to give support to Raymond, and visit the hospital and enquire from the doctor in charge what was ailing her. We returned home on Saturday urging Raymond to phone immediately if mere were any news.

Friday the 26th of January, Auntie Madge passed away of that dreaded cancer. Sunday the 28th we drove to Wolverton to help Raymond who was shattered by the speed of events and the sudden realisation that he was now alone.

At the age of eighty-five, the shock of it all must be beyond belief. Luckily, Reg had, as long as I have known him, done everything to help regarding both Madge and Raymond, and his uncle knows whatever help he needs. Reg will give it. It was obvious that now he was alone and living in a rented cottage, Reg had to find a home that was comfortable for his elderly relative, so he arranged for him to go into it on Wednesday the 31st at Bletchley. Raymond also wished Reg to arrange his affairs, so a visit to a solicitor for Power of Attorney was duly signed and that concern was lifted from his uncle's mind.

Thursday, we went to the Funeral at St. John's Church, then on to the Crematorium. Reg and I drive Raymond to the home. We stayed the night at the cottage, but a dreadful storm blew up, rainwater started to pour through the bedroom ceiling, we tripped downstairs in our night clothes, found an old tin bath, carried it upstairs and used that. We barely slept two hours. The downstairs was also waterlogged. Next day, kindly neighbours offered us a bed as we were both rather shattered. Reg sorted out his uncle's clothes to bring them to his new home, and promised he would do the necessary in a few days regarding getting the gas and electric meters read. Also Reg got in touch with a Women's Refuge to arrange for the furniture in the cottage to be donated and collected, also do the necessary phone calls to the owners of the cottage and explain the situation.

As is the norm in February, snow had fallen and was now slush, the black clouds promised more snow and mid-morning was as dark as evening time. Reg was so tired with lack of sleep, I don't know how he drove all the way home, but we were so pleased to get home, and have some comfort. We were lucky, we had each other but Raymond had to get used to a new home with strangers, it must have been difficult at the beginning.

Reg had to get up early at 5am Monday 12th February. I drove him to Orpington station for 6.15 train. Got back home, still dark at 6.35. Reg was going to Wolverton to close the house down and phoned me from Charing Cross station. Met him with the car at 3pm. Tired but glad he'd done his best for Raymond.

The tempo of life carried on, I was still involved with the Abbeyfield Society in Orpington. One of my friends in the village had lost her mother and her father was in need of a reliable place as looking after himself was not possible, so she asked me details of this Society and I arranged an appointment for her elderly father and herself to be interviewed. On Tuesday the 20th of March at 2.10pm I collected both and we went to the interview. Eventually, it was arranged this lady's father would have a ground floor bedroom at one of the four houses in Orpington and would be comfortable and well looked after.

On the 3rd of April, I went to Chelsfield Park Hospital to consult an eye specialist as I was having difficulties with my right eye. I was told I had Macular Degeneration, I had peripheral vision, but no central vision. When I asked if anything could be done, was told it was age-related, in other words "TEMPUS FUGIT" and since I was going to be fifty-eight in four days, I realised with a jolt that obviously I was getting ancient (in terms of reliable eye-sight) so I felt a little low. Still my left eye was still OK, so I couldn't let it get me down.

On Monday the 16th of April, we had a surprise. Colin and Wendy called in the afternoon, first time since their wedding last June, (that's ten months). I expect furnishing their home, as well as working left little time to spare, but were agreeably surprised when they brought delayed Christmas presents and a basket of flowers for Easter, as it was Easter Monday.

We were both astonished to be told by Colin, that Gladys had cancer of the liver. Didn't seem to know much else.

The next morning, Reg phoned his daughter Penny and was told that for three months her sick mother had stayed at her home. Reg asked why, saying was surprised she had not told him. All I have in my diary is "USUAL EXCUSES", so don't know what was said. However, living apart, when illness strikes you would imagine such news should be told, but apparently his daughter did not see the necessity to inform him. No wonder he felt completely at a loss to understand her extraordinary attitude.

Four days later, we celebrated our first wedding anniversary. The next day we had passport photos made and acquired a year's passport, plus Swiss Francs and travellers cheques.

The Horticultural Society was arranging a 6 day holiday to KANDERSTEG (Switzerland) and enjoy the alpine flowers.

One of our members was attached to an airline and was getting our air tickets and booking the hotel. Of course, we also had the pleasure of having the company of the friends we had made in the village and were looking forward to it. On the Tuesday 24th April, a Safari Supper was organised, and although it was to us first, we joined in the experience In our village, we used to organise a starter in one house, then drive to another house for the main course, then ended our evening in a usually fairly large house for sweets and puddings, as well as coffee. I was asked to help, so did two choices of starters, then on to the next two houses. It was fun and everybody enjoyed the party atmosphere.

On May the 3rd, a Thursday, the evening class of painting at Ripley House, Bickley, was giving an exhibition of paintings by us students and we took our framed paintings. It took place from 7pm to 9pm and Reg drove us to it and enjoyed the different styles of art. He did not want me to sell them, so you just make a notice by the side of the painting as N.F.S. (Not for sale).

Jacqui holding both paintings in the exhibition

The following Tuesday, one of our friends whose husband was arranging the flight and the hotel in Switzerland invited the members of the Society to their home at "Ivy Lane" to meet each other. The date of departure was the 24 of May, Thursday. Looked forward to the visit as I didn't know mat part of Switzerland and it promised to be good.

We arrived from the airport to the Victoria Hotel and we were very pleased with the accommodation. It had its own grounds and we were made very welcome. Judy and Brian Brett did all the organising of this holiday and we often spoke of all the lovely places that we visited. If I recall it was our very first visit to Switzerland with our club and Reg and I often spoke of the colourful flower meadows, the alpine flowers we spotted while walking in the hills, we had a trip by cable car to a restaurant and I still have the photos we took around the table enjoying a good laugh. We returned home the Tuesday 29th of May with a few souvenirs for our home and many memories to cherish of a very pleasant holiday.

On our return, we took up again our bowling practise as matches became booked and we wanted to play as well as possible. June became a month of Barbecues and Barn dances, in between, Reg and I went to our local theatre and enjoyed musicals. On Saturday the 20th June, our good friends Diana and Peter Ball organised a Barbecue for the Horticultural Society and Reg invited six friends to join us. Diana and Peter had a very large garden as well as a Bluebell Wood and had strung coloured lights around the tree branches, so when evening came, it looked so pretty. It was a lovely evening, when we got home, our friends came in for coffee till midnight. So what with the Bowls practise and everything happening in the village, we had little time for ourselves, but we both enjoyed the getting together.

On the 14th of July, the Knockholt Carnival took place, enjoyed seeing all the floats going round the village, all the roads were closed by the police for the time needed and then everyone entered the recreation ground to enjoy the stalls and all the fun of the day. August came and we heard of the news that Gladys passed away on Friday the 10th. The cremation took place on Wednesday the 15th of August. Two women had succumbed to that dreadful disease – may they rest in peace.

24

October came and with it the temperature of an Indian Summer, the French windows were wide open and the scent of roses came wafting in even at this late hour, the heat of the day still felt warm on your face. Reg had sat in the comer of the settee as was his usual habit while I stood at the French window admiring the silhouette of the lovely oak, the pink blush of the sky with the black outline of the branches reminded me of black lace against a pink satin cloth and as always when looking at the back garden I couldn't help admire that majestic tree and the beauty of a Kent sunset.

All at once I was conscious that Reg was looking up at me and seemed to be in a thoughtful mood and I turned to see if he'd spoken to me and I perhaps had not heard. "Did you say something?" I asked. "No darling, I was just looking at you, come and sit by me." I walked over and sat next to him, he took my hand and looked at me very nervously. Was something troubling him? I wondered what he was going to say. I thought it best to say nothing, Reg always thought carefully before saying anything he considered important, so I waited. Then to my surprise he said, "As you know, I have always said to you that what is past is past and only the present is important. Now we are man and wife I believe it's right that some events in my past should be known to you."

He was by now holding tightly to my hand and I had the feeling he had no intention of letting go until he had unburdened himself.

He related the events from joining the RAF and meeting the girl who was to become his wife. After he explained the convoluting events and the advising his mother and aunt of his forthcoming marriage only then did I start to understand how the events of so long ago had continued to fester in his mind and were never really forgotten with time and so often people will confidently tell you that time obliterates all sad events, but ask a grieving spouse if that is so and all who sincerely loved and cherished will tell you it's a blatant lie.

So I became able to understand why even though he loved his children, what took place all those years ago could never be forgiven, so each went their separate ways, though still under the same roof, but on one side, the appearance of togetherness was still played out for the sake of family and friends.

At long last, he let go of my hand and he realised my fingers were sore due to the strength of his grasp.

I told him I appreciated his telling me and as he asked me to keep this to myself I am not divulging his secret. I always keep my promise. We hugged each other and I think he felt relieved to have told me, that is what families have to endure, sad secrets which are such a burden and which their children have not the slightest idea about.

It is a sad thing that children have the idea that their parents are without blemish or faults. How gullible can they be?

I closed the windows and we went to bed. I did not think we would be any closer but somehow the evening talk made me feel even more loving towards him, it must have been another disappointment he struggled with, but at least he knew that my love for him was endless.

The mild Autumn and sunny weather encouraged people in our village and also surrounding areas to organise opening their gardens, doing cream teas and having plant stalls. All the funds were sent to worthy charities. Also, we had joined the Sevenoaks Indoor Bowling Club so that we could in cold and rainy weather practise and get better at the sport. We soon realised how different it was to play on a carpet instead of grass, but it was very good practise. The weather became cold and winter came, we joined the gatherings in the village, Christmas parties were in full swing from the beginning of December.

On Thursday 12th of December, Reg was invited by a parish councillor who was keen on trees and the preservation of them to Vavasseur's Wood. He explained that people in our village were interested in the woods and starting a Tree Society would be the answer.

That wood was long ago the property of the Vavasseur family, the owner had a tall and impressive tower built attached to the house which looked over as far as London. Apparently, in the second world war, that said tower became a recognised beacon for the German Air Force to pinpoint Biggin Hill Airfield and bombing Fighter Command. So the tower had to be demolished. The house fell into disrepair and the Parish Council in the end purchased the grounds, but only the Tree Society which interested many villagers wanted to form, to take care and have the wood looked after, cleared and replanted for the benefit of our village. It was a very difficult task and needed support and a lot of work to do a good job. Reg was very enthusiastic having discussed the possibilities with Peter Ball who also wanted the woods to be cared for, ideas were tossed about and a core of interested people were helping to put the intentions to as wide an audience as possible. The Secretary of the Parish Council at that time, Gillian King-Scott, was willing to do the job of secretary which involved a lot of paper-work, also organising working parties, so a lot of energy had to be found. Many people were willing to be on the committee to get this worthwhile project off the ground.

On Friday, the 21st of December there was a Carol Concert at the village hall and we joined in the gathering.

Reg booked a table for two at the Mange-Tout Restaurant in Downe Village, a restaurant which did lovely food in an intimate atmosphere, having been recommended by good friends, we were looking forward to our Christmas Day lunch.

We spent many occasions in that place and were never disappointed. Christmas Eve we were invited to an open house at "CRTTTLESHAW", the home of Diana and Peter Ball, always looked forward to their party, they both made their guests so welcome and we had a lovely evening. Certainly, the last month of the year, was a round of gatherings and the hospitality was unrivalled. On Boxing Day, lunchtime between 11am and 1pm we went to other friends for drinks and finger food and in the evening our next door neighbour invited us for supper. The next day, I had an appointment to Moorfields eye hospital to see a specialist regarding my eye trouble and Colin, Reg's son, very kindly offered to drive us to London. Naturally, had drops in my eye and couldn't see where Reg and Colin were sitting, lost my sense of direction and made a bee-line for a complete stranger, till Reg quickly took my hand and redirected me to where Colin and his wife Wendy were waiting. We invited them to share our meal, by then the drops had worn off and I could see what I was doing.

On New Year's Eve, we went to the bowls disco at the village hall and ended the year in a party atmosphere. New Year's day Nancy and Peter Leyton, who lived in a pink house called "Rock's Forge", were holding a buffet lunch and we enjoyed the company. And so 1991 started on a note of fun and friendship. Reg and I so enjoyed the social life that was very much part of village life.

25

Colin and Wendy became fairly regular visitors. When the eve of my fifty-ninth birthday came they called with a small flowering shrub and a bouquet of flowers. The next day Reg took me out to lunch and we shared a quiet but pleasant day. No news, either phone call or card from his daughter Penny, wonder I feel surprised. On the 13th of April, Colin and Wendy invited us to their home for supper. Wendy had prepared a very tasty meal and a delicious sweet. Enjoyed our coffee and chatted about the forthcoming holiday in Austria next June, which the horticultural society was organising. They both looked after us well and it made up for the feeling of disappointment being ignored by Colin's sister.

On the 8th of June, we flew with other members and friends to Innsbruck airport and thoroughly enjoyed the alpine flowers growing in profusion and to see the Ibex jumping from boulder to boulder, so sure footed compared to us human beings.

A week later after our arrival, a male-voice choir from Wales were invited to our village and people were asked if we could put up one or two for a long weekend. We offered to put up two singers, strangely enough one was Aneurin Bevan and the other Ronald Colman. Apart from the official concert which took place at Fort Halstead, a mile from our village, the next evening we all met at the village hall and to thank us for putting them up they gave a concert as a thank you, such lovely voices they had, it was pure delight We went to the centre of the village next morning to wish them a safe journey back to the Land of Song. When we returned home we found, on our coffee table, two bone china pin-trays painted with the Red Dragon and a shield with three Fleurs-de-Lys and painted in black around the rim "MYNYDDISLWYN MALE VOICE CHOIR".

On Friday the 2nd of August, we invited Colin and Wendy to join us at our good friends Diana and Peter Ball's house, who were organising a barbecue for the benefit of the horticultural society. They fortunately had a very spacious garden for tables on the lawn and some of us had helped in a small way by bringing either a savoury dish or a pudding to help out, as the hostess was already very busy preparing both food and tables. It was as ever a lovely evening and I have such pleasant memories of those occasions.

On Friday the 23rd of August '91, Reg had his 71st birthday but his new tablets for his irregular heartbeat had an unpleasant effect on him, so suggested I cancel our restaurant booking, took the car and went to purchase something for our evening meal, so that we could dine at leisure at home and avoid driving to a restaurant if not feeling too well. Glad we did, he relaxed and we shared a quiet but intimate meal just the two of us.

Although we enjoyed playing bowls in our new club, 1 realised that although Reg did not seem to look much older, I had to remind myself that he should perhaps restrict his energies a little. As it was we both used to go to Vavasseurs wood once a fortnight to help other members of the Tree Society committee and other kindly helpers to carry on clearing and removing ivy from existing trees as well as planting new saplings. Also we used to play bowling matches three times a week, as well as playing league matches Thursday evenings, so, although a game of bowls looks very leisurely when viewers watch it on TV, after the walking, bowling very heavy woods and concentrating you feel quite tired at the end of the match.

On Thursday 5th of September, I drove to Waitrose to get my weekly shopping, I bumped into a WI friend, Doris Beverton, on my way back to the car and after a quick chat, turned away after saying goodbye, caught my foot on a grating one inch higher than the tar surface they had recently spread in the car-park and fell flat on my face and knees, I was down so fast I felt shaken. I had a bleeding nose, grazes and abrasions over my chin, right knee, a hole in my trousers and both hands grazed. Luckily, I had all the weekend shopping in the boot of the car, someone fetched the manageress who was very kind. She said she would phone my husband and would drive me to the Queen Mary's Hospital in Sidcup. When I arrived, the waiting room was full, were attending a child so I had to wait to be seen. I thanked the lady who drove me and told her to get back.

Thirty minutes later Reg arrived and was, I think, a bit shocked to see the state I was in. While we waited for someone to see to me, Reg explained that he had asked our neighbour, Brian Hickman, to give him a lift to the supermarket, took his spare car keys, drove our car to meet me in hospital. After being attended, was given a tetanus jab and Reg drove me home. I felt shaken though the injuries to my face were sore, I didn't think anything was broken. Reg cancelled our holiday in Bournemouth. Friends called in the afternoon with flowers, phone calls also were received and our Vicar Malcolm Bury who was also a regular visitor came to see me and Reg, much appreciated that kindly gesture.

On Monday, Reg made an appointment with the Doctor as my knee was very swollen and also had an x-ray on my nose in case it was broken or there was a blockage. But there was no damage.

A friend called and took a couple of photos which were developed right away in case a compensation was possible.

December was a month of festivities and we enjoyed the get-togethers. Christmas Day, Reg invited his son and daughter in law to share our Christmas luncheon at the Mange-Tout restaurant and spent the afternoon together. They returned to their home in Bromley early evening.

1992 was a year full of events, pleasant ones mostly with the occasional hiccup, but on the whole it was great.

My good friend Diana Ball was celebrating a birthday on 8th of February and Reg and Diana's husband Peter suggested to have a meal at our favourite place in Downe Village. When Reg and I were alone, Reg suggested that perhaps Diana would be pleased if he ordered a small birthday cake with a single pink candle so that she could be presented with it at the end of the meal. I agreed it would be fun and when we saw the lights dim and someone singing "Happy Birthday" we enjoyed the look of surprise on Diana's face. Reg always had lovely ideas and we enjoyed our evening.

At the beginning of February, rumours were circulating that some villages around the area, as well as our own, were going to be chosen for 150 Travellers to settle in our village, so although our Parish Council tried to have the meeting re-scheduled and moved nearer to us, we nevertheless drove to the Wilderness School in Sevenoaks, over 5 miles away for the Public Meeting to take place on Monday the 30th of March at 7pm. Reg gave a lift to our immediate neighbours and off we went. Our village must have become a ghost town that evening as apart from people working in hospitals or special services, everyone went to the meeting. I remember looking at the back of the large hall, the people were standing as there were no seats left.

We heard a man putting his case forward for the Travellers, then we had Mr. Michael Stevens speaking for the District Council, he was then Chairman of the Planning Committee of Sevenoaks and put the case forward against having the Travellers invade our little village.

He put the reasons clearly and when he finished speaking, everyone clapped him for accepting to champion our case and doing it so well. It was the first time I had attended a protest meeting, and I was proud that our village responded so sincerely and yet vehemently.

Reg was already planning to arrange a special birthday party for the nearest appropriate date after the 7* of April and we chatted about how and what to organise for that day. He made lists galore, how many friends and members of the family to invite, how to decorate our home for that day, how the catering was going to be done, and if we might have to arrange two gatherings as we thought our little home might sag under the weight of too many guests, so Reg and I shared ideas to make my sixtieth birthday a day to remember with joy.

I knew that Reg was a methodical man but until I saw the lists started on the 29th of March for the party taking place on the Saturday the 11 of April, did I realise how each day he had listed items to do with the big day.

His first page was checking napkins, cutlery, crockery, plates, wine glasses, brandy glasses and serving spoons. The next day, lists of wines, spirits to buy. Champagne bottles, tonic, fruit juices for drivers. Next he had a list of invitations to be written and so on ad Infinitum.

Reg was in his study, using the phone, and even asked me what colour scheme I had in mind for the flower arrangements to be done for the reception room. He asked Mrs. Gill King-Scott, who was a skilled flower arranger who had won prizes at the Chelsea Flower show, if she would make the flowers for us. His enthusiasm was contagious and soon we were both involved in the excitement of it all.

The Sunday before the party, Reg and I wondered how to decorate our home to make it festive but not in your face. Party balloons were not for inside our home, but for friends driving from a fair way, we had some on the large oak tree by the side of the road. We used a pink and black theme. We cut out masks in black cardboard and I pleated using pink flowery wrapping paper to make fans and also tied pink ribbons on the handle.

We stuck them on the walls of the sitting room and dining room, also one or two on the large mirror at tile end of the room. It took ages but we prepared them on the dining room table and we thought it was worth the trouble.

When Reg mentioned his intentions of arranging the party, soon after the New Year, I asked him to get in touch with Mrs. Margaret Elliott, she was the WI President on the year 1 joined in 1987 and had a very capable daughter called Emma, who made beautiful cakes and delicious sugar-spun flowers to decorate them, so Reg phoned to ask if it could be done. Those lovely flowers that were on my cake are still as beautiful today. I found a circular dish with a glass dome covering it and have still to this day those pink and white flowers.

I wonder if Emma realises how much pleasure I still have after all that time, and remembers that day.

Thursday the 8th of April, was the General Election and Reg had been asked to be a Teller at the village hall from 10am to 11am. I was secretly pleased to see him go to the hall, at least he got away from his lists and had a break in the fresh air for one hour.

As well as the six members of the family we had 29 guests and Reg organised with a lady in the village who still did catering, to give us a list of savoury dishes and salads, also a most attractive dressed salmon curved in a circle with prawns along its back, eight different sweets, and she certainly did us proud. A week later, we again invited twelve friends and enjoyed another more intimate party. So 1992 was a year when I felt really very spoilt, by Reg, his family and the good friends that came to our home.

A month after my birthday Reg and I sorted out the photos taken at the party, and decided to get a fairly large and solid photo album for just that occasion. Reg and I from the first occasion we took photos on the day of his 59th birthday on the 23rd August 1979, we started to collect memories.

We neither of us kidded ourselves that photography was a gift to either of us, unlike his son-in-law who belonged to a photographic club and obviously was talented in that skill, but strangely, as time went on, we enjoyed taking photos and putting them in albums, adding to the game that lovers and close-knit families play which we call "Do you remember when ..." We put photos of our guests, all in colourful clothes, in our book, also our replies to invitations and even birthday cards are still in that album. I sometimes look at those photos, they were part of the happy memories and time has stood still for each and every one.

At my 60th birthday party, April 1992

Jacqui cutting the cake, my 60th birthday party, April 1992

26

Following the socialising in the month of April, Reg and I spent a fun-time being involved with the sport of bowls and at last began to play and enjoy our new found sport.

Unfortunately, my experience of sport was only the ones I'd learnt at school, so apart from tennis, netball and lacrosse, I had little idea of this new game. On the other hand, Reg had played most sports ever since he was in college and his knowledge of golf and snooker were, so he was told, an advantage, so Reg soon became proficient.

On Monday, the 12th of October 5 992, at the AGM of our bowling club I accepted taking the position of Ladies Match Secretary, and was glad of the help of our Ladies Captain, who had worked closely with our first Match Secretary when our club was re-founded in 1990. There were many tasks involved and it was interesting, though more time consuming than many members thought. Apart from booking matches, home and away, so that one year ahead our fixture books could be printed with the relevant information, we also held special events, drives, matches with barbecues and tournaments with cups to be won. Also, amongst ourselves, different kind of matches were organised and by elimination the Finals took place about three weeks before the season ended and cups and shields were then taken to have the winner's names put on and at the end of the year we organised a special dinner at the Village Hall and the President at that time would present the Trophies all set out on a large table so that all the members could see them and show their appreciation to the winners. Once a month we held a committee meeting in our Pavilion on Wednesdays and discussed any ideas to improve our programme and of course read the minutes.

On the 22nd of March 1993, I decided to phone our Ladies Captain and invited her and her friend who lived opposite her and who was always at hand to show enthusiasm re the bowls club and gave them both my suggestions all being that the Committee would give their blessing to it. So I explained my suggestion. I thought it would be a good idea if we had a "Ladies Rose Bowl" day. I intended to buy a silver rose bowl on a mahogany base, with handles on each side and a crisscross over the bowl for roses to be put in. The Captain thought I meant open to all outside ladies, I said, no, that is for all our ladies to play for. The winner has her name carved on the mahogany base and keeps the trophy for one year, till the next match is played and the next lady wins it. They seemed interested and before the next committee meeting 1 made a large poster and painted in watercolour a Tea rose and one Victorian rose so that I could show it to the committee for their approval.

Reg thought it a good idea and was kind enough to add to the event as follows; I listened intently to the suggestions and right away made notes of ideas which he will mention to the men in the hope that they agree. As I told Reg, the ladies' match would start at 2pm on Sunday the 19th of June 1994 and I suggested I would do the catering for that occasion, at no cost to our ladies and having buttered bread with jam, a choice of five gateaux and to finish strawberries and cream. Reg said he will approach the men and ask them if they will serve the ladies their tea and as a gesture of goodwill wash up afterwards. Reg also said if I would like it he will order ten pink roses for the winner to receive at his own cost.

I am glad to say the men of the club were gallant and kind enough to accept Reg's request. We also asked our friend, Peter Ball, who was an accomplished photographer and a playing member of our club, to take photos of the days event and the "Rose bowl" presentation on our green. Naturally, the men's captain was asked to sort out the scores and find the winner.

So started our first "Ladies Rose Bowl" and at that time even one was enthusiastic about our Day.

Our Finals Day took place on Sunday the 11 of September, starting at 10am and lasting all day. To my surprise, I received a silver plate for the Ladies Pairs and for 6 months had the wooden shield for that event and then passed it on to my partner for the following six months.

By this time our Bowling Club had one hundred and twenty one members and came from Bromley, Chelsfield, Halstead, Orpington and Sevenoaks.

Ladies' Rose Bowl presentation to Jacqui

Bowls Finals Day – I won Ladies' Pairs with June Hayes

27

Men are like wine, some turn to vinegar,
but the best improve with age.

Pope John the XXIII

I feel very lucky that my husband, Reg, who asked me to marry him, was with the passing years, appreciative, mellow and always had loving words for me. Although his birthday was not until August I had many tasks to achieve before that date.

His party would not be a secret, as always I wanted him to share with me all the things relating to that day. Birthdays always caused a lot of fun and excitement to both of us, whatever age we were at the time, so I was busy making a list of surprises and gifts to get.

Now that I was coming up to the age of sixty-three, it was no surprise to me that some jobs, either in the garden or our home, took much longer to do than ten years ago when I used to dash around and plant shrubs, or prune existing ones, or dig over the vegetable plot, with no effort and without tiredness creeping up, so I believe I was wise to plan any jobs well in advance. Time creeps up on you if you don't stay focussed.

As spring 1995 arrived. I made use of warming soil and carefully made a list of colourful plants which would make the borders full of interest and scents coming up to the month of August, I improved on the design of certain parts of our garden, transformed my variegated holly bush into a standard, so that beneath its skirt, more flowers could bring colour. Reg offered to help by digging over beds but, if the lawns had been mown, he often started wheezing and I used to ask him to make us both a cup of tea, so that we could have a sit under the arbour and steal a few moments rest. Being keen to help,

Our back garden

he often ignored the onset of Asthma, so I found different excuses so that he did not do too much.

Faithful to his Zodiac sign (Leo) a fire sign, he loved hot colours, red, orange and sunshine yellow, so flowers of those hues appealed to him. Particularly the salmon-pink of roses or deep velvet red with wonderful scent, so planted them in different parts of the garden, I found Bourbon roses with rich scent, also tea roses like Fragrant Cloud that lives up to its name, the elegant salmon-pink of Paul Shirville with delicate petals. In the shades of Amber and Orange I planted Whisky Mac, Troika and Alpine Sunset, all three with lovely perfume.

Over the arch, modern climbers were wafting their heady scent as we walked beneath into the top garden. Compassion and School Girl, apricot and orange and also New Dawn,

236

silvery blush-pink, supposed to be a fruity fragrance, but to me the roses seemed to remind me of scented face-powder I once used in my salad days.

We were fortunate to have acid soil and so many colourful shrubs could settle happily like Rhododendrons, Pieris and Camellias. Facing south, our pineapple scented shrub with large yellow flowers became laden with them and silvery green leaves were a good contrast. It grew eventually to fourteen feet and Reg loved the sweet and fruity fragrance of it.

Two or three friends in the village had recently celebrated anniversaries and birthdays and mentioned a lady who was sensational in catering for such events, so I went to visit her and she said she would post me a list of either hot or cold dishes and I would then be able to ask Reg what he preferred. She was most helpful and would send two young ladies to help serve and take away dirty crockery and so forth, also remembered that vegetarian canapes and savoury dishes would have to be organised as Reg's daughter was a vegetarian.

Apart from his family, many members of the bowls club were invited as well as our close friends in the village and friends who lived in neighbouring counties.

I ordered a birthday cake and then wondered if there were any job I might need to do in the house. Although I was spoilt by the ability of Reg knowing how to do electrical tasks, doing woodwork and metal work, I felt he had done all that for the past fifty years and anything needed either we employed someone or if I could do easy things like putting a coat of paint or wall-papering, I would do it, no problem.

On May the 19th Reg's bowls league called "Rushmore" was playing Quebec team at the usual time 6.15pm, so once he had departed, I decided to use the time by doing a tedious job which I expected would take most of the time that Reg was away bowling.

Along the right-hand side of our drive, Reg and I had planted, when we first started to set out our front garden, a row of three feet tall golden cypresses, the length of the hedge was just over thirty-two feet. They now were usually about six and a half feet high but were now badly in need of a haircut, sides and top were untidy and needed a good trim, so I got the metal ladder and with my shears started by measuring the height which was nine inches taller than the norm. It took a fair time, bit I was pleased with my efforts and it started to look neat. 1 did not notice it at the time but to keep my balance I pressed my right knee against the tread, and by the time I had completed the side abutting the drive, I was starting to ache. The other side of the hedge was two feet higher as the sunken lawn on the other side was two feet lower, so when I dragged the ladder I found the hedge was eight feet high. I dare not stop because I could be tempted to go in and leave the job unfinished. Still, I carried on and filled two black bags with ail the cuttings. I was so pleased, Reg would be surprised, it was nearly 8pm when I went in, washed and changed my clothes. Bits of vivid golden green pieces of conifer scattered over white hair is no fashion statement, so looked a mess but it was worth the effort. Reg was surprised when he came home, but the next day my right knee was well and truly swollen. Still we were both pleased with the result.

When summer came, I asked Reg to give me some ideas regarding decorating the lounge as it was for his birthday, so didn't want girlie items on the wall. He had a good idea, we cut out in black cardboard top hats and canes and put them together on the white walls, as well as balloons, so we cut them out on the previous week of the party. I asked Reg to give me a list of wines he favoured and went to the wine merchant to get them.

At last things were coming together, the weather was kind to us, so mowing lawns were best tackled before the heat of the day, as heat is not very good for my fair skin, freckles, burnt skin and usually headaches, so once breakfast was done I did prefer to do gardening tasks early. Reg on the other hand, although he also had a fair skin, loved the warmth of the sun and it did not seem to have any adverse effect on him.

Reg's birthday party was taking place on Saturday the 26th of August at home and in the afternoon, Reg was setting out chairs and tables on the lawn and generally getting it all laid out as he wished.

But by the time I came out with cold drinks his cheeks were bright red and advised him to put some soothing cream on his face. We had twenty nine guests and the two young ladies that were sent to help were very helpful, they passed the canapes round and Reg did the honours bringing chilled white wines to our friends.

It was lovely to hear laughter coming in from the garden and we took a few photos before calling them in to the dining room to tuck in to the buffet Towards the end of the evening we brought in the birthday cake and Reg cut the first piece. We toasted him with Champagne.

When the guests had gone, we locked up and sat in our lounge feeling tired but pleased that all went well. Then Reg put his arm round my shoulder and said, "It's been a lovely day, you know how to spoil me, don't you?"

"I do hope so," I replied.

"It's late, bed, yes?"

"Bed, yes."

28

Apart from our shared interest of bowling and working every fortnight at Vavasseurs Wood with members of the Tree Society, Reg and I supported other charities which involved time, money and effort, but when you live in a village any help given to the village is right and as neither of us could stand inactivity, it made life all the more enjoyable. Soon after settling in our home, Reg had been invited to join a club called PROBUS (Professional Business) men, usually retired who met for lunch and enjoyed a good speaker. They took it in turn to bring the wines for their table and once a year organised a special meal and brought their wives to it as well as a week's holiday in the countryside, the club was in Orpington and he enjoyed the fellowship. Similarly, I was invited to join the Wives Fellowship in our village, once a month a meeting took place in each members houses, had tea or coffee with biscuits and had a speaker. 1 also attended the Women's Institute and used to help serve and wash up once a month at the over 60s lunch club. I drove one lady, Mrs Florrie Neave and took her back as she was unsteady on her legs. I did that for ten years. Reg still attended his Lodge though it was a long drive now we were in Kent, as he had to go to Essex which was not too bad when he worked in the City of London, but found it now a little tiring. Eventually, joined a nearer Lodge, but age and health made it difficult to carry on as he would have liked. Also, Reg enjoyed the occasional game of whist at Halstead Village Hall, also we used to play Table Tennis in that same hall, but soon gave that up, time was getting short and so was our energy.

I still carried on with my duties at the "Abbeyfield Society" which I first was asked to join while living in Orpington, if I would like to be on the "House" committee, which then meant a monthly meeting at No. 18, Tower Road, Orpington and also a weeks duty visiting the residents, taking them to hospital for hearing-aid tests or in the summer, Reg used to drive two of them in his car to country places like Boughbeech Reserve, we had already booked the appropriate number of seats and after enjoying the views on the terrace, we all gathered in the tearoom and enjoyed a good tea. I was with the Abbeyfield Society for fifteen years and enjoyed the friendships that one made over the years. I left because the health of my husband was giving me concern and I decided that I would prefer to get involved with things closer to home. Christmas this year, was a time of worry, Reg was feeling unwell and without the consideration shown by our doctor, I don't know how we would have managed. It was freezing cold, car doors were frozen solid, and it seems the worst weather possible was upon us earlier than normal.

On Wednesday, 27th of December, the doctor visited Reg at lunchtime. The next day, Reg was feeling worse. The doctor came again and give him a thorough examination, gave a prescription for water tablets and another tablet. He said, "If dizzy when lying down to phone him even if in the middle of the night." Next Friday, doctor visited again between 1 and 2pm. Saturday was Wendy's fortieth birthday. I sent flowers to their home, had to cancel the restaurant as Reg too unwell. New Year's Day, Colin and Wendy arrive. Gave her a birthday gift and made lunch. After they went Reg felt very tired. We woke up to a freezing fog, Colin knew Reg had an appointment at Chelsfield Park Hospital for a blood test so was given a lift. Our doctor called again at 4.15 and changed amount of tablets.

On the 8th January, Reg had to return to the hospital to see a heart specialist at 9.45 am. Four days later, I suppose after getting results from blood test, our doctor calls. Reg is low in salt and potassium. Under active thyroid, so one Thyroxine tablet a day and two Potassium tablets. Will get them first thing in the morning. Sunday, the sun is warm, Reg is keen for a stroll in the garden but the temperature is too low for comfort. Two days later, icy winds return to remind us that February is a month when cold weather must be taken seriously.

March was also cold and windy, but Reg started to feel stronger and by April the spring sunshine cheered him up a little.

On the 22nd of April we celebrated our seventh wedding anniversary and I am glad to say Reg felt better. I suggested we forego to a restaurant and spent our evening at home. I feel he is not as fit as he's trying to pretend and worry over him. He seems to be in the wars right now, phoned for an appointment with the dentist as he has toothache. Although, like most men, Reg wants to drive himself to Orpington, I urge him to let me drive in case the dentist decides to remove the offending tooth. Just as well I did, the tooth was removed with an abscess attached to it and broke in three pieces. Poor man, there seems to be no end to his problems. At this time, Reg was the Men's Match Secretary at the bowls club as well as Vice President and realising his health was below par, asked another member to come over so that he could help him to take over the job of secretary and how the men's fixtures were organised. He called on the 1st of May and spent the morning here making notes about it and Reg helping with information. Reg is still attending hospital for different tests and feels frustrated that he is not up to scratch to either attend meetings or even put his name down for matches. Slowly, slowly there's no need to rush. Sport is important to some people but health is much more so and he had to find patience from somewhere.

Tuesday the 21st May, I made an appointment for Reg and would drive him to the surgery as his chest felt tight and uncomfortable. I suggested to get the doctor as we got to bed but Reg would not hear of it. Will go after a night's sleep.

At one thirty am, Reg woke me up, pain was worse, and also down his left arm. It was obvious to me that I had to phone the doctor urgently. He told me to phone the ambulance. Dressed at the speed of light, checked house keys and money. Almost within five minutes the door-bell sounded. There stood my doctor who said came to give me moral support and went up to our bedroom. Reg was sitting in his armchair looking pale. He examined him and I noticed the doctor's pyjamas were sticking out under his trousers, he wrote a letter for me to give to the hospital doctor on duty. Almost at once the doorbell sounded and there were the ambulance men. The poor doctor left to go back to bed but I certainly appreciated him coming over so quickly. Reg was well looked after in the ambulance and at 3am we reached the hospital. Reg was wheeled into a side waiting room where another man was waiting on a trolley, gave my precious letter to the doctor on duty. Reg was still telling me his chest was hurting as well as his left arm, when to my astonishment, the doctor who I saw reading the letter in question gave Reg an indigestion tablet. It was now three am and still not even a pulse reading or anything else was being done. Two hours later, another indigestion tablet which made me see red. A blood sample was taken which apparently had to be sent to another hospital about confirming it was a heart attack. I cornered another doctor and asked him to give my husband something to take his chest pains away and at last an injection was given. By then, without the pain, Reg relaxed so I dashed to a phone and asked his son Colin to come over at once and told him what had happened. In ten minutes Colin and Wendy arrived and I was at last feeling that support was at hand.

I won't mention the hospital, anyway it no longer exists, but I was absolutely disgusted with the lax attitude of the chap we saw. Next, at seven am, they decided to take him to Farnborough hospital, Colin and Wendy would accompany him in the ambulance and suggested I took a taxi back home and have two or three hours sleep and visit Reg later in the morning. He was in Jay Ward, bed no. 7. His pulse and heart monitored and told me how he had been looked after so well. Reg was not finding it easy to get into the routine in hospital, but he knew that rest and being looked after was necessary, so we had a long chat and made a note of anything he wished me to bring him tomorrow.

On Friday the 24th of May, I visited Reg at 10am. Four visitors called, as did his son Colin. Many phone calls came at our home from good friends in the village. All day long Reg was having treatment. Next day, Saturday, Reg told me he had been given since 6.30pm last night two drugs, one to thin the blood, the other to dilate the arteries. Had had oxygen mask on all night. He was having a scan at 11am at the Brook Hospital, Woolwich. Reg didn't return to his hospital ward till 3.30pm. Each day I visited more tests were being made.

Monday, the 27th May, Reg explains that he went to the Queen Elizabeth Hospital, just two patients in the ambulance. The Atomic Department was closed and had to be opened for Reg to have a radioactive scan on his lungs. At a later date, he will have a treadmill test and artery scan

Tuesday the 28th, visited Reg at 3pm, received lots of 'Get Well' cards. Our local Rector, Rev. David Flagg, called to see him and had a cheerful chat with him. Will visit him when he returns home. On Thursday the 30th of May, Colin arrives at 10.45 has a coffee and drives our Renault to the hospital to fetch Reg home. Reg is very tired, but so happy to be coming home. Took letter from the hospital and gave to Gill, our Doctor's wife for her husband to see. I was glad Colin went to fetch Reg at the hospital as no doubt there would be waiting for the hospital letter of discharge to be made available, Reg would be given medication and instruction about it, also having given a zip-bag with his outdoor clothes, it would take a while to get dressed and say goodbye to patients in the ward who wished him well.

So I chose to stay home and wait expectantly for his coming home. Today, the 30th May, was too early for roses, but strangely enough, his favourite rose bush had three scented roses on it, no other roses had flowered as yet and I cut all three and put them in water. Although I didn't expect them home yet, I kept going to the porch to see if the car was coming. At last, I heard it come up the drive. Colin walked round to the passenger seat and helped his father out. As Colin was getting the zip-bag out of the boot, Reg looked at the front door and as soon as 1 opened it he smiled at me and opened his arms wide. I gently stepped forward and he put his arms round me, no words were needed. Colin had disappeared into the house, but somehow the relief and the joy of touching him was so great, that we stood rooted to the spot. I suddenly realised that he was probably wanting to sit down and relax. I offered to get a cold drink for Colin, but he refused and seemed to sense that his father was so relieved to be home again. We sat on the settee and I could not quite believe that after those seven long days, although I visited every day, it was so good to have him home again. Was glad to visit every day, but the wires on his chest, those monitors on the side table, if not trained to understand what they mean can be rather frightening. Soon after being home, Reg started to pick up different knick-knacks on the mantelshelf, smell the scented roses I had picked from the garden and placed on the coffee table. I asked him what he was doing, he just said "I have missed the familiar things we have collected over time and enjoy touching them."

I should have realised, that even in that short time away, Reg, tactile and sensitive, was pleased to see the souvenirs we had given to each other these last few years. We both had an emotional day, feeling tired but so happy.

On Monday the 3rd of June, at just after 2pm, our doctor called to talk to Reg about his heart attack. Later in the afternoon our good friend Sue Gooch called to see Reg, also our immediate neighbours visited to welcome him home.

I tried to catch up on my planting annuals in the bed in front of our old conservatory, but started to feel unwell. When I came into the kitchen, Reg noticed I had spots all over my shoulders and back. At ten thirty am next day see the doctor, I have chicken-pox. Must stay home all week as it's contagious. Phoned the Bowls Club as can't play in the leagues till I am clear of it. I am fortunate that my friend Sue, who has had chicken pox, offers to get my prescription and get some shopping for us and I am appreciative of her kindness. Reg is advised by his doctor to gently get back to some form of exercise, but gentle walks before attempting two hours of bowling. Glad to say, he listens to the advice and makes full use of our garden, so that if tired he can have a sit down under the arbour, have a sip of tea and a rest. I did not play many bowls matches, I preferred to be home as Reg was beginning to be little frustrated not playing his new found sport.

July the 7th was our third Ladies Rose Bowl Day and Reg said he would like to support me by being there. It was a lovely sunny day. The usual bouquet of pink roses had been ordered by phone by Reg and I asked the Men's Captain if the ladies could again count on the gentlemen's team to do the honours for us.

Everyone was pleased to welcome Reg back to the pavilion and all the food was already there, as I had brought it in the morning, all the gateaux, strawberries and everything needed for our tea. At two pm the match started. At the end of the match the score cards were collected and the Men's Captain had the task of totting up the points to find the winner. We put a small table on the green with the Rose Bowl, the pink roses and a small little token mahogany plaque with a brass plate "KNOCKHOLT B.C. LADIES ROSE BOWL WINNER 1996". The ladies' captain was advised by her opposite number of the winner. Much to my surprise I won by fourteen points and could not believe it. I tried to play as well as I could and I was pleased for Reg as he was so happy for me. What a perfect day.

29

Slowly July, a sunny month with warm breezes, helped Reg feel a little less fragile, though he still missed not bowling. By August, he asked his doctor if he could pace himself to get back to his sport and was told it would be beneficial as long as he didn't do too much.

Spoke to my good friend Sue and she suggested to drive Reg to the bowls club as I was playing at Petts Wood that afternoon, and they practised bowling together. They played only four ends but Reg was pleased to bowl again.

The following Saturday there was a drive and a barbecue organised at the pavilion and Sue again was kind enough to fetch us for the barbecue, but by 8.30pm we left to go home as we were both tired.

PROBUS club were organising six days at a hotel in Church Straiten in Shropshire by coach and Reg was keen to go and not have to do the driving. We put our names down and left Sunday the 29 of September. We were somewhat surprised to see a lady get in the drivers seat on this long coach but off we went. I have never known a lady drive so well and with such confidence, nothing fazed her and when we reached the valleys and hills of that beautiful county the scenery was stunning and both Reg and I really enjoyed the journey.

We didn't realise that the hotel was on top of a hill and the road leading to the entrance was a tortuous and very difficult road which was obviously made years before enormous coaches had to negotiate it, but it was no problem at all for our efficient lady driver and when she stopped outside the entrance to our hotel, on the spur of the moment, all of us clapped her for her brilliant driving. I thing she was taken aback, but she certainly was an accomplished driver. A few days later our chairman told us that when chatting with her discovered that she had been trained in the army and certainly she knew how to handle a very long and heavy vehicle.

The food and accommodation was good and we were much taken by the lovely countryside. We also had a day in Shrewsbury and enjoyed it all. In surrounding villages we found lovely little shops full of attractive pottery also handmade knitwear as well as book shops we were drawn to.

On free mornings we went for gentle walks and took photos as round every corner views were there to make a picture. We visited Warwick on our last leg home and arrived early evening pleased to have spent a few days in a lovely county.

December brought us sad news. Uncle Raymond passed away in his nursing home on Sunday the 15th. We heard the news on Monday and Reg hired a car to take him to Newport Pagnell, arrange the funeral and do the necessary paperwork. Went first thing in the morning and returned home by four pm. The cremation was taking place on Friday the 20th and it all went well. He was ninety-one years of age and had been a widower for the past six years. We were both sorry to lose him, but felt at least he was at peace and no longer suffered the loneliness.

We were quite glad to see the back of 1996, Reg's heart attack and the sad loss of his uncle, we just hoped 1997 would be kinder to us, though as long as we are together we will be all right.

1997 made its presence known by bitter winds and snow. It's usually at its worst in February, but snow was already covering the road.

My left eye was very painful and after a visit to our doctor was advised to make an appointment with an eye surgeon. Even as early as the 26th of December, Reg sounded very congested and I had to phone the surgery for Antibiotics.

Drive there the next day to get the tablets. Saturday, I feel heady, joints ache and start a bad cough. This time I feel awful and Reg calls the doctor for me. He says that I have got this virulent flu and a temperature. Gives me medicine for seven days, three days later my appointment at the hospital re suspected rodent ulcer has to be cancelled and booked for next Thursday. Four days later I feel worse, it's difficult to breathe, so Reg calls the doctor again. I was given a new course of tablets and an inhalant. On the TV news, the government admits there is a 'flu epidemic. Still it's snowing and Reg had to cancel again my appointment till Thursday the 30th of January. When that day comes, the eye surgeon tells me the rodent ulcer has travelled to the inside, next to the tear duct. It means either radiotherapy or removal of the ulcer, than plastic surgery to follow. He advised me to consult his mentor in London and will send a letter with details this very day. Eye drops are given to me to reduce swelling.

A post office go-slow caused my letter to reach the specialist in London nine days later. The delays were so upsetting but as soon as the letter was received the specialist phoned at our home, and we arranged for a car to take Reg and I to the Chelsea and Westminster hospital.

I think that both Reg and I were apprehensive about our forthcoming visit but the eye surgeon who I first visited could not speak more highly of the Consultant and Ophthalmic Plastic Surgeon and was confident that I would be in good hands.

On Tuesday the 25th of February, Reg and I were taken in his consulting room, although I was a little nervous I was put at my ease and my eye was examined.

He made a sketch to show Reg what the procedure would be and although I told him I was scared that I would not be able to see sufficiently to look after my husband, do my painting and any sport he completely took those morbid fears away. Explained that at St. Thomas' hospital a cancer expert would use micro-surgery and then I would go to the Chelsea and Westminster for the next procedure. Naturally the operation for plastic surgery was going to be performed under a general anaesthetic so I would be unaware of anything. He explained to Reg that just one and a half inch of the inside of my lower lip would be removed and placed where the tumour had been removed, then the skin of the left cheek would be rotated to cover the wound and then the stitching would be completed. Reg was amazed that such a difficult procedure was explained as if it's an everyday occurrence, but soon felt confident about the skill of our surgeon. The day for the first operation was fixed for Tuesday the 11 of March 9am St. Thomas' hospital. Reg, although doing his best to appear relaxed, was so worried about all this, he went quiet and sometimes didn't hear what was said, as he was thinking of what the outcome of the different procedures to be done. He checked and double checked the time our taxi was calling, of course for the past thirteen years our Halstead taxi lady had become a kindly friend and was going to drive us to St. Thomas' then take us to the next hospital and after that take Reg home.

At 6.45am, the car was collecting us and at 9am it all started. It was done with a local anaesthetic. I had three separate procedures, after each one a nurse guided me to a waiting room, while an analysis was taken, then back again for a second one, then a third, then Halleluiah, noon they told me I could join my husband and our good friend Pat Turner, the taxi lady, and go to the Chelsea and Westminster. I remember this gentle nurse guiding me to this outer room. naturally with a thick pad over my left eye and a plastic shield and at last I felt Reg's hand on mine and heard his gentle voice. Apparently I had to sit in a wheelchair and be taken on this long walk of corridors and lifts and eventually got in the taxi. As I told Reg, that's one difficult hurdle behind me, tomorrow's operation will be over when I wake up. We were escorted to room No. 4, and Reg suggested I have a lovely evening meal because tomorrow I will not be able to enjoy food as much.

So after we had kissed each other "Au Revoir" I sat in the armchair and thought of Reg going home to an empty house. Miss Pat Turner, sometime later, told me she knew how concerned Reg was on their journey back to our home, as he went very quiet and sat in the passenger seat, his hands gripping his gloves and his knuckles white.

On Wednesday, the 12th of March at 10 am the surgeon came to see me in his green gown – I did not recognise him. Since 6.30am when a blood sample was taken and 8am when the anaesthetist also called, it had been a busy morning. I was told 12 noon I would be taken down to surgery. At 3pm the operation was over but didn't come to till 4pm. I kept hearing my name called, vaguely remember and as I was lying down thought I had been in a road accident and had forgotten I was having an operation today, so took a long time to realise I was in hospital. The memory can certainly play tricks, can't it? I woke up with an oxygen mask on. Reg phoned at 6pm, but spoke to the sister in charge. It seems that I was advised tomorrow I will be able to go home, but not till after 11am.

The surgeon came to my room and said after an examination, I will be able to wash and dress, after the drip on my arm was removed.

Three other gentlemen (perhaps were students or junior surgeons, I don't know which) were ushered in so that the surgeon could explain what the surgery involved.

Although so many medical terms were used I did manage to understand what a skilled and detailed procedure was done and hoped the three attentive listeners learnt a lot from his explanation. I was given nine items of antibiotics, cream, spare plastic shield to cover the eye and special tape.

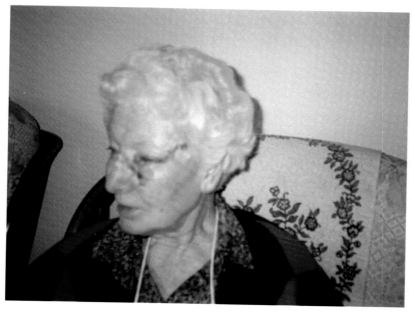

Jacqui's eye surgery

Once free of the drip, I went to the bathroom to have a wash, but more than that to peer into the mirror, getting as near as I could as everything was blurred. Did not really recognise my reflection through the plastic shield, can see a few white stitch tapes, blue/yellow bruising, swollen eye also swollen lower lip, red cut across my left temple and also a half-inch cut down the left side of my nose. What a sight! Hope Reg won't find it too difficult to see. I go and sit in my armchair and wait for Reg to arrive. I have put my watch on my wrist, but I can't read the dial. Feel so excited about going home, but am nervous. Listening for his footsteps. Knock on the door, my usual nurse popped her head in and said, "Your husband has arrived. Just ring the bell when you are ready to go." She disappeared and Reg came in.

He very gently put his arms round me and softly put his right cheek against mine, only forty eight hours have passed, but we have missed each other, but now he's taking me home. I know he will take care of me, as he's always done. We arrive home at 2pm but feel tired, so tired – but very happy.

30

I had been advised by the surgeon, when I go to bed, to put a pillow on either side of my head so that I don't turn over and push off the plastic shield over my eye as advised, we did just that. When we got to bed, I could not see Reg, I could not go to sleep hugging him, all I could do was hold his hand. Told him in the morning I felt like a filling between two buns, still until it all heals and my stitches are removed I guess it's sensible.

My eye was stuck together and I was glad that the surgeon phoned and gave Reg his mobile number in case of any problems during the weekend. Friends called with flowers and the scent of flowers was all over the house. Marjorie, on behalf of the "Wives Fellowship" brought pink roses, the W.I. President came with Freesias and Carnations, Pat Cook and her husband Noel came with a lovely card and Primulas, Sue Gooch with Begonias and Margaret Croston of the Bowls club gave me pink roses. Margaret Elliott gave me six new-laid eggs from her Bantams and Claire Allbury gave pretty primroses. Everyone spoilt me, it was incredible.

Penny phoned, will call tomorrow on her way to London. Barbara and Ray arrived from Orpington also with flowers. Stella Bellhouse who finds walking difficult arrived with an enormous bouquet of home grown flowers.

On Friday the 21st of March, Derek Blundell starts doing our garden, such a help as we are getting on. Worked for two hours and in that time had done all the lawns and edges. We left it to him to decide what was needed and were so pleased with the way he looked after our garden. We felt lucky to have a gardener who took such pride in his skills. Reg and Derek Blundell got on well, and if any particular task was required, Derek did it at once.

My sixty-fifth birthday was as usual a day when Reg spoiled me, firstly I opened the front door to a lady carrying a basket of spring flowers and as well as a lovely birthday card Reg put a pile of letters in front of me at breakfast so that I could enjoy looking at them and putting them on the mantelshelf. Also he gave me a beautiful brooch with sparkling purple stones, wonder whether he knew that purple is the colour of healing? He took my hand and led me to the settee, then said, "I have a surprise for you – I hope you will enjoy it, I thought after all your problems and your eye trouble it will be something to enjoy."

I could not wait to find out what Reg had arranged, but first told me we would start our surprise on Sunday the 20th of April. He seemed to enjoy keeping me on tenterhooks but I eventually managed to find out what the surprise was.

Reg had booked a short break of four days to Holland, going by coach and boat and a visit to the "KEUKENHOF" Gardens. The hotel was booked and he had booked a taxi to get to Orpington to board the coach at 6.10am. Found out the park had eighty acres, six million bulbs, tulips, daffodils, hyacinths and others all in flower. The shrubs were full of blossom, ponds and fountains. It all sounded lovely. We would return home Thursday and we would be able to celebrate our anniversary on the 22nd of April.

On board the coach we could have tea, coffee or chocolate and the courier, a lady, was very knowledgeable of the Netherlands and explained anything we didn't know. Met some lovely people and enjoyed every minute. Took photos whilst walking in that colourful park and they still bring back happy memories.

Whilst I was attending London hospital for post-operative examinations, poor Wendy was having troubles of her own. Pains in her breast caused her to seek advice from her doctor, who sent her at once to hospital and she had her breast removed for cancer. She was very brave and kept herself focused, but I can understand how Colin must have been shattered. Soon after, her right thigh caused problems, a secondary cancer made it imperative that a metal thigh bone was inserted in her leg. On Wednesday the 21st of May, Reg and I went to see her in hospital, and could not take in the speed with which all that had happened. On the 10th of July, more problems in my left eye, had to go to Queen Mary's for a dye injection and take a photo of my eye.

Wendy was now alone, but feeling weaker. The Hospice Nurses were with her for the two nights before the inevitable happened. Colin phoned to say Wendy died that morning, Monday the 14th of July. Only forty-one and a half years old; how terribly young. We said our goodbyes on Tuesday the 22nd of July at a Requiem Mass at the St. Joseph's Church where twelve years ago we saw them married.

I am still under the care of the surgeon and will have to be for the next five years, but on the 10th of September, was told I can now drive again and endeavour to bowl.

On the 22nd of September, we go to Sevenoaks Station and pick up the coach to go to Bruges for three days. Had a good hotel and had many strolls around gardens and canals. Enjoyed the lovely chocolates and saw some made in a "chocolatier" window. It was a short visit, but we used every moment to suit our interests. The beautiful lace shops were lovely, bought a few lace items for our home as well as for friends.

Come October, we both had our flu jabs, but Reg has to go to hospital re: diabetes so will have to take tablets for that.

The 30th of December went to Eastbourne to the Burlington Hotel to spend the New Year Festivities and return home on Friday the second of January. So we said goodbye to 1997 and hoped 1998 would bring happiness instead of sadness.

31

Our hopes were mostly answered as 1998 was a year of happy events, birthday festivities of good friends and short holiday breaks which we enjoyed.

Although January was my least favourite month having suffered two sad losses in 1980 and 1981, this year our very good friend Eileen Jones celebrated her eightieth on the 24th of the month, but also invited us to a tea party on Tuesday the 27th in the foyer of the Village Hall. Eileen made us very welcome when we arrived in this village in 1984, and we had got to know each other well.

I could not believe that time had gone so quickly, it said 80 on her birth certificate, but she was very young at heart, was an accomplished painter and Reg and I were so pleased to be invited to wish her all the best. So many friends in the village were there and as she said in her little speech at the end of our tea, "I know I am celebrating my 80th but in my heart I am still 20 and have to realise that when I am dashing through the village in my car, I must remember the speed limit. Luckily I am blessed with good health so can enjoy many pastimes."

It was an enjoyable occasion and soon after our Bowls Club organised a Bowls Week at Bembridge on the Isle of Wight and so enjoyed five days of sport as well as a very special anniversary dinner in a hotel by the sea a few miles away from Bembridge. Friday the 24th of April we returned home.

Friends of ours had just returned from a holiday in County Cork, Ireland and were full of the places they visited and the beautiful countryside, so Reg booked five days there but decided to go by air as it would have been a long journey to even reach the coast. Mind you, we went via Gatwick by

Turbo Prop and though it didn't bother Reg, I thought it was bit slow. A coach took us to ROSCARBERRY, West Cork and our hotel "CELTIC ROSS". It was very comfortable, but we both smiled when we saw our big bed, it was so wide as well as long, it had three pillows side by side. I guess we will have to get used to the Irish sense of humour.

Many things were somewhat different over there, but it all contributed to a holiday with a difference. Even road signs were sometimes slightly different. The one that amused us and so we took a photo of it, was the sign which in England is an upturned triangle just as you emerge from a small road into a main road. Here in the UK it reads "GIVE WAY" but in Ireland it reads "YIELD" which one does not expect to see.

So many places we visited, but the striking difference was the vivid green of the countryside, and the fascinating brogue that people speak, any accent from the different parts which speak in English enriches so much the time spent in that country. You can't possibly get tired of listening to people explaining their country's ways and customs in the manner of the Irish. The last day of our holiday came and we made our way to Cork Airport.

Unfortunately, I had not been aware that in those planes, the air is recycled and any germs are spread around for any passengers to breathe in and that's what occurred on our journey home. By the time we reached Gatwick Airport, and sat in the taxi, I felt so tired, I fell asleep all the way home. The next morning, I felt so ill, Reg called the doctor. I had a virus and had to take massive pills (large pills which would have suited a horse) every cup of tea swallowed thereafter had a metallic taste and by the end of the day Reg was also feeling bad. Neither of us wanted to eat, only drink. A week later, feeling still rough, we both needed another visit from the doctor and another course of those enormous pills. Nevertheless, however difficult they were to swallow, after fourteen days, they made us well again and it was lovely to be able to enjoy a good meal at last.

September brought some very happy news to us, Reg's grandson Thomas and his young lady, Vicky, announced their coming wedding and invited us to be there and join in the festivities.

Vicky's parents lived in Brighton and the service was taking place at the Methodist Church there and the reception was going to be at the Courtaulds Hotel in Hove.

We were going there by car on Friday the 18th of September and the wedding was the next day Saturday and the reception after. Sunday, the 20th we return home.

Reg came back from a "PROBUS" lunch in Orpington with the news that this autumn holiday trip was taking place in Harrogate for five days and thought he would let his daughter know so that we could meet on one of the days. We were leaving Knockholt on Sunday the 4th of October and would be back home on Friday the ninth. His daughter Penny and her husband Jim had moved to Harrogate because of a new position in the Energy business some years ago and we had not ever seen their new home. We chose one day and excused ourselves not going on one of the trips with our friends, but explained we were going to share a day out in Reg's daughter's company.

So we were invited to coffee and biscuits at their home, then we went to "Betty" for lunch. Afterwards, Penny drove us in the beautiful Yorkshire countryside, were taken to a country garden to see the flowers, though many were not at their best as rain the previous week knocked most of them down.

Had a cup of tea at the tearooms adjoining the gardens and were driven back to their house.

Hopefully, Jim would be back from business. They showed us their spacious home, her husband was particularly keen to show us his new piano which he can play very well. Then we were driven back to our hotel for the evening meal.

After all those years living in Harrogate, it was the first occasion we were invited to their home and wonder when the next occasion will come about.

Two days after our return we received an invitation to a very special birthday party.

Our old friend Sid Bird was celebrating his ninetieth birthday on Sunday the 18th of October and was having a birthday luncheon at Donnington Manor, only ten minutes away from our home.

When Reg was first approached about taking part in resuscitating a bowls club, Mr. Bud Coburn was the person who injected enthusiasm in Reg and they both enjoyed the challenge of trying to start a new club.

When 1990 arrived our friend Sid Bird called at our pavilion and met Reg, asking if he could become a member, so our membership secretary was contacted and he joined our club. Sid was a gentle man and an experienced sportsman who had, similar to Reg, played many sports over the years and was still playing golf. Reg and Sid had many things in common, they enjoyed each other's sense of humour and an appreciation of good food. Sid's wife was a Belgian lady and a wonderful cook. Sid, although now a widower, always spoke with much regard and affection about her and all three men were good friends.

We so enjoyed the lunch party and admired the energy and "joie de vivre" Sid showed, he so enjoyed both friends and family members who came to wish him well. He was always included in birthday parties, New Years Eve parties, he was such a loyal friend.

As soon as the Christmas festivities were over we went to Eastbourne and came home on the 2nd of January.

1998 had been a year full of celebrations and sharing friends happy times, Reg and I thank our lucky stars that since our settling in this Kentish village our life together has been great.

32

1999 was a slightly quieter year, Reg had suggested to me that a five day break this April just outside Paris would be pleasant. We would go by coach and stay in the suburbs and would celebrate my sixty-seventh birthday and reminisce of the exciting visit together way back in 1981. It does not seem possible it was eighteen years ago.

As the coach took us to our hotel, the courier was explaining that the mayor of that particular district was very fond of gardens, so every roundabout or green space on our way to the hotel was absolutely full of flowers very tastefully planted and made the journey very pleasant. The hotel was called "LA CHAUMIERE", it was comfortable and the food was great.

Although there was a programme of visits to interesting places, we had one day to ourselves and took the metro to the centre of Paris and wandered around as we pleased.

The courier was easy-going and certainly knew Paris well. Reg and I discovered a Thai restaurant five minutes walk from where we stayed, we went there on my birthday and enjoyed both the food and the welcome received from the staff. Exploring the area, we also found a lovely park where we strolled and the spring flowers were a sight to behold. We spent a day visiting Versailles and the five days flew by.

Although it was such a totally different holiday to our first trip abroad together all those years ago, we soon made friends and both of us being older we were relaxed and enjoyed it all in a laid back manner. The frisson of excitement of eighteen years ago, was replaced by an appreciation of just being together. However different the Paris holiday was it was as wonderful as our first experience in the City of light.

We went on a boat trip on the Seine and recalled our first trip, having dinner and toasting each other with a glass of wine, but on this occasion we just held hands and remembered it all. Friday the ninth of April came too soon and we returned to England, but we both were looking forward to seeing our home again.

As June arrived, at last, Reg and I made plans to choose and put in a new bathroom suite. It was the last awkward job to be done, bathrooms and kitchens seem to disrupt the whole household but as we had a shower room next to our upstairs bedroom it was possible to, at long last, bid farewell to that appalling "Avocado" suite with the matching tiles dotted about with over-ripe apricot flowers, most of its grout flaking off and when I sat in the bath, as I told Reg, felt as if I was sitting in an avocado salad; not nice at all.

So we enquired from our usual neighbour's son who was skilled at tiling, electric work, plumbing, plastering and all kind of manual skills and he gave us a brochure of from Armitage Shanks' bathroom appliances. Gone had the gaudy colours of the seventies, mulberry, cinnamon brown and electric blues that made your hair stand on end, now soft feminine shades as well as clinical white were on offer and we both decided, as the bathroom was fairly long but not very wide, to choose a light colour. A very pale rosebud pink, bought pale pink wall ceramic tiles, a few with a delicate flower in the centre of it.

A skip was ordered to chuck the offending bathroom suite and remove piping which was very amateurish. Plastering and replacing pipes, boxed in to keep nice lines were done, though the weather was sweltering. Each day, when we are alone, we peer and appreciate the transformation occurring in our bathroom. I must get four rolls of wallpaper and must wait for the delivery of the tiles. In a shop in Orpington I found the perfect material for curtains, tiny pink roses with a background of leaves, and ordered them to be made.

Once the light fittings are done it's ready for the christening. The luxury of relaxing in the bath in a delicate shade instead of that awful green is a joy. And the icing on the cake, Reg brings me a cup of tea and massages my back with Givenchy foam bath. Lovely!

In early October, I was asked if I would take on the task of President of the WI, was very surprised and to be honest did not think I was that knowledgeable of the Women's Institute background to be able to do it, was told that the secretary would help in any way if I was not too sure of procedure.

Mentioned it to Reg and he seemed more confident than I that I could do it, so on the 18th October 1999, I had to take the meeting and take the job on for the next three years.

When you live in a village you meet friends at the village shop, at charity events, at meeting so you become so used to seeing each other that when illness or worse happens, it's as if a member of your family has been touched and this year so many friends have left us.

We were both so shocked by our next door neighbour, Silvia Nightingale, who had welcomed us on our arrival in 1984. At least, she's at peace and no longer in pain. The Christmas season so often brings sad news as well as joyous tidings.

On the 30th of December, we went to Eastbourne for 4 days and saw the new Millennium in. I wonder what it will hold for us.

33

On the day of our return home, Reg was most upset to receive a phone call from his childhood friend. Ray Johnson, announcing that his dear wife Doreen had passed away on New Year's Day. Reg had often mentioned her as she was a petite and dainty lady and Reg had been Ray's best man on his wedding day on the 28th of January 1942.

Quite soon after Ray was posted overseas and although the two friends were the same age, war separated them. The next day, Thursday, another friend, Margaret Elliott's husband, Jim, passed away of lung cancer.

The cruel month of January still brings sad news. As spring arrives and June the 7th, a Wednesday, The Kent West Kent Federation of Women's Institute (KWKFWI) Triennial General Meeting was taking place at Wembley and as the President, I had to be the delegate. I picked up the coach at the "Vine", Sevenoaks. We were told by the W.I. Chairwoman that the Prime Minister, Tony Blair, had asked to address the meeting. When he began to make his speech, it was to boast about the Health Service and sounded like a Party Political broadcast. The members near the stage on my right, started to slow clap and everyone was muttering under their breath, it was so unexpected. The Prime Minister looked very put out and clasping his hands started to walk backwards from the microphone. Immediately our Chairwoman took the initiative and using her microphone said, "Please can members of the WI remember that we must respect the views of our guest, even if we do not necessarily share them and stop this heckling, it is not the kind of behaviour we can allow ourselves to be dragged into."

The Prime Minister hesitantly walked toward the microphone and continued his speech, a low murmur of voices was still coming from the audience, but we listened in silence. Noticed that after the speech he left the stage and I presume left Wembley.

When we got back to the coach, of course everyone was talking about the unexpected events of the day. As soon as the coach started the driver put on the radio and all at once we were given our afternoon's headlines as reported on the BBC.

It is not often that a Prime Minister is booed and slow-clapped by a 10,000 strong audience of women, makes the headlines in the National Press and the next day everyone in our village was buying the Sevenoaks Chronicle to read all about it. As the President, I had to make a report and relate the days happening. I never imagined that my very first visit to a General Meeting of that magnitude would develop into such an amazing event. One thing I did get from this visit, apart from finding the place full of draughts, was a viral infection which laid me up but was eventually cleared by the care of our doctor. One whole week's meetings had to be cancelled, but the medication given and the looking after by Reg, soon got me fit and well.

A few weeks ago, at a WI meeting, names were put in a hat to be drawn, regarding a bursary for Denham College, so that members wishing to take a course in languages or arts and crafts etc, could book for both accommodation and the course of their choice. I was quite surprised and felt pleased to get that opportunity, though I did not know too much about it. Members who had visited the place explained to me all about it. One could get a room in the main house, but dotted around the grounds were cottages with single or double accommodation and also studios where the teaching took place.

I went home so excited about it and explained it all to Reg who having looked through the brochure a while ago, knew I was interested in a short three day course called "Atmospheric

Water-colour Painting". I wrote to the college but it was so popular that two courses were already folly booked and the next available one was in January 2001. I felt a little disappointed but Reg urged me to book it and look forward to enjoy and learn something I get so much pleasure doing. So I did the necessary and was advised to take the coach at Victoria Coach station for Gloucester Green Coach station at Oxford. Taxi to Marcham, only twenty minutes ride. Nearer the time more details regarding accommodation etc, would be sent to me. Today, Saturday the 29th July, the Knockholt Carnival was taking place. As I was walking along Main Road, met Pat Cook who was pushing Noel in a wheelchair. He looked ill, yellow and so thin. I was shaken by his appearance, he was always such a tall, strong man. Kissed him on both cheeks and hurried home while his wife Pat was taking him to watch the Carnival for a while. At 3pm Pat was driving Noel past our house back to the hospital. Reg and I spoke about the many times when going on holiday with the Horticultural Society we all four of us used to share laughter together, it all seems so sad, all the villagers enjoying the fun of the Carnival and a couple sharing anxiety and sadness.

This Millennium coincides with Reg's 80th birthday and the occasion could not be missed to have a celebration on such an important day.

I could not quite believe that Reg was going to be 80, although his health had nudged him and reminded him that quantities of tablets, blood test, vertigo attacks, as well as asthma ones, had become almost a routine, few people, except close friends and family, realised his age. Young at heart, blessed with a sense of fun, he had not as yet any lines on his face. His mother, Vivienne, who used to win "Pears contests for a beautiful complexion, had obviously passed her gene to her son and although his thick mop of hair was now getting sparse on the crown of his head, he had not as yet lost that twinkle in his eyes and that enjoyment of teasing the ladies, though when we returned home or visitors had gone, the serious Reg returned. We used to talk of so many things; sometimes till our sitting room was only lit by the glow of the fire, enjoying the quietness, just holding hands and so grateful to be together.

Two days later Denman College phones to confirm my name is down for the course of painting, will confirm by letter. The date is the 15th of January, 2001.

Mention to Reg that a birthday lunch will be organised at Donnington Manor and would he like to make a list of friends to invite. Top of the list was our Doctor and his wife and also good friends that had been invited to birthdays in the past.

Reg was thinking of an intimate lunch with family members and friends and afterwards gathering at home for the birthday cake and the champagne.

Now that Reg was a diabetic, I thought a light sponge cake would be better than a dark fruit laden cake, so ordered that.

Reg's 80th birthday party at home, August 2000

Unfortunately we received a letter to say our doctor and his wife had booked a holiday to Rhodes, so wished us a happy time, but were sorry to miss the occasion.

Saturday the 12th of August get a phone call from our friend Sue to inform me that Noel had died last night, after being in a coma in hospital. Reg and I were so sorry to hear the news, how sad for his wife and their daughter.

A week before the birthday party, on Monday the 14th of August, the W.I garden parry was taking place in our garden and so organise the food, sweets and asked Reg if he would do the honours and bring the chilled wine to us in the garden and he kindly agreed. When the members were all there and were chatting Reg arrives with a tray of glasses and a white napkin draped over his arm. Everyone enjoyed it and once we had a glass he retired indoors and left us to continue the party. When the hot dishes were ready and before telling everyone to come in I cut some quiches and asked Reg to help himself . He wished me a happy evening and took his plate upstairs to our room and discretely left us to it. I asked our guests to help themselves in the dining room and we all tucked in. Every year in August a member would offer to organise a garden meeting and enjoy the company. We took photos to remember the day and I still look at them and remember it all.

On the 30th of October, trees were down and also power cables, so no electricity and back to candles. By Thursday the 2nd the electricity was back.

This year seemed to be so busy, ever week there was some new task one didn't expect to do. I have been asked to do the reading at the Carol Service at St. Margaret's Church in Halstead, a bit nervous about it, stupid of me it went alright, so I need not have worried so.

On the 18th of December, the WI Christmas party was taking place, the County Chairman, Mrs. Young and her husband had been invited, with Reg at our table the conversation was going well. The committee, who organised and prepared the buffet, excelled themselves as usual and with the pretty flowers on each table, colourful napkins and such a lovely spread it looked very festive. As it was my first Christmas party as President I hoped I would do justice to the evening. Once I had delivered the speech of welcome to our guests I started to feel less nervous and began to enjoy the evening. We had singers to entertain us and they were very good.

We missed one of our members, a gentle and kindly lady called Stella Bellhouse who usually attended with her daughter, Jane, but today her daughter was alone. Her mother was being cared for in Burswood Home and was giving cause for concern to her family and friends, Christmas cards and flowers had been sent to her. Jane wanted to thank everyone present for their kindness to her mother, so I went to her table and brought her to our table as she wanted to say a few words. Afterwards I accompanied her back to her table and she seemed pleased to have spoken of her mother.

We spent a quiet but intimate Christmas, just the two of us, undoing presents, having mince pies and cream mid-morning, taking our time looking at books, I was trying on jewellery, lace lingerie and tasting chocolates. Reg is looking at bottles of wines and spirits making his mind up about which bottle to open, putting CDs of Carols on his new radio, tape and CD recorder which he seemed pleased with.

We have always enjoyed Christmas and have to remind ourselves that we are no longer children, but somehow the magic still is weaving the usual spell on us both.

Christmas morn: our special magical day.
Undoing our presents by the hearth

34

Once Christmas had passed, we used up the film and I took it to be developed. On it were several photos of Reg's 80th birthday party, some taken outside the restaurant, some better ones in our home supping Champagne and relaxed.

I was taken aback by photos taken outside where Reg looked strained, his suit no longer seemed to fit and it appeared he was beginning to lose weight. On the other hand, our photos at home were different. He looked relaxed, his face no longer showed any strain and he looked much younger than his years.

The Denman College course was beginning on the 15th of January 2001, and I was starting to feel that leaving Reg to look after himself was perhaps a little selfish on my part, although he kept telling me that the list of tablets to take daily and pinned on the kitchen wall, was clear and he would follow it to the letter.

Only illness or staying in hospital ever separated us, and thinking back of occasions in the late seventies and early eighties, didn't want to emulate leaving my husband in order to pursue my interests.

He knew something was troubling me and when I told him, said it was a chance I should not miss and we would talk on the phone every morning and evening, so time would pass. He ordered a car for me to go to the coach station and I promised to phone the moment I reached my destination.

He also arranged for a car to fetch me on my return and will be there to welcome me home.

The college gave me very detailed information and it appears I was billeted in 'Willow Cottage', the Hampshire room on the ground floor.

Each front door had a security code which I would be given on arrival. The car was picking me up at 12.45 and laden up with paints etc, and night clothes and toilet bag, Reg and I said our goodbyes at home and said will phone as soon as I arrive.

I reached Gloucester Green coach station in complete darkness, but the taxi soon arrived and when I entered the main house a roaring fire and the welcome that was shown to me was so appreciated. I said I wanted to phone home, was accompanied to the cottage and found a phone by my bedside.

I asked the lady if she could give me five minutes, and Reg answered the phone on the 2nd ring so must have been anxious about me. I said would make it a quick call but will phone after the evening meal.

The programme of learning was quite intensive and the teacher was great, explained and showed us how to get the best of individual abilities.

The class was a good mix of beginners and experienced painters and the time, I am glad to say, whipped by. On the last two days we were given three roughly photocopied sketches, no colour to them, and we had to choose the shades we favoured and by the last day I had finished my favourite subject, an apple tree flanked by a rickety wooden gate with the sun shining from one side. All 28 of us students painted it and each and everyone, pinned on our studio wall, was completely different, size of tree trunk, colour of leaves and grass shades, even the wooden gate was in different depths of brown. It was quite surprising. I hoped that my efforts would please Reg as I tried hard to paint a sunny picture. He got it framed and encouraged me to do more painting. My teacher was selling a video called 'Line and Wash' and I have learnt quite a lot by looking at her technique.

On our last day, settled in the coach, I wondered how I would find Reg, had the time dragged for him and I was so looking forward to seeing him again. The coach arrived on time and as I was putting my luggage down I heard my name called, our driver had seen me and waved. Reg came out of the car and I was so happy to see him again. I snuggled against him in the back seat and felt safe again, just to feel him close.

I am now doing much more driving regarding shopping, taking Reg to the surgery and to hospital for blood tests as notice his driving has been erratic. I have for years had such confidence in his driving and always felt absolutely relaxed due to his efficient way of handling a car, but noticed lately that he was not aware that he was doing 20 miles an hour down Rushmore Hill, no car in front or behind, and when I asked why the slow speed, didn't seem to have noticed, so from that day I used to sit in the drivers' seat and wait for him to get in, hoped he would not be put out, but had to look after him.

Reg must have perhaps noticed that his concentration at the wheel was not as good as it should be, and soon accepted my driving him wherever it was necessary.

I decided that with Reg's health giving me such concern it was time to cancel any commitment which took my time away instead of being home to look after Reg.

So the month before our Abbeyfield chairman retired I advised them that regretfully, after being involved for so long, I would not be able to carry on. They were most understanding but I said I would attend the next meeting to say goodbye to our chairman.

I told Reg I would be back within an hour but felt I had to pay my respects and wish her well in her retirement. Much to my surprise, after the speeches etc, a beautiful arrangement of yellow flowers was presented to me for 20 years service. Was surprised but thought how kind of them to do that. I excused myself and they understood that I could not stay for the lovely tea all laid out by the 'Housekeeper' but wanted to get home.

Monday the 15th of October 2001 I drive Reg to the surgery. See a locum. Apparently tests show a swollen liver. Tomorrow book for a blood test. Eight days later go to surgery. Must get an appointment at Chelsfield Park Hospital for ultrasound on abdomen. Test by Gastroenterologist Specialist. One week later the test show the heart is not getting the blood pumped and it's giving extreme tiredness.

We spent a very quiet Christmas and although I had purchased the food he favoured most, i.e a moist capon instead of a quickly dried turkey, roasted parsnips and King Edward's which he loved etc, poor man's appetite was not good and although I put small amounts on his plate he could not do justice to it. I could not even tempt him for a glass of Chateauneuf-du-Pape he would have usually enjoyed, so I didn't even bother to open a bottle. This was the first Christmas lunch which had no appeal to him and I felt so sad that our favourite festival had this day lost its magic.

Tuesday, December the 27th saw the specialist at the hospital, shows Reg's heart is pumping at 70 per cent efficiency. His heart was damaged when he had his heart attack in 1996. (He was then 76 years old.)

Thursday the third of January 2002 Reg said he felt very cold and I realised the radiators were cold. Looked in every room, all radiators were cold. I went in the garage which houses our Gas boiler to see if it was on, found a terrible smell of gas by the meter and a black pipe next to it. I quickly returned indoors and phoned the Emergency number for gas leaks. Was told to shut off the boiler, don't put any electric switches on etc. It was now 3.40 in the afternoon. I then got a large double blanket and wrapped it round Reg, while I put on a thick winter coat, a woolly hat and could do nothing then but wait. At 7.15pm the gas engineers arrived. I went in the garage and showed him where the smell of gas was coming from and he said, "Just as well I've brought a new gas meter with me, your pipe attached to it is split and I'll put a new one in." The meter was only 60 years old and had been installed in 1942. At last by 8pm all was back to normal and the heat was put on again. We were 5 hours without heating and that was a long time.

35

This year winter was not too unkind to us, though March winds did a certain amount of damage to our garden. April came and its arrival was heralded by the trumpets of the short daffodils I had planted last November, our garden is exposed to the prevailing winds across the fields at the back of our property and noticing in the past years that tallish plants were blown down, I had chosen many varieties of golden daffodils only 8" tall and they lasted a longer time, edged by sky-blue grape hyacinths. The colour of the sky and the gold of the sun looked good together. Even while choosing tulips I chose a multi-stemmed variety which lasted well and did not get their petals ripped off.

Before our conifer hedge grew a fair size, even our sturdy shrubs with thick trunks suffered the indignity of leaning sideways like drunken sentries, even with the large oak affording protection from the force of the wind, small shrubs did not escape the power of nature.

Reg and I had shared many tasks in the garden but although I urged him to leave all that to both me and the gardener; who came once a week, what could not be done got left and that was that, but when I went shopping he showed me, on my return, jobs he should not have attempted but seemed so pleased to be of help to me.

St. Valentine's Day we gave each other cards as we always did. I discovered later that when his son Colin called a few days before he asked him for a lift to purchase a card so that the element of surprise could still happen. Reg always remembered special occasions and cards and flowers were always given to each other, so those days were much appreciated.

My 70th birthday was soon approaching and Reg asked me if there was anything I wanted to do on the 7th April to celebrate, said no, I was quite happy just to stay home, I will make a special birthday meal for us in the evening and just enjoy being home together.

Mid morning, after putting the cards on the mantelshelf, the doorbell rings. A young woman was at the door holding an enormous willow basket with 20 red roses surrounded by lovely foliage and tiny bamboo sticks dotted around the greenery. Reg had ordered them by phone and I was pleased for such a gift knowing his health was not very good. Colin called lunchtime on his own with a bunch of spring flowers and a bottle of Champagne.

Thursday our good friends May and Donald called with a card and a very dainty pottery in the shape of a blue and white bag, ideal for putting tiny flowers in. I had been spoilt by the kindness of good friends.

On a sunny Friday, 17th May, I drove to the supermarket and told Reg I would be back in a couple of hours. Get back home at 11am, the French windows are wide open and as I walk in the lounge laden with shopping bags I see Reg carrying a hanging basket, face as white as a sheet. Drop my bags and run up the lawn. Take the heavy basket off him and put it on the lawn. Reg asks me if there are any glass pieces on his jacket at the back. I immediately look and see, hanging over his jacket, shards of glass. Tell him to keep perfectly still, get a plastic bowl and carefully pick the pieces, when it's done, take him in the kitchen, put the kettle on for a hot cup of tea and then ask what happened. Apparently he had carried the basket but tripped over the greenhouse step, fell against the Chelsea trellis opposite, toppled back against the glass panels of the greenhouse smashing them. I carefully removed the jacket, his shirt had cuts in it, after removing it, was surprised his vest also had cuts but to my amazement not one cut on his skin. By then I gave him a hot cup of tea and soon saw the colour coming back in his cheeks. Told him off (very gently) for tackling jobs in the garden which I can do. Ended hugging him and giving him a kiss, but I think he realised that it wasn't too clever to try to do too much. I guess it could have been worse, I just had to clean a cut on his leg and put a plaster on it.

As the end of August came our gardener's wife, who used to do the housework for us, started to give concern with her health. She had to now inject herself for Diabetes and her arthritis was getting more painful and restrictive in her movements and it was very obvious that the energy needed for her job was beyond her capabilities, so was suddenly without help at home.

I asked a friend in the village if she knew of anyone she could recommend. By the Tuesday 4th of September I had a phone call about a couple (man and wife) who would call to see what needed to be done. They called on that particular morning and after looking upstairs and showing them the amount of rooms to do, we asked them if they could start next week. They agreed and left. Izzy and Paul had answered our prayers. Reg and I looked at each other, then at the same moment, we smiled and said, "They are a nice couple, I feel sure we will get on fine."

On the 11th of November, after discussing together the need to purchase another double bed for the downstairs bedroom, I drove to Orpington to get one, the same make as our own upstairs and after sorting out the paperwork walked back up the main street to get a special cheque from my building society so that it will be all paid for and arrangements for delivery could be done.

On my way, I tripped and fell on pavement and could feel my left arm was broken, so after a passer-by helped me to my feet I carried on to the shop and asked to phone my husband. Was asked to wait, Rhoda and her husband, who live in the village, kindly agreed to collect my car parked in the town (her husband offered to do that) while I was driven to the surgery to confirm it was a break, then on to Queen Mary's hospital to have an x-ray and plaster, with a rubber sling round my neck. I had broken the radius bone just below the elbow. An appointment was made for next Monday for another plaster to have for six weeks. Everyone was so helpful, lifts for getting shopping etc were organised, but doing things one-handed is so different, you do not realise how difficult simple things are to do.

Monday the 17th of November, the hospital cut off the plaster, (what a relief) won't put another on as the elbow would get set, so fix a rubber sling and must exercise arm everyday.

I am very lucky that Jenny Whitelegg, who used to be a physiotherapist, calls on me and shows me different exercises to do which will help my arm to regain its movement.

Received my WI spring bulbs but could not plant them, so my neighbour asked a gardener she knew, as mine was away, to call and plant them all. So at least that was a good job done. It seems that this year we both are in the wars, Wednesday the 11th December, my leg is very painful, I can hardly stand on it. By 4pm Reg phones and talks to our doctor's wife, he will be home in 30 minutes and will call. Takes one look at the large blisters on my thigh and says, "It's shingles, probably the shock of my fall could have brought it on." Made a prescription for anti-viral tablets, paracetamol and codeine tablets for the pain. Phoned Jenny, will call the next day, 10am and get my prescription. The next day, Izabel gives me a lift to Halstead and show her the farm that sells their home-grown vegetables. Also gives me a lift to Cooling Nursery to get two baskets filled with plants and flowers to be delivered to Rhoda and Jenny Whitelegg for all the help they have given me when I broke my elbow. Christmas Eve, my butcher was kindly delivering our capon, bacon and breaded ham, so that was a lot of help. On the 30th December had to go to the hospital for the "All Clear" regarding my elbow and that was how 2002 ended.

36

On New Year's Eve, Reg had a very disturbed sleep, he was a little unsteady on his feet and started to get out of bed, I woke up and helped him to the bathroom and made sure he was back in bed safely. He was short of breath just taking seven steps and I felt very concerned about the weakness in his legs and arms.

He could not settle and had much difficulty in going to sleep. At four in the morning, at last his breathing became regular and eventually I relaxed enough to find sleep.

At 8am, I made a cup of tea, but as Reg was still asleep just let him catch up on it and waited for him to wake up.

When he did he was still very out of breath, feeling discomfort in both chest and tummy. I suggested phoning the doctor as I could not help him, would not hear of it as it was New Year's Day. I said, "In that case, I will contact the paramedic, you must have some help."

It was 12 noon, he arrived at 3pm. Examined him very thoroughly for 45 minutes. Told me to phone for an ambulance and he left. I phoned his daughter Penny in Harrogate to explain how things were, she wanted to know the details, told her I was not given any, expecting the ambulance and packing his toilet bag, so said she would drive directly, also will phone her brother to organise where to stay the night. The doorbell rang and the ambulance men arrived. The usual tests are done and Reg is afterwards taken to an assessment ward. It is now 7.30pm. Tell Reg will take a taxi home and visit him tomorrow.

It appears that Penny was asked to come to her brother's house in Fairlight, a little place in the hills behind the seaside town of Hastings. Thursday the 2nd of January, Penny, her daughter Ele, her brother Colin and his girlfriend arrived to visit Reg. I arrived at 2pm; they had then gone. As I came by taxi I was able to stay a little longer, when I can drive again I have to leave before it's getting dark because of my eyes.

Friday the 3rd, spending the morning sorting out laundry and putting clean sheets on the bed, also answering phone calls from friends in the village asking about Reg, I get a call from the hospital to say Reg will be sent home by car with a letter for his G.P. When he arrives home still in his pyjamas and dressing gown, notice he still has a needle in his arm. Not something to fiddle about with so phone our doctor's wife and she assures me he will call after surgery and remove it. He was a little critical of sending a patient home without noticing it but was as usual kind and gentle with Reg and was given the letter from the hospital. It seems that Reg has fluid in his lungs, also a swollen liver which is causing pain. More blood tests wanted, so our doctor will call and do it, to avoid Reg having to visit the hospital.

The following Wednesday, the 8th, it's snowing again, our doctor called to take more blood samples. He then examined my left wrist, told me not to go in the car for at least four weeks as my wrist is so stiff. It's all happening at the wrong time, as I have to rely on the help of good friends to give me a lift to get the shopping.

On Thursday the 23rd of January, after noticing my eye is giving blurred vision, I get a taxi to my optician and find to my surprise that a skin is nearly covering the lens in-plant that the eye surgeon inserted in my left eye July 1999, but can be removed by laser treatment. He will send a letter to my G.P. The surgeon does the laser surgery on the 4th of February, taxi home and that same evening could read my book easily. Wonderful to see clearly.

The next day we receive a visit from Colin and his girlfriend telling us he has booked a holiday to Canada and

New York for October for the two of them.

Next day I drive for the first time to the supermarket since the 11th of November last when I broke my elbow. At last I can be mobile. In the afternoon Colin called to borrow money Reg, saying his customers owed him money and he was short. Reg being Reg, kind but well aware that that sum of money was a little excessive, gave him the £1,000 he asked for but admitted to me that it was a coincidence with his son's intentions to go on holiday so far.

Very frosty and for the first time ever Reg asked me to buy a Valentine's card for him from the village shop, apologized profusely but don't see the need, I know how much care and time he always chooses his cards for me, but I get two cards, one for me and one for him. I let him choose which one. Only four in the shop so no choice really.

St. Valentine's Day was this year was frosty and icy underfoot and was treacherous. Gave each other our cards.

A week passes, Reg not well at all. I ask the doctor to call. 2.15 examines Reg for 30 minutes. Agrees he wasn't well, knows Reg doesn't want to go to hospital so will try to get fluid off the lungs, liver still swollen and has a chest infection. Gives me a prescription for medicine twice a day and antibiotics. Will call Monday to see if progressing, Friday 4th April, doctor calls again with the result of blood test. Reg is short of salt which makes him feel so tired. Penny visits her dad as on her way to visit her son Tom in north London. Tuesday the 22nd April, our fourteenth anniversary, have to console Reg who is so worried he has no anniversary card or flowers for me, tell him not to worry. Just saying "Happy Anniversary" to me makes me happy.

Our car is having electrical problems, had it seen to twice at the garage and had a hefty bill, but can't be helped.

Towards the end of April Colin phones. Reg told him that he's having trouble with the car and might have to recall the

£1,000 he borrowed on the 6th of February. Saturday the 10th of May the nursery is starting to send the plants I have ordered for the garden which must be potted before they start to go limp, so when Reg is able to have a sleep, perhaps after lunch, I will go to the greenhouse and pot as many plants as have been sent and hope the colours and scent will give him something to enjoy without leaving his armchair.

Friday the 16th of May, poor Reg is having a bad time, the very thing he so dreaded has started. Apart from being out of breath, his tummy is still upset and every other day he is suffering the indignity of being incontinent. Whenever he calls me to the bathroom, he feels he has committed the worst mistake possible. I feel so sorry that it should happen to my husband who is so clean and tidy, yet has to be washed, dried and helped into clean clothes, taken back to bed while the bathroom is thoroughly washed. It's no trouble to me, but he feels so embarrassed. It's difficult to convince him that we will surmount these things together.

Sunday the 20th of July, Tom, Reg's grandson, phones to say his wife Vicky is expecting their first child next January. Reg is so pleased as I am and looking forward to that happy event. Spoke to Tom afterwards and told him Reg is very thin and unsteady on his feet.

August the 18th Reg still can't manage food and his clothes just hang on him. Penny phoned to say will call Saturday the 23rd on Reg's 83rd birthday, minus Jim, after lunch. Colin phoned to say will call in the afternoon. Tom and his wife Vicky also came, it was a lovely sunny day and we all sat on the terrace. Penny gave Reg some videos, Colin nothing. Discovered after they all went that Colin has repaid £500 of the £1,000 he borrowed 6 months ago.

Our top garden past the arch has a fair amount of shade and very little colour, so I suggested to Reg my idea of filling our 5ft square bed underneath the large oak with a mass of spring bulbs which I can plant now so that there is a lot of colour, short red tulips, burgundy trilliums, short white narcissi and in the centre 3 tall Crown Imperials, one yellow, one red, one orange. In all 145 bulbs to light up the left side of the top garden. Reg is enthusiastic, but thinks I shall find tile planting tiring, said it sure is a change from ironing and would enjoy planning. I have already made a diagram of how the bulbs will be planted. I always spend time there whilst he's having a snooze, so can do it a little at a time. Whilst sorting out the bulbs, I get this feeling that perhaps Reg won't be there to see it in spring, yet how do I know. Perhaps he will and still appreciate my efforts to please him. When the job is done I spread a heavy gauge netting over the bed to avoid temptation to curious squirrels.

Thursday the 18th of September, Penny phoned, was calling with Jim on the way to her brother's house because Jim had not yet seen the place. Arrive at 6pm. By the time they go it's well past me time for our evening meal as it's 8.30pm.

Ten days later, as if there are not enough problems, we are plagued with wasp nests, one by the kitchen where the soffits are, one by the front door, so have to hope the man can find time to call as everyone in the village is suffering.

Friday the 10th of October, Reg has a pain in his heart, I call the doctor's wife who lives two houses away who comes round, she phones her husband at the surgery and told to call for an ambulance. Arrive at hospital at 4.15 and after the necessary tests, at 10pm, he is eventually put in a ward. Didn't leave till he's in bed and I have noted the name of the ward. At least he is in the place kindly nurses and knowledgeable doctors know what to do for him.

Saturday the 11th of October, I visit Reg at 10am. I think he realises that at least he is being looked after by kindly and professional staff.

I drive back home to phone his daughter but no reply.

Return to hospital and the doctor is examining him. He thinks he could have a blood clot in his lung and be anaemic, also will ask for another x-ray. On my return home, try again, but still no reply, so leave a message on the phone. Next day, Sunday, still not a word from Penny, so phone her son Tom who tells me his father and mother are at a wedding in Salisbury, so he gives me their mobile number. Phone every 30 minutes, but obviously it's not switched on to receive calls. Knowing her father is so poorly, you would think she would keep it available for calls.

Tuesday the 14th I phone Harrogate, Jim at last tells me his wife left at 11.30 am to visit her dad, better late than never I suppose.

On Thursday the 25th of October, ask the doctor in charge to tell me of Reg's condition. Told me Reg has emphysema and pneumonia and they will test the fluid removed from his lungs, it will take four to five days. 1 didn't tell Reg as he will worry, so keep this to myself.

When I visited the next day, noticed Reg is lying on his side as bedsores are now hurting him. Sunday the 26th at 7.30pm Reg uses his bedside telephone to tell me his grandson Tom and his wife Vicky have just left. Vicky is expecting their first child in three months and live in north London, so have a long drive home. Reg was so pleased to see them both and appreciated their kind gesture. Reg is looking forward to seeing me tomorrow. I understand that the health visitor wants to call at our home to advise re fixing aids around the house to help Reg be safe and mobile, I tell her of course, just tell me day and time and I shall be there. Whatever aids are suggested to be of help. His legs are so weak, he has to be in a wheelchair to reach the toilet. I will bring him a dressing gown as he says he feels cold.

November the 4th, Reg phones me, feels very low, is so wanting to come home but has to have scans, be monitored in so many ways it's difficult to be patient for him but I visit every day, sometimes twice a day and at least he can tell me what worries him. He can phone from his bed, so he asked me to bring a £5 note for a phone card. 8pm Reg phones, tells me Colin tried to ask the nurse about Reg's illness and what was wanted in our house in the way of aids. Was told that Reg's wife knew about that and it was all in hand. Reg's weight is so low now, he was 14 stone, but is now 10 stone 8 ounces.

At long last Reg is allowed home on Friday the 14th of November, after 35 days in hospital. We are both pleased, it's been so long and so distressing for Reg particularly.

As soon as Reg is back home the hospital has made appointments for him to do different tests and when we return home is so tired, he often sleeps for three hours. Reg tries very hard to get dressed while I go to the village shop for bread and milk, but can barely manage, even with his walking stick, to reach his armchair in the lounge. It is such an effort, but will try to do the normal everyday things. Our cleaners, Isobel and Paul, I should now call our good friends, have helped to clean up after accidents that occur and I can't thank them enough for their help, they have been so good to us both.

Reg has started to be very sick and by 7am I can't help myself, I phone our doctor. It's Friday the 19th of December, ten minutes later he calls. Reg is very dehydrated, needs to go to hospital. Writes a letter and the ambulance arrives. It's 9am. He's put on a drip straightaway and given oxygen. I leave Reg in good hands and return home. Next day, Saturday the 20th, I get up at 6.30am, prepare a large Christmas hamper for Isobel and Paul as next Tuesday will be their last working day before Christmas and I had previously decided, that with three daughters to care for, it would be a suitable Christmas gift.

I phoned Reg's childhood friend in Northampton to tell him of Reg's health.

Monday the 22nd, Reg is having an ultrasound, so will be home for Christmas but don't know which day. Sort out many 'get well' cards. Also receive phone calls of which one from Penny who tells me she's travelling to her son Tom on Christmas morning.

On Wednesday at 6pm after a complete mix-up with me ambulance, eventually his son spots Reg waiting in a wheelchair in the hospital hall, so takes him to his car and they both arrive at 6pm. Christmas Day after a very disturbed sleep I eventually tuck Reg up in bed and he managed to doze.

His friend Ray Johnson and his lady Miriam drive to Farnborough hospital trying to see Reg. Eventually a helpful porter found he had been sent home and let him use his phone to ring me to ask if it was convenient to visit. Said nothing to Reg, twenty minutes later they arrived. I took Ray to Reg's bedside, the look of surprise and pleasure on his face was a picture. He was so pleased to see his old friend, I took his lady to the lounge and appreciated her company.

I was feeling tired through lack of sleep, but thought how kind of Ray to drive all the way from Northampton to see Reg.

They were on their way to have lunch with Miriam's daughter and had left their home early to do all that travelling.

Next day. Boxing Day, Penny phones to say will call at 2pm with Jim and her daughter Ele.

"Don't get him up just for us," I said, "can't stand anyway."

2.15 Ele, Penny, Jim and Colin arrive. All in the lounge, bringing packages for each other, (the floor looked like a sorting office at the Post Office) when I had said we didn't want anything as we had not purchased presents, but took no notice as usual. All chatting and laughing whilst I am in the downstairs bedroom with Reg waiting for the ambulance to take him back to hospital.

Eventually, at 4.30, had to ask them to leave as going in the ambulance with Reg. Colin said he will follow in his car. Went into a side cubicle to await the doctor, but Colin came in and sat down, not intending to leave us alone. When we eventually went to the ward Reg was put to bed and the nurse tested Reg's abilities by asking his name, date of birth, address and the usual "who is the Prime Minister?" then looking at us both said "who is the next of kin?" Just as I opened my mouth to reply, Reg's son Colin said "I am" Reg then said "Excuse me, this is my wife Jacqui." So the nurse said "Oh, you are the next of kin then" Colin said nothing, but his father certainly didn't appreciate that remark, only showed what an ignorant man he was.

Colin phoned Reg the next day, saying he can't visit today but will come next Tuesday. Reg told him, "By the way, Jacqui is my next of kin, remember that." Colin slammed the phone down on him. I had gone to the hospital shop to buy a small bottle of water that Reg wanted. I wondered why he looked so upset. He told me about the phone call. I stayed with Reg till 8pm, then was driven home by a good friend up the road.

Monday the 29th of December, I arrive at 11am, Colin is already there. At last. Penny arrived at 4.30pm. The doctor tells me that Reg is not responding to treatment, can only try to make him comfortable.

When I return to Reg's bedside Penny moves her chair and I sit by him and hold his hand. My good friends Isobel and Paul call, he recognises them and puts his hand out to shake both of them. They go and then without a word spoken, Reg raises my hand to his lips to kiss, turns his head to me and gives me a wink. Even feeling so ill, he had given me the message he knew I would understand. So I excused myself and my friend kindly drove me home. I wanted to get home and let the tears flow, I think we both knew that this was 'Goodbye'.

New Year's Eve the telephone wakes me up at 5.20am, Penny tells me my Reg just died peacefully. She will fetch me at 6.30am to see Reg one last time.

While the three of them hang about in the corridor, I go to his bed, kiss him on his right cheek, it's still warm and whisper to him "I love you, we will meet again when the time is right." I return to the corridor and Colin and his girl are going to get some breakfast, and Penny takes me to the car park to get home.

Only an hour later, the mask of pretence was discarded and it apparently was found to be unnecessary to show the slightest understanding towards their father's widow.

The pain and sorrow felt trying to organise the arrangements of a funeral as well as getting the certificates and so on, were completely ignored as immediately on my return from the hospital after saying my last Goodbye, his daughter said she had to return home to her husband.

It was only friends who were kindly and understanding who helped me at this sad time, yet the daughter and son returned home and left me to it.

The charade had been played while Reg was alive, but he was no longer present to shield me, so his daughter and son no longer felt the need to pretend any feelings of understanding for their father's widow in her loss. I now knew that any support or help to organise the funeral would not be given by the Dolan Family, at least I now was aware of the total indifference from them and his son.

37

It is perfectly certain that the soul is immortal and is imperishable, and our souls will actually exist in another world.

Socrates (469-599BCE), Greek philosopher

Thinking back to the months of September 2003, Reg was aware that time was not on his side and he also knew that I realised we would fairly soon accept the inevitable.

He took my hand and said very seriously, "When I am no longer with you …"

"Please don't, I feel icy cold just hearing this." He stopped and said no more. The next day, again he took my hand and told me to listen, "Please listen, when I am no longer with you, I will be watching you in the garden, planting your flowers, protecting you from anyone wanting to harm you."

I suddenly saw that the man who had loved me for the last twenty-five years was more spiritual than I had thought. I now saw why we had always felt on the same wavelength. In many ways from the first day we spoke we noticed we could read each other's minds. I had accepted similar tastes, same likes and dislikes, without question, not realising that it is very rare for two people to enjoy sharing all difficulties that life throws at us, criticising without knowledge, in difference, abuse of kind gestures, but at the same time the friends we met over the years knew how close we are. We both wanted to help any worthwhile projects which would help the village which had adopted us.

Reg always loved our garden; that was why I decided to make a colourful bed of his favourite flowers to be the setting for his casket. I could then go in the garden and when a problem came I could just sit by the bed of flowers with his favourite rose and just pray for his help.

Also, I must mention how a fortnight before he died, Reg asked me to help to go in his study, told him not too long as tiring, but I took him there. Heard him slide the drawer of his metal filing cabinet and shut it. He came out of his room and just thanked me for my help. Only seven days after that fateful New Year's Eve, I realised that I didn't even know the name of his pension office, so phoned his firm to enquire. Then noticed on the right hand side of his desk, Reg had put the last statement of his pension firm and a piece of paper headed "Where" and it listed where the birth and marriage certificates were, pension book, details of shares, list of direct debits and so on. That was what he had removed from the filing cabinet as he wanted to help me even after his going.

Our home was now very quiet. I felt as is half of me had been torn away, I so missed his warm personality, the chats we used to have dotted with humour and a few laughs. So to feel closer to him I took out of my cupboard the very first leather bound diary, it was dark green, a page-a-day book 9½" x 6" and 1½" thick. Reg brought it back from his London Office and gave it to me, hoping I would find a use for it.

That year was a very sad year, my husband Sherry, who had been ill for the last three years with strokes, died on the 3rd of January, that is to say the day after I received my gift, and my mother herself ill with cancer, was feeling shattered as she never imagined seeing her son-in-law leave this world before her. He was a good husband and I will always keep a place in my heart for him.

Reg, as always, was kind and supportive and I will always be grateful for his help to both me and my dear mother.

So I found comfort in reading my diary and read a few pages each day.

Mrs. King-Scott, our village correspondent, wrote a detailed article in the Sevenoaks Chronicle about Reg's passing and I sent a copy to Reg's childhood friend Ray, Penny, his grandson Tom and his wife Vicky. Other friends outside our village were also sent the paper.

On the 27th of January, our kindly doctor called, I found it impossible to stop crying, but was so grateful for his understanding, we spoke of Reg, told him that I was reading my diaries, he feels it's the best therapy imaginable. Two days prior to that visit, I received a communication to tell me that Tom's wife, Vicky, had had a little girl, no names chosen as yet. Reg had so wanted to hear such news, but the baby was born on the 25 of January, 25 days after Reg was gone. The mother and baby are both well, so happy and proud.

Reg's study was very much his domain, phone calls, correspondence, filing receipts etc, so didn't really go in that room except to ask if he wanted a coffee or would prefer to be in the lounge, so did not notice at first the list that was tucked in on the left of his blotting pad.

If he wanted to purchase something or do a particular job, he would put it on the list and draw a line through when done. Sure enough, there was a long list which I had not previously noticed. It contained a list of jobs which he must have known he would not be there to do, so I guess he knew I would carry them out in the order they were listed.

The first was to get a burglar alarm fitted. The surface of the flat roof above our kitchen and the end of the lounge was beginning to pond and could be troublesome. Refit the kitchen fitments, they had been there twenty years. A piece of pine coving fell on my head when opening a wall cupboard, it was a headache literally and being pine was dark, so would do that. The conservatory, which was badly designed, was only 12ft x 8ft. We had sometime ago thought to have it 5ft longer on to our lawn and better designed, and lastly have the outside of our house repainted as flaking was bad, had not been painted for some years. That was a long list, but as often Reg had told me, a home must be regularly looked after before difficulties arise. So I started with the first task, to clear out the eaves cupboards so that electrical cables and fittings regarding alarms systems could be done and there was room for the electrician to work. We had put our cardboard boxes in both attics of personal belongings and it was necessary to get them out and cheek them, so that some order was back.

I knew that Reg was fond of memorabilia but was taken aback by what I found.

We both kept our childhood toys and mementoes of those early days, I hated girly toys (dolls were thrown in the nearest cupboard) only liked boys toys and found Reg's toys were identical to mine. Jigsaws, albums of stamps, other albums of both cigarette cards and albums of actors and film stars in books, his Boy Scout badges and my Girl Guide ones, card games, books on Judo, Enid Blyton books on adventures. Also Matchbox cars, which I loved and Meccano sets which fascinated me. I also discovered an old cardboard box, an oil painting of flowers that Reg had done when quite a small boy, so his love of flowers went back a long way, as was my fascination, when very small, to explore gardens when visiting friends with my mother and enjoying the colours and the scent. Painting flowers has also been my favourite subject. I then found a cardboard box full of cricket items, an old cricket ball, cricket cap, jumper with RAF colours, as playing for the RAF team, I even found a Whit Monday programme of an RAF Association match dated 1948. At the bottom of the box I found a white contraption which I didn't know what it was, a friend told me it was called a box. Why did he keep it, I can't imagine. Sport seemed to have played an important part and he enjoyed many different ones.

After it was all repacked and put in plastic bags, the engineer came and my item on the list was installed on the 23rd of March.

The next day our doctor called to see how I was coping from the point of view of my health. Earlier in the month he explained to me that 12 months of very small amounts of sleep had caused me to experience depression and special tablets must be taken to get fit and well. I did as advised.

Following Reg's list I arranged for our long flat roof to be recovered as it was starting to pond badly, they started on the 14th of April and did a very good job.

April 25th I receive a phone call from Penny. She asked if I had made arrangements regarding her dad's ashes to put them in the Garden of Remembrance when the time is right. Said I will make enquiries as to how both our ashes can be put together and then will decide where. I have, of course, the possibility of going to the Family Vault in Paris, but the formalities are time consuming, so I will decide later. Not quite ready to go yet.

Sunday, the 16th of May, up to my armpits in planting Petunias in the garden, all forty of them and plan how many more Lobelias will be needed for the edges of beds.

Penny phones to tell me she's going to London to stay with Tom and Vicky and wanted to know if she can call at 11 am Wednesday the 19th, perhaps we could have a pub lunch as long as she can leave at 2pm. I agreed and just after 1 1am on that day the doorbell went I got the shock of my life as Penny stood there and said, "I have a surprise for you," Vicky walked up the drive carrying a kind of basket and said, "I have brought my baby Daisy to meet you." I was so pleased, such a pretty little girl, beautiful features, nearly four months old. I offered coffee, but Penny was keen to have an early lunch as wanted to leave at 2pm. I suggested a local pub so that we need not rush and when we returned I took them both into the garden and showed them the bed where I would plant his favourite flowers as well as one of his scented roses as soon as they are in flower. Vicky asked to go to the bathroom to make the baby comfortable, she had all that was needed in a travelling bag. As soon as she left the lounge. Penny asked when I would put the casket in the garden, told her again, when the flowers are out. So she said "Will you let Colin see it?" I answered "of course." Vicky returned to the lounge and we chatted about the new baby. A short while later she returned to the bathroom and Penny pounced on the opportunity of questioning me again. "Will I arrange for the casket to be put in the church again when I die?" She politely enquired, "Definitely not, but I intend to have my ashes put with Reg's, so I might arrange for it to go in our Family Vault in Paris." Penny then said "But I don't know where it is." I replied, "No, you don't, but I don't think I will be going for a couple of weeks, so when the time comes, you will be informed." At that moment Vicky returned to the lounge and we chatted awhile. All of a sudden, without so much as a by your leave. Penny got up from her armchair and walked into Reg's study, I was stunned, I looked at Vicky, wondered what Penny was looking for, but five minutes later she came out of his study, walked in the kitchen and out into the back garden for no reason that I could tell. Five minutes later returned, said it was nearly two o'clock and had to leave. That was the last I saw of her. Still don't understand what she was looking for.

As I got in touch with a firm about the construction of a conservatory, realised that I would need to saw the conifers abutting the old conservatory, but after sawing four of them, found it tiring and decided to continue the next day. Eventually the hedge has gone and only the root-balls must be removed by an expert.

On the 8th June, Reg's bed has been planted, Reg's rose is there already showing buds. I have placed two round stones for me to step on to weed and in the centre a square paving stone for the casket. At the back, against the fence a white jasmine is creating a good background for the colour of other plants. Paul and his wife Izzy help me. The marble casket is very heavy, so Paul carries out and places it so carefully in the centre of the bed. It looks peaceful and I can now sit by that bed and enjoy a little bit of contemplation there.

The 1st of July our doctor calls after lunch regarding my tablets, but they are 10mg instead of 20mg. He is obviously gently getting the dose down.

Had a visit from the surveyor re: the conservatory. Unfortunately it takes eight weeks for them to decide, so that's another delay.

July 21st phone rings, didn't recognise the number so press three. It's Colin, first call from him since Reg's death. Very intimidating. Started to shout as to why he wasn't in the first limousine at the funeral as he's his son, wanted to know why Reg's ashes were supposed to be as told, it was in the church and told him his sister knew Reg wanted to be in his garden. Wanted to know the name and address of my solicitor. In the end had to hang up. So upsetting, tummy upset. I should be used to his bouts of bad temper, but when you are alone and vulnerable it upsets you to hear someone ranting on the phone.

On August the 5th the council seem to take an age to decide if there's a way for me to add 5ft to the length of my conservatory, yet the parish council have no objection. Eventually the councillor calls and sees for himself how things are.

The suggestion that my tool sheds right at the bottom of my garden where my back fence abuts a large field, should be removed and my tools would have to be carried 120ft down into the garage, and if the square footage of both sheds add to the extra length wanted on my conservatory it would be allowed. Hallelujah!

I had to ask Paul to carefully take measure of the offending sheds, he would take a photo of them and I could post them to the relevant council department.

I spent four days carrying garden implements, electric saws and drills, heavy pick-axe to transfer them to the garage.

At last it was empty but the garage was full. I found metal holders for spades and garden forks and managed to screw two of them against the wall to try to get it tidy.

Today, the 21st of August, all the work and time spent on planting our garden in spring is paying off, Reg's bed is full of colour, I planted large begonias called 'Sunset Shades', which look lovely, white small begonias in front, beautiful blue Ageratums, called 'Blue Mist', and on the edge of the bed, Cambridge Blue lobelias interspaced with white ones. Reg's favourite rose which is very scented is on the left of the bed standing guard over the white marble casket of Reg. The busy Lizzies are looking colourful and the Sweet Williams are exuding wonderful perfume. The Pineapple scented shrub which has now stopped flowering was a favourite of Reg and 1 am so pleased that the garden is now full of colour and wherever he is he must be glad I am looking after it as well as I can.

For all this pleasure of seeing the garden in its glory, I feel suddenly uneasy. I have no idea why I should, but as I sit on the arbour seat, I try to fathom what it is that all at once, causes me anxiety. I am taking my tablets regularly as our doctor advised, I try to eat meals that are healthy and I am also very lucky that friends in the village either phone or call to see if all is OK, so why do I feel so very apprehensive. Perhaps it is the fact that in two days Reg's 84th birthday is approaching and I no longer have the fun of giving him a present or a birthday card, cooking a special meal for the occasion. No, it's more than that, I can't dispel this nagging worry. The next day, Sunday, the sun is shining and I spend the first hour reading through my diary and remembering how life was when we first came to this village.

We worked hard in both the house and the garden, but it

was all worth it. Then went in the garden, that's a place I feel close to Reg, but today I felt again this feeling of anxiety. Made some tea and hoped it was just a passing phase, it would go.

The next day Monday the 23rd of August, I must admit I felt so hungry for Reg's presence, but had to put that feeling at the back of my mind. The sun was pouring into my study and I just let in a small chink of light in case visitors called. At 1.15, the doorbell went. I noticed through the crack in the curtain, Colin and his girlfriend standing there. I went cold, didn't want to speak to him. He started to bang the front door with his fist, then he phoned, then saw him run to the back gate, but that was securely bolted. Back to the front door and banged it again. Then they left. I now knew why I had had that feeling, at 2pm back they came. Phoned my friend along the way, who came and told him I was still grief-stricken and perhaps it would be wiser to arrange a day to call.

He said he wanted to pay his respects to his dad and I was being unreasonable. Then he turned on the tears, he should have been an actor, but eventually drove off.

I tried to phone three times the next day to make an appointment for him to call, but I don't want to see him alone. No reply. 4pm I get a call from Jim, Penny's husband, told him I was going away to friends and would be back September the 6th. Told him I am trying to get through to Colin, but because of his temper, will organise for friends to let him see Reg's casket, but I don't want to be alone with him. Jim is so worried about upsetting his wife's opinions, so told him to get off the fence, the only thing he will get are splinters. Write a letter to Colin, saying I shall be staying with friends till the 6th of September, so if he wishes to say a little prayer at the side of his dad's casket, let me know a date.

At 12.15, Colin phones to say can't make it, can only do weekends. So it will have to be Saturday week 12 noon. Will ask Paul if he can help me.

So on 18th September, Colin and his girlfriend arrive. Paul was already parked on the bottom lawn and took them via the back gate to the garden. Paul then walked away from the bed and Colin took photos of the casket, while his girlfriend just wandered up the garden. They went after all of ten minutes and Paul left.

I felt as if a weight had been removed, and trust he will now let me be.

It's nineteen weeks since Penny phoned, so trust she will not now get in touch, I have had sufficient aggravation from both her and her brother. At last the people are coming to start on the kitchen. I have completely emptied all units, put items in cardboard boxes and put them in attic. Wall tiles must be removed, but have already chosen the new ones and they have been delivered. Surprise, surprise get a phone call from the council to say regarding drawings, they will allow my new conservatory to be twelve foot by thirteen foot, as I agree to remove both sheds.

At last, I can now tell the firm that it's fine to start on the job. That was the penultimate task on Reg's list, the last one will be painting the outside of the house, so will have nearly carried out his wishes.

26th of October 2004, doctor called lunch-time and believes I should continue to take the tablets for another two months, and did not realise that depression took such a long time to disappear. March 22nd two chaps arrive to remove the back edging of bricks, use a pneumatic drill. A large lorry arrives with made-up cement and using a wheelbarrow start pouring it in deep trenches so the footings are being made. At last, the work is progressing, though there is much to do, the brick wall is being done abutting my neighbours.

Last week after my two sheds were dismantled and burned on the bonfire in next door's back garden, I managed to find a chap to break up the bases of the sheds. Once that's done

I will ask the gardener to loosen the earth, as I have an idea on how to use that flat bit of ground, now devoid of sheds.

True, the large oak keeps it in the shade, but at the edge of the canopy, near our neighbour's fence, there are 2½ ft which receive the sun, and have measured the piece of land and intend to make it into a little garden of Remembrance, so go to our local nursery and purchase a variety of evergreen shrubs bar one deciduous one which has beautiful leaves to plant against our fence and which will enjoy the rays of the sun.

The men are working hard on the conservatory, they have finished putting the floor surface 12ft x 13ft, but will not be rendering for a week.

Tomorrow, will purchase my choice of shrubs which Reg so loved. In the far comer of the plot, I chose a Photinia 'Red Robin' evergreen, shiny leaves and new growth of red leaves, hence its name, next to it a Moroccan Broom, silvery green leaves which in July have large yellow flowers smelling of pineapple, then I planted a Fatsia Japonica, it has acid green glossy leaves hand-shaped. In autumn, October brings out at its tip, creamy flowers. On its right, my only deciduous shrub is a 'Sambucus Plumosa' with golden leaves and red berries in August. To both of us (we had another one in the garden) the delicate golden leaves were beautiful, even without the berries, they were worth looking at. In the open corner, I planted a shrub shown to me which I admired very much and which I did not know about, by Beryl Stevens, who like me enjoyed and appreciated unusual perennials and shrubs. I believe it was called 'Ilea' it has evergreen leaves resembling holly leaves and long racemes of honey-scented flowers. Very unusual.

On my second side of the plot, I planted two Rhododendrons, one yellow and one pink, a skimmia with shiny leaves, and was given a large Rhododendron by Paul and Isobel with salmon-pink flowers which I put on the open corner of the bed.

It was beginning to take shape and when I think of garden sheds, I am so glad the council imposed their wish to have them removed, because now the small and private Remembrance Garden I am planting will be special to Reg and me.

By the 28th of May, my washing machine was placed in the comer of the conservatory, a white cupboard for vacuum cleaner, cleaning materials and buckets was installed and a white counter covering both was put in. So now the conservatory is complete and the furniture has to be chosen and bought so that it can be comfortable, but my efforts at my top garden is my next venture, I have to wait till the lawn has grown and the rest of the garden, back and front must be planted, pruned and looked after while spring is here.

The owner of the building firm remaking a house instead of a bungalow next to me, has been extremely helpful whilst needing help with the destruction of sheds etc, so when his task is nearly over, will approach him to find out if he will take on the job of painting our house. As long as it's well done, I don't intend to ask if he's busy.

38

2006: a venture into the unknown. In the autumn and winter of 2005, I had to organize the budget which I had in the past entirely left to Reg, his knowledge of business and finances were such that like many wives you have implicit faith in your husband's abilities and leave all those things to him.

But as widows know only too well, when the least expected shock happens and you have to organize everything without wise advice, it is so difficult. But we can all re-arrange and manage our affairs, so with the kind help of knowledgeable people, everything was at last done. My last item on Reg's list was to have the house painted.

The owner of the building firm that had completed the house next door to me, only lived a hundred yards from me and was most helpful. On the 6 of February 2006, he phoned me, will call with a double glazing chap regarding my porch windows and front door next Thursday, the 9th at 9.30am.

The porch will be the first item, then the soffits and new guttering will be installed. Thereafter, all the painting will be done. As March begins, I decide to get my first diary dated 1980 and wonder if I could use it and all the others as a basis for a book telling the story of our meeting, and make an autobiography since I have every day kept that diary that Reg gave me and I think Reg would like our story to be told.

So I started on the 7th of March 2006 to do something that I have never attempted before, only my deep love for him spurs me on to get the story told.

I soon realised that if you want to achieve anything, you need to discipline yourself and write at least two hours a day to make sure as well as the research which must be meticulous so that dates and places are correct. In fact, some days I was writing two hours in the morning and also in the afternoon.

Sometimes, I would wake in the early hours and would use my notebook by my bed and would remember events that must have been put in the back of my mind, as if I had been whispered those things and had woken up because of it. It was strange in a way.

I also found in one of Reg's 'boxes of memories', a velvet covered red book I had given him Christmas '81 called "Love, a Celebration", it contained small love poems, I chanced getting it not sure whether Reg would like it, but thankfully, he often looked at it and read some of his favourite ones when we were together. So I wrote some of them as a heading to chapters.

April came and with it the plants I had ordered from a nursery, so had to combine my time with potting plants and writing my book.

Still had not thought of a title, but it will come to me in good time.

I received a brochure from the hotel Reg and I stayed at twenty-six years ago and I can now carry on the chapter relating to that first holiday together.

The builder is still attending to my house and keeps me informed of jobs to be done. Just attending to soffits and guttering, also will advise electrician repositioning my outside door lights in a better position.

April 27th 2006, three men are busy outside my house and the painter is already starting on my conservatory so that the short walls are nicely painted. I keep my eye on the weeding of our Remembrance Garden and after buying round paving stones, will get the gardener to place them on the lawn, making the shape of our initials JR. It looks great.

By the 2nd of May, it is all finished and I settle my bill for all the work done on our house. Have now completed the last item on Reg's list.

Now I am still working on my book and planting our garden so it will still give Reg pleasure.

It is very difficult when in your seventies to achieve very much, but when I had lost my Reg, I made the decision to organise some things I could perhaps do.

Very soon after the sad event, I enquired from a good friend. May Cameron, who attends our village school to help the children with their reading, if I could do the same.

They were only too pleased of some help, so soon after the beginning of Spring, I started to help with the 4-5 year olds and enjoyed it very much every week.

The next thing I did, was to approach Mrs. Gill King-Scott, secretary of the Tree Society, who had written me a lovely letter from her husband and herself, as well as the committee, and asked if I could donate a seat with an appropriate plaque in memory of Reg, being a founder member of the Society.

From its beginning, Reg and I used to go to Vavasseur's Wood and help to remove ivy from the trunks of trees, plant saplings and generally take part in making the wood a place where you could walk in spring and admire snowdrops, primroses and bluebells. So, it's now there for villagers and ramblers to use as others donated seats for that purpose.

The social life of the village still goes on and the good friends who we met on our arrival here, still keep in touch and visit me.

We are now in February 2008 and I have finished the book. I am lucky that in my home I am surrounded by mementoes that bring back happy memories of times gone by.

This house that has been longed for and then found, has been loved because we have felt protected in it.

Now I feel Reg's presence in it, so his Spirit watches over me and I can just wait for Fate to bring us together again. However long it takes, it will be a wonderful reunion.